Louise Jensen always wanted to be Enid Blyton when she grew up, and when that didn't happen she got a 'proper' job instead.

Several years ago an accident left Louise with a disability and she began writing once again, to distract her from her pain and compromised mobility. But writing turned out to be more than just a good distraction. Louise loves creating exciting worlds, dark characters, and twisted plots.

Louise lives in Northamptonshire with her husband, sons, a dog and a rather naughty cat, and also teaches mindfulness.

www.louisejensen.co.uk

ALSO BY LOUISE JENSEN

The Gift
The Surrogate

The Sister

LOUISE JENSEN

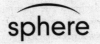

sphere

SPHERE

First published in 2016 by Bookouture, an imprint of StoryFire Ltd.
This paperback edition published in 2017 by Sphere

13 5 7 9 10 8 6 4 2

A CIP catalogue record for this book
is available from the British Library.

ISBN 978-0-7515-7055-7

Printed and bound in Great Britain by
Clays Ltd, St Ives plc

Papers used by Sphere are from well-managed forests
and other responsible sources.

Sphere
An imprint of
Little, Brown Book Group
Carmelite House
50 Victoria Embankment
London EC4Y 0DZ

An Hachette UK Company

www.hachette.co.uk
www.littlebrown.co.uk

To Ian Hawley
Much loved. Deeply missed.

CHAPTER ONE
Now

Stepping out of my car with heartbreak-heavy legs, I zip my jacket and pull on leather gloves before hefting my spade and bag from the boot: it is time. My wellingtons slip-slide across the squelching mud to the gap in the hedge. It's been there for as long as I can remember. I shiver as I enter the forest; it's darker than I'd thought and I take deep breaths of the pine-scented air to steady myself. I fight the urge to go home and come back in the morning, remind myself why I'm here and drive myself forwards.

My smartphone lights the way as I look out for rabbit holes I might fall down. I take giant steps over fallen limbs of trees I'd once have hurdled. At twenty-five I'm not too old to run, but my load is cumbersome; besides, I'm in no rush to get there, I was never supposed to do this alone.

I stop and rest the spade handle against my hip, splay my fingers and shake out my pins and needles. There's a rustling in the bushes and I have a sense of being watched. My heart stutters as two rabbits dart out, bounding away when they see my light. 'I'm OK,' I reassure myself, but my voice seems loud and echoey, reminding me how alone I am.

My rucksack feels tight across my shoulders and I readjust the straps before marching on, snapping twigs underfoot. I'm beginning to think I've taken the wrong fork when I reach the clearing with the lightning-struck tree. I wasn't sure it would still be here, but as I look around it seems nothing has changed – but of course, everything has. Memories of the last time I was here hit me so hard I feel winded. I sink to the ground. The dampness of the leaves and earth seep through my trousers, as the past seeps through to my present.

'Hurry up, birthday girl, you'll be sixteen at this rate. I'm freezing,' Charlie had called. She'd been perched on the weathered gate at the edge of the cornfield, plastic bags strewn around her feet, blonde hair gleaming in the weak coral sun. Never patient, Charlie kicked her heels as I trudged towards her, cradling the box that contained our hopes and dreams.

'Come *on*, Grace.' She jumped down, scooped up her wares and dashed into the trees. I shifted the box under my arm and tried to keep up, following flashes of her purple coat and wafts of the Impulse body spray she always stole from her mum's bedroom.

Branches and brambles grasped at our denim-clad legs, snagged our hair, but we kept going until we burst into the clearing.

'Your red face matches your hair,' Charlie laughed as I dropped the box and hunched over, resting my hands on my knees as I tried to catch my breath. Despite the cool early evening temperature, sweat beaded on my temples. Charlie upended the carrier bags: snacks, drinks, matches, a trowel and a small present, wrapped in sparkly purple paper with a 'Fifteen Today' sticker on it, all scattered over the crumbling earth. Smiling, she handed the gift to me. I sat cross-legged, carefully opening the ends without tearing the paper, and inched the box out. Nestled inside was half a gold heart on a chain engraved with 'BFF'. Tears pricked my eyes as I looked at Charlie. She tugged the neck of her fleece down, revealing the other half of the heart. I fastened the chain around my throat as Charlie began to dig a hole. Always the Girl Guide, I lit a small fire. It would be even colder when the sun went down, and the evenings were drawing in quickly now. By the time the hole was deep enough, Charlie was breathless, her fingernails caked in dirt.

I carried the memory box over to the hole and placed it in the ground. We'd spent a whole Saturday choosing the contents and decorating the outside of the plastic tub, sticking on pictures from magazines of supermodels and pop stars we wanted to emulate. 'You can never be too rich or too thin,' Charlie said. She scooped an armful of dirt and began to cover it.

'Wait!' I cried. 'I want to put this in.' I waved the birthday wrapping paper in the air.

'You can't now, we've already sealed it.'

'I'll be careful.' I slowly peeled back the Sellotape and popped off the lid. To my surprise, sitting on top of a stack of photos was a pink envelope that definitely hadn't been there when we'd filled the box earlier. I glanced at Charlie, who was looking secretive.

'What's that, Charlie?' I reached towards the envelope.

Charlie grabbed my arm. 'Don't.'

I pulled free, rubbing my wrist. 'What is it?'

Charlie wouldn't meet my eye. 'It's for us to read when we come back for the box.'

'What does it say?'

Charlie snatched the wrapping paper from between my fingers and scrunched it inside the box, banging the lid on top. When Charlie didn't want to talk about something there was little point trying to pursue it. I decided to let it go; I wouldn't let her furtiveness spoil my birthday.

'Drink?' I grabbed a cider; it fizzed as I pulled back the ring, and froth spilled over the side of the can. I wiped my hand on my jeans and took a gulp; it warmed my stomach, washing away my unease.

Charlie packed the earth into the hole and pounded the surface with her trowel until it was flat, before coming to sit by my side.

The campfire crackled as we leaned against the horizontal tree trunk toasting pink marshmallows on sticks, and it wasn't until the embers burned out that I realised how late it was.

'We should go. I'm supposed to be home by ten.'

'OK. A pinkie promise we'll come back and open the box together?' Charlie proffered her little finger and I curled mine around it before we clinked cans and drank to a promise that we didn't know would be impossible to keep.

There is only me now. 'Charlie,' I whisper. 'I wish you were here.' Charlie's half-heart, forever on a chain around my neck, spins around as I lean forward, as if it's searching for its partner, desperate to be whole again. I gently lay down the wreath. The overwhelming panic that has plagued me since Charlie's death four months ago bubbles to the surface, and I tug my scarf away from my throat so I can breathe a little easier. *Am I really to blame? Am I always to blame?*

Despite the January chill I feel hot, and as I pull off my gloves I think I hear Charlie's last words echoing through the trees: *I did something terrible, Grace. I hope you can forgive me.*

What did she do? It can't be any worse than what I did, but I am determined to find out what it was. I know I won't be able to move forwards until I do. I hadn't been sure where to begin until this morning, when I received a letter in the post in a pink envelope, which triggered a memory of the letter that Charlie hadn't wanted me to read, hidden in the memory box. Perhaps the letter will hold some kind of clue? It will be a start, anyway. Asking people who knew her hasn't been getting me anywhere, and besides, I'm the one who knew her best, aren't I? I was her best friend.

But can you ever really know someone? Properly know someone?

I sit back on my heels, remaining motionless for an indeterminable time as the air cools around me. Branches swish and sway as if the trees are whispering their secrets to me, encouraging me to unearth Charlie's.

I shake my head, scattering my thoughts, and pull my sleeve down over the heel of my hand before wiping my wet cheeks. Picking up the spade with arms that feel too heavy to be mine, I grip the handle so tightly, rockets of pain shoot through my wrists. I take a deep breath and begin to dig.

CHAPTER TWO
Now

'Mittens?' I call to our house cat. 'I'm home.' Holding the memory box aloft, I squeeze down the hallway into the lounge, without knocking any of my seaside prints from the duck-egg walls. 'There you are.' A grey ball of fluff is nestled on the stool of the piano that Dad taught me to play, hoisting me onto the leather stool virtually as soon as I could sit unaided. We'd sit side by side, Dad and I, his huge sausage fingers surprisingly nimble as he navigated chords, while I picked out a melody. I'll never play again. It's still too painful to be reminded of the time I had a normal life. A normal family.

The lounge is gloomy, despite the light from the French doors. Angry clouds scud across the darkened sky outside. I flick on the light. Winter has been harsh this year and I can barely remember the sunflower summer evenings when I'd sit outside with a tall glass of Pimms, ice cubes chinking, until the solar lights glowed and bats flapped across indigo skies.

The Alfred Meakin plate I keep for special occasions is balanced on a stack of *FHM* lads' magazines, dried egg yolk and ketchup masking its floral pattern. A salt pot lays prone on the floor, white granules mounded on the carpet. Dan has eaten.

I step over a balled-up bath sheet to reach the coffee table, where I slide aside the worn copy of *Little Women* I'm reading to Mrs Jones next door – despite her milk-bottle glasses she can no longer make out small print. I've almost reached the part where Beth dies and it doesn't matter how many times I've read it before, I know it will make me cry. Dried mud crumbles onto the table's cream-painted surface as I set down the memory box and I brush it onto the floor. Aged pictures of one-hit wonders and supermodels, once glued tight now hang dolefully from the plastic box; I can hardly remember half of them. My fingernail picks at the edge of the tape that seals the lid; it has lost its stickiness and lifts easily. I peel it off and smooth it back, pressing down hard with both thumbs. It doesn't feel right opening the box without Charlie – not that I have a choice if I want to find out what's in the pink envelope, and I do. But I feel uncomfortable all the same, as if I'm invading her privacy.

The cottage is too quiet. I put on a record. Nina Simone is feeling good. I'm glad one of us is. Dan downloads all his music but I find comfort in the old-fashioned things I grew up with, even though Grandad's more modern than me now, with his Bose SoundDock and Blue-ray Player. I flop onto the brown leather sofa and sink into the squashiness of my mismatched cushions. The vinyl spins round and round, crackling and hissing, demanding attention, much like my memories.

It doesn't seem as though it's been seven years since we moved into the cottage. I had nothing else to worry about then; my life was finally going the way it was supposed to, and I became a little bit obsessed with soft furnishings. Dan had rolled his eyes every time I brought a new cushion home. 'Dance like no one is watching, another snippet of wisdom stuffed with foam.' He had snatched it from me and twirled it around the lounge, holding it at arm's length.

'Nobody wants to watch when *you* dance,' I'd told him at the time. He'd tickled me until we sank to the floor, tugging at each other's clothes until he was on me, in me, and my back burned from the friction of the red swirled carpet we've since replaced with a chocolate-brown pile. Afterwards, we snuggled in the multicoloured throws that adorned the back of the sofa, and munched on Hawaiian pizza. I'd told Dan to order a pepperoni – he's never understood fruit on savoury food but he knew I loved the sweet and salty combination.

It seems a long time now since we laughed like that. Loved like that. Grief has pushed us apart like repelling magnets: no matter how hard we try to reach each other, there's a gulf between us that we just can't bridge.

Mittens sits up and arches her back, legs rigid, reminding me I have missed yet another yoga class. There's nothing quite as corrosive as guilt; it eats away at you from the inside out. I should know – remorse is my middle name; I should have been born a Catholic. Mittens leaps off the stool, in the graceful way that only cats can, and with a feed-me-now meow, butts her head against my calves.

I trail after her into the kitchen. The stench of stale oil hangs in the air, and the sink, shiny and clean when I left it, is now half-full of stagnant water. A saucepan handle rises up like a signpost: wash me. I reach over and crack open the sash window. Icy air filters through from the back garden; snow has been forecast for tomorrow. I flick on the kettle and scoop up two cracked eggshells, their slime oozing over the wooden work surface, and drop them in the overflowing pedal bin. I'll have to empty it later. I wipe down the work surface and rinse a cup, wishing again that Dan didn't use a clean one every time he makes a drink. We don't have a dishwasher – unless you count me, of course, which I'm sure Dan does. Our kitchen is tiny, or, 'compact but functional', as Dan would say if this were one of the houses he was trying to sell. We barely have room for cabinets, but I love our pantry, which houses everything we need.

I dip my hand inside the tea caddy; it connects with the cool metal at the bottom. The light inside the fridge illuminates almost empty shelves as I open the door. What can I make out of half a tub of goat's cheese and a shrivelled red pepper? Dan will come home after football and expect dinner to be waiting. Actually, that's unfair, he never asks me to cook; it's just assumed that I will. I always do. I push away the memory of the time we no longer talk about. The time when I could barely remember my own name, let alone how to operate an oven. I'm coping now. I really am.

I scrawl 'tea bags' onto the never-ending shopping list that's stuck to the fridge door by the Stop magnet, the one with the picture of the pig on it. Dan bought the magnet for me last year – to support me, he said, as I gave up on yet another diet. The glossy magazines I pore over don't help. Telling me on one page I'm the average size for a UK woman, that size fourteen is not fat, and yet on the next page printing photos of emaciated models, all jutting collarbones and hollow cheeks. I keep the magnet as a constant reminder that I should lose ten pounds. I never do.

Mittens weaves between my ankles, urging me to pick up her empty bowl. There is one pouch of cat food left in the cupboard. I scrape it into her dish and measure out biscuits while she mews impatiently.

I watch Mittens eating unselfconsciously, in the way that animals do. She's been such a comfort to me since Charlie died. I've taken more solace from her silence than I have from Dan's clumsy words. I hadn't intended to get a pet, but three years ago Grandma's neighbour's cat had a litter of six and I went to take some photos to show at the pre-school where I work. The kittens were adorable, and when the smallest one climbed onto my lap and fell asleep I was easily swayed into taking her home. I carried her out to my second-hand Fiesta. She sat on the passenger seat in a Walkers crisps box lined with a faded pink blanket, and squinted in the never-before-seen sun. I drove home slower than usual, parked in the potholed lane outside my cottage and shook my tingling hands. My nails had carved crescents into my palms and I remember shaking my head at myself. I looked after thirty-six four-year-old children every day. A kitten should have been a breeze.

Once inside, I studied her as she padded fearlessly around her new home. What could I call her? As a child I had been obsessed with Beatrix Potter. Dad had read me a story every night before bed, giving all the animals accents. I'd loved hearing the antics of Tom Kitten and his sisters Moppet and Mittens. The kitten's paws were lighter than the rest of her. Mittens seemed the perfect name; a connection to Dad.

The first time we let her out, she was nearly run over by the dustbin lorry. She'd been so scared, she wouldn't go out again. We'd tried to encourage her into the garden, but she got so distressed each time that the vet said to leave her, she'd go out when she was ready – but she never was.

I can't imagine what the cottage would be like without her now. I watch as she finishes her dinner and laps water with her darting pink tongue, before slinking out of the kitchen.

The kettle splutters and steams and clicks itself off, and I follow Mittens to the lounge. We sit side by side on the sofa, staring at the box. I wonder whether she remembers coming home in one.

'Don't worry, nothing living is in there,' I reassure her. But that's a lie. My memories are alive and harder to contain than a wriggling kitten.

I chew my thumbnail, half expecting Charlie to pop out with a: 'Surprise! You didn't really think I'd leave you?' Loneliness engulfs me. I am one step away from tears most of the time and

I don't feel strong enough to confront the memories that I've stuffed away. Afraid that if I begin to remember I won't be able to stop, and there are things I don't want to think about. Not now. Not ever.

The cottage is a mess; I'll clean instead. I always find cleaning therapeutic, often grateful for the opportunity to absorb myself in something other than my own thoughts. I abandon the box and start in the kitchen, roll up my sleeves and squirt washing-up liquid into the sink, twist on the hot tap. While the water rises and froths I wipe grease from the hob. When the bowl is full I plunge my hands in the water, jerk them out and flick the tap to cold to soothe my burning skin.

The pot of hand cream on the windowsill is empty. I'm sure Dan uses my toiletries, although he always denies it. I head upstairs into the second bedroom, where I keep spare lotions. When we viewed the cottage we knew we'd ask Charlie to move in, and I still think of it as her bedroom even though she never got to see it.

I find the hand lotion and rub it into my smarting skin. The lavender scent calms me, reminding me of the small bags my grandma made me as a child, when nightmares prevailed every time I closed my eyes. She would pop lavender bags in my pyjama drawer as well as under my pillow; the scent would gently escort me to sleep and watch over me all night. It has been a long time since Grandma's arthritic fingers could sew, but comfort still smells of lavender to me.

My phone vibrates in my pocket and I reach for it with slippery fingers, wedge it between my shoulder and ear and wipe my hands on my apron.

'Hi Dan. Did you win?'

'Yeah, three-two. I scored in the last minute.'

'You must be pleased? It's been ages since you scored.'

'Thanks for reminding me…'

'I didn't mean…' I pause. Pretend we're a normal couple and choose my words carefully. 'It's brilliant news. I'll get some steak and wine to celebrate.'

'We're already in the bar celebrating. Come down.'

'I can't.'

'You've got to start living again sometime. Why not tonight? Everyone's here.'

Not everyone. I think of the box resting on the table, part of Charlie – how can I go out and leave her? 'I've got things to do.'

'Fine.' I can almost hear the rejection in his voice, and for a split second I wish I was at the club with him, sipping warm cider and laughing at jokes far too rude to repeat. 'Don't wait up.'

He cuts me off before I can reply that I won't wait up. I never do.

The evening stretches before me, long and quiet, and although I haven't yet eaten, I don't feel hungry. In the kitchen, I open a bottle of wine. It isn't like I can have a cup of tea, I justify to myself. I always feel a little strange drinking alone.

It's dull in the lounge and I switch on the table lamps, dimming the harsh overhead light. The apricot glow is warming, and I sit on the sofa, legs tucked under me, resting my hand on Mittens' sleeping form. 'It's just you and me tonight,' I tell her. Looking at the box, I know that isn't true. Charlie is everywhere.

It doesn't take long to drain my first glass of Chardonnay, the icy liquid settling amongst the butterflies thronging in my stomach. I'm halfway through my second glass before my trembling fingers can open the box. The sheet of sparkly purple wrapping paper lies on the top; the letter's underneath, I remember. I place the pink envelope to my nose and inhale deeply, hoping for a scent of Charlie. It smells of damp and earth. The lump I'm endlessly swallowing rises again. How many more people will I lose? Sometimes, my jaw clenches when I hear Dan's key in the lock and I steel myself for yet another argument, but the thought of being alone fills me with horror. Besides, what happened hasn't broken us, so surely it's made us stronger?

My fingers curl around my mobile. I search my recent calls list. Dan is number six. I press dial. Our photo flashes up, the one of us dressed as Superman and Wonder Woman at one of Lyn's parties. She's more of a friend than a boss, and the picture always makes me smile.

'I just want to tell you I love you,' I say.

'I know.' His voice is terse.

'Please be careful tonight, don't drink and drive.'

'What? I can't hear you properly?'

'I said please be c—'

'Grace, the signal's really bad; you're breaking up. Hang on, I'll just…'

The phone cuts out. I press redial and a mechanical voice invites me to leave a message. Frustrated, I toss the phone onto the sofa and lean forward to unpack the box.

Myriads of memories flit across my mind as I thumb through a small photo album. There's Charlie and me posing on the beach, proud in our first bikinis, displaying ironing-board chests; at the school disco, arms covered in silver glitter. There are some of Charlie, Dan and me laughing in the garden as we hose each other down on a scorching summer day, and one of Charlie smiling into the camera as Dan stares at her adoringly. There's me, Charlie and Dan on our last day of term, laughing as we throw school ties we'd never again wear into the air. How free we felt. Another picture, a group one this time: me, Esmée, Charlie and Siobhan. Our little foursome. How close we were. Who'd have thought we'd turn on each other the way we did?

I remove the last photo from the plastic film. Charlie stands in my grandparents' garden, white-blonde bob ruffled in the wind, wearing an orange tie-dye T-shirt and tiny white denim shorts. She'd got into so much trouble for taking those jeans from her mum's drawer, then blunting Grandma's hairdressing scissors by hacking the legs off.

I take down a photo of Dan and me from on top of the piano – we're dangling the keys to the cottage and brandishing a bottle of champagne – and slip Charlie into the silver frame instead.

My mobile rings. I leap on it, hoping it's Dan, but it's an unknown number. My mind leaps to conclusions – Dan's had an accident and it's the hospital – and a film of sweat breaks out on my skin. I answer the call and there's the sound of breathing.

'Hello?' I say. Then, louder, 'Hello? *Hello?*'

But nobody speaks. Eventually, the dial tone whirrs against my ear. This is the third time it's happened today and I switch my phone off.

A wave of tiredness washes over me. Alcohol and emotion collaborate, forcing my eyes shut; I rub them, trying to dispel the past. I take the photo and envelope with me to bed and prop them against my bedroom lamp. The photos have stirred up so many emotions, I'm afraid I'll lose it completely if I open Charlie's letter tonight. I pop a sleeping tablet out of its foil cocoon, place it on my tongue and swallow it down with tepid water. I slip into patchy sleep clouded by dreams of Charlie and my father.

'It's your fault, Grace,' my dream dad says. 'I'd still be here if it wasn't for you.'

'Open the envelope, Grace,' Charlie whispers to my subconscious. 'Don't let me down.'

I wake in the morning to tangled bed sheets and a damp pillow. Dan hasn't come home.

CHAPTER THREE
Then

Little by little, the world stopped spinning and I became conscious of Grandad rubbing my back in small circular motions, his hand warm and solid.

'Breathe slowly, Grace,' he urged, as I puffed out clouds of air like a steam train. I inhaled sharply and the ice-cold wind made me cough. Tears streamed down my frozen cheeks as I breathed in and out for the count of five, the way I'd been taught, until I felt calm enough to straighten up and release my grip on the iron railings. I'd clasped them so hard that specks of moss green paint were embedded in my gloves. I slapped my hands together, scattering the flecks onto the pavement, as I surveyed the monstrous construction in front of me.

'Don't make me go in there.'

'I know the move's been hard on you.'

That was an understatement. It wasn't just the people I'd left behind, my sunflower yellow bedroom, or my school that I missed. It was the noises that make up a home. Waking each morning to the sound of crashing waves; the creak of the third stair whenever someone stepped on it; the screech of seagulls as I walked to school; the crunch of shingle underfoot as I ran across the beach on the way home, salt air filling my lungs.

I'd always loved visiting my grandparents in the school holidays. Watching the quaint Oxfordshire village grow year by year as red-bricked houses were tacked onto its outskirts, A second pub built, a coffee shop, a Co-op. 'All the mod cons,' Grandma said, but still, it didn't feel like home. It didn't sound like home. Never again would I huddle under my covers as the wind and rain declared war upon the cliffs, the flash of the lighthouse blinking through my curtains.

'You'll soon make friends,' said Grandad, ever the optimist.

'I won't if they find out what I've done.'

'Stop blaming yourself. No one will find out anything unless you tell them.' Grandad straightened my hat. 'You have to go to school, Gracie.' He smiled, but it didn't make his eyes crinkle around the edges like normal, and I nodded, guilty I'd made such a fuss. I'd turned nine now; I needed to act like it. If Grandma had been there I'd have been marched straight in.

'Come on.' He proffered a hand, age-spotted and wrinkled. 'Let's get you inside.'

I locked my fingers around his and we slid our way across the barren playground. I'd just finished reading *Gulliver's Travels* and I felt like a Lilliputian as I stopped at the bottom of the concrete stairs and stared up at the huge red building. It seemed a million times larger than my old primary.

Grandad looked as though he might speak but he shook his head instead, gently tugging my hand until my reluctant feet followed him into the rainforest warmth of my new school.

Inside the entrance, an unsmiling receptionist sat behind a desk. GREENFIELDS LEARNING COMMUNITY WELCOMES YOU! was painted in daffodil yellow on the wall above her.

'Grace Matthews.' Grandad patted my shoulder. 'It's her first day.'

The receptionist gestured us to salmon-coloured chairs that could have once been red, and I sank gratefully into the softness. My feet dangled above the floor. I thunked my new plastic lunch box onto a wooden table etched with: MISS MARKHAM IS FIT.

'I wonder if Miss Markham is the PE teacher?' mused Grandad.

I picked at stray bits of thread on my fraying seat as I looked around. No drawings or crafts adorned the scuffed walls. A forlorn Christmas tree stood in the corner, its branches almost bare, a too-short string of gaudy coloured lights twisted around its middle. I never wanted to celebrate Christmas again. A few weeks ago I'd felt like any other nine-year-old, and now I had my own counsellor, Paula. I hated the weekly therapy sessions, talking about my feelings – as if that could ever change anything. Now I wished I were in Paula's office, with its walls so blue it made me feel like I was drowning. I wished I were anywhere but here.

The smell of citrus cleaning products was cloying and my stomach lurched as I was overcome with longing for my old school: the smell of plimsolls and poster paint; my old friends; hopscotch and kiss chase. I rested my head back and closed my eyes. It was eerily quiet. We'd been told not to come until after registration so I wouldn't be quite so overwhelmed, but to me it felt worse. I'd have to join a lesson once it had started. I breathed in deeply, the way Paula had taught me, and tried to transport myself to a happy place. I imagined myself in my bedroom, my real bedroom, the one I'd probably never see again. My fists gradually unclenched and I must have drifted off because the click-clack of high heels roused me. For a second, I had actually believed everything was normal. I was back home and Mum was cooking supper for Dad.

'Here's Mrs Beeton,' said Grandad. 'She's the one I saw when I registered you.'

'Grace, it's lovely to meet you.' The headmistress stood before me, complete with a sympathetic smile. I'd been seeing a lot of those lately.

I stared silently at her, my lips straight and serious.

'If you'd like to follow me, Mr Roberts? I have some paper-work. Grace, we won't be long.'

They hunched over the reception desk, heads close together, and spoke in hushed tones, occasionally throwing worried glances my way.

'I'll see you later, Pet.' Grandad's voice was a little too loud as he waved goodbye a short time later, his smile a little too wide. His footsteps echoed loudly, marching to the drumming of my heart, as I watched him walk out the door.

I trotted after Mrs Beeton through a warren of identical corridors, slowing each time we passed a window, longing for a glimpse of Grandad, head bowed against the wind, gloveless hands thrust into corduroy pockets. My smart new Clarks shoes squeaked on the linoleum and I could already feel blisters forming on my heels.

'Here we are.' Mrs Beeton pushed open a classroom door. A sea of faces turned towards us and I'd never felt smaller than I did in that moment.

'Grace, this is Miss Stiles.'

Miss Stiles pushed her glasses onto the bridge of her nose. She was wearing trousers and was younger than my last teacher, who'd always worn a dress. I prayed she wouldn't ask me to introduce myself.

'There's a spare seat at the back, Grace.'

Heady with relief, I scampered towards the empty chair faster than I should have in my not-yet-broken-in shoes. I splayed my hands to cushion my fall the moment I felt myself slip. My lunch box clattered to the floor and I was sprawled next to it, wishing I could die.

I didn't make eye contact with anyone as I tugged down my skirt to preserve what little dignity I had remaining, and scrambled around retrieving my lunch. My yoghurt spoon was missing, but I didn't care. The lid of my new lunch box hung at an unnatural angle, one of the hinges broken, but I thrust everything back inside and cradled it to my chest. My ankle hurt as I stood and I bit back hot tears.

'I think this is yours?'

A boy tilted his chair towards me, thrusting out a piece of paper.

I shook my head. Limped forwards.

'Don't forget how much we *love* you, Gracie.'

I froze, as the words that could only have been lovingly written by Grandad were mockingly read aloud.

I snatched the paper as the class sniggered.

The boy jabbed a finger at me. 'Look, Ginger's face is as red as her hair!'

'That's enough, Daniel Gibson.' Thankful for Miss Stiles's intervention, I hobbled to my seat, staring at the floor as if it could turn into the Yellow Brick Road, take me to see the Wizard. There's no place like home.

It was two to a desk. I didn't acknowledge my neighbour as she slid her textbook to the centre so I could share it. Hostility I could cope with, kindness would make me cry. I'd done enough of that lately.

I tried to calm myself by imagining I was on a beach, but that made me think of home, and I wanted to rest my forehead on the desk and howl with the injustice of it all. It seemed like hours before the bell rang for lunch.

Miss Stiles pushed her way to the back of the room as the class swarmed towards the door.

'Charlotte,' she said to the girl next to me, who was shoving things into a pink rucksack. 'Can you please take Grace and show her where we eat?'

'OK,' said Charlotte.

'Where are you from?' Charlotte asked, as we weaved through a maze of corridors. She was tall. I had to half run to keep up with her. My ankle throbbed but I didn't complain; I was grateful not to be alone. 'How come you're late starting?'

I'd been expecting this question, but the lies I'd been practising in front of my bedroom mirror seemed to stick in my throat. Charlotte stopped walking and I swallowed hard, thinking she was waiting for my answer, but then I realised we were there, at the canteen. The hall looked like a clip of the prison I'd seen on TV once: rows of plastic grey tables and orange chairs. Lunch had only just begun, but crisps and crusts were already scattered over the parquet floor. I was stung by a sharp longing for my old school, where we had eaten lunch in our classroom, swapping Club biscuits for Penguins, yoghurts for cake.

'Well, this is the canteen. "Hardly the bleedin' Ritz," as Mum would say, but you know…'

I nodded, even though I had no idea what she was talking about.

Charlotte waved to two girls hunkered down in the corner. 'That's Esmée and Siobhan; I'll introduce you later. I usually sit with them, but not today. C'mon.'

I scurried after Charlotte, straining forward to hear her.

'You can come round my house if you like after school, yeah? I can do your hair and make-up. My mum's a singer and has loads of cool stuff. She's hardly ever home so she won't know.'

I couldn't. Grandad was picking me up; besides, Grandma would have a fit if I came home wearing make-up.

'Maybe,' I said, not wanting to sound like a baby.

'Let's sit here.' Charlotte plonked her things next to the boy who'd humiliated me in class. I hesitated, told myself it was better than sitting alone, but I felt my cheeks heat all the same.

'Take a pew.' Charlotte stared at me. Her bright green eyes reminded me of our old cat, Bessie, and something told me I could trust her.

My throat always felt like it was closing whenever I was anxious, but I sat and unpacked my lunch anyway. If I'd still had a spoon I might have managed to swallow some yoghurt. It was apricot, too: my favourite. I scowled at the boy, Daniel, then pierced my carton of apple juice with a straw and took small sips. Charlotte shook her bottle of banana milk.

'Could you fetch me a straw?' Charlotte flashed Daniel a brilliant smile.

'Yeah.' He flushed, scraped back his chair and swaggered across the hall in an I'm-too-cool-for-school kind of way.

'Keep watch.' Charlotte snatched Daniel's half-eaten sandwich and removed the top slice of bread. She grabbed the ketchup bottle from the condiment holder and squirted tomato sauce on top of the strawberry jam, then reassembled the sandwich.

I stiffened as Daniel returned, picked up his lunch and took a large bite. He chewed once, twice, before spitting everything out and rubbing at his mouth with his sleeve.

'Oh, look!' Charlotte pointed at him. 'His face is as red as his sandwich.'

'Who did that?' Daniel stood up, hands fisted by his sides.

'I did. It serves you right for being so mean to Grace on her first day.'

'You're a bloody bitch, Charlotte Fisher.' Daniel swept his lunch into his rucksack, glaring at me, and I flinched. 'I'll get you for this.' He stormed towards the exit.

'Good riddance!' Charlotte shouted.

'I can't believe you did that, Charlotte,' I said.

'It's Charlie, not Charlotte, if we're gonna hang out,' she said. 'Want one?'

My mouth felt too dry to eat, but I took a cheese and onion crisp and placed it on my tongue.

'So why did you move here, Grace?'

And the crisp felt heavy and solid in my mouth. I tried to swallow, but my throat had closed.

CHAPTER FOUR
Now

It took ages to get to sleep last night. Looking through the photo album stirred up so many memories that my stomach churned with regret and my mind refused to still. The sleeping tablets aren't as effective as they used to be. I resolve to go to the doctor on Monday, pretend I've lost my latest prescription. That way I can get some more and double my dose.

When I last checked the time – frantic with worry that Dan still wasn't home – it was two in the morning, and I thought I'd never drift off, but now, looking at my clock, it's past six so I suppose I must have. I jump out of bed so fast my head spins, thrust my feet into slippers and yank my dressing gown off its hook on the back of the door. There's a chance, I tell myself, that Dan has crept in and crashed on the sofa, so as not to wake me, but as I run into the lounge and turn on the light, only Mittens is there, blinking at the sudden brightness.

I pull open the curtains. My temples throb as I try Dan's phone for the umpteenth time, a slideshow of despair flickering across my mind: Dan in a ditch, car upturned, wheels still spinning; Dan mugged and left for dead in an alleyway; Dan bleeding and broken at the side of the road.

There isn't much to see past the front garden. It's still wintery dark and the fog hangs heavily in the air, snaking fingers swirling towards me, rendering the lane invisible. It wasn't until we moved here that I appreciated how powerful the weather is: now you see it, now you don't. I shiver, although I'm not cold, and wrap my dressing gown a little tighter. There's a packet of Polos in the pocket and I slip one onto my tongue. The medication I'm on leaves a foul taste in my mouth that seems to linger all day, no matter how many times I brush my teeth or how many mints I eat.

I check my watch again, as if I can somehow make time go faster. It isn't yet seven, too early to really panic, but still, it doesn't stop me thinking the worst – I always do. Paula used to say it stems from a fear of loss, Dan says it stems from being up-tight. I pace in front of the lounge window, carpet pile flattening under slippered feet, a tiger in a cage, backwards and forwards, coiled with tension.

When did Dan and I begin to unravel? My life seems split into two: before Charlie's death and after. I think we were happy before, but it's hard to properly remember. Sometimes it feels like I've pushed him so far away it will be impossible to pull him back, but although I'm terrified I'll lose him, I can't stem the almost constant irritation I feel. I tell myself it doesn't matter if he makes a mess, if he doesn't do the things he's promised, but I nag him all the same – almost goading, wanting him to bite back sometimes.

I shiver as the wind howls and rattles the gate. The latch doesn't hold and it swings wide open before crashing shut again. I've asked Dan to fix the catch so many times. I hear a car and strain my eyes to see. Headlights poke through the fog at the end of the lane, like cat's eyes, and I wait for the car to properly appear. It must be Dan. Our lane only leads to fields. When we bought the cottage I had visions of sheep grazing, or horses hanging their heads over the five-bar gate, but the land is arable. Wheat is farmed here, and every time I eat Weetabix I feel strangely proud, as though I've grown it myself.

The car emerges from the fog. It's too small to be Dan's and is barely moving. I wonder whether the driver is lost. There are only two cottages along here. Ours and Mrs Jones's. She doesn't have a car and only has visitors at Christmas and on her birthday; besides, who would visit at this time in the morning? It's not even properly light yet.

The car crawls closer and closer until it stops virtually outside the cottage, but it's too foggy to see inside it. The engine thrums and the lights illuminate our apple tree, but no one gets out. Time ticks past and I wonder what they're doing. *Who they're watching.* The words run through me with a chill. It isn't the first time I've felt I'm being watched, and I tell myself I'm being ridiculous. Who would watch me? But I can't tear my eyes away all the same. The last time I'd requested a repeat prescription, my doctor asked whether the sleeping tablets were causing any side effects. I said no, but a sense of unease has burrowed its way inside me; my skin crawls and my mind hops and it's hard to stay focused. I really should stop taking them. I'm edgy and paranoid and barely recognise myself.

It's just a car.

A second set of lights appear now and Dan's ancient Land Rover chugs into vision. I scoot over to the sofa, casually recline and pick up my book with a hand that still shakes. I will be calm. Dan shuffles into the room, slings his jacket on the sofa near my feet and glances at me through bloodshot eyes. He looks terrible. My inner fury and joy wrestle: fury wins.

'Where the hell have you been? Who's with you?'

'With me?' Dan looks over his shoulder.

'The other car?'

'Other car?'

'Are you just going to repeat everything I say? Why didn't you call?'

'I lost my phone.'

'Where?'

'If I knew that it wouldn't be lost,' he snaps.

'Don't…'

He holds both hands up in front of him, fingers splayed. 'Sorry. I should have called you from Harry's but I fell asleep on his sofa.'

There's a stabbing in my gut as I imagine Dan, Harry and Harry's girlfriend, Chloe, curled up in front of Harry's log fire with a case of Budweiser and bowls of tortilla chips and salsa, the way we all used to on a Saturday night before Charlie died.

'I was worried.'

'You always are. I'm going to clean up and crash for a couple of hours.'

Avoiding my gaze, Dan strides out the room, thumps up the stairs. A moment later I hear the creak of the bathroom door opening and the gurgling of pipes as he turns on the water.

I wonder whether he'll come back down after his shower, suggest a Sunday morning snuggle. I wonder why I don't feel I can suggest one myself. Before long, the bedroom door opens and closes. The bedsprings squeak.

In the bathroom, steam rises and hangs, a cloud of uncertainty hovering over me. I open the small window and pick Dan's towel off the floor. Stepping into the glass cubicle, I turn the shower on and shiver while I wait for the water to heat. My eyes close as I remember how we both used to squeeze in here. My palms would be flat against the wet tiles. His hands on my hips. Afterwards, he'd massage shampoo through my hair as I leaned my body back against him. Was he really at Harry's all night? I wash with lavender shower gel: the familiar fragrance, my childhood comfort, dissolves my fears, until one by one I wash them down the plughole. I've no reason to believe Dan has lied to me. Grief has skewed my judgment. My grasp on reality feels tenuous at best. Paula always encouraged me to process my thoughts rationally rather than submitting to fear. 'The mind can create multiple possible scenarios from one thought and the majority of them won't be true,' she'd said. I'm too tired to think about it properly

I step out of the shower, away from my thoughts, and pull my pyjamas back on. I'll leave Dan to catch up on his sleep. I'm afraid of what I might say if I stay, afraid of what I might hear, and it isn't until I'm walking downstairs I think to check if that car is still outside – but it's gone.

It's freezing in the shed; my breath mists before me. I flick on the heater and pull on grey fingerless gloves. The telephone table I've sanded rests on sheets of newspaper, ready to be painted. It's for Mrs Jones's birthday. She always admires my own table. I dip my brush and stroke pistachio chalk paint over the bare wood. Dan can't understand my fascination with old furniture, but I love to upcycle, to preserve a little piece of history. I always wonder about the original owners: what were their lives like, were they happy? The sweeping of the paintbrush soothes me and by the time I'm finished, tension has released its grip on my shoulders, my fears tightly packed away where they can't be seen. My phone beeps and I swipe the screen. It's Grandad confirming lunch is at one – not that I could forget, we go most Sundays, but since Grandma bought him a mobile phone for his seventieth birthday last year, he texts me all the time. I punch out a reply that's far more upbeat than I feel, and slip the phone into my pocket. I'd better wake Dan up.

The gravy is thick and smooth. I pour it into a white china gravy boat, wiping the drops that trickle down the sides with my finger. Grandad carves the roast beef while Grandma heaps vibrant, steaming vegetables into serving bowls. My mouth waters at the smell of Yorkshire puddings. I'm ravenous. I'd skipped breakfast, feeling too rough to be hungry. Do NOT DRINK ALCOHOL is written on the side of my sleeping tablet bottle, but it's just a stock warning, isn't it? And we all ignore those. I fork the meat into my mouth, and my nose streams from the horseradish sauce. Grandma passes me a tissue and carries on telling us about the 'nice young man' who came to set up their new computer, and how she rides the Google every day.

My shoulders shake with suppressed laughter and I try to catch Dan's eye. He's hunched over his plate, pushing his food around, and doesn't look up as I begin to clear the table. I carry the dirty plates through to the kitchen and balance the crockery next to the sink. I've often tried to persuade my grandparents to buy a dishwasher. They can afford one and have the space. They always say they'll consider it, but they like the washing-up routine I think: standing side by side, Grandma washing, Grandad drying, discussing how big the marrows have grown, identifying the birds on the feeder.

Grandad's voice filters through the wall, low and gravelly. If you didn't know any better you'd think he smoked. Dan laughs and it takes me a second to identify the sound, it's been so long since I heard it. We've grown up together and sometimes I wonder whether it's natural that we've grown apart, whether it would have happened anyway and circumstances aren't to blame.

Grandma stirs home-made custard for the apple crumble that is warming in the oven. I stand on tiptoes and pull down the jug from the top of the dresser, the pink one with the picture of cows grazing on it. Swill it under the tap.

'Gracie, I got an email from my friend Joan the other day. It's on top of the fridge for you.'

'You printed it?'

'Yes. She sent a recipe I wanted to forward to you.'

I open my mouth to explain what 'forward' actually means, and close it again. It's enough for now that she's got to grips with composing an email, even if she does put 'THIS IS FROM GRANDMA' in every subject line, and then rings me to make sure I've got it.

The recipe is for a butternut squash risotto; it sounds delicious. I'll try it for tea next week, although I'll have to cook a steak for Dan or he'll lift up vegetables with his fork and ask where the meat's hiding.

'And, I saw Lexie.'

I freeze at the mention of Charlie's mum's name.

'Drunk again, could barely stand.'

Lexie always liked a drink when Charlie was alive, but has gone off the rails completely since her daughter died. Grandma turns the gas ring off and faces me. 'I didn't know whether I should tell you, Grace. The last thing I want is that woman upsetting you.' Grandma has never held Lexie in very high regard.

'Tell me what?'

'She wants to see you.'

My pulse skyrockets at the thought of facing my best friend's mum. I haven't seen her since Charlie's funeral. The funeral I had to leave after Lexie told me she'd never forgive me for the death of her daughter.

What happened before Charlie died wasn't my fault. It wasn't Charlie's either. How could it have been? *So why did Charlie run away?* whispers the voice in my head and I ignore it, but it won't go away.

Grandma slops custard into the jug and hands it to me to carry into the dining room. It sloshes as I walk, hot liquid splattering my hand, but I barely notice. Grandma follows me through with the apple crumble that I now can't face eating. I sit at the table, gripping my spoon. The hum of voices surrounding me become more and more distant until they're indecipherable. I smile and nod at what I hope are appropriate moments, while all the time the same thought swims round and round my mind: what does Lexie want with me?

CHAPTER FIVE
Then

I hopped from one foot to the other, rubbing my arms as I peered down the road waiting for Charlie to appear. She was coming to tea. I'd thought very carefully when Grandma suggested I invite a friend home at the end of my first week at school. Esmée was lovely, Siobhan more guarded but still nice, even Dan had been OK with me after the first day, but there was already a strong bond between Charlie and me. No one had ever stood up for me before; hadn't really needed to, I supposed.

'You'll let all the heat out,' grumbled Grandma from the hallway.

I pulled the front door closed behind me but remained on the step, standing on tiptoes each time I heard a car. But when Charlie appeared, twenty minutes late, she was walking alone.

I ushered her through the front door. 'We'll go upstairs to my room.'

'Not with shoes on, young lady, you know the rules.' Grandma bustled into the hallway, wiping floury hands on her apron.

My scalp prickled with embarrassment as Charlie kicked off her faded blue trainers. Grandma picked them up and placed them on the shoe rack, clicking her tongue as she noticed the soles were almost worn through at the toes. Charlie and I thundered upstairs and flopped onto my bed.

'What do you want to do?'

I still hadn't properly unpacked. In the corner of my room were boxes of games and books. Charlie walked over and picked up Mousetrap, and shook the box. The contents rattled inside.

'Here.' She passed me it and I popped off the lid. It wasn't one of my favourites, some of the pieces were too fiddly.

'How come you live with your grandparents?'

I'd been expecting the question but still felt unprepared for it. 'My parents can't look after me. What colour mouse do you want?' I held out my hand.

Charlie took the green one and looked at me steadily. 'Why not?'

'They're dead.' The lie lodged in my throat and I picked up the pink plastic beaker of Ribena that Grandma had put in my room, and gulped it down as though I could wash my words away, screwing my nose up at the syrupy sweetness.

'Dead?' Charlie's forehead creased.

'Yes.'

'How did they die?'

'I think I'll be blue.' I tossed the other mice back into the box. 'Do you have brothers or sisters?'

'No,' said Charlie. 'It's just Mum and me. I used to get so lonely I had an imaginary friend.'

'Really?'

'Yeah, her name was Belle. She'd whisper to me to do naughty things and Mum would go mad and shout, and Belle would laugh when I got into trouble. I got a Barbie for Christmas once and Belle made me cut off her hair and paint nail varnish over her face. She was fun though, too.'

'Did you name her after Belle in *Beauty and the Beast*?'

'Suppose. I grew out of her though, like I grew out of Disney.'

'Me too.' I hoped Charlie wouldn't open the box with my videos in. I'd been a bit princess obsessed until recently. I'd grown up now, though, after what had happened with my parents. Anyone would have.

'You're lucky to have grandparents.'

'I know. Don't you have any?'

'Nah. Mum says we don't need anyone else. It's me and her against the rest of the bleedin' world. But we've got each other now, haven't we? You and me are the same, with no dads. We'll be best friends.'

Charlie reached for her coat and pulled out a Kit Kat. She slid off the paper and scored the foil with her thumb before snapping it in two and holding out half. I took it gratefully.

'Let's play Mousetrap – you'll be much more fun than Belle, even if I'm not guaranteed a win.' Charlie grinned and shook the dice. 'And smile! You, me, Siobhan and Esmée, we'll be like a little family at school. I'll make sure of it.'

We were deep into Mousetrap and it was Charlie's turn to play when Grandma tapped at the door. Flour from her hands dusted the carpet. She rubbed it in with the toe of her slipper.

'Phone, Grace.'

'Don't cheat, Charlie. I'll be back in a minute.'

Downstairs, Grandma disappeared into the kitchen. I picked up the receiver and twisted the telephone wire round and round my finger, listening to the static on the other end. I didn't speak. I already knew who was there and I had nothing to say.

'Grace? Grace?' Mum's voice sounded far away and I slammed the phone down.

'That was quick?' Grandma called as I stamped back upstairs.

'We were cut off,' I shouted.

Charlie handed me the dice as I sat down again. 'Who was on the phone?'

'No one,' I said, crossing my fingers. 'There was nobody there.'

CHAPTER SIX
Now

I lie awake all night, wondering why Lexie told Grandma she wanted to see me. I yo-yo between thinking she might apologise for her behaviour at Charlie's funeral, to convincing myself she wants to kill me. My mind buzzes like a hive of bees, busy and noisy, and by the time the sun rises, tingeing the sky a fiery red, I've drunk three cups of tea and still haven't decided whether to see her.

I know Lexie stopped singing in the local pub, and is rarely seen in public at all now except at the supermarket, pushing a trolley containing more alcohol than food. Dan thinks her unhinged – he did even before her behaviour at the funeral – Grandma's more compassionate. 'She shouldn't have spoken to you the way she did,' she said. 'But people grieve in different ways.'

By the time I arrive at work I'm exhausted and puffy-eyed.

'Morning, Grace.' My boss, Lyn, is always cheerful. 'Ready for the onslaught?' Lyn unlocks the front door and holds it open, greeting each parent and toddler by name.

A sea of children floods into the cloakroom, trailed by weary mothers, stamping booted feet and shaking umbrellas. Droplets of rain pool on the floor. I make a mental note to remember to mop, or someone may slip. Emily dashes over and wraps her arms around my knees. I shouldn't have favourites, and I do love all the kids, but I have an extra-special bond with Emily. I unzip her raincoat and ease it off her shoulders, revealing a pink *Dora the Explorer* shirt underneath.

'Morning, Sarah,' I say. Emily's mum looks pale, violet smudges under her eyes. 'How are you?'

'Tired. This little one was screaming all night.' She rocks the pram. I peep at the sleeping baby splayed out like a starfish, hands bunched into fists. 'I've been struggling to sleep anyway, since…' Her eyes meet mine above Emily's head, and I know she means since Greg left. Sarah warned us several weeks ago that Emily might be unsettled, missing her father. Sarah kicked him out after catching him in bed with his secretary, a cliché that until then I had never quite believed actually happened.

'I'm off for a nap anyway,' Sarah continues, 'before she wakes.' She plants a kiss on the top of Emily's blonde hair and walks towards the door, one hand pushing the pram, the other pulling her hood up.

I spend a happy morning at the arts and craft table, observing the children creating their glittery masterpieces, utterly absorbed in what they're doing.

'Look, Grace.' Emily pushes a piece of paper in front of me, depicting two stick figures. Blue paint drips onto my black trousers.

'It's beautiful, Emily. Is that you and Lily?'

'Yes.'

'It must be fun having a sister?'

'No. She cries all the time. Mummy says when she's bigger she'll be more 'tresting.'

I smile at her mispronunciation. 'I'm sure she'll be very interesting.' I peg the sopping paper onto the washing line above the table. 'Mummy will love it. It should be dry by the time you go home.'

Emily darts over to the dressing-up corner and I study the image of the two little girls. Growing up, I always wanted a sister, someone to share things with – and then I met Charlie and I thought we'd always have each other. Grow white-haired and walking-sticked together, sucking humbugs on a park bench as we compared our aches and pains. Laughed about the good old days.

'Penny for them?' Lyn lightly touches my arm.

'I don't think they're worth that much.'

'I'm sure…' She trails off, interrupted by the buzzer. The noise is relentless: either someone is keeping their finger pressed on the button, or it's broken.

'Keep the children in here,' Lyn instructs Hannah, and I follow her into the corridor, closing the activity room door behind me.

Emily's dad releases the buzzer when he sees us, slapping the door with his palms instead. Rain streaks down his furious crimson face.

'Let. Me. In.'

Lyn presses the intercom and speaks in her normal tone, and it's only because I know her so well that I can detect a slight quiver in her voice.

'What do you want, Greg?'

'Emily.'

'You need to go home and calm down. I can't let you in like this.'

'Open the fucking door.' He begins to kick it. Muddy footprints haphazardly imprint the glass like the children's potato print patterns, and the frame rattles. But it remains secure, for now.

'You'll scare the children. If you don't leave, I'll call the police.'

'I have the right to see my daughter, you fucking bitch. You're all fucking bitches.'

I wonder how long the police will take to arrive. The room next door is silent. I can picture the children's faces, pale and anxious, small hands covering their ears. Anger nudges out my fear. How dare he? Dads are supposed to be protectors. Long-forgotten feelings ignite as I slip through the staffroom and out of the back door, gasping as the wind blows freezing rain into my face. My shoulders are hunched and my head is down as I arc my way around the building to the front door.

'Greg.'

He swings around. The vein on the side of his head is pulsing. 'Where's my fucking daughter?'

'I'm not bringing her out.' Ice-cold water snakes down my back and my purple 'Little Acorns' T-shirt clings to my skin.

Greg darts forward, raising his fist. I flinch. The muscles in my thighs tremble; they feel too weak to support me. I think of Emily, pink tongue between her teeth as she concentrates on her painting.

'If you don't let me see her, Grace, I swear you'll be sorry.' His jaw tics.

'Do you really want her to see you like this?' My voice is mea-sured, belying my fear.

His arm suspends mid-air as his eyes lock onto mine. Distant thunder rumbles. His legs crumple and he drops to his knees, his face wet with rain and remorse. He covers his eyes with tremu-lous hands.

'I miss her. I miss them both, so much.' He lowers his fore-head to the ground as if pleading to a God that isn't listening.

I reach out and touch his shoulder, not sure whether I'm try-ing to comfort him or steady myself.

He raises his head, looking at me through bloodshot eyes. 'I can't cope with the pain I've caused.'

But he can. We all have to carry the consequences of our own actions, no matter how heavy they are. I know that better than anyone.

'Please. Let me see her, Grace.'

'I can't.'

'Then I'll make you feel the way I feel right now. How would you like that?'

Lyn queues for our drinks, while I bag a table by the window. I unwind my scarf and shrug off my coat. I'm wearing Hannah's gym clothes. My wet pre-school uniform is scrunched up in the boot of my car. I lean back in the tub chair and slide forwards on the faux-leather material. There are hordes of people scurrying past the window and I wonder where they're going: home; picking up children; meeting a lover, perhaps? Feet slap against the wet pavement as coats are zipped around shivering bodies, scarves wound a little tighter. We haven't yet had the forecasted snow but the January air is biting.

Across the road, under the street light, stands a lone figure: black padded coat, hood up, face shrouded. They're looking directly in the coffee shop. At me? I shift uncomfortably in my seat and look away, but when I glance back they're still there. Still motionless. The same feeling I'd had on Sunday, when the strange car sat outside my cottage, creeps up and down my spine.

'Here.' Lyn plops mugs of steaming chocolate on the table. Cream trickles down the sides and she licks her fingers.

'See that person across the road?'

'Where?' Lyn squints without her glasses.

'There.' I stand and press my palms against the window. My forehead touches the window and my breath fogs the glass. I turn my head to her. 'Do you see them?'

Lyn puts her glasses on and stands, forehead creased, peering into the darkened street. 'Who am I looking at, Grace?'

I turn my head back, but the figure is gone, and I wonder if they were ever there at all.

'It doesn't matter,' I say. 'I think Greg's unnerved me. Thanks for this.' I sit and pull my mug towards me, half listening as Lyn recounts a mix-up with the order. My eyes are drawn out onto the street again. There is definitely no figure and I berate myself for my paranoia. My senses have been on high alert since Charlie died. It's odd how many sides there are to grief: tears and sadness, confusion and anger. I reach forward and open the bag of mini muffins, pull one out and take a bite. The sugar rush goes some way towards restoring the energy the day has drained from me.

'What a day.' Lyn picks chocolate chips out of a muffin with her fingernails and pops them on her tongue.

'At least Emily's safe.' I'd found the number of Greg's sister from the emergency contact book and she'd come to pick him up. Despite everything, I didn't think he deserved to be arrested. I know how it feels to have guilt sit in the pit of your stomach, gnawing away. A dull ache that never quite goes. Greg is human, as flawed and repenting as the rest of us, and we all make mistakes, don't we? Only some mistakes are harder to forgive.

'Do you think Sarah will take him back?' Lyn asks.

I shrug and spoon cream into my mouth, savouring the velvety sweetness as it dissolves on my tongue.

'It's so nice to sit down,' says Lyn. 'I danced so much at Steve's niece's eighteenth on Saturday I've got blisters on my blisters. I wish you'd come.'

'I know. It's just…'

'Too soon after Charlie.' Lyn pats my hand, reaches for another muffin and leans back.

It's been over five months now and I'm trying to rebuild my life. Sometimes I fleetingly feel something close to normal, but my grieving feet are not yet ready to dance, however much I appreciate Lyn's attempts to get me out. I'm trying to let people back into my life, grateful they're still here. I'd fallen apart after we buried Charlie; couldn't seem to wrench myself out of bed. It was only as my grandparents stood over me with fake smiles and brightly wrapped gifts on my twenty-fifth birthday that I really noticed the worry etched into their faces. After that, I started to piece myself back together. I tell myself I'm coping but I'm not. Not really. Take away my sleeping tablets and I would shatter.

'Grandma saw Lexie, Charlie's mum. She wants to see me.'

'Why?'

'I don't know. Only one way to find out, I suppose.'

'Is that a good idea? She was awful to you, Grace. Driving you out of your best friend's funeral.'

'I know, but she's Charlie's mum and she has no other family. I really should check she's OK. She probably wants to apologise.'

'Probably,' said Lyn. But she looks as unconvinced as I feel.

The washing machine rinses my uniform as I stab holes in the film covering the fish pie I found languishing at the bottom of the freezer. I'd meant to go shopping, but the events with Greg and the sense of being watched had unsettled me, and I'd come straight home after leaving Lyn. I put the pie in the microwave and slosh some wine into a glass. Dan has football training on a Monday and always has dinner in the bar afterwards. He's texted to say he's found his phone; I'm glad we hadn't replaced it already. I'll eat and have an early night.

I flick through my albums, trying to find one that matches my day. The TV is rarely on when Dan isn't around. I lower the needle and listen to the static before the singing starts. Ella Fitzgerald croons 'Stormy Weather'; I'm ready for some sunshine of my own. Even though it's early, I put on my fleecy pyjamas, the tartan ones that Dan says make me look like Rupert the Bear. Charlie's pink envelope stands between my bedside lamp and a stack of books I have yet to read. I pick the letter up carefully, as if it may explode, and take it downstairs, where I stare at it while eating out of the greasy plastic container to save washing up. I'm curious to know what Charlie's written, but equally reluctant to open it, scared of the emotions it may engender. This is the last new memory I can form of Charlie. Once I've opened it, everything else will forever be re-runs.

I place my tray on the floor, swing both feet up and stretch out on the sofa, pulling a patchwork throw over my legs. Picking the envelope up between thumb and finger, I ease it open.

CHAPTER SEVEN
Then

'Bulbs are coming up. Daffodils already.' Grandad washed his hands at the sink, while Grandma wiped splashes of water from the stainless steel taps with her 'J'Adore Paris' tea towel. She'd never been to France, never been out of England at all, but she loved tea towels, always buying one when she visited somewhere, and often bought them as gifts. She had a drawer full of places she'd never been. It wasn't like I'd been abroad either, but at thirteen, I thought I had all the time in the world.

I sat at the pine kitchen table, squeezed next to the Welsh dresser crammed with blue and white crockery. Only a few crumbs remained from my slab of lemon drizzle cake and I pushed my plate away, slid the stack of photo albums towards me.

I opened the brown crinkly pages. My hand rose to the stabbing in my chest. Seeing my fractured family always left me breathless. It was something I usually avoided, but I needed some photos for a school project. Grandad stood behind me and placed his hands on my shoulders as I silently turned the pages. I traced the faces with my fingertips. We looked like an ordinary family: Mum, Dad and me. Quality Street Christmases and sandcastle summers. We *had been* an ordinary family. I missed that. I paused at a photo of Mum and Dad grinning on the beach, holding me up proudly between them like a trophy they'd won, their hair blowing in the wind. I must have been about two and had ice cream dripping off my chin as I thrust my cone towards the camera. The image captured the moment in time so perfectly I could almost feel the sun, see the crashing waves, hear the seagulls. The sense of home. There was a grainy photo of Dad and me. We were sitting at the breakfast bar, nestling mugs of hot chocolate topped with whipped cream and flakes. Dad used to make me proper hot chocolate, 'None of that powdered rubbish for my girl.' He'd a special pan just for milk, and would stir chunks of Cadbury's round and round until the milk was smooth and brown.

'This one.' I eased it out from its plastic cover and added it to the pile of photos of my grandparents, Mum and various aunts and uncles I didn't think I'd ever met. Scrawled names on Christmas cards I never recognised.

'You must miss them.' Grandad sat next to me. 'It doesn't have to be this way. Your mum rang again last night.' He covered my hand with his. His palm was warm and moist.

'I don't want to talk about her.' My stomach twisted when I thought of what I'd done and I snatched my hand away.

'You should talk about her. Get things straight in your head.'

'I talked to Paula at the time, didn't I? What was the point of having a bloody therapist if I have to talk to you too?'

'Don't swear, Grace.'

The chair legs screeched on the tiled floor as I pushed back my seat and stood. 'I'm going to Charlie's.'

'Wait.' Grandma held up a hand the way a policeman might stop traffic and I leaned against the door frame, drumming my fingertips on the wood as she placed a huge slice of sponge on a piece of foil and parcelled it. 'That's to take with you. That girl needs feeding up.' According to Grandma, nobody ate properly except us. 'You might want to ask her on holiday with us this year, we're going abroad.'

'Really? Where?' Curiosity lifted my mood. I crossed my fingers behind my back: *Disneyland, Disneyland, Disneyland*. Esmée had been to stay with her aunt in Paris last year and hadn't stopped talking about it since.

'The Isle of Wight.'

'Ivy, it's not abroad. I've explained this to you.' Grandad winked at me and I couldn't help smiling back, my outburst all but forgotten.

'If it's not abroad then why do we need to catch a ferry to get there, eh? Explain that.'

The Tesco carrier bag stuffed full of photos and cake bumped into my legs as I sprinted through the village, past humming lawnmowers, and garden hoses spraying grubby cars. My trainers smacked against the concrete as I ran faster and faster, trying to drive out Grandad's words, which were circling around my mind. My life seemed split into two. Before and after.

My T-shirt was damp with sweat by the time I got to the high street and I slumped against the postbox to catch my breath. A peal of laughter floated across the road. Siobhan. She'd come out of Boots with her younger sister, Abby. I began to call hello but Siobhan cupped her hand over her mouth and whispered in Abby's ear. They both looked over and giggled. I snapped my jaw shut and studied the mail collection times, conscious my cheeks were probably the same colour as the postbox, wishing I'd cut across the park – but Grandma didn't like me going there alone. 'Undesirables,' she said, but in the day the park was usually full of sticky toddlers and fraught mothers. I wasn't sure what Siobhan had against me but she'd never welcomed me the way Charlie and Esmée had, and the older we'd got, the unfriendlier she'd become. Abby and Siobhan ducked into the coffee shop and I scurried passed the window, head low, shoulders hunched.

Charlie's house was sandwiched in the middle of a row of Victorian terraces, red-bricked and chimney-stacked. These were where the employees of the old textile factory used to live. The factory was long gone, it was a primary school now, but the houses remained.

The grass was knee-length and full of nettles and I kept my hands raised as I picked my way towards to the front door. Ignoring the doorbell – I'd never known it to work – I banged the knocker. Specks of black paint flaked off, fluttering onto the step. I waited, and just when I was about to knock again I heard stilettoed footsteps, the jangling of bangles, and the door swung open with a creak.

'Hi Lexie.' Charlie's mum flattened herself against the wall while I squeezed into the hallway. Lexie flapped her hands.

'Wet nails. Shut the door, Gracie-Grace.'

I pushed the door shut behind me and bent down to pick up the post from the mat.

'Any red ones take them home with you,' said Lexie. 'I don't bleedin' want them.' She blew on her ruby red nails. 'How's it going? Got a boyfriend yet?'

'No. I…'

'You're better off without one. They're no bleedin' good, the lot of 'em. Charlie's in the kitchen – she's cooking tea. Hungry?'

'Starving.' I'd run off the lemon drizzle cake.

Charlie was shaking chicken nuggets and chips onto a baking tray that was ginger with rust.

Lexie almost never cooked. Charlie practically lived on pizza, burgers and chips – it was a wonder she was so skinny. 'Lazy food for lazy people,' Grandma said, but my mouth watered all the same.

'Do me a favour, light me a ciggie. Don't wanna smudge me nails.' Lexie nodded towards her packet and I tapped a cigarette out and held it up. She closed her scarlet lips around it. It took me three attempts to spark the lighter to life and as Lexie leaned forward I was worried that her hair, dry and straggly from years of dyeing, would catch alight. She inhaled and the tip of the cigarette glowed red.

'Watcha got there?' Lexie nodded towards my carrier bag.

I shifted a pile of letters that had spread all over the table like paper ivy and tipped my photos out. 'It's for our history project. The family tree one? Stupid idea but it's compulsory. Charlie needs some pictures too.'

'Not sure if I've got any suitable. They're publicity shots. A bit risqué, if you know what I mean?'

I didn't, but I laughed along anyway to her cackle. 'What about Charlie's dad?'

'What about him?' She frowned, flapped smoke away from her eyes.

Charlie scowled at me, clanked the nuggets in the oven.

'Do you have any photos? We need the whole family. It's ridiculous but…'

'I am her whole family. Aren't I bleedin' good enough?' Lexie ground out her cigarette.

'Yes, but…'

'But what?'

'We're supposed to have pictures. Did you lose them in the fire?'

'What fire?'

'Charlie said she remembers a fire, here, when she was younger.'

'Charlie's got a bleedin' overactive imagination.'

'But Mum… I remember…'

'You remember nothing, you lying little madam. There never was no fire.' Lexie pushed her chair backwards. It thudded against the wall. 'I'm going out.'

'Mum, I'm cooking…'

'I'm not hungry.' Spiked heels echoed down the hallway. The house vibrated as the front door slammed shut.

'What did you do that for?' Charlie stood, hands on hips.

'What?'

'I've told you how she gets when I mention my dad.'

'You've a right to know; anyway, we need…'

'*We* don't need anything. Siobhan's right, you can be a real pain in the arse sometimes, Grace. Just because your family's a mess – stop interfering in mine.'

My chair toppled over with a clatter as I sprang to my feet, fists balled. 'I can't believe you said that. You're supposed to be my best friend.'

'Well maybe we shouldn't be friends any more. I don't need a dad and I don't need you, Grace Matthews. Just fuck off.'

Charlie jumped up and rocketed out the door. Footsteps thundered up the stairs and the light above me shook as Charlie ran into her room. There were no carpets in this house to cushion the sound. I remembered Charlie once saying they'd all been ripped up when they were smoke-damaged, and I couldn't help but wonder why Lexie denied having a fire. What was she trying to hide? But as I scooped my photos back into my bag I knew Charlie was right about one thing. My family was a mess and it was all my fault.

CHAPTER EIGHT
Now

I hold the letter in my hands. The notepaper has a jagged edge. It's clearly been ripped from an exercise book and I can almost hear our primary school teacher, Miss Stiles, shouting: 'Charlotte Fisher! What do you think you're doing?' Charlie had so often been in trouble.

I pick up my wine glass, rest back and begin to read.

ONLY GRACE AND CHARLIE ALLOWED TO READ THIS SO IF YOU'RE NOT ONE OF US, RE-BURY OUR BOX AND BUGGER OFF!!!

So we're not fifteen any more and we're all grown up and fabulous and here is my list of things to do, if I haven't already:

1. *I want to find my dad. There, I've admitted it. I'm so bloody sorry for being such a whining bitch, Grace, when you were trying to help me before, but Mum's so against it and I feel so torn. I thought writing it down would be easier than saying it but I'm feeling so guilty for even thinking it. Mum's a mad cow sometimes but she's all I've got and I don't want to upset her. But you know what it's like not having your dad around, don't*

you, Grace? There's always a hole, isn't there? A sadness under the surface that just won't go away, and it's getting harder and harder to ignore.

I seem to spend more and more time thinking about him lately. I wonder if I look anything like him (my gorgeousness has to come from somewhere), if we share the same humour (something needs to explain my obsession with Monty Python*) and if he hates beetroot as much as me. I'm half of someone I don't know, and I want to. I want to know who I am and where I came from, and I want him to know me too (only the good bits though!).*

Hopefully by now Mum will have come clean and told me who he is (I'm NEVER going to lie the way she does BTW) and we've already found him and holidayed in his Hollywood mansion by the pool. (Is it too much to hope he's a millionaire movie star too?)

2. *Don't get fat!!! We'll be spending lots of time in bikinis (see above)!*
3. *Stay friends forever. Grace, Siobhan, Esmée and Charlie. Our fab four. I love you all (but especially you, Grace. My BFF).*

Charlie xxxx

I read the list twice more while I finish my drink. I'm still no nearer to uncovering the meaning behind her last words. There's nothing here to help me understand them and disappointment sours in my stomach. I don't know what I was expecting, really. A letter-labelled clue? A big black arrow with 'start here'? As I read it again, it hits me that we never did find her dad, and I stand and pace the floor. Where did she go when she disappeared? Could she have found her dad? Might he know what she did that she thought was so terrible?

I close my eyes. *Think, Grace.* If I could find him, I could ask him. The only problem is there's only one person who knows his identity. Lexie.

CHAPTER NINE
Now

Rain-laden clouds hang heavy in the slate sky as I drive towards Lexie's house, and I'm not quite halfway there when they burst. Fat raindrops machine-gun down, bouncing off my windscreen. I switch my headlights on, although it is not yet four o'clock.

Despite my pleading, Dan's refused to accompany me. I've tried to explain to him that I need to make peace with Lexie, she's my only real chance of finding Charlie's father, but he doesn't understand why I feel so compelled to track him down. At best, Charlie's dad met Charlie when she disappeared and can provide some answers. At worst, he didn't meet her, but in that case at least I could tell him all about her. Honour her memory.

Besides, I need to unravel the meaning behind Charlie's last words: *I did something terrible, Grace. I hope you can forgive me*. I have to start somewhere.

My mobile trills and I pull in at a bus stop to see who's calling; if it's Grandma, I'll answer it. A red Corsa slides in behind me. The call is from an 0843 number and I think it's probably a cold call and reject it. I indicate and pull back onto the road, leaning forward in my seat, squinting to see through the downpour. It's a relief when I reach Charlie's street.

Lexie's front garden is saturated and by the time I've made my way through the overgrowth to the front door, the bottom half of my jeans are soaked through. It doesn't seem seven years ago that my palms stung as I slapped them against the door, tears streaming down my face, screaming for Charlie, demanding the truth. I never had an inkling then that I wouldn't see Charlie again for years, and that the next time I knocked on the door would be to take Lexie to Charlie's funeral.

The door knocker is stiff, and as I yank it upwards it creaks in protest. I stamp moisture from my shoes while I wait. A clap of thunder startles me; at first I think it's a car backfiring and I turn around. A red Corsa is parked behind my car, but it's too dark for me to properly see the driver and I wish I'd noticed the number plate of the car at the bus stop. How many red Corsas can there be? Hundreds probably, but the hairs on the back of my neck stand up as I wonder whether it's the same car that sat outside the cottage last Sunday.

I knock again. Hard and fast.

'Who is it?'

'It's me. Grace.'

The door swings open and I try and hold my smile in place, as Lexie's lined face peeps around the door. Tiny red blood vessels streak the whites of her eyes.

'I don't answer it any more unless I know who it is. I'm sick of bloody do-gooders. I wasn't sure you'd come.'

'Neither was I.'

I step into the hallway, prepared to defend myself if she starts shouting, but to my surprise, she opens her arms and her behaviour at the funeral doesn't seem quite so important any more. She's Charlie's mum and she's hurting. We both are. Her hipbones dig into me as we awkwardly hug – she's never been tactile – and I turn my head away from her hair. Her dark grey roots contrast with bright red split ends, it smells as though it hasn't been washed in weeks.

I follow her down the narrow hallway, my shoes leaving wet imprints on the naked wood.

'Take a pew.'

The kitchen is pungent. Rubbish piled high against the back door, spilling out of carrier bags. Hot shame fills me. This is Charlie's mum and no matter what happened at the funeral I should have visited before. She has no one else. I pull out a chair. The legs wobble, and I sweep crumbs from its seat before sitting.

'Tea?'

'Thanks.'

The sink is stacked with dirty crockery like a giant game of Jenga and as Lexie pulls out a mug, cutlery falls. The clattering shatters the uncomfortable silence.

'Sugar?'

'No thanks.'

Lexie rinses the stained cup under the cold tap and pours not-yet-boiling water onto a tea bag. I push away a pile of post and an overflowing ashtray to make room for the drink slopped before me. I don't bother asking for milk.

I raise the mug, hovering it in front of my lips, and pretend to sip. 'How have you been?'

Lexie shrugs and glances around the filthy kitchen, as if that should tell me all I need to know – and it does. The uncomfortable silence returns.

'I get by, I suppose. Your grandma sends over enough casseroles and cake to feed the street.'

I mask my surprise. Grandma has never been Lexie's biggest fan. I'm touched by the gesture.

'So.' I take a deep breath. 'You wanted to see me?'

Lexie lights a cigarette with shaky hands. She carries the ashtray over to the back door and aims the contents towards an already full bin bag. Ash spills to the floor. 'I'm taking a lodger in. Need the cash. Haven't worked since… You know.'

I nod.

'Gotta clear Charlie's room. Can't do it on me own.'

Lexie picks up her gold Zippo lighter, flicks it open and snaps it shut, over and over. I clench my jaw. I want to cover her hand in mine and still her, but I don't.

'You want me to help?'

'Yeah. They move in tomorrow.'

'Tomorrow?'

'Yeah. Will you help me?'

Her question hangs in the air, demanding a response, but my mouth is dry and I can't speak. I don't want to go back into Charlie's bedroom.

Her grey eyes lock onto mine. 'Please.' The word is whispered so softly I almost miss it.

I open my mouth. The word 'no' sits on my tongue, like a caged bird waiting to be released, but my guilt has other ideas. 'Yes,' I say.

The door feels cold and hard against my palm, as if it knows it's guarding a room that has lost its heart. As I push it open, I'm not sure whether it's dust or old memories that make me choke. The faded purple curtains that have never quite met in the middle are drawn, and I swish them apart and open the window. I gulp air as though I've been underwater for a long time, welcoming the splashes of rain that splatter against my face.

Charlie's bedroom wasn't used in the six years leading up to her death but she left so suddenly that most of her things are still here. Barely an inch of floor space is visible beneath the chaos that was once Charlie, but the room feels empty somehow. Hollow.

Lexie lingers in the doorway, not quite crossing the threshold, chewing her thumbnail.

'I'll get a rubbish sack,' she offers.

I nod, although I feel we will need at least a roll of sacks, and possibly a miracle, to empty the room today.

The corkboard, covered in photos, still hangs skewed against the Artexed walls. Charlie had hated her room: 'Who has walls like a ceiling?' I remember the weekend she gave up asking Lexie to hire a plasterer, and we painted the nicotine-stained walls bright pink. It looked even worse. Charlie came back to mine and cried as she picked paint from her hair, complaining her room now looked like a giant marshmallow. Grandma cooked us shepherd's pie while Grandad silently fetched his roller and ladders from the shed. By the time Charlie went home the following day her walls were crisp white, but the Artex remained.

I unpin a photo and my abdomen contracts as I gently trace the outline of Charlie's face with my finger. 'I miss you,' I whisper.

'I miss her too.' Lexie hands me some sacks and a cardboard box. 'I'm drinking the last lager so we can use the box.'

I swallow my sarcasm. She is trying. 'Where do you want to start? We should probably divide it into sections. Stuff to keep, things for the charity shop and rubbish.'

'I'll strip the bed, put the laundry in the machine. You start with the drawers. Anything you think you might wear you can keep.'

I kneel. My kneecaps press into the wooden boards and I'm glad I've worn trousers. The top drawer is unyielding and I have to yank it open. The handle comes off in my hand and I think about asking Lexie to try and find a screwdriver, but I place it in my pocket instead. I've got a small toolbox in my boot. Crumpled inside the drawer is a glorious rainbow of tiny T-shirts. Even if I wanted to wear them, they'd be too small. I pick out several that I think Lexie might like to keep – an orange tie-dyed T-shirt, Smartie-coloured vest tops – and fold the rest into a sack for the charity shop. There's a floral shirt in the bottom drawer. 'This is mine,' I tell Lexie. 'Wonder what else I'll find?'

A ghost of a smile passes Lexie's lips.

'What?' I ask.

'When Charlie was about five or six she went through me drawers playing dress-up. I was making dinner in the kitchen when she came in waving me vibrator. It was buzzing away in her hand. "What's this, Mummy?" she asked.'

'What did you tell her?'

'Told her it was a special shoulder massager I used when I had a hard day.'

'That was quick.'

'Didn't think any more of it but about two weeks later when I went to pick her up from school, Miss Johnson, her teacher, asked if she could have a quick word. Said she'd told the children the day before she had a stiff shoulder and couldn't write on the whiteboard properly. Charlie had brought my special massager for her to borrow. She handed me my vibrator in a Tesco carrier bag. I nearly bleedin' died.'

'Oh my God. What did you say?'

'I said thanks, and I hoped she got some relief soon.'

I snorted. 'Poor you, and poor Charlie. Was she in trouble?'

'Nah. She was only trying to help. Wasn't as bad as the time charity collectors knocked on the door asking for donations for the sick children in Africa.'

'What happened?'

'I was in the shower but Charlie decided to give them one of my plants. "These are herbs that make you get happy. Give them to the children," she told them, as she handed over me home-grown cannabis.'

'Lexie! You're lucky you didn't get arrested.' I can't help laughing. The air doesn't feel quite so thick now.

'I don't think they knew what it was. They told Charlie they just wanted money. "Oh we never have any bleedin' cash in this house," she told them. She must have been about five.'

'I can't imagine her being small. Do you have any photos?'

'A few. I'll show you later if you like.'

'Yes, please.' I imagine Charlie at five, pigtailed and fearless. I'll never forget the way she stood up for me the first time we met.

'Grace, I owe you a big apology…' Lexie tails off.

I smooth creases from summer dresses, fold winter jumpers. Clothes for seasons Charlie will never see again. 'The funeral was stressful. You don't have to apologise.'

'It's not just the funeral.' There is the flick of the lighter, a waft of smoke. 'It's complicated…'

'We don't need to talk about it today.' I pull the last thing out of the drawer. 'These were yours once, remember?' I hold up tiny white denim shorts.

'I loved those jeans. Little madam.'

I place them with the things I'm setting aside for Lexie.

The drawers are empty. I stand and brush my knees, and open Charlie's jewellery box. Tinkling music spills out as a pink-tutu-ed ballerina twirls incessant pirouettes.

The other half of my heart necklace lays inside the red velvet lined case. I lift it out. It spins around, just as mine did in the woods, as if searching for its missing partner.

'You should have that,' Lexie says. 'She was wearing it that day. She'd want you to have it.'

I nod, too choked up to speak. I unclasp my chain and slide on Charlie's half-heart until it nestles against mine, not exactly fitting together: a broken heart that will never quite be whole again.

We work in silence until the moon rises, casting a creamy glow on rows of black sacks lined up like soldiers against the grubby walls.

'I'll drop these off at the charity shop on Monday.' I heft a bin bag over my left shoulder and carry one in my right hand. I feel like Santa Claus as I inch down the stairs, careful not to slip. I fold the back seats in my car down and somehow cram Charlie's entire life into my boot, except for the sack of bits I think Lexie might wear. That, I tuck inside her wardrobe.

I say goodbye to Charlie's bedroom. Faded outlines of posters and the sticky remains of Blu-Tack are the only visible signs of a life that once was. How quickly we can erase someone's physical presence, while their memory forever lingers. I flick off the light and join Lexie downstairs.

'Drink?'

'Please.'

I sit on the cracked leather sofa, tucking my feet under me, and sip from a glass of Merlot. I wait for the sharpness of the alcohol to soothe my anxiety. I'm going to take this opportunity to ask about Charlie's dad. I have to get this right. This is my chance to get a name, an address even.

'I had my first glass of red wine here,' I tell Lexie. 'Charlie told me it was blood and dared me to drink it. I cried when I got home. Told Grandad I'd turned into a vampire.'

'She was a little bugger, Charlie was,' Lexie says fondly.

'Can you show me those baby photos?' My tone is casual but my heart is pounding. I take another sip, bigger this time.

Lexie rummages through the sideboard and I cross my fingers behind my back.

'Here they are.' She drags out a brown A4 envelope with 'CHARLOTTE' scrawled on the front in black felt tip, photo corners poking through split seams.

'Always meant to put them in an album.' Lexie tips them out between us.

A toothless Charlie grins at me from the kitchen sink, hair frothy with shampoo.

'Very cute.' I pick up an old Polaroid. A pink-haired Lexie wearing a spotted gown, hospital band on her wrist, sleeping baby nestled against her. 'Was this the day she was born?'

'Yeah. Fourteen hours of labour. Christ, I was knackered. Did love that gas and air though.'

'Was Charlie's dad there?'

'No.' Lexie gulps her wine.

'Why not?'

Lexie shrugs. 'He didn't wanna know. Fucker did a runner as soon as he found out I was pregnant.'

'He never met Charlie?'

'No.'

'It must have been hard for you. Alone with a baby.'

'You don't know the half of it.'

'Tell me about him.'

'He's a bastard. She was better off without him.'

'I'm sure she was.' The lie trips off my tongue. 'I'm just curious.'

The silence between us stretches tighter and tighter until it snaps.

Lexie exhales deeply. 'OK. What do you want to know?'

She shakes the last drops of wine into her glass – it's almost overflowing – and reaches down the side of the sofa. She waves a new bottle and raises her eyebrows at me.

'I'm driving.' I cover the top of my glass with my hand and fidget in my seat. The air is clouded with cigarette smoke and secrets. Lexie flicks through the photos and pulls out a dog-eared print of a man. He's raising his pint to someone off-camera. A cigarette dangles from his lips. He's the spitting image of Charlie.

'His name's Paul Lawson. I met him when I was sixteen. I was hanging around The Folk Lore all the time. That was a great music venue. They had in-house bands that changed every few weeks. Think it's shut down now.' Lexie scrunches her forehead and I lean forward, willing her to carry on. 'I used to sneak in through the back door without paying. Stand at the back watching the bands, wishing it was me singing on stage. One day Frank, the owner, clapped me on the shoulder. I nearly shit myself. Thought I was gonna be thrown out. He said, "If you must insist on sneaking in, the least you can do is make yourself useful and collect some glasses."' Lexie smiled at the memory. 'Paul was a singer. It was his first gig and he was fan-fucking-tastic. I fell in love with him on the spot.'

Lexie paused to light another cigarette. Her smoke swirled around my face as her words swirled around my head. She'd loved Charlie's dad? Really loved him?

'He were twenty-two. Not a big age gap really, but he felt a lot older than me. A proper man, you know? I fancied him like mad. He'd bright blonde hair and the greenest eyes.' Lexie's cigarette flutters ash onto her leg. She doesn't seem to notice.

'Here.' I hand her the ashtray. 'So you had a relationship with him?'

'The first night he sang, he came off stage on such a high. Picked me up and twirled me around so fast I thought I might chuck. He asked me to celebrate, but Frank told him he wouldn't serve me, even after hours.' Lexie unscrews the new bottle and tops up her glass. 'Paul bought a bottle of whisky to take out and we went to the park.' Lexie wraps her arms around herself, as if holding the memory close. I've never seen her look so vulnerable. 'I didn't like whisky, thought it was fucking horrible. Didn't say that though. I spat half of it back in the bottle rather than swallowing it.' She shuddered. 'Never try and change yourself for a man, Grace.'

'What happened?'

'He told me I was special and I fell for his crap. We had sex on his coat. It was me first time. Classy, eh?' Lexie glugs her wine.

'Then he dumped you?'

'Nah. We had the next six weeks together. But then he disappeared. Didn't even say goodbye. Haven't seen him since. Don't fucking want to.'

'And you were pregnant when he left?'

'Yeah, but he didn't know.'

'Surely you could have found him? Told him? He had a right to know about the baby.'

Lexie fumbles with her cigarette packet, delaying her answer, as if she's formulating the words in her head before she says them. 'I did tell him. He didn't want us.'

'I thought you said…'

'He didn't know until I told him, I meant. He didn't want kids. Wanted me to have an abortion. Bastard.'

'Does he know you didn't? That he had a daughter?'

'Course.' Lexie swung her legs down, knocking over the wine. 'Shit, shit, shit.'

I fetch a cloth and kneel. Dab the threadbare rug, mopping up the claret liquid. 'So what did he say when you told him about Charlie?'

'I don't bloody know. It was twenty-five years ago. Can barely remember what I did yesterday.'

'Does he know Charlie died, Lexie?'

Lexie stares at the crimson stain, her eyes brimming with unshed tears. 'I don't wanna talk no more.'

'But Lexie, it's important…'

'Don't ruin it, Grace. It's been nice seeing you again but I'm tired.' Lexie holds out her hand and I pass her the sopping cloth, pull on my shoes and gather my coat and bag.

'We will talk again soon,' I tell her.

She nods and we hug our goodnights.

As I climb into my Fiesta, I feel Charlie's drawer handle in my pocket. I never did screw it back on. Still, it will give me an excuse to go back. I'll need to return the picture of Paul that I slipped into my pocket while Lexie wasn't looking. As I drive away, I can't help but feel a frisson of excitement. I have a plan.

CHAPTER TEN
Now

My muscles ache. I'm balanced on the edge of the mattress, teetering like a high-wire walker. Dan's still asleep, lying on his back, mouth slack, forehead smooth as a pebble. Sleep's erased the lines that furrow his brow the moment he wakes. Cold white sheets stretch between us, a gulf I still cannot cross no matter how much I want to. I'm not sure how he feels about me any more. I watch the rhythmic rise and fall of Dan's ribs as his lungs expand and contract. I long to place my head on his chest. To feel the prickle of his dark hair against my cheek; hear the beating of his heart.

Grief is crushing, isolating, lonely. We have both lost Charlie, but Dan doesn't know how I feel, not really, and how can he? At first I was mute with shock, unable to contemplate the simplest of tasks, to operate appliances I'd used a thousand times before. My toast was burned, clothes wrinkled. I lost my ability to communicate. Words knotted themselves on my tongue until I swallowed them, and they collided with the mass of emotions swirling inside me. If I couldn't pinpoint how I felt myself, how could I express it to him? Dan began to work later and later, often rolling through the front door at midnight. The stairs creaked under his heavy tread and I'd screw up my eyes and lie still and silent as he fumbled with his clothes, flopping into bed beside me, the smell of alcohol so strong it was as if I'd drunk it myself.

It has been different lately. There has been a shift. He's home more and I am back at work. Mixing with people as though I am one of them, as though I have not had the very fabric of my universe changed.

The windows rattle as the wind whips against them. The garden gate creaks open and thuds shut. I sit up and lean to reach my slippers. My neck cracks. I slip my feet inside faux fur and unhook my dressing gown, pad downstairs and open the front door. The apple tree is hunched over like an old man, braced against the wind. My slippered feet tread carefully on the frosty path and I yank the gate shut, latching it, knowing that it won't hold.

In the kitchen, I switch on the ancient heating system that gurgles and chugs to life, and pull bacon from the fridge. We used to take it in turns to make each other breakfast in bed on a Sunday and I can't remember when we stopped, whether it was after Charlie died or before. I cut thick slices from a white loaf and slather them in butter and brown sauce. The bacon hisses and spits, and Mittens purrs at my feet, telling me that she likes bacon, too. I cut off the fat. I will give half to her and half to the birds.

'Morning.' Back upstairs, I rest the tray on the foot of the bed. The mugs chink together and tea sloshes onto the plates.

Dan sits up, props pillows vertically behind him and sweeps magazines and wine gum packets to the floor. I pass him his breakfast.

'Thanks. You were late last night. How did it go with Lexie?' He bites into his sandwich. Grease trickles down his chin. He wipes it away with the back of his hand.

'She has a lodger moving in. I helped clear Charlie's room and then we had a drink. She told me about Paul.'

'Paul?'

'Charlie's dad.'

'Fucking hell. I never thought she'd tell you. I didn't think she actually knew who it was, to be honest. She's such a slapper.'

'Not always. He was her first and she really loved him.'

'Lexie in love. Who'd have thought? What happened?'

I rub my eyes. 'I'm not sure. She said he didn't know she was pregnant but then changed her story, saying that he'd run away when she told him. She was pretty cagey. Still, we can find him now, can't we?'

'Are you sure you want to?'

'Yes. We don't know where Charlie went when she disappeared. If she met him, he might know what she did that she thought was so unforgivable.'

'You might never find out. It's a long shot. And if you do, you might not like what you hear.' Dan chews his sandwich.

'I won't know if I don't try. Please, Dan.' I'll find Paul Lawson with or without Dan, but it will be easier if he helps.

'You've had a lot to deal with lately, Grace. I don't want anything else upsetting you.'

'Then help me. I want to move on, Dan. I really do. I want things back the way they were, as much as they can be. I want *us* back.'

Dan finishes his sandwich and wipes his fingers on the quilt. Pinpricks of grease seep into the white cotton and I take a sip of tea to stop myself from snapping. He reaches over and curls his fingers around mine.

'Me, too. OK. I'll help. Where does he live?'

I sigh. Suddenly the task ahead seems enormous. 'I'm not sure.'

'So, how can we tell him?'

'His name's Paul Lawson and he's a folk singer. I thought you could find him online somehow?'

'Because I'm a genius?'

'Because we splashed out on an all-singing, all-dancing Mac-Book, which you claimed was worth the over-inflated price tag because it can do everything.'

'It might not be able to perform miracles. Let's go downstairs though, and I'll Google him.'

The laptop balances on Dan's lap as it whirrs into life, screen glowing bright. Dan hunches over the keyboard. I sit as close as I can, our thighs pressing together. It's the most physical contact we've had in months. I hand him the picture I took from Lexie's last night. I hope she doesn't notice that it's missing.

Dan's fingers fly over the keyboard. 'Paul Lawson you said? Folk singer?'

'Yes.'

'There's links with either "Paul Lawson" or "folk singer" as keywords, but nothing with them both.'

'Let's look through them anyway.'

Dan laughs. 'You don't quite understand the Internet, do you? There are forty million results. Be my guest if you want to trawl through them all.'

I take the laptop from him and click on page after page. The knots in my shoulders pull tighter and tighter until I have to stand up, link my fingers behind me and stretch out my arms.

'Let's try websites dedicated to tracing people.'

The afternoon flashes by as we visit site after site: The Salvation Army, Missing Persons; it seems that everyone is looking for someone. I read stories of children who have run away, of husbands who went to the shop never to return, of mothers who vanished.

The bacon sandwich that had tasted so delicious feels weighted in my stomach. Its greasy tentacles rise up through my body.

'OK.' Dan scratches his nose. 'No one will help us find Paul as we aren't related to him, right? They might help Lexie, though, if they knew the circumstances. Is there any chance…'

'No.'

'That just leaves social media, I think.'

'But we've already done that.'

'We've searched social media, but we can post in some groups. There's loads of music-related ones. Someone must know him.'

Optimism rises. I nod.

'Go fetch the Chinese menu, woman, and leave me to work my magic.' Dan waggles his fingers like a cartoon villain contemplating a dastardly scheme. I go and find the takeout leaflet to choose what we want, even though we always end up picking a House Special Chow Mein and Egg Fried Rice.

The coffee table is strewn with the remnants of our Chinese dinner. My half-full foil containers nestle inside Dan's empty ones. Mittens bats at a noodle as it dangles from the side of my plate. Her eyes flick from left to right as she watches it swing, like a Wimbledon spectator following a rally.

'We'll post the photo you took from Lexie's house. What do you want to say?'

I crunch another prawn cracker. 'How about: "Are you Paul Lawson or do you know him? If so please get in touch as a matter of urgency. We have some important news for you"?'

'Not sure about that. It sounds as though he might have a windfall. We don't want every nutter replying, pretending to be him.'

'OK. What about: *We are trying to trace Paul Lawson for a matter unrelated to finance. If you know Paul, please contact us.*'

'Now it sounds like he's done something dodgy. I wouldn't reply to that.'

'That's because you're too suspicious.'

'I have to be, when you're so trusting.'

'Try: *I am an old friend of Paul Lawson's from the music business and would love to know what magic he's creating with his guitar now. Do you know him?*'

'Better. It's friendly. It should pique his curiosity. I'll set up an email account just for this, something music-related without a name.'

I lean back against the arm of the sofa and watch the screen illuminate Dan's face. He is utterly absorbed: my techie geek. I haven't felt so content in a long time.

'Finished.' Dan shows me what he's done, before snapping the lid of the laptop shut and sliding it under the coffee table.

I pick up my wine glass. The distance between us is evaporating. I wonder if he feels it too. I take a deep breath and am about to suggest an early night when Dan's phone vibrates. He pulls it out of his pocket, and frowns at the screen.

'I wish work would leave me alone on a Sunday.'

'Switch it off.'

'I can't. The survey's thrown up a problem with the house I'm trying to sell on Easton Road. The buyers want to pull out. I need to make a phone call. I'll speak to them while I nip to the corner shop. I'll pick up more wine.'

'We've still got quarter of a bottle. It *is* a school night.'

But the phone is pressed to his ear and he doesn't hear me.

The house is quieter without Dan. Emptier. After a while, I cross to the window. Scoop back the curtains. There are no mystery cars or figures, but I still hope Dan has locked the front door. I go to check. My hand stretches for the handle but I hear a noise. Freeze. There's a shuffling on the porch. Footsteps? I press my ear to the door and think I hear breathing, but I know that's impossible over the sound of my heart. *Clatter.* Something – I think the umbrella stand – has been knocked over. I tell myself it's a fox, but a voice says, 'Shit.' It's whispered, so I can't tell if the speaker is a man or woman.

'Who's there?' There's a quaking in my voice and I'm almost too scared to move, but I reach forward and switch the outside light on. I press my ear against the door. Silence. I imagine someone on the other side doing the same thing. A hand snaking through the letter box, grabbing me. A fist shattering the decorative glass panel. I'm torn between fetching my phone from the lounge or a knife from the kitchen, when I hear the rumble of Dan's car. His shoes slapping against the path. The front door creaks open and I practically snatch the wine bottle from Dan's hand, peering over his shoulder into the blackness, but there's nothing to see.

CHAPTER ELEVEN
Now

The week passes quickly and it's Friday already. I've worried all day that I'll have nothing to wear for my night out, but when I get home from work there's a Royal Mail card on the door-mat: a package has been left for me at Mrs Jones's. I tap on my neighbour's glossy green door, tuck my hands deep in my pockets and rock from foot to foot for what seems like ages in a bid to keep warm. Crouching, I peer through the letter box and see Mrs Jones, grey head bowed as she shuffles up the hall. I straighten as the door swings open.

'Hello, Grace dear, it's lovely to see you.'

'You too, Mrs Jones. How are you?'

'I mustn't grumble, dear. Everything's working and still where it should be.'

'Have you taken a parcel in for me?'

'It's here on my new telephone table. I'm ever so pleased with it, dear. It's a lovely colour. That pretty Kirstie Allsopp had one just like it on her programme last night.'

'It was my pleasure; I really enjoyed restoring it. I'm glad you like it.'

Mrs Jones squeezes my package and looks at me expectantly. 'It's a squashy one.'

'It's a dress, from eBay.'

'Going anywhere nice, dear?'

'It's Hannah's hen do, from work. We're going to Pizza Express.'

'Lovely, dear. It will be your hen night soon, I expect?'

I grin wryly. 'Have to wait until he asks me, first.'

'A lovely young girl like you? I'll tell that young man of yours to get a move on, shall I? Before somebody else snaps you up.'

I smile at the old lady I've grown so fond of.

'And is he better now?' she continues.

'Who?'

'Dan. I saw him go to work on Monday and then come home again about an hour later. I thought he must be ill. It's unusual for you to not have the same holidays. He got changed out of his suit and then went out again. Doctor's, was it?'

I hesitate. If I admit I've no idea Dan was off work or why, the whole village will know by teatime. Mrs Jones must keep BT in business, the amount of phone calls she makes – repeating 'have you heard' and 'you'll never guess what'. There's no maliciousness in her, though; just loneliness, I think.

'Stress, is it? All you young people seem to have it. It didn't exist in my day. I've heard him shouting at someone on that cordless phone of his. You should do what my granddaughter does.'

'What's that?'

'She chillaxes.'

My laugh sounds forced, even to me. 'We'll definitely try that.'

I take my package and step over the picket fence that divides our properties. My parcel feels light compared to the ton of questions I want to ask Dan.

The pale blue shift dress fits perfectly and I'm so pleased – it was such a bargain. I can't afford to shop in Coast normally, and this looks barely worn. I smooth the fabric over my hips and twist from side to side as I check out my reflection: stomach in, chest out. Ella Fitzgerald sings 'Someone to Watch Over Me'. Mrs Jones has certainly been watching Dan. I practise turning my rose-painted mouth into a happy smile.

The front door closes with a crash. Keys chink into the bowl on the telephone table; shoes thud against the wall as they are kicked off.

I find Dan in the kitchen, sleeves rolled up and tie loosened. He is rooted in front of the sink, staring at the garden, ice-cold lager in his hand, beads of condensation dribbling down the can.

'You OK? I thought you were driving me into town later?'

'It's just the one. I've had a shit day.'

'Do you want to talk about it?' I place my palm on his shoulder, feel the muscles under his shirt tighten as he shrugs me off.

'There's nothing to talk about.'

'Mrs Jones says you seem stressed lately.'

'Don't talk about me with the bloody neighbours, Grace.' His fingers clench the can. It begins to crumple.

I tense up. 'I wasn't. She mentioned she heard you shouting on the mobile. Who were you talking to?'

'A client. Christ.' Dan bangs his drink onto the draining board. Lager fizzes and froths, pooling on the gleaming surface. 'Can't a man have a drink after work without an interrogation?'

I flatten myself against the fridge as Dan pushes past me, and I remain motionless long after the front door has slammed. It isn't until my heart has stopped thumping quite so loudly that my trembling fingers dial for a taxi.

The jalapeños on my spicy meat pizza are volcano-hot, and I knock back chilled wine to cool the flames. Lyn tops up my glass with Pinot Grigio as I check my mobile again. No messages from Dan.

'I can't believe Charlie wanted to find her dad. It's so sad,' says Lyn.

'I read a story in *Take a Break* this week about a Mum who gave her son up for adoption.' Hannah reaches across the table for a slice of garlic bread. Her sparkly sleeve brushes against the pizza, and I dab the cheese that sticks to the material with my napkin. It's funny to see her so dressed up, and not in her in her 'Little Acorns' T-shirt and leggings. 'She spent her life waiting for him to knock on the door. Imagine if he's waiting for Charlie, thinking he'll meet her one day. Have grandchildren.'

'I know. That's why I want to find him. To tell him the truth.' *And to find out the truth*, I think, but I don't say that.

'Do you think Lexie gave you his real name?' asks Lyn.

'Paul Lawson? Yes. She seemed really relieved to talk about him. She doesn't have any female friends or family. Probably kept it all bottled up for years. She was really cagey when I tried to find out whether he knew about Charlie, though.'

'Does she know you're looking for him?' Hannah asks.

'No. She resents him for running out on her when she was pregnant. It probably wouldn't have occurred to her that she should tell him his daughter has died.'

'I don't blame her. He sounds like a bit of a bastard,' says Lyn.

'We haven't heard his side.'

'So what next? He may not be Internet-savvy. A lot of that generation aren't.'

'I'm not sure. I will find him, though. One way or another.'

I signal to the waiter, brandishing our empty bottle.

'Grace.' Lyn covers my hand. 'Don't take on too much. I'm worried about you.'

'Don't worry about me.' I shake free and pick up my glass.

'And you're drinking a lot. I didn't think you could, with the tablets. Have you stopped taking them?'

'Nearly.' I don't tell her about the strip I carry in my handbag. The way I break each pill into quarters that I take whenever life gets on top of me. Not enough to send me to sleep, but enough to create the warm haze I've become so reliant on. I will stop. I really will. Just not yet.

I change the subject. 'A toast to Hannah.' I raise my glass. 'To eternal love.'

'I can't imagine love being any other way,' says Hannah.

The conversation turns to the wedding, and it is gone eleven before we pay the bill and stumble out into the inky darkness. After the warmth of the restaurant, the cold air takes my breath away and I button my coat, ease fingers into gloves.

'Shall we go to a club?' asks Hannah.

'If that's what the bride-to-be wants,' says Lyn. 'Which one?'

'I dunno. Which one have you booked the stripper for?'

'You'd kill us if we had.' Hannah only has eyes for Andy.

'I'm just grateful you haven't made me wear L-plates and carry a blow-up cock. Let's try Rumours. They play lots of '80s and '90s music.'

We link arms and weave along the pavement. It's the first payday since Christmas and people are out in droves: men with designer stubble, girls who look too young to drink. Tiny dresses, fake tans, bare arms and legs. I feel old as I shiver in my layers. The queue for the club is long and we stamp our feet in the cold air.

Bouncers in black ties appraise us before nodding at the door. We pay our entrance fee to a bored-looking bleached blonde and navigate our way down a dark staircase. It isn't easy in heels; I hardly ever wear them. The pounding bass rumbles below us and the staircase shudders, making my toes tingle. I blink as my eyes adjust to the glaring neon brightness. The cocktails sign winks on and off; shiny black tables reflect flashing strobe lights.

'Sex on the beach?' screeches Hannah. I'm glad her wedding isn't for another couple of weeks. I think we'll all be hung-over in the morning.

I squeeze against the sticky bar and wait for ages to be served, despite waving my £20 note.

'What can I get you?' The young barman leans his forearms on the bar and stares into my eyes. Too many buttons are undone on his bright white shirt, displaying a tanned, hairless chest.

'Three cocktails please. Sex on the beach.' I'm glad it's dark in the club. I can feel myself blushing.

I wend my way through the crowd to Lyn and Hannah, who are perched on high stools near the dance floor. We shoulder boogie as we drain our drinks. The cocktails are smooth and sweet.

'Let's dance.' Hannah shimmies her way over to the DJ.

Three songs later and I'm panting. I gesture to our seats.

'Not yet,' Hannah clutches my wrist, shouts in my ear. 'I love this one.'

Madonna's throaty voice invites us to strike a pose. My body stiffens as the dance floor vogues. The thrum of the club slows and fades. I don't need to close my eyes to see Charlie's face. I can almost hear Grandma yelling up the stairs that we sound like a herd of elephants as we perfect our moves.

I feel a hand, hot on my arm. See Lyn's worried face. I remind myself we're supposed to be having fun and summon up a smile. 'Going for a wee,' I mouth and point over to the back wall.

I fight my way to the toilets and join the queue of over made-up girls in tiny black dresses. I squeeze into a cubicle and rest my forehead against the cool door. Toilet paper is caught on my heel and I use my other foot to knock it off. I want to go home, but I don't want to ruin Hannah's evening. Someone bangs on my door, shouting for me to hurry up, but it takes a while before I feel ready to emerge. I run my wrists under icy water; reapply my lipstick. The door leading back to the club is heavy, and as I pull, someone pushes from the other side. We fall into each other and red wine splatters the front of my new dress.

I wave away apologies and step back out into the fug of the club. I must look a state: my blue dress stained crimson, jostling my way through the throng, pulse beating in time to the music. I can't see Lyn or Hannah.

I unclasp my bag to fish out a tissue, thinking that maybe I can soak up the worst, but then I notice the illuminated screen of my mobile. It's a text from Dan: *We've found Charlie's dad.*

Lyn and Hannah aren't ready to leave, but I can't wait to talk to Dan and I say my goodbyes, claiming exhaustion. They know I don't sleep well and I can see the sympathy in their eyes. The night breeze cools my hot cheeks. The smell of frying onions from the burger van fills the air, greasy and sweet. I tap my clutch bag against my thigh impatiently as I scour the street for a taxi. The clubs haven't kicked out yet and there are no cabs to be seen. The rank isn't too far. I decide to walk.

The street is deserted – everyone's still partying. I turn off the main road, and as the thumping of the bass quietens and fades, I hear footsteps behind me. I stop. Fiddle with my bag and glance over my shoulder. There's no one in sight, but the shop doorways cast shadows and I wonder what they're hiding. Who they're hiding. I move again. My heels click-click-click against the pavement and there it is again. The slap of shoes on concrete.

I speed up. So do the footsteps. Alcohol churns in my stomach and I calculate the quickest route back to the main road. Run at full pelt. My breath wheezes and my mouth hangs open in a silent scream. Fight or flight has kicked in: I'm definitely the latter. My heels slow me down and I wonder whether I've time to kick them off – they're hard enough to walk in, let alone run – but the footsteps are getting closer and I can't afford to stop. There's hot breath on my neck. Something brushes against my shoulder. I shrug it off, hurl myself around the corner and wham into something solid. A policeman. I cling to his arm, crying with relief, turning around to point – but there's nobody there.

CHAPTER TWELVE
Then

The school toilets always smelled of cigarettes and cheap perfume. I tried not to inhale too deeply as I stuffed my shirt into my bag, pulled on a fitted T-shirt and rolled over the waistband of my skirt until the hem was way above my knees. I was desperate to look older than fifteen.

I joined Charlie in front of the mirror and picked up her Boots Seventeen mascara.

'Forest?' I asked. 'Or pocket park?' We were making the most of the balmy evenings.

'Park. Esmée and Siobhan are meeting us there.'

I sighed, long and hard. 'Someone took my history homework from my bag. I'm sure it was Siobhan. She really doesn't like me.'

Siobhan was always inviting Charlie and Esmée round hers without me, saying her mum was really strict and would only let her have two friends in the house at a time. 'Sorry, Grace,' she'd say, pulling a face, but I knew she wasn't sorry, not really. 'You'd understand if you had a mum.' And I wanted to smack her. Hard.

'Well, me and Esmée like you. Siobhan will get used to you.'

'Charlie, I've lived here six years now!'

'Yeah.' Charlie grinned. 'She's a bit slow.'

'I heard her saying I was boring. Do you think I am?' I never quite understood why Charlie stayed friends with me. We were polar opposites.

'You're not boring. You're calming. Mum says if it wasn't for you I'd have gone off the bleedin' rails. Stop analysing everything, Grace. I love you, and Siobhan doesn't know what she's talking about. Anyway, it won't be just us. Dan and Ben are coming tonight.'

My feelings for Dan were changing. The sight of him made my insides crackle like space dust. I hadn't told Charlie yet. I kept my feelings close to me, revelling in the deliciousness of the unknown. I was half-terrified, half-hopeful that he liked me too. At night I'd lie wrapped in my quilt, dreaming of the day he'd catch me in his arms as I whizzed down the slide, praying my bottom wouldn't get wedged halfway down. 'You're the reason I come here every day,' he'd murmur, before giving me my first taste of a boy's lips.

Charlie had kissed half of our year already. 'What's it like?' I'd asked her, both curious and repelled.

'It's OK until they shove their tongue in your mouth and poke it around. Ethan's was like an eel. He ran it around my teeth. Cleaned out the salt and vinegar crisps stuck there, though.'

'Charlie!'

'You asked. They mainly taste of fags though. You should try it.'

I'd practised on my hand, but that didn't taste of anything. I was waiting for the right boy. I was waiting for Dan. If Charlie knew I liked him she'd try to push us together. I wasn't quite ready – too scared of being rejected, I suppose.

Be careful with your heart, Grandma had told me. *You only get one and it's precious.*

If you can't be good, be careful, Lexie had told Charlie, in contrast, while giving her condoms. The condoms had torn, one af-

ter the other, as we'd rolled them down a banana. I'd washed my
hands three times afterwards. The smell of rubber had lingered
for hours.

'Dan's asked me out,' Charlie said now, as she smothered her
lips in gloss. I slipped with the mascara wand, and went into a
cubicle to get some tissue. CHARLIE FISHER IS A SLAG was written
on the back of the door. I'd scrubbed over a similar statement last
week. This time, I left it. My eyes sprang tears as I rubbed at my
cheek with the tissue until my skin felt as raw as my emotions.

I blew my nose. 'What did you say?' I asked, coming out of
the cubicle.

'I told him I might.' Charlie slicked pink gloss over her lips.

'You like him?'

Charlie shrugged. 'Never really thought about him that way.
He's just Dan, Dan, the ketchup man, isn't he? I want to do it
though.'

'Do what?'

'Sex. God, you can be so naive sometimes. I'm not sure
whether to do it with Dan, though. I think Siobhan fancies him.'

'Does she?' I felt sick at the thought.

'Yeah. I might let her have him. I'll find someone, though. It's
time we got it out the way.'

*Once your virginity's gone, you can't get it back. Give it to some-
one special,* Grandma had told me.

Don't get knocked up, Lexie had told Charlie.

'I'm going outside. It stinks in here.' I nodded at the cubicle.
'Someone's called you a slag.' I saw Charlie's mouth fall open and
I let the door slam shut behind me.

Dan and Ben were already at the park. Dan stood on top of the
slide and waved a bottle of vodka like it was the Olympic torch.

Charlie, never one to hold a grudge, turned to me and grinned, hitching her skirt up even higher. Bare legs already tanned. Although it was June, my skin was January pale.

'Well done, Danny boy,' Charlie called up to him. 'Let's have a swig.' Dan slid down and landed in front of us. 'Something stinks.' Charlie wrinkled her nose.

'It's Old Spice.' Dan grinned. 'It's sexy.'

'To who? You smell like an old man.' Charlie covered her nose with her sleeve and quaffed the vodka before passing it to me. My throat stung and I swallowed hard to stop myself from choking.

'Look.' I nodded towards the gap in the hedge. Siobhan sashayed through, trailed by Abby, who mimicked her big sister's walk, swinging her hips and pushing out her non-existent chest. With them were five older kids. I'd seen them around, although they didn't go to our school. Always dressed in black, skin pale, hair rainbow-bright. The Walking Dead, we called them. Grandma always crossed the road whenever we passed them on the high street. Why was Siobhan talking to them?

I took another gulp of vodka so Siobhan wouldn't notice my smile as she wobbled towards us, heels sinking into the grass, ankles turning.

'Got any cash?' Siobhan stood, hands on hips, shadowed by her mini-me Abby. She wasn't given an allowance. Her parents poured every spare penny into a savings account so Siobhan could go to uni – she wanted to be a lawyer. 'Bloodsuckers' was what Grandad called lawyers. Siobhan would fit right in.

'Nah. I'm skint.' Charlie never had any money. 'How about you, Grace?'

'Some. Why?'

'They've got weed.' Siobhan jerked her head towards the Walking Dead, barely visible, huddled next to the dark hedge.

'I'm not buying drugs!'

'You don't have to. I'll do it.'

'No.'

'You're so boring sometimes, Grace. Get a life.'

'Yeah, get a life,' Abby said.

'I have a life, thanks.' I gulped back the clear liquid. It smarted as it went down my gullet and I coughed until my eyes streamed.

Siobhan snorted. 'Loser.'

'At least I'm not a wannabe junkie.'

'At least I never killed anyone.'

I sprang forward, hands like claws, and raked my nails down her face. 'Take that back!'

Dan wrapped his arms around my waist and yanked me backwards. I leaned against his solid frame, panting, itching to dart forwards again.

'Siobhan, don't be such a bitch,' he snapped. 'Grace told us about her past because we're her friends.'

'And you know that's not how it was.' Charlie's voice is so low she's practically growling at Siobhan. 'Shut up or fuck off.'

'Sorry,' Siobhan mumbled to the floor.

I didn't speak for the rest of the night but I watched Dan watching Charlie, and Siobhan watching Dan and I drank vodka until I couldn't see anything any more, but Siobhan's words still rang in my ears. Did I actually kill him? Is that what they all thought?

CHAPTER THIRTEEN
Now

It's one of those rare February days that could pass for April: blue skies and cotton wool clouds. Apricot sun pours through the coffee shop window, making it feel far warmer than it actually is. I shrug off my coat. I'm lucky to find a vacant window table. The cafe is busy with Sunday fathers, their shirtsleeves rolled up, lifting whining toddlers out of buggies. Couples stare into each other's eyes, oblivious to the world around them. Two teenage girls discuss who Nick really fancies.

The cream melts into my hot chocolate as I dissect a muffin. My stomach is rolling with anxiety. The aroma of freshly ground coffee is oppressive.

I can't quite believe we've traced Paul Lawson – or rather, found someone that knows him. Anna's email was sparse, but she has agreed to meet me, to answer my questions as I will answer hers, as best I can.

My phone rings – an unknown number. As I answer, I pray it's not Anna cancelling. There's the sound of breathing, of static, and then nothing.

The bell rings as the front door of the coffee shop swings open. My head jerks around, but it's a man and I try not to be disappointed. So far, she's only five minutes late. But by twelve twenty my drink is cold and I have shredded my muffin into enough crumbs for Hansel and Gretel to find their way to Neverland.

My phone vibrates, skittering across the wooden table. It's another worried text from Dan. He didn't want me to come alone. I fire off a response: *I'm fine, she's not here yet*, and just as my thumb presses 'send', a shadow falls over my screen.

'Grace?' The voice is soft. There is the trace of an accent. Northern, I think, but I can't be sure.

I nod.

'I thought so, you're the only redhead here.'

'Anna.' My voice sounds small and high. I rub my palm on my jeans before taking her hand. Long fingers grip mine. 'Thanks for coming. Hope you haven't travelled too far?'

'No.' Anna slips off a baby-pink leather jacket, which I instantly covet, and hangs it over the back of the chair. She smoothes her skirt over narrow hips and I resolve to start another diet on Monday.

'Want another?' She nods towards my mug. I shake my head, grab my purse and start to stand.

'It's OK.' She gestures for me to sit again, and weaves her way to the back of the queue, glossy blonde hair swishing across her shoulder blades.

I shred the stack of napkins on the table as I watch her. I was expecting someone older, someone Paul's age, not mine. *Who is she?* I sift through the pile of tissue as if I can find the answers buried at the centre.

'That took ages.' Anna places her Americano on the table. Her cup wobbles on the saucer but she doesn't spill a drop. No cake for her. She can't be more than a size eight, probably never eats carbs, probably never eats anything. I brush my muffin crumbs and envy onto the floor.

'Not the place to come if you're in a rush, but you know what you get here.'

'Overpriced commercialism?'

'I was going to say good cake, but yes. That too. I used to work here when I was doing my A levels. Just part-time.' I'm babbling. 'It's not as if we have a great choice here in the village.'

The term 'village' is a bit of a stretch; it's expanded enormously in the fifteen years I've lived here. It's a small market town now, really, with a good selection of shops, but we cling to our rural roots all the same.

We fall into silence. Anna stirs her drink. The sound of the spoon chinking on china jars me. I'm searching for words, staring out of the window, at the floor, as if I might find them written there.

'So.' Anna rests her elbow on the table, chin cradled inside cupped palms. 'How do you know my dad?'

I lean back in my chair so suddenly I thwack my head on the wall behind, but if it hurts I don't register it.

'Paul is your dad?'

'Was. He died when I was eight.'

'Sorry.' I scrape my chair back and rush to the toilets.

I lean against the sink, steadying myself against the porcelain, and take slow, deep breaths. My anxious face stares back at me from the streaked mirror. Charlie's dad is dead. Anna is Charlie's half-sister. How can I tell her she has lost another relative? I twist the cold tap and cup water into my mouth. It dribbles down my chin and I wipe it away with my sleeve.

'Are you all right?' Anna's come to find me.

'Yes.' I talk to her reflection. There are similarities to Charlie. I don't know why I didn't see it before. Her hair is a darker blonde, and she's not as tall, but her eyes are the same green.

'So, who are you?'

I turn the tap off, dry my hands on a paper towel and consider lying, but I'm not very good at it.

'Paul, your dad, was also the father of my best friend, Charlie.'
'I don't understand?'
'Charlie is – was – your half-sister.'
'Was?'
'I think we'd better sit down.'

It takes some time to tell Anna about Charlie and Lexie. I talk slowly at first, recounting how Paul and Lexie met. Anna asks the odd question but for the most part she is silent: face pale, brow furrowed. I explain how Charlie grew up never knowing who her father was, how she always felt there was a piece missing. Anna blows her nose and wipes her eyes.

'Did she try to find him?'
'She wanted to. Lexie got upset.'
'She wouldn't help?'
'No.'
'What a bitch.'
'I think she had her reasons. She thought it was for the best.'
'What reason could she possibly have for separating a family?'
'I don't know.' I shift uncomfortably in my seat. 'She probably wasn't aware you existed.'

She frowns. 'Anyway tell me about her, this sister of mine.'

And I try. Falteringly at first – words like 'beautiful', 'funny' and 'amazing' are too generic; they don't capture the essence of Charlie.

I tell Anna about our school days, about our history project on powerful and inspiring women. Charlie snuck Grandma's jam funnels into her rucksack and turned up at school the next day with a home-made conical bra, proclaiming Madonna to be the most influential woman in the world. I talk until my jaw aches and my throat is sore.

The barista clears our cold drinks away, returning with a cloth to wipe the table. He scrunches up the rubbish and stuffs it into his apron pocket. 'We're closing now.'

I check my watch. 'It's half past four. I can't believe we've been talking so long.'

'What's the pub like down the road? Fancy a drink and an early dinner? I really want to hear more about Charlie.'

'That would be great. I've never eaten there, I usually go to The Hawley Arms by the park, but I'm sure it's fine. I must just text my boyfriend and let him know.'

'Oh, let him wait.' Anna links her arm through mine and we walk towards the door. Anna chatters as we walk through the village and I'm glad I'm not alone. The fear I'd felt last night while being chased rests beneath my skin, ready to speed up my pulse, heat my blood. I don't know who it was and I try to ignore the thought that they'll come back, but no matter how hard I push it away, it creeps back in.

The pub is quiet. Faded striped carpet sticks to the soles of our shoes as we tramp towards a chipped wooden table in the corner. It wobbles as I rest my bag down, and I stuff beer mats under one leg to steady it. A chalkboard menu hangs behind the bar and I squint to read it.

'You ready to order?' The waitress hovers over us, pad poised, chewed biro in hand. Black ink stains the corner of her mouth. Her grubby once-white shirt strains at the buttons.

'Lasagne and chips for me please.'

'And a chicken salad for me,' Anna adds

I am aware of my thighs spread over the chair and I cover my lap with a paper napkin.

'Drinks?'

'Glass of wine?' I venture.

'Sod it, we deserve a bottle. White?'

'Perfect.'

'I'm just nipping to the loo.'

I take the opportunity to check my phone. There are several texts from Dan, each one more frantic than the last. I reassure him that I'm fine. That Anna is lovely, not an axe-wielding murderer.

The waitress plonks a bottle of lukewarm house white and two glasses on the table. I pour our drinks but before I can take a sip, my phone rings. It's an unknown number again. As I say hello, the dial tone fills my ear. I glance around the pub, mute the ringtone on my phone and stuff it in my bag.

'What's the wine like?' Anna slides back into her seat.

I take a sip and pull a face. 'If they don't have any vinegar for my chips this will do nicely.'

'That good, huh?' Anna laughs.

'What happened to your dad? I understand if it's too painful to talk about.'

'It's OK. It was a long time ago.' Anna twirls her wine glass. 'We were going on holiday and I was so excited we were going to see the sea. Mum bought a pack of jelly babies for us to eat on the way. I loved the orange ones; I'd bite the head off and work my way down. Of course, I ate too many and began to feel sick. Mum told me to get some fresh air. I hung my head out of the window like a dog until I felt better, but then I heard buzzing. I thought a bee had flown right into my ear. I shook my head and screamed. Dad looked around to see what was wrong and that's the last thing I remember. Apparently he veered onto the wrong side of the road and we hit another car head-on. Mum and dad died instantly.' Anna lowers her head and I reach over the table, covering her hand with mine. 'I was only nine. I blamed myself: if only I hadn't eaten so many sweets; if only I hadn't opened the window; if only I hadn't screamed. I wish I'd just let the bee sting me.'

'You lost both parents at once?'

'Yeah. Little orphan Annie, that's me. I just need your red hair and I could sing about the sun coming out tomorrow.' She pats my hand and offers a wry smile.

The waitress slops two plates in front of us. Yellow grease pools out of the lasagne. Anna forks salad into her mouth as I push chips around my plate.

'Where did you live afterwards?'

'Let's move onto something a little more cheery, shall we? Save that tragic story for another time.'

I gulp my wine, grateful now for the sour taste, which diverts attention from the aching sadness that threatens to overwhelm me.

'What do you do?' Anna asks.

'I work in a pre-school. I love it. Do you like kids?'

'No.' Anna sloshes wine into my glass. 'You're lucky to do something you enjoy, though. I'm working as a secretary and I hate it.'

'Why?'

Anna's face contorts. 'Let's just say I call my boss "the octopus" for good reason.'

'That's horrible. Can't you report him?'

'It's only a small company. Another job will turn up. It's not exactly a vocation. I didn't grow up dreaming of taking notes for some middle-aged man while he drooled down my blouse.'

'What did you want to do?'

'I thought about being a nurse. It would be great to be able to help people who have accidents, you know?'

I nod. 'What stopped you?'

'Money, I guess. I had to support myself as soon as I turned sixteen.'

As we continue to chat, I think about how different my life might have been. At one point, after the waitress has cleared away our plates, I reach out to squeeze Anna's hand, but a dessert board is slammed between us.

'Well?' the waitress demands.

'Black coffee for me,' says Anna.

I think of my thighs and resist ordering sticky toffee pudding.

'Do you have hot chocolate?'

The waitress sighs. 'No.'

'A tea then, thanks.'

We sip barely warm drinks from chipped china mugs and I settle the bill.

'I'll get the next one,' Anna says.

'That would be nice. I hope it hasn't been too shocking for you today?'

'It's a lot to take in, losing a sister I never knew I had. I feel so alone sometimes. The thought that I could have had a sister, a family…' Anna shrugs. 'I feel like I've found a friend, though.'

'Me too. How about coming to mine for dinner next week? I can show you some photos of Charlie. You can meet my boyfriend, Dan?'

'That would be great, thanks.' We hug our goodbyes and Anna sashays off, reminding me of the half-sister she never knew. I wonder what Dan will think of her. Will she remind him of Charlie too, and if she does, is it a risk inviting her into our home?

Darkness is blanketing the village. We've had every other street lamp turned off and it's gloomy and Sunday-night-still. Families are huddled in front of fires, around TVs, weighted with Yorkshire puddings and thoughts of Monday morning. I walk briskly, stopping when there's a buzzing inside my bag. My phone is vibrating. Dan must be getting impatient; I've been gone hours. The number's withheld and I answer it, say hello.

There's the sound of breathing on the other end. I hear someone swallow. Sniff. I hang up and the screen lights up almost immediately with an incoming call. An engine purrs behind me. Someone is driving very, very slowly and I duck behind the wall of the church, almost holding my breath as the car crawls past. It seems ages before the sound gets fainter and I uncurl my body, stamp my numb feet. As I stand, I think I see a flash of red disappearing around the corner but I can't be sure, and I run as fast as I can in the opposite direction, not stopping until I'm home.

CHAPTER FOURTEEN
Now

Usually I'm wrenched from a medically-induced sleep by the trill of the alarm. Not this morning, though. Excitement has nudged me awake early. It's Thursday. Anna is coming to dinner.

'Are you asleep?' I stage-whisper.

'Not any more.' Dan pulls a pillow over his head.

'You will be home on time tonight, won't you?'

'Yes. Calm down. It's only Charlie's sister. Not the bloody Queen.'

Sister. I hug the word close, as comforting as Dan's old fleece that I wear around the house. Anna and I have been texting all week. Dan sighs whenever I pick up my phone, but I already feel a strong bond with her. Not a replacement for Charlie of course, but something fresh, a new beginning. I slip out of bed, shower and dress at Olympian speed, bound downstairs and pirouette into the lounge. 'What shall I cook?' I ask Charlie, smiling at me from her silver frame on top of the piano.

The kitchen is cast in a daffodil glow. The thin curtains that Grandma made are no match for the early-morning sunshine. I swoosh them open and the birds tweet their good mornings. Everyone is happy today. Mittens purrs, rubbing her face against my legs, as I refresh her water and squeeze a pouch of meat into her bowl, scatter biscuits on the top.

I flick through recipe books as I spoon porridge into my mouth, honey sweet on my tongue. I scribble a list and fuss around the cottage, straightening cushions and refolding throws. It's still early. If I'm quick, I can call into Waitrose on the way to work.

I tilt forward and push the security buzzer with my nose. The muscles in my arms tremble from the weight of my shopping, plastic bag handles slicing into my palms.

'Goodness.' Lyn opens the door as wide as it will go as I inch forward like a cowboy, one hip at a time.

'Thanks. I didn't want to put this lot down to find my key.' I stagger into the staffroom, drop the bags on the floor and massage the indentations on my hands.

Lyn raises an eyebrow at the mountain of food and wine spilling over the lino. 'Are you sure you've bought enough?'

'Anna's coming for dinner,' I say, as though she could forget. I've talked of nothing else all week. 'I daren't leave this lot in my car all day. Don't want to poison her.'

'Not on your first dinner, anyway. It's probably colder outside at the moment than it is in the fridge.' Lyn picks up a bottle of Chardonnay as it rolls across the floor. 'I hope Ofsted don't turn up to do a spot check today. How much alcohol have you bought?'

'Just three bottles. I had to buy red, white and rosé, and some orange juice in case she doesn't want to drink, and sparkling water in case she doesn't like fruit juice. I got some real coffee too, and herbal teas and after-dinner mints, although I'm sure she won't touch those. Did I tell you how tiny she was?'

'Several times.'

I kneel down in front of the tiny staff fridge and Lyn passes me a bag of leaves. I have to pierce the plastic before I can squash it in the fridge.

'Rocket. Very posh. Look, Grace, I know how much this means to you, but really, if she's anything like Charlie she won't want a fuss. A bag of chips and can of lager will do.'

I lean back on my heels, picking up a box of silver candles. 'Dan says I'm acting like the Queen's coming to tea.'

'It's natural that you want her to like you, that you want that connection to Charlie, but we all love you just as you are. Give Anna the chance to get to know you and she will too.' Lyn unpacks four shallow glass bowls. 'What sweet treat is going in these?'

'They're finger bowls. We're having garlic bread.' I hold up a stray lemon. 'Too much?'

'Much too much. Slice the lemon into a gin and chill out a bit?'

'Shouldn't we wait until lunchtime or shall we share with the children?'

'I bet a few mothers would welcome a G&T. Probably not this early, though.' Lyn checks her watch. 'It's time to open up. You finish tidying this lot, Nigella, and I'll unlock the doors.'

I slot a bottle of balsamic vinegar in the fridge door, wishing I had bought a jar of Hellman's mayonnaise instead.

I paint my face like a tiger for the kids and spend the day prowling and pouncing. By the time the last mother has left, I'm exhausted. I'm clunking the toys back into their brightly coloured storage tubs that are stacked against the wall when Lyn hefts my shopping – neatly packed back into bags – into the room.

'Oi. Stripy. I'll finish up. You get home and iron your napkins.'

'The butler should already have done it.' I pull on my coat and fish car keys from my pocket. 'Thanks, Lyn. I really appreciate it.'

'Hope it goes well. If it doesn't, you've got enough wine here to drown your sorrows.'

'And an emergency-sized bar of Dairy Milk. See you tomorrow.' With the bag handles cutting fresh grooves into my hands, I bustle my way to the car.

Everything is ready. The newly lit candles hiss and flicker before the flames glow tall and strong. Fairy lights twinkle around the lounge window.

'Can you open the wine?' I ask Dan.

The cork is pulled with a squeak and a pop.

The doorbell chimes and I rush to answer, smiling brightly as I pull open the door. There's no one there. I step forward.

'Anna?'

The lane is dark. Quiet. I shiver and shut the door.

I fill a glass with water and swallow down half a tablet. It's just because I'm nervous. Anyone would be. The smell of garlic and basil triggers a deep rumble in my stomach: we've normally eaten by now. I scroll through my classic iPod before settling on Einaudi, *Islands*. I hum along to the piano music as I polish already gleaming cutlery. There's a rap on the door and I answer, cloth and knife still in hand.

'Wow. Is this a rough area?'

'I was just…'

'I'm kidding. At least you're not telling me to fork off.'

Anna steps into the hall, thrusts a box of chocolate-covered Brazil nuts into my hands and brushes a sprinkling of snow from her coat. 'Something smells delicious.'

'Spag bol. Is that OK?'

'One of my favourites.'

'I've gone a bit overboard on the garlic, I'm afraid.'

'That's OK. Rest assured I'm not a vampire.'

'I can tell that by the way you stepped in uninvited.' I grin. Our friendship feels easy already. Natural. 'Did you pass anybody on the lane?'

Paranoid Polly, Grandma would say.

'No. There was a car, though.'

I stiffen. 'What sort?'

'Don't know. It was red I think. Why, have you…' Anna's speaking; I watch her mouth move and I hear the sounds but I can't understand what she's saying. There was a car. A red car. It must be the Corsa from the other day. *Someone is definitely following me.*

'Hello?' Anna swooshes her hand up and down in front of my eyes. 'Earth to Grace.'

'Sorry.' I plaster over my fear with a smile.

'I said you've not fixed me up with a blind date, have you?'

'No.' I remind myself how to act. 'Come and meet Dan.' I lead the way into the lounge. Dan stands, hands in pockets, shuffling from one foot to the other.

'Hello, handsome man.' Anna opens her arms and Dan half hugs her in that one-armed way you do when you feel uncomfortable. He's put a shirt on and made an effort, but damp patches are visible under his arms. Poor Dan. He isn't really a dinner party type of guy.

'Look what Anna brought.' I rattle the box.

'You're allergic to nuts.' Dan frowns.

'I'm sorry. I…'

'Don't worry, Anna. It was a lovely thought. Dan will eat them. Drink? Glass of wine?'

'Please.'

'I'll get them.' Dan seems relieved to have something to do. Small talk is not his forte. He returns a minute later with two glasses of white wine and hands one to Anna.

'Is white OK for you?' I ask. 'We have red and rosé too.'

'I didn't think to check. Sorry,' Dan mumbles.

'It's OK. White's my favourite.' She takes a sip. 'Better than that paint stripper they served at the pub.'

'It couldn't be worse.' I scrunch my nose as I remember.

'So, is it rude to ask why you are orange?'

I touch my cheek. Despite my scrubbing with a flannel, the face paint hasn't quite come off. 'I was a tiger today.'

Anna grins mischievously. 'Lucky Dan.'

Dan's neck turns red and blotchy. I rub his forearm and frown encouragingly at him. I don't know why he's being so awkward. I really want this evening to be a success.

'Anyway, make yourself at home.' I motion towards the sofa where Mittens is asleep on the faux-fur throw draped over the arm.

'You have a cat.'

'Mittens. I've had her since she was a kitten.'

'No Tom or Moppet?'

'You're a Beatrix Potter fan?'

'My dad used to read them to me.'

Memories explode in psychedelic colour. I hurry to the kitchen, lean my hot face against the fridge, trying to cool away the images of Dad and me on my bed, giggling our way through the tale of the naughty kittens.

'Are you OK?' Dan stands in the doorway. 'This was a bad idea. I'll ask her to leave?'

'No. I'm fine,' I say. 'I'm just tired and over-emotional. I want everything to be perfect.'

An expression I can't quite read flickers over Dan's face, and then it is gone.

'Everything's good. Honestly. You go and sit with Anna.'

'I'll stay and help you.'

'It's rude to leave her own her own.' I half push him towards the door. It doesn't take long to plate the food up and we cramp around our bistro table, which creaks under huge bowls of pasta, garlic bread and sauce, eating with our elbows pulled firmly into our sides.

'You're a good cook,' says Anna. 'This sauce is divine. What make is it?'

'It's not shop-bought. Grace grows her own herbs,' says Dan. 'The garden's her pride and joy.'

'Very clever. I live on salads. It never seems worth cooking for one.'

'Well, you look fabulous on it. I'm always saying I need to lose ten pounds. Dan gets bored of hearing it, don't you, Dan?'

'I'm sure he likes curvy women, not sticks like me. What do you say, Dan?'

'I say, I'm going to fetch some cheese.' Thin-lipped, he rises from his seat. He has hardly touched his food.

'Very tactful,' says Anna.

'He's learned with age. He wasn't that sensitive when we met, believe me.'

Dan returns with a bowl of Parmesan.

'Have you known each other a long time?' Anna's expression is quizzical.

I twirl spaghetti. 'Ages. We met at school. Our first meeting didn't go well, did it, Dan?'

'Why?'

Dan groans. 'That's a story you really don't want to hear.'

'Of course she must. It involves Charlie, too.' I relay the details of our first meeting. Anna's eyes widen as she hears how her half-sister took revenge for me.

'Dan, Dan, the ketchup man,' she splutters. 'That's so funny.'

Dan shrugs. 'I was only ten. I learned my lesson pretty quickly. Don't mess around with girls.'

'No, you shouldn't.' Anna scrutinises Dan over her wine glass.

'Look.' I pass Anna the photo of me, Charlie, Dan, Esmée and Siobhan. Ben had taken it outside school. 'We went to the pocket park and decided it would be a good idea to burn our school ties. We had a pile of old newspaper and some matches. Dan lit the fire and tipped some whisky he'd stolen from his dad's shed over the flames to make them bigger. It had been such a dry summer that the fire spread quickly. The flames were enormous. We had to ring the fire brigade in the end.'

'Were you in much trouble?'

'Huge. The police came around to our houses to tell our families. I was so scared; I'd never been in trouble before. The policeman was really stern. We were lucky they didn't charge us with arson. The pre-school wouldn't have employed me with a criminal record.'

'Did you actually burn your ties?'

'No. We lost the moment after that. Dan and I still have ours in the wardrobe.'

Anna picks up the silver candlestick and waves it around. The flames splutter and wax drips onto the tablecloth. 'Go get them. Let's finish what you started.'

'I think we'll give the smoke alarm a rest. It worked hard enough when I forgot the garlic bread in the oven earlier. What about you? Do you have a wild side?'

'If I did, I'd do something suitably nasty to my boss.'

'Anna calls him "the octopus",' I tell Dan.

'I'm sick of him trying to put his hand up my skirt or peer down my blouse.' Anna looks utterly dejected.

I feel so awful for her. 'I don't know how you cope.'

'I have to until something else comes up.' Anna's eyes fill with tears. 'You say I'm thin, but that's because I'm too knotted up to eat half the time. I go to bed at night and can't sleep, playing the day over in my head, all the innuendos he has made, the times he's physically touched me. I spend most of my time worrying about what's to come, how far he'll go. My muscles are always so tense, I have constant neck pain.'

I pass her a box of tissues.

Anna blows her nose. 'How embarrassing. I'm not usually like this.'

'Can't you find something else?'

'I'm trying but it's difficult. I work long hours and he won't give me time off for interviews. The rent on my bedsit is extortionate. If I could manage without an income for a couple of weeks I could find something else. It's so hard when you don't have family to fall back on.'

I squeeze her hand. 'You have us now. You're Charlie's sister and you must ask for help if you need it, mustn't she, Dan?'

Dan grunts, swipes the empty bottle off the table and leaves the room. He's always uncomfortable with tears.

'Could I stay with you? I really can't face that awful man again. It would just be for a week or two while I find something else. This is nearer to Oxford than where I am. It'll be easier for interviews. I want to be closer to you. Find out more about Charlie. You're beginning to feel like family already.'

Dan crashes plates around the kitchen.

'Of course,' I say. 'It'll be fun. I'm happy to help.' But that isn't the only reason I want her to move in – the sense of being watched is getting stronger, especially after the red car in the lane. But I can't admit to being scared of being alone, not even to myself.' With: 'If Anna is here and Dan goes out I won't be alone. Feel afraid. I'll be safe, won't I?

CHAPTER FIFTEEN
Then

The heat from the fire pushed us back and we watched from a distance as it spat and crackled. Charlie never liked to get too close. Always said she was too scared after being trapped in a fire, even though Lexie said she was making it up. I saw the terror in her eyes as she watched the flames: that fear had to come from somewhere. Guy Fawkes slumped in the middle of the burning logs, head hanging to one side as though wracked with guilt, resigned to his fate. Flames licked around his feet and the crowd cheered as his trousers ignited.

'Hot dog?' Charlie tugged my sleeve.

I nodded and we pushed our way through the throng – most of the village had gathered on the green for the annual fireworks display – and joined the queue at the snack van. Onions covered my cremated sausage and I zigzagged ketchup down the middle.

'Coke?'

Charlie shook her head 'Let's go to the beer tent.'

'There's no way Mike will serve us.' The landlord of the village pub knew us.

'I'm eighteen now.'

'I'm not.' I still had ten days before I could legally drink.

'You practically are. I'll get them; you wait outside. It's so busy he won't know. Then we'll find the others.'

'OK.' I stayed close behind as we sidestepped children with sparklers looping their names in the air. I wished Siobhan wasn't coming tonight. I faded into the background whenever she was around, lost behind her fake laughter and hair flicking as she thrust her boobs towards Dan at every opportunity. My boobs were growing bigger, but the rest of me was as well. I'd started forging letters from Grandma to my teacher, pretending I had a bad knee so I didn't have to do PE and get changed under Siobhan's scornful gaze. She was so thin. Her sister was a bitch, too. If I passed Abby in the corridor at school she'd look at the floor and scurry away, but when she was with Siobhan she was fearless.

We reached the beer tent and I swallowed the last of my hotdog, licked my fingers clean, pulled my gloves back on.

Charlie shouldered her way towards the bar and I hovered in the entrance to the marquee, stamping my booted feet. The air was biting and my breath clouded before me. I watched the curling Catherine wheels, which were nailed to the fence, while I waited. They spun faster and faster until they were a blur of blue and gold, the sparks shooting through the sky like falling stars.

'Gracie Grace!'

I jumped as two arms encircled my waist. Sour breath warmed my neck. 'Lexie.'

'This is Ant. Isn't he handsome?' Lexie giggled and stroked the blushing face of the boy next to her. He worked behind the counter in the Co-op and couldn't have been much older than me. Lexie slung an arm around my shoulders. Lager sloshed from her plastic pint cup, saturating my scarf. I tried to soak it up with my gloved hand.

'This is Grace. Isn't she beautiful? She's never given me any trouble, this one.' Lexie staggered and I shifted my weight to steady us both.

Ant shrugged.

'Don't bleedin' shrug.' Lexie tried to stand tall, swayed like a tree in the breeze. 'She's lovely, is Grace. Good as gold she is, too.'

'And I'm not?' Charlie thrust a cider towards me. I stepped away from Lexie. She lost her footing and lolled on the frosty grass, clutching her cup.

'Didn't spill a drop. Woohoo!' She lay on her back, raised her beer and kicked her legs in the air like a dying fly.

'Mum,' Charlie hissed. 'Everyone's looking.'

Lexie clasped Charlie's outstretched hand and clambered to her feet. Ant mumbled something and shuffled off.

'That's right, fuck off. Didn't like you anyway. You're a boy; I need a man. Any takers?' Lexie raised her pint and spun around, landing sprawled against the side of the beer tent. Pegs pinged out of the hard earth and guy ropes flapped in the breeze. Charlie and I dropped our cups, grabbed one of Lexie's arms each and hoisted her to her feet.

'I'll have to take her home.'

'I'll come with you.'

The crowd thinned out as we reached the edge of the green. Siobhan, Abby and Esmée were silhouetted in the distance, and as they drew closer my jaw clenched.

'You leaving?' Esmée asked.

'Yeah, gotta take Mum home.'

'Want a hand?' said Siobhan.

'Nah, me and Grace can manage.'

'Of course, Grace will be more help; she's much bigger than me.'

'Don't be nasty.' Esmée elbowed Siobhan in the ribs.

'I wasn't. I meant she's stronger, that's all. Anyway, best let you go.'

We staggered forward a few steps with Lexie.

'Oh, Grace?' I twisted my head around. Siobhan was smiling menacingly. 'I'll give your love to Dan, shall I?'

'Cow,' I muttered.

'Ignore her,' said Charlie, as they walked away. 'I'm getting sick of her. She must be freezing her tits off in that mini skirt. Ben says Dan doesn't fancy her anyway.'

'Really?' Charlie and Ben were going steady. I had visions of them double-dating with Siobhan and Dan, while I sat at home in plaid pyjamas watching *Bridget Jones* on repeat and stuffing myself with sour cream Pringles.

The fifteen-minute walk to Charlie's house took nearly half an hour as Lexie alternated between lurching forwards and stumbling backwards. By the time we reached Charlie's, my arms were burning with the effort of keeping Lexie upright.

Charlie propped Lexie against the front door. 'Grab the key, Grace.'

I lifted Brian the gnome. Grandma had taken Charlie to a garden centre to choose a birthday present for Lexie years ago. Lexie wasn't one for plants and flowers – 'All that bleedin' weeding' – but Charlie had fallen in love with the little fishing figurine. Lexie had screeched with laughter when she'd unwrapped him – 'He's so bleedin' ugly no one will ever steal him' – and he'd guarded the spare front door key ever since.

Charlie inched up the stairs backwards, dragging Lexie by both hands as I followed behind, hands on Lexie's back, pushing her forwards.

'I'm sorry,' Lexie mumbled into her pillow as I tugged off her shoes.

'It's OK, Mum.' Charlie drew the duvet up to Lexie's chin.

'My girl, all grown up. I wish you weren't. I wish you were still little.' Mascara ran in rivulets down Lexie's cheeks.

'Just sleep, Mum.'

'My life's a mess.'

I rooted around in my pocket and found a tissue under a half-eaten packet of Polos. It was clean, and I unfolded it and handed it to Lexie.

She blew her nose. 'I didn't mean it. I don't know how to make it right. You know how it feels, don't you, Grace? To make a mistake.'

'It'll be OK in the morning.'

'It won't be. It can't be. I shouldn't…'

Lexie's mouth hung open. I exchanged a worried glance with Charlie, but Lexie's jowls shook as she juddered out a snore.

'Thank God for that.' Charlie flicked off the light and we crept downstairs.

'Want to go back to the green?'

'Nah. I'd better stay near Mum. Wanna watch from the front garden?'

I nodded. We fizzed open cans of Stella from the fridge, and went to sit outside, where we dangled our legs from the crumbling brick wall.

We oohed as burning streaks of bright light shot through the sky, bursting into millions of gold and silver particles. It looked as though someone had thrown handfuls of glitter up in the air. We aahed as myriad colours rippled across the sky, popping and fading into blackness.

'I wish I was a firework,' said Charlie.

'Why?'

'I'd fire myself far away from here.'

'What's up?' I downed the last of my lager, scrunched up my can.

'It's Mum. I dunno what's up with her. She's been like this for about a month.'

'Drunk?'

'Pretty much 24/7.' Charlie kicked her heels and dry plaster crumbled to the ground.

'Why didn't you say?'

Charlie shrugged. 'Embarrassed, I suppose. She's stopped going out, keeps the curtains drawn all the time. She was sick all over herself on Monday. I had to hose her down in the shower. It was disgusting. I don't want to whinge all the time, anyway. It's not like you've had it easy, is it?'

'No, but you're entitled to have problems too. Why do you think she's doing it?'

'I dunno. She goes through phases.'

'She was saying about you being eighteen. Perhaps she's worried you'll leave home. Grandma's the same. Thinks I'll go off to uni after sixth form and forget about them. She's worried they'll never see me again.'

'Maybe. Perhaps she wishes she were still with me dad. Whoever he might be.' Charlie jumped down; her trainers smacked against the grey concrete. 'Wanna go find the boys?'

'What about your mum?'

'Oh, let her choke. I don't care,' Charlie said. But I knew that she did, and when the sounds of the fireworks died down and were replaced with tormented screams, Charlie thundered up the stairs towards her mum.

CHAPTER SIXTEEN
Now

There's nothing quite like waking to the smell of bacon. Breakfast in bed always feels like such a treat. I sit up as I hear the telltale creak of the loose floorboard at the top of the stairs, and the squeak of the bedroom door being nudged open. Gritty sleep is lodged in the corners of my eyes and I rub it away. I fumble with my pillows, propping them horizontally behind me, and I lean back against them, my hands resting in my lap, as though I am in hospital and she is a visitor.

'Morning.' Anna is wearing my apron. China clinks together as she hands me a tray. 'Thought I'd make a good impression on my first morning here.'

'You've certainly done that.' I gulp orange juice. The sharp tang of citrus washes my grogginess away.

'The bacon is crispy,' Anna says, 'the bread lightly toasted and there's lots of brown sauce. The tea is sweet and milky.'

'Just the way I like it.'

'I know. I asked Dan before he went to football practice.'

Anna perches on the bed as I bite into my sandwich. The saltiness of the bacon mingles with the sweetness of the sauce.

'This is so good. Thank you.'

'It's the least I can do. I'm so grateful you're letting me stay. The last few months seem like a bad dream already.'

I chew my food as Anna peruses the books on my bedside table. 'Little Women. Are they all short?'

I laugh. 'Haven't you read it?'

'No. *Fifty Shades of Grey* is the last book I read.'

'It's a bit different to that. It's about a group of sisters. The eldest, Jo March, is my heroine. She's so strong.'

'So are you, Grace. It can't have been easy, losing your best friend.' Anna flicks through the book before tossing it on top of my endless reading pile. The books teeter and topple; my bottle of tablets rattles to the floor.

'Sorry.' She picks them up.

'Sleeping tablets,' I offer, although she hasn't asked. 'I haven't slept properly since Charlie died.'

'Do they work?'

'Too well. If it wasn't for Dan I'd sleep through my alarm half the time. The doctor doesn't like giving them, though. Thinks I should try antidepressants instead.'

'Grief isn't an illness though, is it?' Anna's face crumples. 'It's not as if you get better, like you do with chickenpox. It's been years since I last saw my parents but I still want to tell them whenever anything happens, good or bad. I forget they're not here. When you said I could move in, I thought I must tell Mum and Dad how lovely you are. Stupid, isn't it?'

'I think it's natural. It's so hard to process the fact there are people we'll never see again. Our minds block it out.'

'I remember when I'm asleep.' Anna sits on the edge of the bed and lowers her head so her chin touches her chest. 'I still have nightmares about the accident. The funeral. Even to this day.'

I swallow the last of the sandwich. It gets stuck in my dry throat and I force it down with a mouthful of tea.

'Sorry, but I'd better get up. I'm going out this morning.'

'Out?'

'Yes. Sorry. If I'd have known you were coming to stay I wouldn't have arranged anything, but I've promised Lexie I'll take her to Charlie's grave.'

'Lexie? Charlie's mum?'

I nod.

'I'll come with you. I want to meet her.'

I hesitate.

'I'd like to meet her. She's my half-sister's mum. I want to see where Charlie's buried, too.'

'Of course,' I say. 'And I'll take you to the churchyard, but not today. Lexie's fragile. She's not coping well. She doesn't know you exist.'

'It might cheer her up. A link with Charlie.'

'It might, but I'll need to talk to her first. Prepare her. I can't just turn up with you.'

Anna nips her bottom lip between her teeth. A shadow passes across her face.

I touch her arm. 'I'm sorry. I'll be back by twelve. I'll dig out the photo albums. We can have a proper girls' afternoon.'

'OK.' Anna picks up the tray. 'I've got unpacking to do anyway.'

I've never quite equated cemeteries with death – my grandparents shielded me as much as they could – but as I stand at the entrance to the graveyard, I'm giddy at the thought of all those bodies. This is the place that Charlie, Esmée, Siobhan and I used to run around, climbing trees and making dens, and I feel a sense of shame that we weren't more respectful – not to the dead, but to the mourners huddled around headstones, bewildered expressions on their pinched faces. What must they have thought of four shrieking girls, darting in and out of bushes playing hide-and-seek?

I cup Lexie's elbow, guiding her down the frosty path as though she is blind, and we pick our way down mossy paving slabs, eyes lowered, not wanting to see anyone else's pain. Beyond the crumbling headstones etched with dates too faded to read, there is a large rectangle littered with crosses and shiny plaques: memorials to those recently departed. I was surprised when Lexie had requested a burial here; I had been unaware she'd been brought up a Christian. But an interment of ashes was all this church – already overcrowded – could offer.

Lexie's bony hand grasps my arm and I pat it. There's nothing to say, no words that will make this easier. I'd like to be able to tell her the first visit is the worst, but I can't: it isn't true. The black plastic vase I'd filled last time is full of stagnant water and withered scarlet roses, and as I pick it up, brown leaves scatter before me. I only brought them a week ago, and I make a mental note not to bring roses again.

'I'll be back in a minute.' I'm not sure whether Lexie has heard me. She doesn't seem to notice as I leave. There's a yellow bin at the back of the church specifically for old flowers. The lid doesn't quite close and I thrust the roses on the top, too wary of the thorns to push them down. I bend and rinse out the vase under the outdoor tap, and fill it with fresh water. As I stand, I see a figure at the top of the overgrown path: black padded coat, hood covering their face.

There are hundreds of black coats in the world. It's probably not the person who was watching me from outside the coffee shop, I reason, but I'm rooted to the spot. Unsure what to do. The figure is still, and although I can't see their face, I feel they're staring straight at me. I don't know whether to confront them or run. I notice a bunch of flowers hanging from the figure's hand. They're visiting a grave.

It's probably seconds later – but it feels like minutes – that the figure drops their flowers, turns and runs back down the path towards the gate. I wait to compose myself before returning to Lexie.

She's standing where I left her, clutching her bunch of pink carnations tightly between her fingers. I ease them out from her grasp, arranging them in the too-narrow vase as best I can.

'That's brightened it up,' I lie. The plot still feels as stark and black as the hole Charlie has left.

'Thanks for bringing me, Grace.' Lexie's voice is small and quiet and I tilt my head so I can hear her. 'I don't deserve your kindness.'

'Of course you do.'

'I don't. I've been awful. Everything's such a mess.' She presses balled fists into her eyes as though she can change the scene in front of them. 'I haven't been here since the funeral. It's horrible.'

I nod. It is. The smattering of words on a colourless stone do not comfort me. How could they? Charlie is not here. My logical mind knows that, but I come every week all the same, afraid that if I don't, she might think I've forgotten her.

'Do you want to go home?'

'No.' Lexie's tears spill onto her pale cheeks. 'Can we go for a drink?'

'Just the one,' I tell her, but one turns into two, into three, into four, and, by the time I drop her home, it is nearly half-past four.

The house smells of comfort. I lift the lid off the saucepan and breathe in home-made soup.

'I've used up all the vegetables in the fridge. Hope that's OK?'

I start. I hadn't heard Anna come into the kitchen.

'Yes. It smells great. I thought you couldn't cook?'

Anna's blonde hair is piled up on top of her head; she tucks a stray tendril behind her ear. 'Not can't, just don't. It's a treat to have someone to cook for. I want to earn my keep. I feel so bad that I'm not paying rent.'

'I wouldn't dream of taking your money. You're a guest. Besides, it's only for a few days.'

'How was Lexie?'

'Not good.' I flick on the kettle, pull mugs from the cupboard. 'I'm sorry I'm so late. I took her to a pub afterwards. Had a job to get her to leave.'

'Is that usual?'

'Sometimes. She goes through phases. Charlie said Lexie lay on the lounge floor once for hours – Charlie couldn't wake her, but was too afraid to leave her.'

'That sounds like an awful childhood.'

'It wasn't always like that. Lexie had her moments, but seemed OK when I met her, right up until we turned eighteen. I'd be surprised if Lexie can remember any of that year.'

'Any idea why?'

'No.' I fight to keep my breathing measured. I don't want to talk about that year, still don't like to think about it, and not just because of Lexie. 'She cleaned herself up, though, and has been sober ever since. Well, sober-ish. Until Charlie…'

'Are there no relatives to help? Aunties? Uncles?'

'No. Lexie moved here when Charlie was small. She doesn't have any family.'

'But she has you.'

'Yes. And my grandparents help her out. You'll have to meet them. They loved Charlie.'

'It sounds like everyone did. Hungry?' Anna ladles thick soup into my bowl. It splashes on my shirt and I dab it off with the dishcloth, hoping it doesn't stain.

*

We sup soup sitting at the table, its surface smooth and gleaming under the electric light.

'Have you dusted?'

'Yes. I wanted to make myself useful. It didn't take me long to unpack. I'll show you what I've done in the garden when we've finished. I didn't use polish on the piano – it looks really old. I didn't want to damage it.'

'It was Dad's. He taught me to play.'

'Are you good? I wish I was musical.'

'I was. Haven't played in years, but I can't bear to part with it.' Whenever I look at the worn leather stool I can almost feel Dad, my small body leaning against his large frame. Smell his Aramis aftershave. Feel his fingers touching mine as he guided me to the right keys. Whether I'd played 'Twinkle, Twinkle Little Star', or later, 'Ode to Joy', he'd always clapped with the same enthusiasm.

Bowls rinsed, coats on, I follow Anna through the French doors into the dusk. Mittens sits inside, watching us, pink nose smearing the glass. We wind our way across the stepping stones towards the greenhouse. I stop. Gasp. Spin around in a slow circle with my hand over my mouth.

'My borders!'

'They were a mess, weren't they? I've tidied them all up for you.' Anna gestures to shrubs and perennials she has wrenched from the ground, roots exposed, leaves curling.

'Anna, what have you done?'

I drop to my knees, lifting plants as gently as I would an injured child.

'They're all dead, aren't they?' Anna kneels next to me. 'Grace?'

'They're not dead. You've pulled up nearly everything. It's taken me years to establish them.' I bite back tears, tell myself they're only plants, but I stack this loss against my others all the same.

'But there's no flowers, no colour in them. They look like weeds.'

'It's winter; they're supposed to look like that.'

'I'm so sorry. I've never had a garden. Can we put them back?'

'We can try but the shock might kill them, if it hasn't already.'

Anna stands, brushing soil from her knees. 'I'll fetch some tools.'

The ground is hard, a frost forming already. Anna angles a flashlight towards the solid earth as I stab a fork in, pressing on it with one foot and then two in an effort to drive it down. There is a throbbing in my lower back and I am sweating, despite the evening chill. I almost cry with relief as I hear Dan call out, see his solid frame lumbering towards us. I gratefully hand over the fork and as he loosens the soil I'm able to scrape holes with my hands. It doesn't take too long before the plants are back in their earthy homes, drooping and withering.

Anna's apology runs on a loop and it isn't until we're sitting cross-legged on the lounge floor in front of a crackling fire, brandy snifters in hands, that I tell her not to worry and I mean it.

'You were trying to help. We'll find this funny one day.'

I tell her about the time Charlie tried to bake me a cake. She'd carefully measured out the ingredients, put them in the food processor and switched it on without the lid. The chocolate mix went everywhere. Grandad had to paint the ceiling and Grandma's curtains still have brown splodges, even now.

Anna and I laugh but Dan sits apart, nursing his drink, an emotion on his face I can't identify. A shiver runs through me and I'm not sure why.

CHAPTER SEVENTEEN
Then

My eyes sprang open. The day I'd thought would never come had finally arrived. *I'm eighteen!* I leapt out of bed and bounced downstairs like Tigger.

'Morning.'

'Happy birthday, Gracie.' Grandma and Grandad lined up in the kitchen to give me coffee-flavoured kisses. The table was strewn with multicoloured envelopes and while Grandma cooked breakfast I sliced them open, read out the messages inside the cards and handed them to Grandad. He balanced them between the Wedgwood on the dresser.

'Tuck in.' Grandma placed a plate before me, piled high with bacon, sausages, eggs, mushrooms, tomatoes and beans.

'Thanks.' I picked up my cutlery, wondering where to start.

By the time I forked the last mushroom into my mouth and pushed my plate away, my jaw ached from chewing. 'No wonder I'm popping out of my clothes with portions like that,' I said, leaning back on my chair. 'It's a good job I'm going to buy a new dress for tonight.'

'Women nowadays are too thin,' said Grandma. 'You look like a woman's supposed to.'

'In the 1950s maybe.'

'Men like a few curves.'

Did they? My love life was dismal. I was too hung up on Dan to consider dating anyone else. I wondered sometimes whether he still fancied Charlie, but she said he'd only ever asked her out the once. He didn't seem interested in Siobhan, thank god. Even though she practically threw herself at him: leaning forwards every time she talked so he could see down her top; touching his arm and giggling at everything he said, even when it wasn't meant to be funny. Charlie had started calling her 'Jessica Rabbit's evil twin'.

Charlie burst through the back door. 'Don't tell me I've missed breakfast?' She was red-faced and panting, hefting a large present in polka dot wrapping paper.

'I've saved some bacon for you, dear,' said Grandma. 'You need some meat on your bones. Turn sideways and we struggle to see you.' Charlie did seem to grow taller and thinner by the day.

Grandma buttered thick white bread and slathered the bacon in ketchup, just the way Charlie liked it. 'Sit down. We're about to do presents.'

Charlie thudded the box onto the table and shoved it over to me. She picked up her sandwich, took a bite and licked her fingers.

I carefully removed the ribbons and bows and peeled the tape away from the paper, trying not to rip it. I planned to glue the paper and bow from each present into my scrapbook later, and write details of the gift and who sent it underneath. It was important to me to preserve my memories. Dad had so much stuff. I never knew where it came from or what it meant to him and it never seemed important to ask while he was here. Afterwards, it pained me to think I knew so little about the man I'd thought I knew so well.

'You'll be nineteen before you get it open at this rate.'

Inside the box was an assortment of vinyl records: Billie Holiday, Etta James, Bessie Smith. The music I'd grown up with that Charlie didn't quite understand. I shook my head to dislodge the lump in my throat and stood up to hug her. She squeezed me with her forearms, her greasy hands splayed out to the side.

'Where did you find them all?'

'Car boot sales, eBay, Amazon. I've been saving my babysitting money and collecting them for the past year.'

Grandad took the albums through to the dining room, and as the strains of Etta James drifted through the open door, he came back and proffered his hand.

'Ginger?' He pulled me to my feet and I giggled as he Fred-Astaired me around the kitchen, twirling me around in his pin-striped pyjamas.

'This is from Grandad and me,' Grandma said, as we sank, breathless, into our seats. She pushed a sparkly silver-wrapped box towards me.

I rotated it in my hands, looking for the best place to open it.

'Here we go again,' said Charlie. 'You do know the shops shut at five-thirty?'

'Very funny.' I slid the present out of the paper. Diamond stud earrings.

'They were my mum's,' Grandma said. 'I've had them cleaned for you.'

I tilted the box towards the window and my great-grand-mother's earrings sparkled in the light. It was hard to equate something so beautiful with the frail old woman who smelled of pear drops that I remembered visiting when I was small.

'They were a present from your great-grandfather on their wedding day.'

'They're so beautiful, thank you.'

'And buy yourself something nice to wear tonight when you go to town.' Grandad pressed notes into my hand.

I was suddenly overcome by emotion. 'I love you all.' My voice caught.

'And we love you, too.' Grandma gave me a hug and then began to shoo me out of the kitchen. 'Now go and put some clothes on, unless you're planning on shopping in your pyjamas?'

I scooped up the wrapping paper before Grandad could recycle it and ran upstairs to get dressed.

The sofa was heavy. Charlie pushed as I pulled. Together, we wedged it into the corner of the room and slid the coffee table against the wall. The sideboard had been cleared and I flapped open a sheet and covered it up, ready to set the buffet on.

'Are you sure your mum doesn't mind me having a party here?'

'Nah. She's looking forward to it. I made her promise she won't embarrass me.'

I ripped open packets of Wotsits and flung them into bowls as Charlie made a punch in a giant glass bowl I'd brought from Grandma's. The liquid turned orange as Charlie sloshed fruit juice into the mix and gave it a stir.

'Try this.' She held a teaspoon to my lips and I slurped.

'God, that's strong. What's in it?' My eyes watered.

'Everything.' Charlie grinned and unscrewed the top from a half-open bottle of gin she'd found at the back of the cupboard.

'It's a good job my grandparents aren't coming,' I said.

I had invited them, but they'd said they'd leave us 'young 'uns' to it.

By nine o'clock my head was fuzzy, my step unsteady. Half the sixth form were crammed into Charlie's tiny house and the walls vibrated with the thump-thump-thump of the bass. Disco lights flashed red, green and blue, and I had a sense of detachment as I watched bodies sway on our makeshift dance floor to the playlist

Charlie had created. Dan shuffled his feet to 'Sex on Fire', waving a beer can in the air, as Siobhan raised her hands high and shook her head from side to side. Her chest wobbled. She didn't have a bra on under her spaghetti-strapped top. *Slut.* I swiped a cocktail sausage and bit it in half, wishing I could stab Siobhan with the stick. It was my birthday. Dan should be with me.

Beside me, Lexie ladled punch into a pint glass. 'You should go get him, girl,' she slurred, as she nodded at Dan. 'You're only young once. Just don't do what I did, Grace. Don't fuck it up.'

'What did you do?'

But the opening bars to 'Mamma Mia' rang out and Charlie yanked my arm.

'Let's boogie.'

I swigged what was left of my drink and fought my way into the middle of the lounge. Esmée clasped my left hand, Charlie my right. I lost sight of Siobhan and we were spinning and spinning and flying and falling. We heaped on the floor, arms and legs tangled, giggling, but then I felt sick.

The queue for the toilet snaked down the stairs and I pushed my way into Lexie's darkened bedroom instead. There was a pile of coats on the bed and I sat cross-legged on the floor, pressing my palms into the floorboards, wishing the room would keep still.

The door banged open and I was cast in a rectangle of light streaming in through the landing. Charlie tottered towards me.

'Are you OK?'

'Yeah. Too much punch I think.' I rubbed my eyes. 'Do I look a state?'

Charlie clicked on the bedside lamp. 'A bit.' She rooted around in Lexie's drawer and pulled out a handful of Rimmel make-up.

'Do you miss your dad, Charlie?' The alcohol had made me emotional. 'I miss mine.'

'Your face I can fix,' she said. 'Your dad…'

'I know.' I sighed. 'I'm OK, mostly, but days like today… How do you cope?'

Charlie shrugged. 'Can't miss what I never had.'

'But what if you found him? You could have a whole new family.'

'That might be a good thing. Mum's pissed again.'

'I noticed.'

'Suck your cheeks in.' Charlie dipped a brush into bronzer.

'We could find him.'

'How?'

'I don't know, but we're eighteen now. You can get a copy of your birth certificate if your mum still won't give you one. There are organisations that will help trace him. Google.'

'I dunno. We're supposed to be focusing on our A Levels. It's our last year. With Mum and Ben and everything…'

'I'll do it. It's not like I have a love life to occupy me.' Excitement welled up in me. Here was something I could change. Something I could do right. 'I could do with something to focus on.'

A groan came from the bed. Charlie peeled back coats.

'It's Mum. Out for the count, again. Let's go downstairs.'

The crowd had thinned. Charlie disappeared into the lounge. I crunched down the hallway towards the kitchen – someone had trailed pretzels over the floor – and filled a glass with water.

I jumped as Dan appeared behind me, reflected in the kitchen window.

'Look.' He wrapped an arm around my waist and pointed at the night sky. 'It's Orion.'

I squinted at the mass of stars. They all looked the same. 'Where?'

'You see that cluster that's brighter than the others, just there?'

'Yes.'

'That's Orion.'

'Is it?'

'I'm not sure. Got a telescope for my birthday but haven't used it yet. You were impressed though, weren't you? Admit it.'

I jabbed him in the ribs with my elbow, but he kept his arm around me. I leant back into him, fumbled around for something interesting to say and wished I hadn't drunk so much. I wasn't sure if it was alcohol or anticipation making my head spin.

'How's work? I haven't seen you in ages.' *Work?* I mentally kicked myself. No wonder Siobhan got all the boys. How did you learn to flirt?

'It's OK. I show people around houses they have no intention of buying most of the time. I miss school and the laughs we had. I miss you.'

I studied his reflection in the window. I couldn't make out his expression. 'We miss you.'

'I mean, I *really* miss you.'

My body felt weightless, as if I could float away if he weren't holding me.

'Charlie too?' My voice squeaked.

'Not in the same way. Look, Grace, I can't stop thinking about you. You've always been there in the background, and I took that for granted. Now you're not, I find myself missing the conversations we had. Charlie was a crush, someone to flirt with, fun. But what I feel for you, it's different. Real. Natural. I want to be with you. Do you want to be with me?'

He spun me around and locked his gentle eyes onto mine. I coaxed my nervous tongue to form an answer.

'Yes,' I whispered.

Dan brushed my hair away from my face and ran his finger down my cheek.

'Happy birthday, Grace.' His lips feathered across mine.

'No!'

We jerked apart. Siobhan stood behind us, hands on hips.

'Siobhan,' I started, 'I'm…'

'No fucking friend of mine, Grace Matthews.' She turned and ran down the hallway towards the front door. 'You'll regret this,' she yelled over her shoulder.

A pang of guilt shot through me. I knew she really liked him. 'I'd better go after her.'

The garden gate was swinging open by the time I got outside. Siobhan was nowhere to be seen. I put a hand on the stone wall to steady myself and let the icy air fill my lungs. The moon drifted in and out of focus and nausea churned up inside me like a tornado. The ground was hard and damp as I dropped to my knees and vomited Charlie's punch into the hydrangea.

I heard heels clicking down the pavement towards me and I thought Siobhan had come back to gloat.

Hands bunched my hair behind my head as I vomited again, and cool fingertips stroked my brow.

'Grandma said I'd find you here, Grace.'

I looked up and gasped. It wasn't Siobhan. It was Mum.

CHAPTER EIGHTEEN
Now

'Where were you last night?' The breakfast table is heavy with preserves and accusations. Dan unscrews a jar of marmalade, plunges his knife in. I try not to tut as butter seeps into the orange jelly. I dip a clean teaspoon into the strawberry jam and heap it onto the side of my plate.

'I went for a quick drink with the lads.'

'Until midnight?' I don't want a row before work, but my head throbs and my eyes are gritty with tiredness. I'd lain in bed, muscles tense, eyes wide open, until I heard the scratching of Dan jabbing his key in the front door lock, his unsteady tread as he stumbled his way up the stairs. He'd undressed with exaggerated slowness and, when he'd tumbled into bed, I'd turned away from his alcohol fumes, wanting to avoid a late-night row. I'd been conscious of Anna sleeping in the next room.

'I was worried, that's all – I wish you'd left a note.'

'I didn't think you'd notice.'

'What's that supposed to mean?'

'You're usually with Anna, hunched over photo albums. If she spent as much time looking for a job as she does quizzing you about Charlie, she'd have gone by now.'

'You want me to throw her out?'

'It was only supposed to be a few days. It's been three weeks. We're nearly in March.'

'I know.' I pour tea. It has brewed for too long and is dark and unappealing.

'I just thought we were going to concentrate on us.'

'I'll talk to her.'

'No.' Dan swigs tea, screws up his face. 'I'll do it. You've had enough stress.'

'Morning.'

We both jump. Anna usually stays in bed until after we've left for work. I wonder how much she's overheard. I lower my head, letting my hair fall over my burning face, studying the table as if it's the most interesting thing I've ever seen.

Dan pushes his chair back, fastens his top button and eases the knot on his tie upwards. 'See you later.'

'Grace, can I borrow your laptop?' Anna asks. 'I want to send off some more CVs and look at some flats for rent. I don't want to outstay my welcome.'

'Borrow away, and you're more than welcome to stay as long as you like.' I mentally apologise to Dan as I sweep toast crumbs and guilt into my cupped hand.

There's a staff meeting after work, but I find it difficult to focus my busy mind. I don't want Anna to move out, but Dan and I do need some quality time together. I wonder whether we should book a weekend away. We still haven't resurrected our sex life. I'm too aware that Anna could overhear our creaking headboard and squeaky springs.

The muscles in my back are tight as I drive home. Rain lashes against my windscreen and my wipers swish at double-speed, but it's still difficult to see. I drive carefully. Puddles form at the side of the road and fat drops of water bounce off my bonnet. I hold my hand in front of the heating vent. The air hasn't warmed yet and I'm freezing. I can't wait to step into a warm bath and scrub the poster paints from my fingernails, wash the glitter out of my hair. I decide on a Chinese for tea; we can curl up on the sofa with the laptop and check out country hotels. Anna might be glad of a few days to herself; she could look after Mittens.

Glaring white light slices through my thoughts and I squint through my windscreen. I can barely see the road. I flash the on-coming driver. *Dip your lights, idiot.* In my rear-view mirror I see the car screech to a stop. It spins around in a U-turn. I turn the radio down. Concentrate on the winding road ahead of me. An engine revs. Headlights flash. The car has caught up with me. It's so close it's almost touching my bumper.

My palms are damp with sweat. I remove my hands from the wheel, one at a time, and wipe them on my jeans. My foot squeezes the accelerator. I weave through the country lanes I know so well, but the car stays on my tail. There's a horn. A flash. And I'm scared. Really scared. I don't like driving fast. Don't like driving in the dark at all, especially in this foul weather. I'm push-ing eighty now. Far too fast for these wet roads with their sharp corners and potholes, but I can't bring myself to slow down. We squeal around corners, tyres slipping. I think of a film I saw once with a serial killer chasing a driver, and I lean forward as though I can make my car go faster. As I reach the lane, I slam my foot on the brake, make a sharp right and screech to a halt. My car skids sideways as the tyres lose traction. The other car doesn't turn but it stops at the top of the lane, engine put-put-putting. The orange glow of the lamp post illuminates its bonnet. It's red and I know with certainty that this is the person who's been fol-lowing me.

My left hand grips the steering wheel. My right rests upon the door handle. *C'mon, c'mon, c'mon.* I could step out of the car. Ask them what the hell they're playing at. My fingers twitch and my lower back aches where I'm twisting around in my seat. There's a beat. The interior light floods the red car as the door cracks open. A shadowy figure moves, but with the rain pelting down I can't see them properly. I know I should go home but I'm transfixed. The snake and the charmer.

A horn. A bus grinds to a halt behind the car, bus driver beeping impatiently. The car door closes. The interior light darkens, and as the car pulls away, I feel I've escaped something – but I don't know what. I rest my forehead on the steering wheel momentarily. Then I urge my trembling legs to move, press my feet against the pedals and speed towards the cottage.

'Dan!'

The smell of roast beef greets me as I push open the front door. In the lounge, the candles are lit and the table is set for two. There's a large vase of baby-pink roses on the coffee table.

'You're late?' Anna bustles towards me, wiping her hands on my apron.

'I had a staff meeting. Where's Dan?' I'm panting.

'He's gone out. It's just you and me.'

'Did he say where he's going?'

'No. Just "don't wait up". Are you OK? You look pale.'

I open my mouth to tell her what happened, but I think how ridiculous it sounds: *There was another car on the road and I got scared. I think I'm being followed.* An overactive imagination, Grandma would say.

'I need a drink.' There's a bottle of Shiraz on the table. Not my favourite, but it will do. I twist the cap off, slug some into a large goblet and knock it back in one. The alcohol burns my throat and my head swims.

'Grace, are you OK?'

'Fine.' I pour another glass. 'Look out of the window, Anna.'

'What am I looking for?' She crosses to the window and parts the curtains.

'A car.'

She looks right and then left. 'There's just your car.' She steps back and the curtains fall from her hands, coming back together like magnets. There's still a strip of light shining through and I press my back against the wall, scared someone might be looking in.

'What's going on, Grace?'

'Never mind. I'm going to get changed.' I pause by the front door on my way to the stairs, make sure it's locked, but I've only climbed three steps when I come back down, rattle the handle and put the chain on. *You're safe – you're safe – you're safe.*

There are no missed calls or texts from Dan when I check my phone – so much for our chat about communication. I swallow a fragment of a tablet, strip off my uniform, drop it in the laundry bin, and jump in the shower. Rinse away the cold sweat and dread that had covered me during the journey home. By the time I'm dry and dressed, I'm encased with the familiar warm medicated feeling and the terror has seeped away.

I take the wine Anna proffers. I'm feeling fuzzy, but it's Friday. Everyone has a drink on a Friday, don't they?

'Good day?' I ask.

'A productive one. I've applied for quite a few jobs. There are some nice flats on the market too. I'll need a hefty deposit, though, and the first month's rent in advance.'

'I might be able to lend you some.'

'Don't be silly. I'm used to taking care of myself. Now, I have a surprise for you. A little thank you for all you've done for me.' Anna passes me an envelope.

'What is it?'

'Open it.'

I run my finger under the seal and peel it open. Inside is a gift voucher for a spa day.

'It's for tomorrow. I hope you're not busy? Dan says he'll be at football.'

'I don't have any plans. This must have cost a fortune?'

'Not really. It was a Groupon offer. Virtually free.'

'Thanks.' I'm genuinely pleased. I read aloud the list of treatments on offer as Anna serves the food. 'Chocolate mud wrap, orange zest facial…' My mouth waters. 'They all sound good enough to eat.'

'Try this instead.' The roast beef is pink, goose-fat potatoes crispy, and when I'm finished I don't think I can possibly eat dessert, but then I'm presented with tiramisu covered in cream and dusted with chocolate. It tastes just as good as it looks.

'Dan doesn't know what he's missing.' My jeans feel tight and I slouch back in my chair, unfasten my top button.

'No. He's a moron.' There's a bitterness in Anna's voice that I haven't heard before. 'Grace, I don't know how to put this, so I'll just come out and say it.'

I sit up straighter.

'I heard Dan talking on the phone before he went out. Arranging to meet someone.'

I freeze but then shake myself. *Don't always jump to the worst conclusion, Grace.* I look at Anna steadily. 'It was probably Harry.'

'Does he always call Harry "babe"?'

The room suddenly feels cooler and I wrap my cardigan a little tighter. 'Are you *sure* that's what you heard?'

'I think so. I wasn't going to tell you, but I thought to myself, what would Charlie do?'

Brandy and cream tap-dance together and I feel sick. Why do I always overeat?

'I could have misheard. The TV was on. I'm sorry, I shouldn't have said anything.' Anna springs to her feet and begins to stack plates, clattering cutlery. I squeeze my eyes shut, and when I open them, she has gone into the kitchen. The candle flickers and hisses, fighting to stay alight in its diminishing pool of wax. Black shadows prowl around the walls, the strangers from my nightmares, the monsters under the bed. Chills run down my spine and I blow out the candle and switch on the light.

Anna is running steaming water into a bowl. Bubbles froth and multiply, out of control, much like my thoughts.

I pop the lid of the bin open, begin to scrape the plates. Beef fat and stray peas land on a piece of lined paper. Recognising Dan's handwriting, I fish it out and shake off a piece of potato peel that's stuck to it.

Going for a beer with Harry. See you later x

'Anna, did you put this in the bin?'

She reads it. 'No.'

'Why would Dan write me a note and throw it away?'

'Maybe he was afraid you'd check with Harry? Catch him out? Or maybe it just blew in there. I had the back door ajar when I was cooking; the bin lid was open for the peelings. I did shut the door when I thought I saw a figure in the garden, though.'

'There was someone in the garden and you're just telling me this now?' I snap, tossing the cutlery into the bowl. Frothy water splatters up over the tiles. I cross to the back door, rattle the handle to make sure it's locked and peer out through the glass into the garden.

'I wasn't sure if I imagined it. It was so dark.'

'But still. You'd know if you saw someone, surely?'

'Or something. I'm not used to the country. Easily spooked. It could have been a badger squeezing under the hedge.'

I pull the roller blind down on the back door and draw the kitchen curtains. We finish cleaning the kitchen in silence, then head upstairs to bed. I read my book, and have just got to the part where Mr Rochester makes Jane Eyre cry, when I hear a hammering on the front door. I bang the book shut and test the weight of it, as if I can use it as a weapon. *They've come back.* The figure Anna saw in the garden earlier. I should have rung the police.

A bang. A thud against the window. A voice. 'Grace?'

It's Dan. I remember I pulled the chain across, and I run downstairs to let him in.

'Why's the chain on?'

'Where have you been?' I cross my arms over my chest.

'Out with Harry. I left you a note. Didn't you see it?'

'And you call Harry "babe", do you?'

'Of course not. What are you talking about?' Dan pulls his trainers off. 'Are you OK? Your eyes are really bloodshot.'

'I'm tired.' Nothing makes sense. 'Anna heard you on the phone calling someone "babe".'

'Did she?' Dan throws his trainers onto the mat and they thud against the front door. Fragments of mud stipple the carpet.

'And I suppose you expect me to hoover that up?'

'I don't *expect* you to do anything except believe me over some mad bitch you've only known *five minutes*.'

'Keep your voice down.'

'Why? In case precious Anna overhears and twists things around? I can shout if I want. This is my bloody house.'

'Our bloody house. So where were you?'

'At the club with Harry. Ask Chloe, if you don't believe me. She was there. There are still girls around who actually want to spend time with their boyfriends.'

'Well, maybe their boyfriends don't go around calling other girls "babe".' I stomp back upstairs and lie rigid in bed, listening to the muffled sounds of the TV drifting up through the floor as

Dan watches a late-night film, all squealing tyres and gunshots. It seems ages before sleep tugs me under. My dreams are strewn with torn-up notes, red Corsas and a figure in a black padded coat hiding in the bushes.

CHAPTER NINETEEN
Now

Everything is stark white: my fluffy robe, slippers, the floor and wall tiles. If it wasn't so warm I'd think I was in the Arctic. I stuff my belongings into a locker and drop the key into a canvas bag that is already bulging with my towel and a book, *Jane Eyre*. Anna's cubicle door creaks open. She steps out, swamped in her robe. I pull my belt a little tighter.

'Ready?'

'Ready.'

'Sauna first?'

'I've never had one before.'

'Never? Let's do that, then. You should leave your necklace here. The metal will heat and burn your skin.'

I finger the gold hearts. 'I never take this off.'

'I've noticed; did Dan buy it?'

'No. Charlie.'

'It will be safe in your locker. You won't want it on for the massage anyway.'

I carefully take the necklace off, fasten the clasp and put it inside my jacket pocket.

'Let's go.'

We hang our bags and robes on the hooks outside the sauna. Anna tugs the glass door and the rush of escaping heat takes my breath away. I trail her through the gloom and copy her as she spreads her towel out on a wooden bench and kicks her slippers off.

'Are you OK?' she asks.

'I wasn't expecting it to be quite so hot in here.'

'You'll get used to it pretty quickly. I was wondering, Grace, if we can go and see Lexie tomorrow?'

'I'm sorry, Anna. I haven't talked to her about you yet. I will, I promise, but I haven't had a chance.'

'We could surprise her?'

'I don't think that's a good idea. She's very fragile.'

'But I might cheer her up?'

'Maybe. I'll talk to her. How about you come and have Sunday lunch at my grandparents' tomorrow? They're dying to meet you and they have lots of Charlie stories.'

'OK.' Anna lies back and closes her eyes and I do the same. Sweat runs in rivulets down my body and, when Anna suggests a swim several minutes later, black dots dance in front of my eyes as I stand. I grip the bench to steady myself before I walk. It's a relief to take a shower and plunge into the cold pool. I swim lengths until my breath rasps, then I flip over and float on my back. Anna climbs out the pool before me. Her thighs are covered in puckered scars I haven't seen before. I wonder what happened to her after her parents died. She can be so guarded sometimes.

I shuffle across the poolside, conscious of the slippery tiles. Lots of the guests have brought flip-flops and I decide that if I ever come again, I'll do the same. It's so warm I don't bother drying my skin, but I rub my hair with my towel as I perch on the edge of Anna's lounger.

'Can I ask you something personal, Anna?'

'You can ask. I might not answer.'

'Where did you go? After your parents…'

'I was fostered for a while, but it didn't work out.'

'Why?'

'Some children are hard to love, I suppose. I was very angry. I wanted my mum. Hungry?' Anna stands and folds her towel into a square and I feel hurt that she doesn't feel able confide in me.

Lunch is a buffet. I feel virtuous following my swim, and heap my plate with colourful salads and cold rice. I can't resist the dessert table, though, and eat two slices of cheesecake, telling myself I can swim it off later. However, by the time we've finished our coffees and nibbled on after-dinner mints, I'm too full to exercise, so we sink into the Jacuzzi instead. The water comes up to my chin.

'How many foster homes did you have?' I can't help probing.

'Not as many as the calories you've just eaten. Look at the body on him.' Anna nods towards a guy spreading his towel on a lounger.

'His biceps are huge.'

'That's not the only huge thing, looking at his Speedos.'

I avert my eyes. 'Not my type.'

'I don't really have a type. I want someone who can make me laugh.'

'Dan's funny.' I catch her expression: she looks slightly scornful. 'No, really, usually he is; he was, anyway,' I persist, not sure why I'm feeling so defensive.

'What do you mean, "he *was*"? What happened?'

'I couldn't cope when Charlie died. It was such a shock. I began to wonder if I was cursed. I couldn't sleep, couldn't eat. I snapped at Dan constantly, hating him for not knowing how to make me feel better. He started going out drinking every night just to avoid me. He's never been one to talk about feelings. Anyway, it has got a bit better lately. Relationships are hard work, and you've got to take the rough with the smooth, I guess. I want to make it work. We both do.'

'I'm sure you will.'

'How long have you been single?'

Anna fiddles with her hair. 'Not long enough!'

'Bad break-up?'

'Is there such a thing as a good one? I don't know if I believe in all that happy ever after stuff. It's not the way it works in real life, is it? I have this idyllic memory of my parents, but maybe they just died before it could all go wrong. Relationships don't last, do they? Between anyone?' She looks at me intently.

'My grandparents are doing all right. It's their golden anniversary this year.'

'They're the lucky ones then, or maybe more tolerant than the rest of us. Living with someone's faults, accepting their mistakes, forgiveness – that's true love, wouldn't you say?'

'Suppose.' I wonder, should you compromise to accept someone for who they really are, or is that settling for less than you really want? I'm not sure.

'How about your parents?' Anna asks.

But before I can answer, a girl in a black tunic sashays towards us, clipboard in hand. She looks barely old enough to have left school and I wonder how it is her thick make-up doesn't melt in this heat. I don't often bother with make-up but when I do it doesn't take long before my nose is shiny, mascara smudged and there's lipstick on my teeth. I'm lucky Dan prefers the natural look, but is that something men just say? The women they seem to look at in magazines, in movies, on the street, are the glamorous, the über-thin. Not like me. Not like most of the women I know.

'Grace Matthews?'

'That's me.'

She smiles, teeth impossibly white. 'I'm Caroline. I'll be doing your aromatherapy massage. If you'd like to come this way?'

The room is in semi-darkness; wall lights in the shape of candles cast a mandarin glow over the therapy couch. Pan pipes stream from an iPod dock. I undress and lay on my front on a chocolate faux-fur throw that tickles my skin. Caroline covers me with a soft fleecy blanket and I breathe in essential oils, praying my bottom won't wobble too much once the massage starts. Caroline warms lavender oil between her palms, and her fingers start to unknot long-neglected muscles. I stop worrying about my cellulite as the heels of her hands slide either side of my spine. My eyelids flutter and close.

'Grace, it's time to get dressed.' A whispered voice and a gentle hand on my shoulder stir me. I sit up, blinking and disorientated, feeling like I've just come out of the cinema into blazing sunlight. Caroline passes me a glass of water and I take a sip.

'That was magical. Thank you.'

It feels like I float back to the poolside. 'You're up,' I tell Anna.

I flop onto a lounger; I don't want to swim and wash the oils off. My skin feels so soft. I close my eyes and doze, until Anna gently shakes me awake.

'Time to go home, sleepyhead.'

'Do we have to?' I yawn and heave myself upright. 'I could happily stay here for the rest of my life.'

'You'd get bored.'

I'm not convinced I'd ever tire of this, but I follow her to the changing rooms all the same. I fish my key from my bag and open my locker, bundle my belongings and find an empty cubicle. My arms feel heavy as I guide them into sleeves. I can't remember ever feeling this relaxed. I drag a brush through my hair and reach into my jacket for my necklace. It isn't there. I've barely taken off the heart since Charlie gave me it on my fifteenth birthday and I feel light-headed. I check again. The pocket's empty. All the pockets are empty. Panic wells. Where is it? Fingers of dread twist my insides and I bang open the door, scouring the floor as I rush back to the locker I used. The necklace isn't there.

I chew my lip. *Think, Grace.* I rummage through my hand-bag. Everything is still there.

'Are you OK?'

Anna stands behind me, shower-wet, dripping over the floor.

'My necklace has gone.'

'What do you mean, gone?'

'Gone, as in it's not there.' I bite my lip hard to stop myself from crying.

'It must be.' Anna checks the locker and my pockets. 'I don't understand. Has someone taken it?'

'How? The door was still locked. I left the key with you when I went for a massage. Did you go in my locker?' I cross my arms.

'No. Of course not. Let's think. Have you let the key out of your sight at all?'

'No.' I sit down heavily on a bench. 'Well, I did fall asleep after my massage. My bag was on the floor next to me.'

'Someone could have taken your key then?'

'And stole my necklace but left my phone and purse, and put the key back before I woke?'

'That's pretty implausible, isn't it? Let's go and talk to reception.'

I stand tapping my foot as Anna dresses, then we rush back to the entrance I had floated through so happily, just hours before.

'Sit down,' Anna says. 'I'll fetch the manager.'

I sit on the edge of a high-backed chair and grip the table in front of me. My knuckles are chalk white. *Charlie, I'm so sorry.*

Anna murmurs in a low voice to a woman in a black pencil skirt and white blouse, who glances over. Her forehead is Botox-smooth and glossy, eyebrows rigid and arched. It's impossible to see if she's shocked. She totters over to me, thrusting out her tanned hand. 'I'm Tina. Let's go back to the changing rooms, shall we?' She leads the way. 'Which one was yours?'

I point to the locker on the bottom row.

'Look. There's a slight gap between the door and the base. How thick is your necklace?'

'It's quite thin.'

'It's possible then that if you didn't put it in your pocket properly, or if it slipped out when you pulled your jacket out, it could have fallen down there?'

My heart sinks as I examine the gap, thinking of the way I dragged my clothes out: bundling them together, trying to carry everything at once. 'I suppose so.'

'I think that's the rational explanation. We've never had an experience of theft here.'

'So how do I get it back?'

'Is it valuable?'

'It has great sentimental value.'

'Rest assured that when we next renovate and replace the lockers, we'll find it. If you want to leave your name and number, we'll contact you.'

'When will that be?' I feel so desperate.

'I don't have an exact date, but we're always improving our facilities. That's why our customers return again and again. Did we give you a membership leaflet?' I turn away from her dazzling smile.

Anna rubs my arm. 'I'm so sorry, Grace. I know how much the necklace means to you. We'll buy another one.'

'It won't be the same. It won't be from Charlie.'

'No, but it will be from me.' Anna smiles and I feel grateful she's there, wonder what I would do without her.

CHAPTER TWENTY
Then

It was the early hours of the morning by the time Mum and I had walked back from my eighteenth birthday party at Lexie's. We sat at Grandma's wooden table, steam curling from the mugs of coffee in front of us. My hair, wet from my shower, was making my shoulders damp, but at least it smelled apple-fresh now, not of sick. I felt self-conscious in my pyjamas and tugged my dressing gown to cover my knees. It was freezing. I'd flicked the heating on and there was a click-click-click as the pipes warmed.

'You should dry your hair. You'll catch a cold.'

'You do *not* get to come back after ten years and tell me what to do.'

'No.' Mum raised her cup to her lips and blew. 'I don't suppose I do.'

'Why are you here?'

'To talk.'

'I don't want to.'

I didn't want to deal with this now. I felt ashamed and I wasn't sure if it was my past actions or present words making me feel that way. I gulped my drink to try and wash my confusion away. The liquid scalded my tongue and tears sprang to my eyes as I jumped to my feet. I yanked open the freezer and cracked an ice cube from the tray, let it melt in my mouth.

'Well, I do. Darling, I'm so sorry I left, but you're old enough to understand. It wasn't that I didn't want you. I wasn't well. It was hard to cope with what happened.'

What happened. It was as though I were expanding. My lungs were pushing against my ribs. My skin stretching. And then I was back there. Back in the day I'd tried so hard to forget.

I'd woken swathed in a honeycomb glow as pale sunlight penetrated my thin yellow curtains. It was early. It was coming up to my ninth birthday and I was too excited to sleep. I shed my pyjamas and pulled on jeans and a jumper, then scraped my hair into a ponytail before padding barefoot downstairs. Mum was already in the kitchen, Radio 2 playing as she whisked the batter for our lunchtime Yorkshire puddings. 'Morning,' I called as I walked past the open kitchen door, heading towards the dining room and the tinkling of the piano.

I sat next to Dad on the worn brown piano stool, resting my head against his shoulder. 'Can we go to the park today, Dad?'

He gave me a hard, Paddington Bear stare over the top of his glasses. 'You should really practise for your exam next week, Grace.'

'We could practise after lunch?'

'OK.' He smiled. 'Have some breakfast and wrap up warm. It'll be colder than it looks out there.'

I scuttled to the kitchen and munched on Marmite toast as Mum peeled parsnips for dinner. On the radio, ELO promised 'Mr. Blue Sky'. Dad brought me my coat and boots. 'It's a beautiful new day,' he sang along. 'Hey, hey.' We were ready to go.

'Be back by one, and don't fill up on ice cream,' Mum started.

'Or there'll be no pudding for you,' chorused Dad and I. Mum kissed Dad goodbye and handed me a bag of bread for the ducks.

We rustled through the orange and brown fallen leaves, walking with my small hand wrapped inside Dad's giant one, making up stories. The biting air nipped at my exposed face, the rest of me wrapped tightly in my pink Puffa jacket. We adventured down the road in wellington-booted feet, jumping bravely into every pile of curling leaves that carpeted the pavement. Each one had the possibility of containing a portal to another world. There would be a parallel universe, we decided, containing carbon copies of us. 'Although without the tummy,' Dad said, patting his rounded belly.

At the park, we headed straight for the duck pond and opened the bag of stale crusts.

'I'm foregoing my bread pudding for you,' Dad told the snapping birds. 'I hope you're grateful.'

I hid behind his legs as the geese jostled the ducks out of the way. I'd had my finger nipped the week before. The bread was soon gone and we headed to our usual bench and watched fathers and sons whizz remote-control boats around the water, leaving foamy snail trails behind them.

Dad produced a packet of strawberry bonbons and for a while we sat toffee-tongue-tied. The church bells chimed twelve and over the hill I saw a flash of yellow.

'Ice cream!'

'It'll spoil your dinner.'

'Just a small one. Please?'

Dad pushed his glasses onto the bridge of his nose and nodded, and off I raced. Arms pumping. Boots slip-sliding on the damp grass.

'Wait at the road for me,' Dad called.

By the time I'd got to the top of the hill I was breathless. The van was double-parked and a queue was forming already. I looked left and right and shot across the road. There was a squealing of brakes. A flash of silver. My feet felt glued to the spot. I've never forgotten the image of the driver's face, his mouth a silent scream as he forced himself back in his seat, gripping the steering wheel with both hands. I felt boiling hot and freezing cold at the same time. And then I was flying, twisting, crashing. Sprawled on the pavement, jeans torn and palms scraped. Behind me, Dad was lying in the road. He'd pushed me out of the way but he was motionless. Blood pooled under his head. His spectacles lay shattered beside him. Fragments of glass glinted in the sun.

A woman in a bright red hat ran towards Dad. 'Someone call an ambulance,' she cried.

People scurried over to where my father lay; they gripped each other's arms. Some covered their mouths unable to look away, others covered their eyes, peering through splayed fingers as though watching a scary film.

There was a stillness. Utter silence. Even the wind had stopped blowing the leaves. Pigeons landed and pecked the scattered bonbons that had rolled out of Dad's pockets. I crawled over to him.

'Wake up,' I whispered. His unseeing eyes, hazel like mine, gazed back at me as if trying to impart one last message that I couldn't quite decipher. And then the air was full of sirens. Full of 'Oh my God's and 'Did you see?'s and I was wrapped in an itchy orange blanket and bundled into the back of an ambulance.

He wasn't dead. Not his body, anyway. But his mind was gone, they said, and I never understood how he could look the same, feel the same, although the essence of him was missing. Where did it go?

Mum consented to turn his life support off and went to stay with her sister. I felt I'd lost them both.

'It was my fault,' I sniffed. 'No wonder you couldn't bear to look at me afterwards.'

'Oh Grace, is that what you think? I was ill. I'd been with your dad since I was sixteen; the thought of carrying on without him was unbearable.'

Mum passed me a tissue, and as her sleeve rode up, I spotted it. A sliver of silver puckered skin across her wrist.

'You tried to *kill* yourself?' Scorching hot anger erupted. 'You had a *child*.'

'I had a breakdown. Grandad found me in the bath a couple of weeks after we moved here. Grandma sent me to a clinic. Didn't want me around you. She'd watched her own mother having a breakdown. We wanted to shield you. And when I was discharged, I went to stay with Aunty Jean. I kept ringing you, darling, but when you kept hanging up I gave up. I shouldn't have done. I'm sorry.'

'You had "nerves", Grandma said. I thought that meant I got on your nerves.'

'I wasn't capable of looking after you.'

'And afterwards? You got better?'

'It took a long time before I felt able to be your mum again, but by the time I did, you were settled here. School. Charlie. You were happy. We talked about me moving here, but I know what Grandma's like. She'd have fussed and fussed, got involved in every single decision, and I'd never have properly felt like your mum. You wouldn't even talk to me on the phone. I went back to Devon. I felt closer to your dad there.'

'But further from me? He was gone. I was *still here*.'

'I know. It seemed the right thing to do at the time. For all of us, but if I could go back and change things, I would. Not a single day has gone by when I haven't thought of you. Grandma sent me all your school reports, photos, home movies. I've watched you grow. You just never knew.'

'I can't believe Grandma never told me you wanted me back.'

'She did what she thought best. She watched her own mum go in and out of clinics for years. She didn't want to put you through the same thing. She loves you. We all do.'

I tried to speak but a sob escaped my throat. Years of bottled-up grief poured out of me as I cried so hard I thought I'd never stop. Mum stood next to my chair and wrapped her arms around me, pulling my head into her chest, stroking my hair over and over. She still smelled the same. Of Opium perfume and Elnett hairspray, and I never wanted to let her go.

'I killed him. I killed Dad.'

'You didn't, Grace. Never blame yourself.'

But how could I stop feeling the way I'd always felt? Enough people had told me it was an accident. Grandma; Grandad; my counsellor, Paula. Even Charlie. But my heart? My heart felt differently. Guilt permeated into every cell, multiplied, until it was as much a part of me as my skin. My bones.

'If…' I took a breath. 'If I hadn't run out in front of the ice-cream van. If he hadn't run out to save me, I'd be dead now. Not him.'

'He wouldn't want that. I wouldn't want that. None of us would want that.' Mum reached across the table to me but I leant backwards.

'But I killed him.' I slammed my drink down. Coffee sloshed over the pine table.

'You didn't. I was the one who consented to turn off his life support. I hope you can forgive me for that.'

'I hated you for that.' I squeezed the handle of my mug so tightly I was surprised it didn't splinter.

'It was the hardest thing I've ever done.'

We sat in silence. I dabbed the spilt coffee with my tissue. Grandma would be furious if it seeped into the wood. You'd think it'd be quiet in the dead of night. Still. But the fridge hummed, the clock ticked, the world turned. My world shattered long ago, but I had a chance to put it right now.

'I'm sorry I wouldn't talk to you afterwards, when you used to ring me, but I hated myself, and when you disappeared I thought you hated me, too.'

Mum twisted her gold wedding band round and round her finger. 'I could never hate you, Grace. Never.' She pushed a small gift bag into the centre of the table. 'This is for you. Happy birthday.'

Inside the bag was a small box. I placed both thumbs on the lid and popped it open. Nestled on a red velvet base was something I hadn't seen for many years. 'It's your engagement ring.' I began to cry again as I ran a finger over the sparkling diamond.

'I wanted you to have something your dad played a part in, Grace. He'd be so proud of you. I am, too. Is it too late to start again?' She stretched out her hand across the table.

'We can try.' Our fingers laced together and they stayed that way as we talked until the sun came up.

CHAPTER TWENTY-ONE
Now

No matter how many times I tell myself it doesn't matter that I've lost the necklace, the necklace that linked me and Charlie, that I still have my memories, I can't fight the blackness swirling around my veins. I paint on my happy face every day before work and laugh and play with the children, but it takes every ounce of energy to pretend to be something I don't feel. By the time I arrive home, my eyelids are heavy with exhaustion although it's only six o'clock.

Anna cooks every night and Dan makes the effort to finish work earlier, but the atmosphere at home is tense and thick and I know I am mostly to blame. Dan is snappy with Anna and I hear them stage-whispering in corners, angry and frustrated conversations that cease when I enter the room. I think they're thinking of ways to lift my mood and I am grateful that they care.

While talking to Mum on the phone last night, I broke down. Choking, angry sobs that burned my chest. Mum asked me to go and stay with her in Devon. *The sea air will do you the world of good,* she said, and although I long for the salt stinging my lips, the wind whipping my hair, the sand seeping into my shoes, I can't leave Anna. I've only just found her.

Lexie has taken to telephoning me every day, sometimes lucid but often rambling, her voice slow and thick with alcohol. I stay on the line, listening to her racking sobs, knowing that ten minutes after she hangs up she won't remember calling, and will likely ring again.

Today, I pull up outside the cottage, relieved it's Friday, when my mobile rings. I cringe at the thought of talking to Lexie again today and I'm tempted to ignore the phone, but then berate myself and reach to answer. Esmée's name flashes on the screen and I relax, glad of the chance to immerse myself in someone else's news. Esmée's life has always seemed far more exciting than mine, even before she moved to London.

The line is crackly and I switch the engine off to hear her better. Esmée describes her most recent foray into the world of speed dating and my smile is genuine for the first time in days.

'It's lovely to talk to you, hun, but I do have a reason for calling,' Esmée says. 'It's no biggie, but I think someone's hacked your Hotmail account.'

'Hacked?'

'I've had a few links come through.'

'For what?'

'Porn. It's pretty hard-core stuff. I clicked on the first one thinking you'd sent me a link to shoes or something. I've deleted them now, but you need to change your password, hun.'

I'm mortified when I think of the people in my email address book. My grandparents, my mum. Have they all received these links?

'I'm so sorry, Esmée.'

'Don't be. It's really common. It happened at the Gallery last week. Two hundred prospective clients opened an email from us expecting an invitation to an exhibition, and found a half-price offer for a penis extension instead.'

I promise Esmée that I will visit soon – we both know I won't – and then I sit in the car, cold and uncomfortable, too sluggish to move. Headlights shine in my rear-view mirror and I wait until Dan cuts the engine, opens his door and pulls a suit bag from the back seat. We walk into the cottage together. Anna is dusting the photos in the hallway. I can't remember the last time I had to clean.

'New suit?' I ask Dan.

'Nah, got the old one dry-cleaned – for tomorrow.'

'Tomorrow?' I root around in my memory banks.

'The annual Estate Agents' Dinner,' Dan sighs. 'It's on the calendar, Grace, and I mentioned it last week.'

'I lost track of the date.'

Anna raises an eyebrow. 'Is that as fun as it sounds?'

'It's a black-tie event held the first weekend in March each year. They give awards to the best agents in the county, and there are speeches. Long speeches.' I pinch the bridge of my nose.

'It's important. I'm up for an award this year.'

It is discomfiting that I didn't know this and I plaster over my shame with fake enthusiasm.

'You deserve to win,' I say. 'You've worked so hard.' But I can't remember the last time we celebrated a sale. Is business bad or has he just stopped telling me about his day? Have I just stopped listening?

'What are you going to wear, Grace?'

'I'm not sure I feel up to it. How about you take Anna instead?' The thought of making polite conversation over a three-course meal fills me with dread.

Dan's eyes narrow. 'Everyone's expecting you, Grace. It'll be fun. We're sitting with Harry and Chloe.'

'My hen night dress is ruined – I couldn't get the wine stain out – and I don't know if my others fit me any more.' I think of all the empty Hobnobs packets stuffed inside my glovebox, my bag, my bedside drawer, and conclude that they probably won't.

'I don't mind coming,' Anna says.

'No.' Dan's voice is terse. 'I'm sure you've got job applications you could be filling in.'

'Dan!' I'm embarrassed.

Anna smiles at me. 'It's OK. How about I take you shopping tomorrow, Grace? I know some fabulous boutiques, and I can ask if they need any staff while we're there. I *am* trying, Dan.'

'Yes.' Dan stuffs his suit back into the bag. 'You are.'

The lights in the changing room are muted and golden but that doesn't soften the horror I feel as too many mirrors reflect angles of my body that I never usually get to see, and never want to see again. My Bridget Jones pants and bra, once white, look far greyer than they did at home. I wrap my arms around my belly, fingers sinking into soft flesh, and wish I were anywhere else but here, half-naked with a personal shopper appraising me.

'Hmm,' Tamsin, the stylist says. 'A pear. Never mind. I will fetch dresses to make you look fabulous, yes?'

She swishes the red velvet curtains with the gusto of a magician. I sink into a gilded chair upholstered with maroon velvet, and sip orange juice. My hand hovers over the plate of complimentary chocolates.

'It's incredible here, isn't it? I feel like a star.' Anna bursts through the curtains with an armful of cherry-red silk and taffeta on a size eight hanger. I snatch my hand away from the plate.

Anna sheds her clothes and steps into the delicate material.

'How do I look?'

'Stunning.' She does. Her blonde hair shimmers around her shoulders. Tears prick my eyes as I think of all the formal dresses Charlie will never wear.

'Do you think I need a necklace with this? I'm going to see what they have.'

The curtains part and Anna dashes out as Tamsin totters in, three hangers held high above her head. The dresses look beautiful, stylish, and very, very, expensive. The type of gowns you see in magazines, not on a pre-school assistant.

'Which one first, Grace? They are all stunning, yes?'

'I'm not sure. I don't usually wear stuff like this.'

'Where do you normally shop?'

'Mainly eBay.'

Tamsin scrunches her face, as though she has found a cater-pillar in her salad. 'Never mind. You're here now.' She slides a floor-length olive-green dress from its padded hanger. 'This is the new spring line.' She holds it out for me to step into. I straighten my spine as she zips the back. The dress is heavy, pressing tightly against my ribcage.

'I have to eat in this, you know.' I turn to look in the mirror. All thoughts of food vanish as I gape at my reflection.

'It is good, yes? I have chosen well.'

Marilyn Monroe has nothing on me. I look old-school Hollywood glamour: curves accentuated, bulges hidden.

'It's incredible.' I stroke the material. 'I'd never have picked this in a million years. Mum wears a lot of green, but I never thought it suited me.'

'This is why you need me,' Tamsin says. 'eBay? Pfft. Now, accessories…'

A gold choker is fastened around my neck, a matching bangle looped over my wrist.

Act confident, Charlie used to tell me. *Fake it till you make it*. I feel confident in this dress. Sexy, even. Who knew clothes could be so empowering? I lower the tone of the boutique by taking a selfie and texting it to Esmée.

The curtains swing open. 'Look, Anna.' I twirl. 'What do you think?'

'Honestly?' She wrinkles her nose.

'Honestly.' My hands flutter towards my tummy as if I can hold my confidence in place, stop it escaping.

She looks me up and down. 'I always think bigger girls should stick to black. Much more flattering.'

I close my eyes to escape my many reflections. How ridiculous to think I could be anything other than what I am.

'I disagree,' says Tamsin.

'But you're trying to make a sale, aren't you? I'm speaking as her best friend.'

'I think Grace has a beautiful figure. Many of our customers are a size fourteen.'

'Grace is beautiful on the inside; that's the most important thing.'

'Can someone unzip me?' I snap. I'm hot and uncomfortable, and feel like an overstuffed pillow – shapeless and bumpy.

'I'll try the black one please, Tamsin.'

I feel boring in the black.

'That looks great,' Anna says. 'It really disguises your tummy rolls. I think you should get it.'

My phone beeps. Esmée: *Hun, you look gorgeous.*

'Esmée likes the green.'

'Esmée isn't here,' Anna says. 'You can't see all angles from a photo. It's up to you, though; I'm just trying to help. The black one will last you for years; it's a classic, and you don't look as lumpy as you did in the green.'

'I don't choose dresses that make people look lumpy.' Tamsin gives Anna a withering look. 'This one, it's not as stunning as the green,' says Tamsin, 'but it's perfectly acceptable, yes?'

'I did like the green.'

'Good for you, if you think you have the confidence to carry it off,' says Anna. 'Honestly, Grace. Dan will be proud to have you on his arm, however you look.'

'If you want to try both on at home you have fourteen days to make a return, as long as the item is unworn and the tags are still on it.'

'I'll take both.'

At the till, the dresses are folded, wrapped in scented tissue paper and placed in a box, silver stars sprinkled on top.

'Do you want the red silk dress?' Tamsin asks Anna.

'I can't afford it, and I don't know where I'd wear it.'

'It never hurts to have a formal dress in case an opportunity presents itself. It is a one-off. Very beautiful, yes?'

'It is. I'll have to pass, though.'

'Let me buy it for you,' I say.

'I can't let you pay; you've done so much for me already.'

'I want to. It's a thank you for all you've done for me, actually. Meeting you has really cheered me up and I loved the spa day. God knows what I'd be wearing tonight if you hadn't brought me here.'

'Thanks, Grace.' Anna hugs me, scurries off to fetch her dress.

'You are good friends, yes?' asks Tamsin.

'Yes,' I say. 'We are.'

The boutique door swings shut behind us and I stand blinking in the sunlight, gulping fresh air, not quite believing I've just spent nearly £300. I hope I can intercept the credit card bill before Dan sees.

'Let's get a coffee,' says Anna. 'My treat.'

'Yes. Shall we go to…' I tail off. On the opposite side of the road, a figure in a black coat is staring at me. Is it the same person who was outside the coffee shop, and at the cemetery that day with Lexie? The driver of the red car?

I clutch Anna's arm. 'No time for questions, but can you make out whether that's a man or a woman over there?' I point.

Anna squints, and slides her sunglasses from the top of her head to cover her eyes. 'I can't see anything. It's too bright. Hang on.' She dashes across the road, but by the time she gets there the figure has gone and I'm not quite sure if they were ever there at all.

CHAPTER TWENTY-TWO
Then

The empty hangers in my wardrobe rattled together as I pulled out another dress, held it against myself, and discarded it on the floor. Despite my lack of sleep – Mum and I had stayed up talking until dawn – and my hangover, I wanted to look my best this evening. Who'd have thought I could end up with Dan and rebuild my relationship with Mum all in one night?

I touched two fingers to my lips. They tingled when I thought of last night's kiss, and happiness bubbled inside me like champagne. Charlie and I were only going to the local pub to meet Ben and Dan but I'd taken extra care with my make-up: eyes lined a little darker, lips glossier. It may have been a Sunday evening, but it felt like a special occasion – and to top it off, I was legally old enough to drink now. No sitting in the corner nursing a Coke, sneaking vodka in my glass while Mike, the landlord, wasn't looking, from a half-bottle Charlie had hidden in her bag.

There was a tap on my door. 'Come in.'

Mum perched on the edge of my bed, patted the space next to her. 'I'm going soon, darling; it's a long drive back to Devon.'

'I wish you could stay.' I sat next to her and rested my head on her shoulder.

'I'll be back before you know it.' She hugged me. 'Christmas with my girl. I wanted to tell you that now you're eighteen you've come into a trust fund. Daddy left us very well provided for in case the worst ever happened.'

'Mum?'

'Yes.'

'How will I know I've met the one?'

'Do you remember when you had ballet lessons, you used to teach Daddy the steps?'

'Yes.' I smiled at the memory of us wrapped in old pink bedroom curtains, dancing around the lounge.

'There was this big, strong, dependable man that we all looked up to. He spent all day in the surgery diagnosing illnesses, saving lives and listening to the lonely and sick. He was very well respected. Always fundraising for the village and on the local council.' Mum squeezed my hand. 'He'd come home, put a pink skirt on and dance to *Swan Lake*, just to make his little girl smile. All he ever wanted was for you to be happy, Grace. When you meet someone, ask yourself, "Would they wear pink curtains for me?" and you won't go far wrong. Have you met someone?'

'Yes. I think so.'

'I have something else to tell you.' I could guess what was coming. 'I've met someone too. Oliver.'

I waited for the stabbing pain to come. The tears. The sense of betrayal. Instead, I pictured my strapping Dad pirouetting around the lounge.

'Dad would be glad.' And I believed that. He wanted the best for her. For us. Always.

'Thanks, darling. I would like very much for you to meet him. I could bring him when I come back next month?'

'I'd like that, too.' And I found that I meant it.

I had to redo my make-up after Mum left, removing streaks of mascara with cotton wool pads steeped in baby lotion. I'd chosen one of Mum's old 60s tunics: the aqua swirling pattern looked like water being sucked down a plughole. I spun around, checking my reflection from behind, hoping that my bottom was covered. Although I was wearing black opaque tights and leather boots, I felt self-conscious, and I practised flicking my hair back, to exude a confidence I didn't really feel. My nails were cherry red, a daring choice for me, and I blew on them, wanting the varnish to harden so I could check my mobile again. It had buzzed so frequently with texts from Dan I'd had to plug it in to recharge.

Charlie thundered up the stairs and burst into my room, a silver gift-wrapped box tucked under her arm.

'This is for you. I found it on the step.'

'Ooh, a late birthday present. Wonder what it is.'

'GRACE' was scrawled across the paper in felt pen, in spidery handwriting I didn't recognise.

'You could always try, I dunno, opening it.'

'In a sec. Wet nails.' I sat cross-legged on the bed, splayed out my fingers and shook my hands. 'I can't wait to see Dan. We've been messaging all day.'

'You had a better night than me. Bloody Mum. She was more pissed than all of us put together.'

'How is she?'

'Really weird. Didn't want me to come tonight. She's gone out, though. Want me to open the present?'

'No.' I checked the tackiness of my thumbnail with the pad of my index finger. Picked up the gift. 'It's light.'

'Maybe it's full of kisses,' Charlie grinned.

A white envelope fluttered to the floor as I eased the cardboard shoebox out of the paper.

'Shoes: very Cinderella,' said Charlie. 'Think Prince Charming sent them?'

I rested the box on top of my bed and opened the envelope, unfolding the sheet of lined A4 paper inside.

'Is it from Dan?'

My hand flew to my throat.

'Who's it from, Grace?'

I handed Charlie the note, too shocked to speak.

'What the fuck?'

I chewed my thumbnail as she studied the paper. Unlike the label, it wasn't handwritten. Letters had been cut from a newspaper or magazine, glued together to form the word BITCH. It looked like a ransom note. It looked like a joke – but I wasn't laughing.

'Open the box, Grace.'

'I can't.'

Charlie reached over and lifted the lid, then recoiled as the stench of dog shit filled the room. She slammed the lid down, but it wasn't square and the box tipped on its side. Excrement fell onto my bedspread. I gagged. Charlie wrenched the cover from the bed, bundled everything together and flew downstairs. I flung open my window and took huge gulps of cold November air. Damp circulated around my lungs, causing me to choke.

'Breathe, Grace.' I'd been so lost in my thoughts I hadn't heard Charlie come back in the room. She rubbed my back and I felt myself relax under her warm palm.

'Where did you put it?'

'In the bin. Do you want me to tell your grandparents?'

I sniffed. 'I don't know. Grandma will notice the bedspread's missing. She made it herself.'

'Who do you think sent it?'

'I can't think of anyone I've upset, except…'

'Siobhan.'

'Yes. But surely she wouldn't do this? I know she fancies Dan, but…'

'She's fancied him for years. She did catch you kissing. The paper looked like it was torn from a school exercise book.'

'What shall I do?'

'We'll ask her. She might be there tonight with Esmée.'

We fell silent. I shivered and slammed the window shut.

'C'mon. It'll be fine.' Charlie clasped my hand and tugged me through the heavy wooden door to the Hawley Arms. I kept my eyes fixed on the floor as we walked towards the bar, taking deep breaths of stale, musty air.

'Badger's Bottom?' Charlie raised an eyebrow as she studied the optics.

'You may laugh, but we have the best selection of real ales for miles.' Mike, the landlord, was polishing pint glasses. He held one up to the light and rubbed a smear with his cloth. 'Tony said you might be in.' Mike and Grandad had been friends for years. 'You're in for a treat tonight.'

'Squirrel's Tail to go with the Badger's Bottom?'

Mike scratched his beard and appraised Charlie, before turning back to me. He leaned forward. The smell of stale smoke clung to his clothes. 'Karaoke.'

'Really?'

'It's what they're all doing in London. Got to move with the times. Look,' he gestured behind him. 'We sell Scampi Fries now as well as crisps. New in today.'

'Really forward-thinking.'

I kicked Charlie on the ankle. 'That's great, we'll have two bags of Scampi Fries and two Strongbows for now, please, Mike.'

I stuffed the snacks into my bag and picked up my pint. The glass was slippery with condensation, and so full I had to take a sip before I could carry it to the table in front of the fire.

As we drank, the warm bloom of alcohol spread through my veins and my muscles began to unclench. Charlie nudged me in the ribs and my cider sloshed over my hand. I licked it off and followed her gaze to the bar. Dan was pulling change from his pocket, paying for drinks for himself and Ben. I tried to pretend I hadn't seen him as he walked towards us, but I could feel heat rising through my body.

'Room for two more?'

'You two?' My voice was small and high.

'No, I thought the two bearded guys sat at the bar.'

Dan squeezed between Charlie and me and the hairs on my arm prickled as our thighs touched. We'd been messaging all day but I felt uncomfortable with the shift in our relationship. I didn't know how to act, who to be.

I gulped my drink, draining the glass, and stood to get another.

'Let me.' Dan touched my arm.

I clunked the empties into the middle of the table to make way for the tray full of pints and Walkers crisps that Dan came back balancing in his hands. The sleeves of his white shirt were rolled up and his forearms were covered in fuzzy dark hair that I hadn't noticed before.

By the time nine o'clock came and the karaoke started, I was no longer stiff and uncomfortable. Siobhan hadn't turned up and I pushed my thigh against Dan's, laughing too loudly at his jokes. Charlie sprang up to sing 'Hit Me With Your Best Shot'. We whistled and cheered as she strutted up and down the makeshift stage. Afterwards, she sat on Ben's lap, their mouths locked together, her hands entwined in his hair. Dan turned towards me. 'Let's find somewhere quieter.'

He picked up our drinks and I followed him through to a tiny round table in the corner of the lounge.

'Tell me something I don't know,' he asked, once we were settled.

'You know everything; I've known you for years.'

'Not like this.' Dan sandwiched my hand between his; my fingers tingled.

'Tell me about your dad, Grace.'

I didn't think I wanted to, but once I started talking, words began to pour out of me in an uncontrollable flow. By the time Mike rang the bell for last orders, Dan knew almost everything about me. The fabric of our relationship had changed into something that I didn't yet understand. As he rubbed his thumb across the contours of my knuckles I felt a tug of longing I hadn't experienced before.

'Can I walk you home?'

'Yes, please.'

'How about I get some bottles to take out? If we leave now we'll catch the chippy before it shuts?'

'Great.' I was really hungry. I'd been too busy replaying the events of my party to eat dinner. Grandma had grumbled as I'd pushed roast potatoes around my plate.

I told Charlie we were leaving. She smiled through bee-stung lips. 'Don't do anything I wouldn't.'

'That leaves me with plenty of scope. I'll call you tomorrow.' I kissed her goodbye and as I walked towards the door I was aware of Dan's hand resting on the small of my back, his warmth penetrating my winter coat. There was a frost, and I linked my arm through his as we hurried down the high street, lit by street lamps and the blue glow of television sets from the row of net-curtained stone cottages. The smell of frying fish wafted up the road and I thought about what I was going to have. I always found it difficult to choose between mushy peas or curry sauce.

The chip shop was warm despite the glass door being propped open, and I pulled off my gloves as we joined the back of the queue.

'What do you fancy?' I asked.

'You,' said Dan, tilting my chin, brushing his lips over mine.

'Chips, Grace? Aren't you fat enough already?'

I spun around. Siobhan stood behind me, hands on hips, scarlet lips twisted into a sneer. Abby giggled, a couple of steps behind her.

'Siobhan, I...'

'Grace isn't fat, she can eat what she wants.' Dan looped his arm over my shoulders.

'Of course she can. I wouldn't eat chips from here, though. They taste like shit.' Siobhan flounced out of the door.

The vision of the box, the dark brown excrement splattered over the cardboard, was suddenly vivid in my mind. My stomach rolled as I gulped in the oily air.

'Next,' called the man behind the counter. I stumbled from the shop, doubled over and vomited four pints of cider onto the icy pavement.

'You shouldn't have crossed my sister,' said Abby, as she stomped down the road after Siobhan. 'Watch your back, Grace.'

CHAPTER TWENTY-THREE
Now

The figure stands as still as stone. It may be broad daylight but the sun, the people, don't make me feel any safer. I pull Anna into the nearest coffee shop. It doubles as a wine bar in the evenings. I slide into a tan leather booth, cradling our shopping, and while I wonder what to do, Anna joins the queue for drinks.

'That was quick.' Anna hands me a mug of hot chocolate.

'They do proper chocolate here, none of that powdered rubbish.'

'Thanks.'

'I hope I didn't offend you in the boutique, Grace. You did look beautiful in the green dress. I just preferred the black. I can't wait to wear mine; I've never owned anything so gorgeous.'

'It's OK. I'm on edge anyway, Anna. I think I'm being followed.' It's a relief to tell someone.

Anna's expression is inscrutable. 'By who? Why?'

'I don't know.'

I slurp froth from the top of the drink. The chocolate is bitter – not like Dad used to make – but I drink it all the same, not wanting to appear ungrateful. I tell Anna about the person in the black coat, the red car, and being chased outside the club.

'You should tell the police,' Anna says, firmly.

'Tell them what...' I stop talking and touch my lips. They're tingling. I rub them with my fingers; they feel numb. My nose streams, throat swells. I fight panic as I realise what's happening to me.

'Anna.' My tongue feels thick and I start to cough.

'Are you OK?'

'Allergy,' I gasp, through strangled breath.

'Oh my god! Shall I call an ambulance?'

I tip my handbag upside down. The contents spew over the table, clatter onto the floor. My EpiPen rolls to the edge and I catch it, wrench the cap off. I'm barely aware of the figure brushing past, the crunching as they stand on my compact.

'What can I do?'

Anna's voice sounds as though it's coming from inside a tunnel and I ignore it, clasp the pen in my fist and plunge it into my thigh. There is a click and then epinephrine courses through my body. My leg stings as I remove the needle.

Beads of sweat gather on my forehead. *Breathe in, breathe out.*

'Can I help?' Anna asks.

'Water.' I close my eyes.

'Here.' Moments later, Anna places a cool glass in my hand. 'Are you OK? That was really frightening. I've never seen anyone have an allergic reaction before.'

I nod and sip my water. I'm still coughing and feel cold and jittery, but the worst is over.

'Should we go to the hospital?' Anna's face is pale and worried.

'Strictly speaking, yes, but I think I'm OK now. I have a second pen in case I need another dose.'

'It's better to get checked out though, surely?'

'I don't want to miss tonight. Honestly, I'm fine. It's happened before. The doctors would just send me home in a few hours anyway, with anti-histamines. I've got some at home.'

'Is everything all right here?' a waitress asks.

'Yes.' I hold my empty glass towards her. It feels far heavier than it should.

'We're leaving now.' Anna stuffs my belongings back into my handbag, gathers our shopping and supports me by my elbow as I stand.

'I'm allergic to nuts,' I tell the waitress. 'Could my drink have been made with nut milk? It tasted funny.'

'The hot chocolate?' She frowns. 'It had hazelnut syrup in it.'

'Idiot.' Anna pushes me towards the door. 'I asked for hazelnut syrup in my coffee. We won't be coming back here again.'

'But…' the waitress begins, but Anna has steered me outside.

'Good God, Grace. They could have killed you. We could sue.'

'I'm fine. I just really want to go home and have a nap. Can you drive my car?' My head is fuzzy and it's an effort to keep my eyes open.

'Of course.' Anna peers at my lips. 'You look a bit like Donald Duck. What a shame you'll miss tonight.'

'I'll see how I feel after a sleep.'

'Of course. Fingers crossed you'll be OK.' Anna smiles, rubs my arm. 'Let's get you home to rest.'

My feet don't quite feel like mine as I weave through the multi-storey towards the car, and I hope I don't look drunk. In the parking bay, next to my Fiesta, is the red Corsa.

'Anna! That's the car!' I point.

'Hold these.' Anna thrusts her bags into my chest and runs towards the car, but before she can get there the engine revs and its tyres squeal as it speeds away.

A tapping wakes me.

'Grace?' Anna pushes open the bedroom door. 'I've brought you some vegetable soup. You missed lunch.'

I yawn, pick up my phone. It's five o'clock.

'Thanks.' I pat my mouth. 'How do I look?'

'Back to normal. That's lucky.' Anna rests the tray on the bedside table. 'Eat up. I made it especially for you. Then I'll help you get ready.'

By the time I've mopped up the last of the soup with thick granary bread, Dan's home. He explodes as I tell him about the mix-up at the cafe.

'How the fuck did they get that wrong?' He sits on the bed, clasps my hand.

'It happens, I suppose. They're only human.'

'And you were clear it was only to be syrup in one of the drinks?'

'I think so. Anna ordered.'

'Did she?' The muscle in his neck pulses. 'I'll talk to her.'

'Please don't. The atmosphere between you two is tense enough anyway.' I rub my thumb over his knuckles. 'I know it's not easy, sharing our space, but I'm enjoying having her here. Anyway, everything's fine: I'm fine, my dress is better than fine. I can't wait for you to see me.'

The shower is hot and I shave my legs before exfoliating my body. My skin is pink as I sit wrapped in a towel at my dressing table, painting my nails my favourite cherry red, while Anna dries and straightens my hair. We're talking about perfume. I tell her how obsessed Charlie used to be with Lexie's Impulse body spray and how I can't stomach the smell any more. But then, without warning, my stomach spasms and I lurch forward. Nail varnish streaks down my finger and spots of red drip from the brush to the carpet. I straighten, but my belly clenches again and there's a movement in my bowels. I spring up and sprint for the bathroom, making it to the toilet just in time.

'Grace?' Anna knocks on the door.

'I'm not well.' It's an odd combination, shivering and sweating, and I stretch towards the sink and wring out a flannel with cool water, place it on the back of my neck.

'I'll get Dan.'

I groan as another wave of pain engulfs me. I lean forward with my elbows on my thighs, careful to avoid the bruise from my EpiPen. This is probably my body's way of expelling the excess adrenaline.

'Babe?'

'I'm sick, Dan.'

'What can I do? We need to go soon.'

'I don't think I'm going anywhere. Sorry.'

I rest my cheek against the cool tiles and think of my beautiful dresses. I never did decide which one to wear.

It's thirty minutes before my stomach begins to unknot and I'm feeling brave enough to leave the sanctuary of the toilet. My legs are weak and I grip the banister tightly as I head towards the sound of raised voices.

Anna and Dan are in the kitchen. Anna is stunning in her red dress. Her hair is in a chignon with tendrils whispering against her face.

'What's going on?'

'Grace.' Anna blushes. 'I thought Dan might like some company tonight; gives me a chance to wear this dress.'

'I've said no.' Dan's voice is steely. 'I go with Grace or I go alone.'

'I don't mind. You've two tickets and Anna's ready. I'm going to have a bath and an early night.'

'Thanks, Grace.' Anna tucks her clutch under her arm. 'Ready, Dan?'

Dan opens his mouth and closes it again without speaking. He snatches his keys and wallet and strides to the front door.

I wave from the doorstep as they drive down the lane. *I'm alone.* I lock the door and loop the chain and, although I was feeling better, my stomach churns again and doesn't stop until they are home.

CHAPTER TWENTY-FOUR
Then

The door to my locker clattered open and I rummaged through the piles of paper, sweet wrappers and books I had accumulated over the term. I'd have to take in a plastic bag and clear it out before I left sixth form in a few months' time. The tangerine cover of my English book caught my eye and I yanked it towards me; I hated being late. An envelope fluttered from between the pages, gliding to the ground. I scooped it up, and felt hot as I recognised the spidery handwriting on the front.

The note was longer this time but had the same cut-out letters as before: WE DON'T WANT YOU HERE. I scrunched the letter in my fist and glanced around. The corridor was deserted. Lessons had already started. I slammed my locker door and twisted the key. My footsteps echoed down the corridor as my feet pounded the parquet flooring. I crashed open the classroom door and sank, breathless and sweaty, into my seat. *Pride and Prejudice* was one of my favourite books, but the words blurred into each other and I read the same paragraph three times. My fingertips drummed on the desk as I urged the hands on the clock to rotate a little faster. Finally, the bell rang, and I shoved my things into my messenger bag and skidded towards the door.

Esmée and Charlie were already in the common room, Charlie waving her baguette around as she talked, pieces of tomato and cucumber sliding to the floor.

'Look.' I thrust the note at Charlie.

'What's that?'

I showed Esmée, told her about the first note and the shoebox, explained how I hoped it had been a one-off. That she wouldn't need to get involved, feel she had to take sides.

'I can't believe Siobhan would do that. We've known each other since we were five.'

'She's been a bitch since Grace and Dan got together,' said Charlie.

'She's never liked me, anyway,' I said sadly

'Yes, but…'

Esmée fell silent, staring past my shoulder. I turned. Siobhan was framed in the doorway.

'I've brought crisps.' Siobhan shouldered past me and held two bags of Walkers towards Esmée and Charlie. 'Cheese and onion, or chicken?'

'I don't want anything from you.' Charlie stood.

Esmée bit her lip, stared at the floor, trying to keep out of it.

'What's your problem?' Siobhan straightened her spine but Charlie still towered above her.

'You. Sending crap like this to Grace.' Charlie pushed the note into Siobhan's chest, and Siobhan stumbled backwards.

Siobhan glared at me and opened up the letter. 'I didn't send this.'

'Suppose you didn't send a box of shit either, the night after Grace's party?'

Siobhan's eyes widened. 'No, and I can't believe you'd think I would. We've been friends for years. Long before she came.'

Charlie's face was twisted into a grimace. 'Well, we're not friends any more. Fuck off, Siobhan.'

Siobhan opened her mouth, closed it again. Esmée shuffled backwards.

'Esmée?'

Esmée's eyes filled with tears; she shrugged.

Siobhan turned to me, her hatred so thick it was almost as if I could reach out my hand and touch it as she spat out her words. 'Do you really want to make an enemy out of me, Grace?'

And of course I didn't, but I knew it was too late. The fragile friendship we'd formed was irreparably damaged and I was scared to think what she'd do next.

CHAPTER TWENTY-FIVE
Now

'Grace, can you help out in the baby room today please? Hannah's rung in sick,' says Lyn.

I scuttle into the blue room before she changes her mind. As much as I adore the three- and four-year-olds usually in my care, I'm excited to spend the day with the babies. Sarah is first through the door with Lily, Emily's sister. This is her first day.

'Grace, I'm so glad you're here – although Emily will miss you like crazy; she talks about you all the time. It doesn't seem two minutes since she was like this.' Sarah nods towards Lily.

'I know, it flashes by. Do you want me to take her?'

Tears spring to Sarah's eyes as she hands over the sleeping bundle, swaddled in a cream Winnie-the-Pooh and Piglet fleece blanket. She is heavier than she looks.

'She'll be OK,' I say.

'I know. It's just I wasn't planning on leaving her yet, but I've been offered good money to ghost-write a book and wouldn't be able to concentrate with her at home. It's not easy, being a single parent.'

'It'll be time to pick her up before you know it.'

We sidestep as a stream of mothers flows past. Sarah passes me Lily's changing bag and an inordinately long list of instructions, kisses Lily goodbye and leaves.

My steps are astronaut-like as I take slow strides towards the beanbags with my precious cargo and ease myself down millimetre by millimetre, careful not to wake her. My muscles tremble with the exertion, and I think that I really must get back to yoga. Dark eyelashes graze Lily's porcelain skin and I ease her blanket off, revealing ten perfectly formed fingers with paper-thin nails. 'What will you achieve with those hands?' I wonder aloud.

Lily softly snores as I cradle her to my chest and inhale her newness. I can't resist sniffing the top of her head, her perfect baby smell. She's gorgeous. Mum keeps dropping hints about becoming a grandmother every time we speak, but I'm not ready yet. Neither of us are.

Lily's body stiffens as she stretches out – almost doubling her length – and yawns, pink toothless mouth open wide. With eyes still screwed tight she begins to grizzle. Murmuring soothing platitudes, I carry her to the tiny kitchen to warm through her bottle. I give it a shake and tip milk onto my wrist to test the temperature. 'Perfect,' I tell her. Once we're sitting down, I rub the teat over her lower lip until her crying subsides. Her fingers grasp mine fiercely as she clamps her mouth to the teat, sucking noisily, draining the milk as if she hasn't been fed for days. When the bottle's empty I put it on the floor. 'That's it until lunchtime.' I gently rub her back until she lets out a loud burp. 'Lily! Your sister would be impressed with that one,' I tell her. A small dribble of sour milk trickles from her mouth and I dab it with her Peppa Pig bib.

We spend the next hour thumping bright plastic toys with flashing lights and too-loud noises, and reading stories she can't yet understand. I work hard to gain one of Lily's gummy smiles.

'Grace, can you pop Lily in a cot and go outside? It's warm enough for the children to have a run around before lunch,' Lyn says. 'Cara will be all right in here on her own for half an hour.'

I lay Lily on the yellow gingham changing mat. 'Let's change you before your nap.'

She squirms as I undo the poppers on her dungarees: her legs are rigid, knees locked. 'Come on Lily, I'm supposed to be outside now.' I pull funny faces until her muscles relax and I can remove her pungent nappy. 'Lily, I can't believe how stinky you are.' I clean her, put a fresh nappy on and blow raspberries on her podgy tummy. She giggles and I do it again before fastening her vest and dungarees. She rests her head on my shoulder, my hair entwined in her fist, as I carry her over to the cots. She smells of talcum powder and baby shampoo. I wind up the sun, moon and stars mobile. The melodic sound of 'Twinkle, Twinkle Little Star' fills the air and I watch her eyes begin to flutter. Piercing screams from outside jerk Lily awake, her screwed-up face magenta, as her tears begin to fall hot and fast.

There's a beat where I hesitate before running out into the courtyard. A crowd of crying children encircles the swing set. Pushing through to the front, I see Emily on the AstroTurf, her arm at an unnatural angle. My eyes blur. Emily morphs into my dad lying on the road so many years before. I begin to sway and drop to my knees.

'Grace?'

I look up at the nearest child, remind myself that I'm the adult in charge.

'It's OK. What happened?'

'She was standing on the swing and she fell off,' William informs me. 'Lyn's phoning an ambulance.'

Emily's forehead is clammy as I brush her fringe away from her screwed-up eyelids. Her face is deathly pale. 'Emily, it's OK, the ambulance is on its way. Keep still and everything will be fine.'

Emily stops screaming, whimpers instead, and that's worse somehow. I'm not sure she's even aware I'm here. The pain must be unimaginable and I feel utterly helpless.

Lyn appears with a blanket. We lock eyes across our young charge.

'Where were you?' she whispers.

'I had to change Lily's nappy.' I lower my gaze, not wanting Lyn to see the guilt in my eyes, as I try to comfort Emily with inadequate words, holding her good hand between mine, rubbing it. It is chilled despite the warmth in the air.

My forehead and underarms prickle as adrenaline courses through my body. My hands and feet are numb. 'Sarah's on her way,' Lyn says. 'Lucky they only live around the corner. I'm going outside to wait for her and the ambulance.'

Sirens blast and sweat flows freely down my body, but it doesn't wash away the regret I feel or the memories that have resurfaced. My chest tightens and I gasp for air. I haven't had a panic attack at work before and I fight to calm myself in front of the already stricken children.

A hand pats my shoulder. 'Who's the patient then?' A balding paramedic kneels down beside me, opening his box.

'This is Emily,' I tell him, as his face swims in and out of focus. 'She fell from the swing.'

'Hi Emily, my name's David. I'm here to look after you.'

'Emily, Emily!' The anguish in Sarah's cries is palpable as she rushes to her daughter's side. I can't look at her. In caring for one daughter I've neglected the other. I begin shepherding the other children inside. Some of them are still crying. We watch out of the window as Emily is lifted onto a stretcher and wheeled to the waiting ambulance.

'Will she be dead?' I'm asked. 'Will they make her come back alive again?'

'Emily's fine, she's just hurt her arm.' I try to project a confidence I don't feel. 'Let's all go to the story corner and choose a book.' I somehow make it across the room on wobbly legs and sink into the beanbags. *The Gruffalo* is chosen again. My voice is shaky but I throw myself into the story, imitating a fox, a snake, an owl. Pretending is something I'm good at.

Once the children have gone home, I straighten up the disorderly books and wipe down sticky surfaces until Lyn calls me into the office. 'Sarah's rung from the hospital. Emily has a broken arm. They're keeping her in overnight as she banged her head, but she's going to be fine. Greg's there too. Emily's probably thrilled to have both her parents back in the same room.'

'Thank goodness.' I sit down, legs unwilling to support me any longer.

'We need to fill out a report form stating what happened. Sarah needs to sign it and then we can send copies to Ofsted and the local child protection agency.'

I can hardly bear to look her in the eye. 'And then what?'

'It will be investigated. If Ofsted find us at fault, they'll publish the incident on their website along with any action they had to take, or action we need to take to meet the legal requirements for registration.'

'I'm so sorry, Lyn. I should have gone straight out to supervise instead of changing Lily.'

'It was an accident, Grace. It could still have happened if you were outside. I know how good you are with the children.'

'Ofsted won't.'

'Emily's going to be all right, that's the main thing. Hopefully no fault will be found. We've never had an incident at Little Acorns before, although I can imagine parents will pull their children out in droves if Ofsted publicly blame us.'

'I'm so sorry.' The words are stuck on a loop.

Lyn checks her watch. 'Why don't you go home? We need to speak to the children and the other staff before we can do the report. We've fourteen days to file it, anyway.'

'You go, Lyn. You look exhausted. I'll finish off tidying and lock up.' I'm often the last to leave.

'No. I'll do it.' Lyn's tone is firm.

I want to ask if she still trusts me but I'm too scared to hear the answer. I collect my bag and coat and slip out the front door. The tracks of the ambulance tyres are still entrenched on the small lawn outside, the turf torn apart. In time the grass will heal, there will be no outward signs of the trauma suffered today. Can the same be said of Emily? I wonder. My scars are no longer visible but I carry them all the same.

I drive home on autopilot, startled to find myself outside the cottage with no conscious recollection of my journey. It takes three attempts to stop my hand shaking enough to insert my key into the lock. I thunk my bag to the floor, kick my shoes off on the mat, pad into the kitchen and pour a large glass of Chardonnay. I keep one hand on the bottle as I stand by the sink, sipping my wine and watching the birds on the feeder. I envy them. Free to fly away and start again somewhere new. However can I face Lyn again? I've let Emily down. Let myself down.

I drain my glass and pour another. My mobile rings again and again with an unknown number. I ignore it. I'm sick of answering to find there's no one there. The front door slams, and as Dan walks into the lounge, I allow my tears to torrent.

'Grace. What's wrong?'

I can't find the words. He looks stricken as he guides me into the lounge, settles me on the sofa and kneels before me.

'Grace?' Colour has drained from his face.

'It's work.'

He puffs out air. 'Is that all?'

'All?' I wipe my face with my sleeve.

'I didn't mean that. I'm just glad it isn't anything more serious, that your grandparents are OK. What's happened?'

A shadow falls as Anna stands over me. I hadn't heard her
come in. 'Grace.' She sits next to me and places an arm around
my shoulders. My muscles are so tense they feel tender and I
shrug her away.

I recount my horrific day.

'It's not your fault.' Dan squeezes my knee.

'Well, it kind of is,' says Anna. 'I know you'd never hurt anyone
on purpose, but if you should have been outside supervising…'

'Anna.' Dan's voice is sharp. 'Accidents happen. Sometimes no
one is accountable.'

'She's right. I should have been outside.' I wipe my eyes.

'Even if you'd been outside, Emily would still have climbed,
probably still have fallen.'

'Maybe.'

'Almost definitely.'

'I don't know how I can face everyone tomorrow.'

'With your head held high. Honestly, Grace, you've nothing
to be ashamed of.'

'Ofsted will be the judge of that.' I pick pieces of the wet
tissue I'm holding and watch them flutter to the floor. Confetti
when there's nothing to celebrate.

'Will they shut you down?' Anna asks.

'Unless we're found at fault it won't be made public, thankfully. I couldn't live with myself if I affected Lyn's business.'

'But the parents will be informed?'

'The children have probably told them by now that an ambulance came, so if they ask we'll say there was an accident, but

otherwise, I'm not sure. It's up to Lyn how she handles it. I hope they don't find out. They trust me.'

'They still will,' says Dan. 'You're great with the kids. They adore you.'

'Thanks.' I lean forward; our foreheads touch. 'I love you, Dan.'

'I love you, too. Why don't you go and have a bath. I'll sort out dinner?'

'You?'

'Yes, me. I'm quite capable you know, I've done it before. Cod and chips for three?'

The alarm trills a brand new day, jolting me from a disturbed sleep. I peep out beneath heavy lids. My mouth is dry and sour; I regret last night's greasy fish and chip supper and wine. I stagger into the bathroom and grab my toothbrush, retching as I brush my back teeth. I can barely face myself in the mirror, my eyes streaked red, my face morbidly pale. I momentarily consider calling in sick, but instead shower, dress and kiss Dan goodbye. Anna's door is closed and I'm glad she's not up yet. I was hurt by her reaction last night, even if she was voicing what I was thinking, even if I really am to blame.

Downstairs, I pull open the curtains in the lounge, wincing as light streams through the window. Mittens is curled asleep on the sofa amongst the fish and chip wrappers. Two empty bottles of wine stand on the floor. Did I drink them both? Dan's empty lager bottles lie on their sides. Our glass recycling tub will be overflowing again. I hope the refuse collectors don't judge us the way I sometimes judge myself.

The drive to work is over too quickly. I am pensive as I arrive, half expecting to see a row of angry parents lined up outside with placards – 'Justice for Emily' – but of course, it's just another day. The car park is empty, save for Lyn's car. I let myself in the front door, relieved that my key still works. I haven't been banished.

'Come here.' Lyn opens her arms. 'You look terrible. Please don't worry. It was an accident. Today's a new day.' Her smile splinters my fears; they fall to the ground. I step over them, atoned, and am enfolded in a bear hug.

The morning is much like any other, apart from Emily's absence. The children don't mention the accident or the ambulance. It's an ordinary day. At lunchtime, Lyn and I read through the report as we share Lyn's egg sandwiches. I'd felt too rough this morning to even think about preparing food.

'I think it's pretty straightforward. Our staff-to-children ratio is good, and all our previous reports are excellent. The equipment isn't faulty. It's unfortunate, but I don't think they'll take it further.'

'I hope not.'

'Emily's fine, that's the main thing. And if they don't take it further and it's not made public, it won't affect our reputation at all. It's business as usual. Now go and make me some coffee.'

I make Lyn a coffee and wash two paracetamol tablets down with a large glass of water. Much of the afternoon session is spent making cardboard hearts that we decorate with glitter, tissue paper and paint. I peg them on the line to dry. My arms ache. I've been extra-vigilant all day and am utterly exhausted. It's a relief to lock the doors and tidy up.

'I'm off now.' I stick my head around the office door. Lyn's face is white and pinched.

'Is everything OK?'

'You'd better sit down.' Lyn nods at the chair, not quite meeting my gaze.

I sit down. My watch strap is fraying. My nervous fingers pick at the pieces of cotton, pulling them off. I watch them drift to the floor.

'You need to see this.' Lyn hands me her iPad, her twitter app is open.

Negligent nursery worker breaks girls arm. @littleacorns #getgraceout

'Is this…'

'Scroll down. There's more.'

Don't send your children here it's not safe. #littleacorns #getgraceout

Why haven't you fired Grace? #littleacorns #getgraceout

Grace belongs in jail. #littleacorns #getgraceout

There is tweet after tweet, all baying for blood. My blood. The local newspaper has retweeted and there have been some really nasty comments by people I've never even heard of. I feel sick. The iPad swims in and out of focus.

'Who's done this?'

'I don't know. They're from new accounts. There's no personal information or photos.'

'Could they be from the same person?'

'I don't know.' Lyn beats a rhythm on the side of the desk with her pen. 'I wonder if it's Greg.'

'Maybe. He said he'd make me sorry. He's got a temper, we know that, and he is Emily's dad. What should we do?'

'We can't keep it quiet. There have been phone calls this afternoon. Word has spread amongst the parents. They're concerned.'

I wait for her to continue.

Lyn leans back on her chair and sighs. 'The local press rang. They're going to run a story tomorrow. They wanted a comment.'

'What did you say?' My voice is barely audible, even to my ears.

'I said no one had been found at fault, the investigation is ongoing but until Ofsted reach a conclusion, you're suspended.'

My eyes flood with tears.

'I'm so sorry, Grace, but I can't risk parents pulling their children out. I have to act in the best interests of the nursery.'

'I know. I'm sorry.' That word again, but I can't think of anything else to say.

'As soon as Ofsted make a decision we'll get back to normal. This will blow over.'

I rummage in my bag and pull out my key. 'Here.' I offer it to Lyn.

'You hang onto it. You'll need it when you come back. You will be back, Grace.'

I heave my body out of the chair. It feels heavy. Weighed down with guilt. I walk through the playroom, looking at the row of paper hearts, and feel like mine is breaking.

CHAPTER TWENTY-SIX
Then

Nestled amongst the Christmas cards that plopped onto the mat that morning had been another letter. I'd stuffed it into my schoolbag to show Esmée and Charlie at lunchtime. I was the first into the hall. Why did it always smell like boiled cabbage? We never had vegetables. Despite all the talk of healthy lunches, hot dog and chips were one of the only recognisable things served by grumpy women in pink overalls and hairnets, who looked as though they'd rather be anywhere but here. I pulled a poor excuse for a salad out of the chiller. Iceberg, tomatoes and cucumber with a smidgen of tuna sprinkled on top. It wouldn't fill me up but I wanted to lose half a stone before Christmas, when I knew I'd scoff my body weight in Quality Street and mince pies.

As I queued to pay for my food, I couldn't resist adding a cup of hot chocolate. I deserved it for all the calories I'd saved with the salad. By the time I got to our usual table, Esmée and Charlie were already there.

'Have you heard about Siobhan?' Charlie jigged up and down in her seat.

'No.'

'She's been expelled.'

'What? Why?' Siobhan was the cleverest of all of us.

'Stealing one of the laptops.'

'That's ridiculous. She wouldn't. She has a laptop.'

'She was caught on CCTV. There was a police car here earlier.'

'What about uni?'

'She won't be able to go. She can't sit her A Levels.'

'God.' I was stunned.

'I can't believe it.' Esmée chewed her lip. 'I feel like I never really knew her.'

'We didn't,' said Charlie. 'Look at what she did to Grace.'

'Still doing. I got another letter today.'

'Bitch,' said Charlie.

'She is,' I agreed, but as I looked over at Abby, sobbing in the corner, flanked by concerned 'friends' digging for information about her wayward big sister, I couldn't help feeling sorry for her.

It was a relief not to see Siobhan every day. Rumours were rife. She was part of an organised crime ring. Her dad was one of the Mafia. Stephen Brown in my class said she'd offered to sell him a laptop for £100. He couldn't afford a new one but had no idea she'd steal one. That, I believed. Siobhan didn't have a job like the rest of us. I worked in the coffee shop on Saturdays, Charlie baby-sat and Esmée helped her mum deliver Avon books. Siobhan's parents didn't want her distracted from her studies. What did she need money for so badly?

Stationery, most likely. Letters were arriving almost daily and I was snappy and tired. Charlie wanted to start the search for her dad but I was struggling to keep up with my coursework, my concentration marred. We'd tried dropping hints to Lexie, pretending we'd seen a Jeremy Kyle show where a girl demanded her mum tell her who her biological father was, and concocting a story about a girl at school who had just traced her dad, but Lexie lit another fag, poured another drink and ignored us.

*

We cut across the park on Friday on the way home from school. A lone figure sat on a swing, blonde corkscrew curls tumbling out of her bright yellow bobble hat. Siobhan.

'Let's go the other way.' I tugged Charlie's arm.

'I'm not leaving because of her.' Charlie crunched across the frosty grass, breath billowing out in front of her. 'Oi. Thief.'

I tensed, waiting for Siobhan to erupt, but when she turned around I inhaled sharply and the icy air made me cough. Siobhan's eyes were streaked with blood vessels, her face pale and spotty.

'I didn't steal anything.'

Charlie stared hard at Siobhan. 'I believe you.'

'Thanks.' Siobhan reached out a hand and Charlie swatted it away.

'I believe you like I believe you're not sending letters to Grace.'

'I'm...'

'Save it. You were seen on CCTV. Needed the money for stamps did you? You're pathetic. Dan loves Grace. He wouldn't look at a skank like you.'

Siobhan sniffed and wiped her nose with the back of her glove. 'Please. We were friends once.'

'More fool us.' Charlie grabbed my wrist. 'C'mon, Grace. Let's go and meet the others.'

'Let me come.' Siobhan clasped her fingers together as if she were praying. 'My parents hate me. Even Abby won't talk to me.'

'Drop dead, Siobhan.' Charlie's voice was hard, but as we walked away I could see the tears in her eyes.

CHAPTER TWENTY-SEVEN
Now

I can't believe I have to go home and tell Dan that I have more than likely lost my job. My Fiesta is in the 'Staff Parking Only' space and I scuttle to the driver's door, head down, key in hand. I throw my bag onto the passenger seat, swing my legs into the car and lock the doors. I feel uneasy; there's someone out there who clearly hates me. Is it Greg? Is he the person who's following me?

It's not the first time I've had an enemy. My mind flashes back to the time I was eighteen. I think how that ended and I want to cry. I call Mum. Perhaps when I've said the words out loud, things won't seem quite so bad, and it will be easier to say them again, to Dan. The phone rings and rings and I'm waiting for the voicemail to kick in when Mum answers.

'Hi, Grace.' Her breath rasps down the crackly line. 'You OK?'

'Are you? You sound like you've been running?'

'Oliver's daughter is here with her kids. We're playing hide-and-seek. Did you want me?'

Jealousy rips through me. She never played with me growing up, yet now she's playing with Oliver's grandchildren. Although I understand why, it hurts all the same.

'Nothing important.' I swallow hard to keep my voice from cracking. 'Get back to the kids. I'll call you next week.'

I grit my teeth and start the engine, jumping as noise floods the car. I'd turned the volume up high this morning as the local radio station played a plethora of 80s hits. ELO's 'Mr. Blue

Sky' fills the car and I jab the stereo off and rest my forehead on the steering wheel. I can almost hear Dad's warbling voice, *It's a beautiful new day. Hey, hey*. If only he were here to talk to. There's a stillness fractured only by the sound of my ragged breath, and I wish I could remain cocooned in my car forever.

Lyn taps on my window and I raise my head, smile and nod – I'm OK – and reverse out of my spot. If there are any other cars on the road, I'm not aware of them as I drive. The wheels spin round and round, propelling me forward, and all too soon I am home.

The sound of raised voices hits me before I'm properly through the front door. I clatter my keys into the bits and bobs bowl on the telephone table and call out, 'Hello!' in a loud voice.

The TV is on in the lounge; engines roar as Formula One cars race around the screen.

Dan is perched on the edge of the sofa, head bowed, PlayStation controller in hand. Anna towers over him, hands balled at her sides.

'What's going on?'

'Dan's a sore loser. He doesn't like playing games do you, Dan?'

'Not yours, no.' His eyes are dark. His voice low.

'That's because...'

'Shut up, the pair of you. This is the last thing I need today.' I aim the remote, mute the set. 'I've been suspended.' I sit next to Dan, rest my head on his shoulder. Mittens jumps onto my lap and I scratch her neck, glad of the distraction.

'What? Why?'

I recount my day. 'But Lyn's being lovely. She told me to keep my key as I'll be going back to work. It's just a matter of when. But I don't know, it depends what Ofsted think.'

'That's terrible,' says Anna. 'Someone's really got it in for you. Any idea who?'

'Someone without their own fucking life,' says Dan.

'Lyn thinks it's Greg, Emily's dad. I had a confrontation with him a few weeks ago.'

'But you don't?'

'I don't know. I've been thinking I'm being followed for a while.'

Dan looks doubtful. 'Are you sure? You know how... suspicious you can be.'

'It's true. I've seen them,' says Anna. 'I chased their car.'

'Why the hell didn't you tell me?' Dan looks furious

'I didn't want to worry you.'

'If I catch anyone following you they'll have me to deal with.'

'Quite the knight in shining armour, aren't you?' says Anna.

'Anna?'

'Yes, Dan?'

'Shut the fuck up.'

'Will you two give it a *rest*!' The silence is thick and uncomfortable, more oppressive than the shouting. 'I want a bath and a peaceful evening.'

'I won't be here. Football practice.'

'I'm going out, too.' Anna looks mutinous.

'Anywhere nice?' I ask her.

'A date, actually.'

Dan stands up, the muscles in his neck twitching. 'Shame it's not an interview. I'll see you later.' He kisses the top of my head. I try to catch his hand, but I grasp air as he disappears out of the door.

'Sorry you came home to that, Grace. I'm quite competitive.'

'So is Dan.' I inhale deeply. 'And I think he's finding it difficult, sharing our space. I love having you here, we both do, but it would be nice to have some idea of your plans.'

'Of course. Sorry. I know I can't stay here indefinitely. I'll sort something out soon. I promise. It's been so lovely getting to know you though, learning about Charlie. I just wish I could meet Lexie. Hear some baby tales and see some photos. Anyway, I'll run you a bath. I've got some lovely oil that will relax you.'

'Thanks, Anna.'

She tramps upstairs and the tension in the room dissipates. I close my eyes and stroke Mittens, lulled by her soft purring. 'What would I do without you? You don't care what people say, do you?' She pats my hand with her soft paw.

'Bath's ready,' calls Anna.

My phone beeps. It's Dan. *She has to go.*

I can't wait to wash away the day.

Anna's unearthed a bag of tea lights and the bathroom flickers and glows. A fluffy white towel hangs over the warmer; my robe is on the back of the door. A chilled glass of white wine stands on the windowsill, next to my iPod and headphones.

'Here,' Anna hands me *Jane Eyre*. 'Anything else you need?'

'I think you've thought of everything. This is fabulous, I feel like I'm in a rom-com.'

'We all need looking after every now and then.'

'Thank you.'

'You're welcome. Do you want me to get you any food before I go?'

'No, thanks. There's a pizza in the freezer if I get hungry. Who's your date with?'

'Just a guy I met online; we're going for a bite at the Beefeater.'

'Enjoy it. Don't do anything I wouldn't do.'

'Now, where would be the fun in that?' She smiles, then leaves me alone with my bath and my thoughts, rough and jagged. The water acts like a sander, smoothing away the edges until I'm able to close my eyes and relax.

I lie in the bath until the water cools and my fingers prune. Emotionally drained, I skip dinner and go straight to bed, falling into a dreamless sleep. I don't hear Anna or Dan come home.

Dan drops his towel to the floor and yanks a shirt from a hanger. I can't remember the last time I saw him naked. I usually leave for work before him, and often at the weekends he dresses in the bathroom, leaving early for football practice. He senses me watching, turns.

'I talked to Anna yesterday,' I whisper, although it is unlikely she can hear. 'She'll be gone soon. We can…'

'We can.' Dan pads over to the bed. His palms rest on my shoulder, weighted, pushing, and I lie back against the pillow. He kisses my neck, his hand snaking under my top.

'What about Anna?'

'What about us? It's been too long.'

He tugs down my pyjama bottoms and my nails claw his back as I bite my cheek to stop myself from crying out. I swallow blood, dark and salty. It's over in minutes but I'm giddy with relief that he still wants me. That I still want him.

Dan sits up, brushes the hair from my eyes. 'I've missed that.'

'Me too. I love you.'

'I love you, too.' Dan rubs my lips with his thumb. 'We could do it again later?'

'We could.'

'We should take a break. Have a long weekend with your mum. I'm owed some hours at work. Fish and chips on the seafront?'

'What about all the stuff with the pre-school?'

'There's nothing we can do right now. At least the signal at your mum's is so rubbish you won't be checking Twitter every five minutes.'

'I'll ring her later and arrange it.'

We kiss goodbye – a proper lingering kiss, none of the short, sharp pecks we've grown used to – and it's ridiculous to think that with everything going on at work I could be happy, but I do feel lighter. Part of a team again. I know whatever happens, Dan and I will deal with it together.

The day spans before me and I think I'll spring-clean. Bessie Smith croons 'Downhearted Blues' and I hum along as I hoist up the sofa to hoover beneath it. There is enough fur there to make a new cat. My heart springs into my mouth as someone taps my shoulder.

I spin around. Anna switches the vacuum off at the wall and I pull out my earbuds. There are two policemen behind her.

The room tilts and shifts and I feel as though I've gone back in time. 'Is Dan OK?'

'Grace Matthews? I'm PC Dunne and this is PC White.' A badge is flashed at me. I nod wordlessly, hands on cheeks.

'Do you mind telling us where you were last night?'

'Last night?' My voice breaks. I run my tongue over dry lips and start again. 'Last night? I was here.'

'Was anyone with you?'

'No. Why?'

'I believe you work at Little Acorns?'

I nod.

'Last night, someone vandalised the place.'

'What? Who?'

'That's what we're trying to find out. There was no sign of a break-in; whoever did it probably had a key. Do you have a key, Miss Matthews?'

'Yes.' My voice is barely a squeak.

'Do you mind checking if it's still in your possession?'

I'm followed into the hallway. I bunch my keys, picking out the one to Little Acorns.

'Here.'

'We'd like you to come down to the station and make a statement, please. Can you get your shoes?'

Anna fetches my trainers. It takes two attempts to slip my feet inside, but my hands are shaking so much I can't knot the laces.

'Let me.' Anna kneels and ties them. 'Do you want me to call anyone?'

I stare blankly. 'I don't know.'

'Miss Matthews?' PC White opens the front door. I walk outside to the squad car, past the rows of daffodils and bluebells poking through the verge.

Mrs Jones is standing on her step. 'Is everything all right, Grace?'

I don't answer.

I climb into the back seat, hardly believing I'm in a police car again. Memories roll by, along with the country views I usually find so soothing. Today they're cold and hostile. I close my eyes and the Twitter feed flashes through my mind. *Grace belongs in jail.*

CHAPTER TWENTY-EIGHT
Then

The snow was falling lightly and I brushed it off my windscreen with my gloved hand. My grandparents had bought me a second-hand Fiesta for Christmas and I loved it. It was grey – the colour of fungi, Dan said, and joked that there 'wasn't mush-room in it'.

Stuffed under the windscreen wiper was a letter. My skin prickled and I checked to see if I was being watched before I crumpled the envelope into my back pocket. There had been no more 'gifts' since the shoebox, but letters continued to arrive, each more threatening than the last. I tried not to let it get to me but it was hard. I didn't know why Siobhan was still doing it, but at least I didn't have to see her at school every day.

The lounge curtains twitched and I saw Grandma's lined face peering out. I forced my mouth into a smile and waved. I'd kept the letters hidden from her; she worried enough now I was driving, and I didn't want Mum finding out either. It had been lovely, her spending Christmas with us, but our relationship was still new. Fragile. I didn't want anything to put a strain on it. I was scared of losing her again, so I smiled brightly at her jokes, keeping our conversations light.

The muscles in my upper back felt like stone as I chugged through the village, gripping the steering wheel tightly. Dan found it amusing that I adhered to the speed limit at all times, but he'd been driving a year longer than me. *The tortoise always got there in the end*, Grandma said. I indicated as I turned into Charlie's street, despite the roads being deserted.

The engine thrummed as I sat in the car checking my mirrors, making sure I hadn't been followed, before I stepped out and hurried down the path. I was constantly edgy, jumping at the smallest of things: the tree in the front garden casting shadows in my bedroom, dogs barking. I tried to tell myself that the letters couldn't hurt me, but anxiety had taken up permanent residency in my stomach, leaving little space for food. At least I was losing weight.

Ice crystals scattered onto the wooden floor as I stamped my booted feet. 'It's me,' I called as I headed towards the kitchen. Lexie couldn't afford to heat the whole house 'all the bleedin' time', but a fan heater blasted out warm air in the kitchen, clicking on and off as it tried to regulate the temperature.

'I've got another one.' I dropped the envelope on the table, then slumped into a wooden chair that was just as uncomfortable as it looked.

'What's it say?' Charlie picked it up. 'You haven't opened it yet?' She sliced open the envelope, pulled A4 lined paper out and smoothed it open.

LEAVE OR YOU'LL REGRET IT. The letters were uneven, cut from a magazine just like all the others.

'Fucking Siobhan.' Charlie tossed it down onto the table.

'She says it's not her.'

'She would, wouldn't she? Who else can it be?'

'For you.' Lexie slopped a chipped mug of milky tea on the table. I pressed my spine back against the chair, turned my head away from her stale alcohol breath. She slid a packet of cookies towards me with a hand that was shaking so violently I was surprised the biscuits weren't crumbs.

'It must be bleedin' awful. Don't know how you're concentrating on your exams.'

'I'm not.' I yawned.

Lexie picked up the letter. 'Why don't you?'

'Why don't I what?'

'Leave? I don't mean for good, but you could go and stay with your mum in Devon, give that Siobhan one a chance to cool off?'

'No.' I couldn't even contemplate being so far from Dan. 'It's only words. Sticks and stones and all that.'

'Doesn't want to leave Dan either. I've barely seen her the past few weeks,' said Charlie, and she was right. 'You're turning into one of those girls who dumps her friends when she gets a bloke.'

'I'm not. It's just…'

'You look bleedin' knackered, Grace.'

'I am, but this is an important year. I've got exams. I can cope with a few letters.'

'She's promised to help me with something important, too.' Charlie's voice softened. 'In fact, Mum, I need…'

'Bugger!' Lexie said, as her mug clattered to the floor. She grabbed a grey cloth that could once have been white and dropped to her knees, soaking up coffee. She stood up to wring out the cloth. Mud-coloured liquid splattered over the ketchup-encrusted plates piled in the sink.

'We'd better go.' Charlie scraped her chair back. 'We have an appointment.'

'We do?' I asked.

'We do. Wanna leave your car here? Town will be rammed with all the sales on and you're crap at parking.'

'Thanks for that. Yes. Let's get the bus.'

I huddled on a bench on the high street, stamping my feet to keep warm. Charlie had leaped off the bus last minute – she'd forgotten her purse. I hoped she'd had time to go home and find it and run back to the stop in time to catch the bus that was trundling towards me. It slotted into its bay, and I was relieved to spot Charlie waving out of the window. There was an almost manic atmosphere in town as crowds hurried from shop to shop, hunting for the elusive New Year's Eve outfit. The it-doesn't-make-me-look-like-I've-eaten-a-million-mince-pies dress. Clothes marked at fifty per cent off were tugged from hangers, bundled towards the till.

Charlie weaved through the throng. I kept my eyes on her green hat and tried to keep up. Despite questioning her, I had no idea where we were going.

She stopped in front of a peacock blue doorway. A neon pink sign flashed: Tattoo Parlour.

'You're kidding, right?'

'I thought we could have matching tattoos.'

'Yes. And then we can grow beards,' I said.

'Nothing masculine. Look, I drew this.' Charlie pulled a piece of paper out of her pocket and unfolded it. It was a butterfly. 'We can have them somewhere discreet. On our shoulders?'

'You're serious?' I was absolutely never getting a tattoo, I was sure of that.

'I am. New Year, new start.'

'What will your mum think? Ben?'

'I've dumped Ben.'

'What! Why?' It was selfish, but I was disappointed we wouldn't be able to double-date any more.

'Got my eye on somebody new.'

'Who? Ben's lovely…'

'But boring.' Charlie flashed a smile and pushed open the door. The reception area was white and clinical. Christmas songs blared from a Roberts radio.

'Charlie Fisher?' I couldn't help but stare at the woman behind the desk. Tattoos crawled like vines up her bare arms, snaking around her neck.

'That's me.'

'Hi. I'm Nancy. An appointment for two small tattoos, isn't
it?'

'You can make it one.' I sat on the bench, crossed my arms.

'Charlie said she thought you'd back out.'

'Back out?' I said. 'That would imply I was ever in.'

'Spoilsport.' Charlie showed her drawing to Nancy.

'That's cute. Did you design it yourself?'

'Yeah. I wanted something that represented freedom.'

'Come through,' Nancy said. 'You can watch if you want,' she
added, to me.

'Are you doing it?' I was surprised. I'd anticipated a man:
black T-shirt and too many piercings.

'Yeah. Expecting someone else?'

I shook my head, embarrassed.

The back room was not the dingy, dirty place I'd expected.
Posters of fifties girls hung from stainless steel frames on stark
white walls. Nancy snapped on gloves as Charlie lay, face down,
on a black leather bench. Charlie twitched as the needle touched
her skin, inhaled sharply.

'Does it hurt?' I was fascinated.

'Yeah. Take my mind off it. What did you do last night?'

'Saw Dan.'

'I don't need to be Einstein to figure that out.'

'We took his telescope to the forest. It was quite a clear night.'

'You must have been freezing.'

'We lit a fire, toasted marshmallows. Kept each other warm…'

'I bet you did! You seem really happy?'

'We are. I thought it would be strange making that transition from friends, but it isn't. I know we're only young but I think he's the one, Charlie.'

'God. You'll be getting his name tattooed on you in a minute.'

Sixty minutes later, Nancy was finished. She leaned back in her chair and tugged off her gloves, dropping them into a waste bin as she ran through the aftercare instructions. Charlie sipped water, the colour gradually returning to her cheeks.

'How about you?' Nancy looked at me. 'Are you tempted?'

'I don't think it's really me. It's beautiful, though.'

'You should spread your wings and fly, Grace,' said Charlie.

'Maybe one day,' said Nancy.

'Maybe.' But I doubted it. I liked having both feet firmly on the ground.

We hopped off the bus, carrier bags bumping our shins. I'd spent the Christmas money Mum had given me in Topshop, on an off-the-shoulder purple dress to wear to the New Year's Eve party at the pub the following night. I couldn't wait for Dan to see me. Charlie had bought a postbox-red Lycra dress and a lipstick to match.

'Do you want to come back to mine?' I asked.

'Yeah. I'll grab my stuff and tell Mum.'

'I'll wait in the car.'

I fished my keys from my bag, walked around to the driver's door and froze. The word 'BITCH' was carved in large, uneven letters onto the side of my car.

CHAPTER TWENTY-NINE
Now

'Do I need a solicitor?'

I hope Anna has rung Dan and told him where I am. I'm not sure if I get a phone call or if that's just in the films. The glaring brightness of the artificial lights hurts my head and the smell of cleaning products is nauseating. The air in this windowless room is stagnant and far too warm for a winter's day. Never in my wildest dreams did I think I'd ever see the inside of an interrogation room again. I wait for someone to speak. There's the shuffling of paper before heads are raised, eye contact made.

'Miss Matthews, you're not actually under arrest. At this stage, you're just helping us with our enquiries.'

At this stage.

I reach for the plastic cup in front of me. There's a bang outside, the sound of shouting and I blanch. Water sloshes over the table.

'I'm sorry.' The lukewarm liquid drips onto the grey linoleum.

'Let's start from the beginning. Answer each question honestly, and if there's anything you don't understand, you can ask us to repeat it. Are you clear?'

'Yes.' I need to tell the truth. I've nothing to hide. I've sat in a room like this before and lied to the police. Lived in fear of being found out. I can't do it again.

'How long have you worked at Little Acorns?'

'Seven years.'

'And could you describe the events of the past few days?'

I tell them about Emily, how I hadn't gone straight outside when Lyn asked me to, how she fell. I didn't tell them how I still hear her scream when I close my eyes, how I still see her body, twisted and pale, lying on the ground.

'And I believe there's been some backlash against you?'

'Yes.'

'And have you any idea who started that?'

'There was an incident a few weeks ago. With Emily's father, actually.' I tell them what happened.

'And does anyone else you know of have a grudge against you?'

'No.' I want to tell them I'm being followed, but am scared they'll think I'm making it up.

'Does anyone else you know have a reason to break into the nursery?'

'No.'

'And you were home alone yesterday evening?'

'Yes.'

We run through my story again and again, and then I'm left alone. I pull a tissue out of my sleeve, wipe sweat from my underarms and then wonder whether I'm being watched, whether hidden windows and two-way mirrors are just for TV. I place my palms flat on the table and close my eyes. Footsteps echo in the corridor outside and the door clicks open.

'Thank you, Miss Matthews. You're free to go, for the moment.'

For the moment.

Mrs Jones's net curtains twitch as I step out of the police car outside the cottage. I hurry up the path, berating myself for not taking my phone. The door's locked. I ring the bell, peer through the letter box. Anna doesn't answer. My fists throb as I bang my frustration out on the solid wood, before sinking onto the cold stone step, shivering in my thin hoodie. What should I do? I can't face Mrs Jones and the scores of questions she'll have if she comes outside. It seems ludicrous to hide, but I do, jogging down the side of the house and slipping through the back gate. The greenhouse is freezing and as I sit cross-legged on the floor, dampness seeps through my tracksuit. It isn't long before my bottom's numb.

Dan's the first home. I hear the chugging of the Land Rover and run around to the front of the cottage.

'Grace, been for a run?'

I hurl myself into his arms.

'Grace? You're shivering. Let's get you inside.'

He leads me to the sofa. Clumps of compost fall from my trainers onto the newly hoovered carpet. I don't pick them up.

'Grace, I'm so sorry.' Anna sweeps into the cottage, still in coat and boots.

'I couldn't get back in.' I'm tearful now.

'I was out looking for Mittens.'

'What?' My eyes dart around the lounge, searching for the ever-present grey ball of fluff.

'When you'd gone, Mrs Jones came around and started asking questions. I didn't want to let her in, so I stood with the door open. Mittens ran past me. I couldn't catch her.'

'Mittens never goes outside.'

'I know. She must have seen a rabbit or something.'

'What have you done, you fucking bitch?' Dan's voice is low, quiet. He steps forward.

Anna moves towards the door. 'Accidents happen. Sometimes no one is accountable.' Her footsteps pound down the hall; the front door slams.

'Dan?'

Dan rests his chin on the top of my head. 'I'm sorry, sorry, sorry,' he whispers into my hair.

I push him away. 'What's going on? Where's Mittens?'

He takes my hand. His palm is sweating. 'Grace…'

CHAPTER THIRTY
Then

My beautiful new car was ruined. The road blurred and Charlie's voice sounded muffled but I somehow managed to drive home safely, angled the car so the damaged side couldn't be seen from the house. I didn't want my grandparents to find out. Charlie and I kicked our shoes onto the mat and were tiptoeing up the stairs when the lounge door creaked open.

'Want a cup of tea, you two?' Grandad asked.

I opened my mouth to answer but my sobs caught in my throat, forcing the words back down.

'What's happened?'

I shook my head. Charlie took Grandad's hand, led him outside, and I watched from behind the lounge curtains as Grandad ran his fingers over the letters scratched into the paintwork. Charlie gestured wildly, I knew she was explaining about the letters, most likely about Siobhan catching me and Dan kissing, and I felt ashamed.

They turned towards the house and I stepped back from the window, sank into the sofa and buried my face in my hands.

'C'mon.' Grandad's voice was hard. I splayed my fingers, peeked at his face.

'I'm sorry.'

'We're going to Siobhan's,' said Charlie.

'What?' My hands flopped into my lap. 'Why?'

'She can jolly well pay for the repairs, that's why.'

'Can't the insurance do that?' I hated myself for wanting to avoid a confrontation, but I did.

'And let my premium go up?'

I swallowed hard. My grandparents had sold premium bonds in order to afford the car; it wasn't fair to expect them to foot the bill for this.

'I can pay. I've got dad's money now.'

'You're not paying. That's for your future. I'll drive.'

Sometimes there was just no arguing with Grandad. I stood and dropped my car keys into his open palm.

I fidgeted in my seat during our silent journey as we wended through the village towards Siobhan's house on the new estate. She lived in a large detached house, built so close to its neighbours it could almost be classed as a terrace. A fir tree stood in the bay window, fairy lights twisted around its middle, flashing on and off like they were sending out an SOS. Charlie squeezed my hand as Grandad pressed the bell. 'Good King Wenceslas' rang out and Charlie stifled a giggle.

Siobhan's mum opened the door. Her magenta lips twisted into a sneer when she spotted me.

'What do you want?'

'We're here about the letters Siobhan's been sending Grace, and the damage to her car.' Grandad's voice was firm.

'She didn't send any letters.'

'Could we see her, please?'

'She isn't here.'

'That's convenient.'

'She told me about your accusations.' Siobhan's mum jabbed a finger at me and I shrank back. 'How you've turned everyone against her. She's been really upset. It's your fault she got expelled. Taking that laptop. She wasn't in her right mind.'

'It wasn't Grace's fault.' Charlie stepped forward, standing shoulder to shoulder with Grandad.

'We're here about the car.' Grandad's voice was firm.

'I don't know nothing about your car.'

'It was scratched today, deliberately.'

'Today?' Siobhan's mum snorted.

'Yes.'

'Siobhan's in Brighton. Spending the day with Jeremy.'

'Jeremy?'

'Her boyfriend. Not that it's any of your business.'

I flinched as the door slammed.

Back in the car, Charlie busied herself with her phone as we drove away in silence.

'Bloody hell.' Charlie held out her phone. 'Look who Jeremy is!' Siobhan had uploaded a selfie to Facebook that morning of herself and the leader of the kids we'd dubbed the 'Walking Dead', huddled on Brighton pier, his turquoise hair blowing in the wind, her dead eyes fixed on the horizon. Neither of them were smiling. 'If she's in Brighton, it can't be her sending the letters.'

'No.' I shivered. *Who did this?*

The Touche Éclat Mum had bought me for Christmas tried its best to mask the deep shadows under my eyes, but I already looked like I'd partied all night as I got ready for the New Year's Eve bash at the pub. I wasn't Siobhan's biggest fan, but if she hadn't sent the letters, I felt I owed her an apology. Talking Charlie around would be difficult, though. She detested liars: years of Lexie being economical with the truth had left its mark, and regardless of whether Siobhan had sent the letters, she'd been caught on camera stealing.

The doorbell rang and Dan's low voice drifted up the stairs. I ran the straighteners through my hair one last time, although I knew by the end of the evening it would be a frizzy red mess, and sprayed vanilla perfume onto my pulse points. In front of the mirror I drew my navel towards my spine. It was too late to regret that last piece of Christmas cake. I was ready to go.

Dan wolf-whistled as I tottered downstairs, and I blushed and stared at the floor as he assured Grandad that as he was planning on drinking, he wouldn't be driving home. We picked Charlie up on the way to the pub and Dan wound down the window and sucked in fresh air. She always overdid the Impulse body spray.

The car park was busy and Dan parked under a light. 'See you tomorrow, darling.' I rolled my eyes as he patted the bonnet, then we pushed our way into the bar. It was three deep and we bought two rounds to avoid queuing again – but then drank them twice as fast. The evening flashed by. Dan recounted a showing he'd done that week, where he'd taken an elderly couple to see a supposedly empty house only to find the owner having sex in the master bedroom.

'It wouldn't have been quite so bad if it had been his wife he was in bed with!' Dan laughed.

'It's nice we're all together,' I said. 'Well, almost all together.' Esmée always spent Christmas in France and wouldn't be back until the following week. 'Do you think we should call Siobhan? Apologise?'

'No.' Charlie slammed down her pint. Cider sloshed over her fingers but she didn't seem to notice.

'She didn't send the letters.' We'd accused Siobhan of something she hadn't done. Everyone hated her because of it. Despite the way she'd treated me over the years, guilt burrowed under my skin and it was getting harder and harder to ignore.

'We don't know that for sure.'

'How could she, if she was in Brighton?'

'Abby wasn't. She hero-worships Siobhan. She could easily have delivered the letter and scratched your car.'

I considered this. 'Possibly, but Siobhan said none of her family are speaking to her, including Abby.'

'Even if it wasn't her, or Abby, she's still a thief and a liar. Stop sticking up for her,' Dan said. 'You're too nice.'

'Just suppose it wasn't her,' said Charlie. 'Who could it be?'

It was unnerving to think there was someone else out there who hated me. In a way, it was easier to believe it was Siobhan.

'OK. Let's drop it.' I leaned back in my seat and puffed out air. This was supposed to be a night of celebration. New beginnings.

'I'm going for a wee.' Charlie stood, swayed, and I watched as she fought her way through the crowd. I didn't recognise half the people here.

'Do you know why Charlie and Ben have split up?' I asked Dan.

'No. He's gutted though. He wouldn't come tonight. Doesn't want to see her ever again.'

'Not easy in a village this size.'

'He's planning on going to Africa, once the exams are over. Volunteering to build a school. He'll go straight to uni from there.'

'It's such a shame.' I didn't like change. I'd seen too much of it, I supposed. 'Charlie says she's got her eye on someone else, but she won't say who.'

Charlie returned quickly. 'Bloody queue was ridiculous. I went in the men's.' She flopped down, picked up her pint.

The bell rang. 'I'm closing the bar for the countdown,' yelled Mike, covering up the pumps with towels. 'We'll serve again next year.'

'Next year?' someone shouted.

'Yep. In about sixty seconds.' Mike aimed the remote at the flat-screen TV above the bar. Trafalgar Square was rammed. *Ten… Nine… Eight…*

'I haven't got anyone to kiss.' Charlie looked stricken as she stood on her stool and looked around for an available man. 'We'll have to share Dan.'

Seven… Six… Five… Dan took my hands in his.

Three… Two… One… Our lips met. My ears roared with whistles and cheers until the sounds faded away and all I could hear was the beating of my own heart. When I opened my eyes again, Charlie had vanished.

I was pulled to my feet by Mike's wife, Liz, and a man I recognised as our postman but whose name I couldn't remember. My head spun and I stumbled into our table; the sharp corner dug into my hip and my drink toppled over. Before I could set the glass upright, my hands were criss-crossed over my body and I was jostled around the pub to 'Auld Lang Syne'.

I lost sight of Dan; he hated singing so was probably hiding out somewhere. I bellowed out the words, even though I only knew the first verse, which didn't seem to matter. There was an almost manic atmosphere; I'd never experienced anything quite like it. Usually, we'd stay up until midnight and toast the New Year – Grandma with a sherry, Grandad with a port, and me with a hot chocolate – and then we'd go straight to bed. It was always strangely disappointing. Watching the clock, waiting for the hands to tick-tick-tick to midnight and then realising that even though it was a brand new year, everything was exactly the same. Grandma would rinse the cups before bed, Grandad would make her a hot-water bottle, and I was reminded to clean my teeth just the same as every other night. New Year's Day was much like any other, too, although we'd always have roast lamb.

But this? This was amazing. I felt weightless. Invincible. And who knew I could sing? 'Auld Lang Syne' finished and Mike put on a compilation CD. I belted out Destiny's Child: *I am a survivor!* I stumbled around the pub, laughing, hugging strangers with beaming smiles and shining eyes. But where were Dan and Charlie?

Someone caught my arm and I spun around, revelling in the attention. Everyone wanted to talk to me; it should be New Year's Eve every day. Abby stood before me, her face fraught with worry.

'Cheer up!' I said. I loved everybody that night. 'It's New Year.' I staggered backwards, leaned against the wall for support. The floor appeared to be moving.

'Have you seen Siobhan?'

'She's probably with Jeremy funky peacock-head,' I giggled. I could sing, *and* I was funny. My new-found talents would make this the best year ever.

'Grace.' Abby grasped my shoulders and shook me. The contents of my stomach sloshed and all of a sudden I didn't feel quite so good. 'Siobhan is missing. If you see her, will you ask her to ring me? I've been a real bitch to her and I'm worried.'

Abby's face swam in and out of focus until she had two heads. My stomach was spinning like the Catherine wheel we'd watched on the village green. I clasped both hands across my mouth and bolted towards the toilets.

Charlie and Dan were in the corridor. His arms were wrapped around her. Whenever he held me, my head would rest on his chest, but Charlie was so tall their foreheads touched.

'I'll tell Grace tomorrow,' Dan was saying.

I crept backwards towards the door. I didn't want to hear what he had to say. Didn't want to believe what I was seeing. Dan and Charlie? Tell me *what* tomorrow?

Hands grasped at my waist; leery voices demanded New Year's kisses as I fought my way to the exit. After the warmth of the pub, the icy air slammed into my chest and I leaned forward, hands resting on my knees, sure I'd be sick. But after a few moments, the nausea passed, although sharp pain sliced through my temples whenever I moved my head. I was absolutely never, ever drinking again. My body felt heavy and stiff, like the Tin Man from the *Wizard of Oz*, although he was lucky he didn't have a heart, I thought – he'd never feel the hurt I felt in that moment.

My boyfriend and my best friend? Half of me was desperate to confront them; the other half wanted to go home, crawl under the duvet and never come out again. Why did everyone leave me? Dad, Mum… Was Dan going to do the same? Charlie? I felt so ill. It was hard to believe that ten minutes ago I'd been having the time of my life.

I started to totter down the high street. My heels seemed higher than they had all evening. I held my arms out to my sides for balance. A tightrope walker, although with my frizzy red hair, I probably looked more like a clown. It wasn't far to walk, but it was late. Dark. And someone out there hated me, wanted me to leave. But most of the local taxi drivers were in the pub and it wasn't fair to ask Grandad to drive after his port and lemon. I'd be OK, I reasoned. I'd walked home a thousand times before.

A crash. A shadow. A movement in the post office doorway. I froze. Felt like I might burst: my bladder too full, my heart too fast. Green eyes shone. A cat darted out of the doorway and across the road. I shook my head at my stupidity, but there was another movement. A groan. The sound of a throat being cleared. I kicked my heels off and ran, tearing around the corner onto Green Road, my stockinged feet slapping against the cold pavement. I didn't see the broken glass but I felt it rip through my flesh and I screamed and sprawled onto my knees. Warm blood oozed over the pavement and I whimpered as I tried to stand. There was a ringing in my ears and it took a few moments to realise it was my mobile. I hoped it was Grandad. Dan. Anyone who would take me home. I wanted to be tucked up in bed, safe and warm.

It was Siobhan. The pain in my foot fuelled my anger. What did *she* want? Dan and Charlie thought I was pathetic, wanting to forgive her. No wonder they'd gone off together. It was all her fault.

'Leave me alone!' I screamed into my phone.

'Grace.' Siobhan was crying. 'Please don't hang up. Help me. I don't feel well.'

'Good.' I hung up and hobbled home on my heel, keeping the weight off the ball of my foot. My phone rang again and again, but I didn't answer.

CHAPTER THIRTY-ONE
Now

Dan has promised to help me find Mittens. We've been out looking for hours. The sky rearranges its shading – blues, pinks, greys – until it's jet black, stars hidden above invisible clouds.

'Let's go home, Grace. It's too dark to properly see, and it's freezing.'

The spring warmth has disappeared with the sun and Dan's breath billows out in front of him.

'I want to find Mittens.'

'I know you do, but you're exhausted. You haven't eaten all day. We'll have some food and an early night. We can start again first thing.'

'We?'

'Work can do without me for a day; you need me more.'

I slip my hand inside his, squeeze his fingers.

It's a relief to find the cottage in darkness. I push open Anna's door: her room's tidy, the bed's made. I yank open drawers. Clothes are neatly folded, socks matched. I don't know what I'm looking for but I can't quite believe that Mittens would have run out of the house. But why would Anna have deliberately let her out? It doesn't make any sense.

I stand under steaming water. The smell of the police station seems to have permeated every pore and I scrub at my skin until it's pig-pink. I shiver as I step out of the shower, towel myself dry and hurry downstairs. Dan's warming tomato soup, slicing bread. I'm too on edge to swallow anything solid but I'm grateful for the thought, and we sit at the table spooning steaming liquid into silent mouths. There's only the chink of spoons on bowls to be heard as we eat our supper. I push my dish away. Shake my head as Dan offers to refill it.

'Where do you think Anna is?'

Dan plunges bread into his soup; white turns to orange. 'Far away, I hope.'

'Do you believe that Mittens ran out the front door?'

'I don't know, it's odd.'

'I'm going to call her.'

I place my palms against the table edge, am about to push my chair back when Dan covers both hands with his.

'Leave it for tonight, Grace. Let's try to get some sleep and we can be out at first light. We'll talk about Anna properly when we've found Mittens.'

'OK.' It's probably for the best. I don't know what I'd say to her. I don't know what I think any more.

It's dark and cold when I wake. The rain lashes against the windows and I picture Mittens wet and shivering, tucked under a bush, wondering where home is.

I stretch my legs, ice-cube feet seeking out the warmth of Dan's body, but he's not there. I pad downstairs and find him sitting at the table hunched over his laptop, the screen illuminating his face.

'What are you doing?'

'Look.' He angles the screen towards me. There's a picture of Mittens with 'MISSING' captioned above her photo. Underneath, a plea for people to check their outbuildings, along with our telephone number. 'We can put them up around the village and I'll print smaller leaflets for letter boxes.'

I make tea, and nurse it until it grows cold. Scud forms on the top as I sit on the sofa listening to the printer whirr and click, spewing out image after image of Mittens's adorable face. Dawn breaks and I shower and dress, force myself to chew and swallow toast; I need all my energy today.

The cars slosh by on the high street, headlights on. Drivers impatiently tap their hands on their steering wheels as the bin lorry holds them up. Everywhere I look, there are dangers for a cat who has never been outside. My grandparents wait for us in front of the post office door, rubbing gloved hands together and stamping booted feet. Grandma looks tiny, wrapped inside too many layers. We hug our hellos and divide the pile of leaflets in two. Dan unfolds a square of paper from his pocket. It's a map of the village.

'I thought you could take the roads I've marked in yellow, Tony,' says Dan.

Grandad traces the fluorescent streets with his finger, nods his approval. Grandma unhooks a carrier bag from her arm, thrusts it into my hands.

'Rock cakes. Keep your sugar levels up.'

Posters are sellotaped to shop windows and lamp posts, pinned to noticeboards in the community centre and library.

At lunchtime, Dan and I buy ham salad sandwiches from the bakery, then walk to the pocket park.

I tip a swing seat upside down, shaking off the drips of water before smoothing a carrier bag over the seat to protect my jeans. I sit, balancing my lunch on my knees.

'It's been years since we were here,' I say. 'Do you remember the stupid things you used to do to try and impress Charlie?'

'What can I say? I was an idiot. I still am.' Dan runs his fingers through his hair.

'I don't blame you for loving her. She was easy to love. I miss her.'

'I didn't love her; it was a stupid, childish crush. You're the only girl for me. You know that, don't you?' He picks off bits of crust, throws them to the pigeon that's strutting around his feet.

'I was expecting Anna to be like Charlie. I wanted her to be like Charlie, but she isn't, is she?'

'No.' His voice is hard. 'C'mon.' He stands, scrunches his sandwich bag into his fist. 'Let's get going again. We can try knocking on some doors.'

By six o'clock we still haven't found her. We have run out of posters, rapped on doors until our knuckles are sore. Grandad texts to say they've gone home and that they will call me later. Rain is once again pelting down, bouncing off pavements, running in rivulets into overflowing drains.

'Let's call it a day, pick up a takeaway. We'll come out again tomorrow.'

The Chinese is warm and steamy. Evocative smells drift from hissing woks. I unwind my scarf, unzip my jacket, and sit, thumbing through the papers while Dan orders our food at the counter. The bell rings as the door pushes open. I glance up at the blast of cold air. It's Harry and Chloe. Chloe smiles, pulls out the chair opposite me. Harry leans against the counter next to Dan, both their heads cocked towards Sky Sports on the giant TV suspended over the till.

'How are you?' Chloe asks.

I tell her we've been searching for our cat all day.

'That's terrible. Have you put a picture up on Facebook?'

'Not yet.'

'Send me one; I'll share it. I'm going to put the photos up later from the Estate Agent's Dinner. It's a shame you missed it.'

'I wasn't well.'

'I know, Anna said. I was surprised to see her there with Dan.'

'Do you know her?'

'Only from the club.'

'The club?'

'The football club. She worked behind the bar. I thought that's how you knew her?'

'When was that?'

'She started last autumn, when you didn't come out, after… You know. Charlie. She's left now though. I didn't know Dan had kept in touch with her?'

'So Dan's known her for months?'

'Yes.'

They knew each other when I introduced them, and yet they pretended they'd never met.

I can't breathe. I spring up from my seat, stumble towards the door, almost tripping over my Dr Who scarf as it falls from my lap.

My feet pound through puddles, arms pump by my sides. The icy air burns my lungs, but I don't slow down until I reach our lane. I need to be at home. Get my thoughts straight before I confront Dan. I bang open the gate, fumble through pockets for my keys.

'Grace, dear.' Mrs Jones is standing on her front step. Light from her hallway illuminates the pathway. She hobbles forward and holds a small cardboard box over the picket fence.

'I'm so sorry, dear. The postman found her at the side of the road.'

'No!' I press my hands together as though I am praying.

'I thought Dan could bury her for you.'

I want to bury Dan. I want to bury Anna. I want to crawl into a hole myself and never, ever, come out again. I take the box silently and carry the cat that had loved me – that had never hurt anyone – inside for the very last time.

CHAPTER THIRTY-TWO
Then

So much for New Year, new start. I sat up, opened my eyes and the light from my bedside lamp sliced through my brain like a cheese wire. I must have slept with it on. I clicked it off before Grandma could find out, could point out that there were villages in Africa without any electricity. My mobile phone was under my pillow and I pulled it out. Nine missed calls. I scrolled through all the 'Happy New Year!' messages, searching for texts from Dan.

I'm sorry, please call me. He'd sent the same text six times and I deleted them all. There were texts from Charlie, asking where I'd disappeared to, but nothing else from Siobhan. I felt terrible about ignoring her and not keeping my promise to Abby. I should have let her know her big sister had got in touch. I vowed to call them both later. I replied to Mum's text, wishing her and Oliver a happy New Year, and tossed the phone onto my bedside table. My tongue was stuck to the roof of my mouth. I swiped for my water glass and missed, sending it crashing to the floor. I stood to get a cloth. My foot throbbed and stars exploded behind my eyes. I hoped there weren't fragments of glass in it. I wrapped my dressing gown around myself and teetered to the kitchen on Bambi legs.

Grandad was sat at the table while Grandma fussed around a frying pan. The smell of bacon flooded my mouth with saliva. I just made it to the sink before I vomited, until there was nothing left but the bitter taste of bile stinging my throat.

'Gracie?' Grandma rinsed her Empire State Building tea towel in cool water and soothed my brow.

'I'm not feeling well.' I stated the obvious. 'I think I've got food poisoning.'

'Alcohol poisoning, more like,' Grandma tutted. 'We heard you trying to fit your key in the lock. Get yourself back to bed.'

I willed my muscles to carry me back upstairs, where I fell onto my soft mattress. Still wearing my dressing gown, I screwed my eyes tight and prayed for the world to keep still.

The sound of my door opening wrenched me from fitful dreams.

'Are you awake?' Grandma asked. 'I've brought you some lunch.' I glanced at the clock, surprised to see it was one thirty.

Heinz tomato soup wafted from the tray Grandma held out. The smell of comfort. I blinked away tears – someone still loved me – and sat up, arranging the pillows behind me. My sweat-drenched pyjamas clung to me and I loosened the tie on my dressing gown to shrug it from my shoulders.

'I'll run you a bath while you eat; it smells like a brewery in here.' Grandma cracked open the window.

I checked my phone. There was a barrage of texts from Dan again. I didn't text him back. Nothing new from Charlie.

The soup was scalding; it burned my tongue and I welcomed the sudden rush of pain, which drew my attention away from my self-pity.

'Bath's ready,' called Grandma and I put my half-empty bowl on my bedside cabinet.

The water was hot. The steam revived my nausea and I washed as quickly as I could, dabbing dried blood from the sole of my foot. The cut wasn't as bad as I'd feared. Dizziness engulfed me as

I stepped out of the bath; I clutched the towel rail until I stopped swaying.

I was cleaning my teeth, trying not to gag as the brush went to the back of my mouth, when Grandad rapped on the door. I winced as the sound penetrated my throbbing temples.

'Dan's downstairs,' he said.

I wobbled down the staircase and beckoned Dan through the kitchen into the utility room. It was the only place we could have any privacy – Grandma didn't allow boys in the bedroom.

'You look like I feel,' he said, running his hands through matted hair. 'Look Grace, about last night…'

'So you're the one?' I said stiffly, sidestepping out of his reach.

'The one?'

'The one Charlie dumped Ben for.'

'What? No!'

'I saw you in the corridor. Holding her.'

'Good God, Grace. How could you think that? I love you. Charlie's your best friend. She was feeling low. Lexie's being bonkers. It was a hug between friends. Nothing more, I swear.'

He stretched a hand towards me and I shoved it away. 'So why send me texts apologising?'

'Because I didn't know why you'd left, but I'm a man. I suppose I thought I'd ballsed it up. Upset you somehow. I was really worried, so I came here. I could see your light was on. I tried ringing but you didn't answer; I even threw a stone at your window.'

'Just the one?'

'Didn't want to risk waking your grandma.'

I leaned back against the tumble dryer. It was stifling in the utility room. My skin was damp and I wouldn't have been surprised if cider was running from my pores instead of sweat. My stomach churned in time to the freshly laundered clothes, and my head felt too fuzzy to make sense of what I'd seen. I remembered what I'd heard. Could I have got it wrong?

'You said to Charlie, "I'll tell Grace tomorrow". Tell me what?'

Dan wiped his forehead with his sleeve before tugging his jumper over his head. His T-shirt rode up and I longed to touch his bare skin. Instead, I turned and cracked open the window.

'I didn't want to tell you like this. I'd planned to cook a nice lunch today, be a bit romantic. A cottage has come up in the village. It needs some work, but it's a good price. The owners are going into a residential home and they want a quick sale.'

'So? What's that got to do with me?

'I was asking Charlie whether she thought you'd want to move in with me.'

'What?'

'She knows you better than anyone. And for what it's worth, she thought it was a great idea. Even talked about her renting the second bedroom. You, me and Charlie living together. What do you think?'

A flash of shame streaked through me. How could I have thought the girl who'd stuck up for me on my first day of school, my best friend, would betray me? I knew in my heart she wouldn't.

'But we can't just *buy* a cottage,' I said.

'We can. I've given it a lot of thought. Property doesn't become available here often, you know that – especially traditional houses like this one. I valued it and took the photos. It could be great with a little work.'

'But I'm still at school.'

'I know, but you finish in May, except for exams, and then you've got the job at pre-school.'

'That's ages away. I only work part-time at the coffee shop now.'

'My basic salary may not be much, but the commission is great and I am good at what I do. Charlie will pick up work somewhere.'

'Would we get a mortgage?'

'We shouldn't need one. You've got the life insurance from your dad now you're eighteen, and my parents will lend us some money to do it up.'

'You want me to spend the money?' Instinctively, I bristled. I knew that Dan was thinking about *our* future, but that money, it was precious, and I didn't like that Dan had just decided how I should spend it.

'Not if you don't want to. I'm sure about what I want, Grace, and I'm worried about you. All these letters, your car being vandalised. What's next? If we lived together, I could look after you properly. Make sure you're safe. Your grandparents would probably love some time on their own, I know my parents would.'

Would they? I'd never felt in the way, and it was disconcerting to think I might be.

'I'd have to speak to Mum. It's only fair, with the money coming from Dad.'

'Does that mean you'll think about it?'

'There's no harm in looking.' It didn't mean I'd agree.

'Really?' Dan picked me up and swung me around. I clutched his shoulders and buried my head into his neck, hoping I wouldn't be sick.

'You smell like a Polo,' I said.

'I've used half a bottle of mint shower gel and brushed my teeth three times. I stank. God, I felt rough this morning.'

'Me too. I still do.'

He put me down and swatted my bottom. 'Go put some shoes on, woman. We've a cottage to view.'

'Now?'

'Some fresh air will sort your hangover out. There's no time like the present. The sons are pushing for a quick sale. We'd better walk. I think I'm still over the limit. If we go the long way around, we can sober up a bit and swing by the office for the keys. Do you want to call Charlie? Ask her to meet us there?'

We trudged through the village. Grandma had bandaged my foot and given me some paracetamol. It didn't hurt any more. Our wellington boots stamped footprints in virgin snow, past skeletal trees and squealing children dragging toboggans behind them. It seemed impossible that we were going to view a cottage, could potentially be buying a home together.

Charlie wasn't answering her phone. Where was she? Probably still in bed with a hangover, but Dan said if I liked it then Charlie could see it tomorrow. The crisp air drove out my pounding headache, and then we were there, standing in front of two tiny cottages tucked away on the outskirts of the village. Icicles hung from the eaves.

Dan pushed the gate; it squeaked open. The front garden was coated white; I couldn't properly see whether anything was growing, but there was a tree I thought to be apple, and two trellises hanging either side of the faded red door.

'Are they roses?'

'Probably. It's called Rose Cottage.'

I clapped my hands, hangover forgotten.

'It's your domain, anyway. Woman gardens, Man decorates.' Dan thumped his chest like Tarzan before turning the key with a creak. I stamped the snow from my boots and stepped over the threshold onto a flagstone floor. The hallway was narrow and musty; faded yellow paper curled from the walls. There were brighter rectangles where light hadn't dulled the colours, where picture frames would have hung. I could imagine rows of photos of chubby baby boys lining these walls. Toddlers who grew into men to be proud of, clutching scrolls and tossing mortar boards into the air.

There was a flight of stairs in front of me but I headed down the dark passage and stepped into the room on my left. The living room was larger than I'd expected, and bright despite the low beamed ceiling. Winter sun poured in through the French windows, pooling on the dusty grate of a real fire. Light in the summer and cosy in the winter. I bounced up and down on tiptoes as I looked around. There'd be room for a compact table and chairs as well as a bookcase and a sofa. If we got a sofa bed, Mum would be able to come and stay. I envisaged an old-fash-ioned sideboard to house my record deck. It was perfect. The garden stretched long and thin, a greenhouse at the bottom.

'My grandparents will love this.'

'There's a vegetable patch too, somewhere under the snow.'

The kitchen was opposite the lounge, smaller because it was tucked under the staircase. There was a sink under the window, overlooking a paved patio area and a bird table.

'You can watch the birds when you wash up.' Dan grinned, held his hands up before I could thump him. 'Just kidding. I'll buy some Marigolds.'

Upstairs housed a large main bedroom, a smaller second bed-room that would be Charlie's, and a bathroom with a roll-top bath and a small, glass shower cubicle in the corner.

'I can't imagine owning this. It feels so grown-up.'

'You are all grown up.' Dan stood behind me and slid his hands up my top. 'Do you like it?'

'That's an understatement.' This was somewhere I could live. Somewhere I could love.

'Thought you would. We can make an offer if you want?'

I looked around the empty bedroom, imagined lying here on a Sunday morning in bed with Dan for the rest of our lives, reading the papers and eating bacon sandwiches. I was sure he was the one. I recalled Mum's words.

'Dan. Would you wear a pink tutu for me?'

'What? Why?'

I took his hands in mine. 'It's important. Would you? If I asked?'

'I'd wear anything for you… But not in public, though.'

I grinned. 'How soon can we move in?'

'Not for a few weeks, but we can christen the place now.'

And the wooden floor wasn't the only thing that was stripped.

I kissed Dan goodbye on the high street; he wanted to go to the office and phone the vendor. Hopefully they'd accept our offer – I was so excited. My wellies slipped as I ran towards the pocket park and the shortcut home. The skin on my heels would be rubbed raw but I didn't care. I wanted to get back as quickly as I could, but when I hared around the corner I skidded to a halt. A policeman stood, hands clasped behind his back, at the entrance to the park. Yellow 'Do Not Cross' tape was stretched between the gateposts.

The snow was turning to mush as I stuck to the main roads. Slush splattered over my legs as my booted feet pounded the pavement. My jeans were soaked by the time I turned into our road. There was a police car outside our house. Despite the temperature, I was filled with boiling hot panic as I ran towards the front door. Grandma and Grandad were sitting on the sofa as I burst into the lounge. Two officers stood by the fireplace. I wanted Grandma to tell me off for not taking off my wet boots, for staining the carpets, but instead she stared at her hands in her lap and it was Grandad that spoke.

'Sit down, Grace. We have something to tell you.'

CHAPTER THIRTY-THREE
Now

The cardboard box sits on the coffee table, small and still. The first time Mittens came home in one, it rocked as she stretched and wriggled inside, eager to break free and explore her new surroundings. Now, her exploration days are over. My eyes sting with tears that I gulp away. I will not break. Not yet, anyway.

I sprint up the stairs, burst into Anna's room. It feels different somehow, and as I fling open the wardrobe doors, empty hangers jangle together. The drawers I yank open are bare, apart from the rose-scented lining paper I'd bought especially for her. My mobile rings – Dan. I reject the call, try Anna's number. Her phone is switched off.

The gate bangs shut and I race downstairs. I am sitting on the sofa, outwardly calm by the time Dan has unlocked the front door. Inwardly, I want to kill him.

'Grace? Are you OK? Chloe said you looked like you might be sick.'

I stare at Dan. 'I am sick. Sick of your lies.'

Dan puts the Chinese food on the table next to Mittens's box. Grease seeps through the paper bag and the smell of chow mein sickens me.

'What's going on?'

'You tell me, Dan.' I am icy calm.

He fingers his keys, stares at the carpet, saying nothing.

I help him out. 'Chloe told me Anna worked behind the bar at the football club.'

Dan sits heavily in the armchair and slumps forward, his head in his hands.

'Dan, you knew her before she came?'

'Yes.' Dan's voice is so quiet I can barely hear him.

'Sorry, what? I can't quite hear you?'

'*Yes*, Grace. I…'

'Is she really Charlie's sister, or is that another lie?'

Dan mumbles but I can't make out his answer.

'Who is she, Dan?' I snap.

Dan's shoulders shake; he presses his palms to his face and I wrench them away, my nails puncturing the thin skin on his wrists.

'Who the fuck is Anna?'

'I'm so sorry, Grace.' Tears fall but they're not mine. I rest back on my heels. Not quite believing, not quite understanding. Dan wipes his nose with his sleeve. 'I'm going to get us a drink.'

I'm too stunned to protest as he walks to the kitchen, and as he returns with two glasses and a bottle of Merlot it could be just another cosy night in – if it weren't for the dead cat on the table, of course.

We sit at opposite ends of the sofa. Dan glugs wine into a glass and I drain it in seconds, thrust it towards Dan for a refill. The silence between us feels suffocating and I wrench my jumper off.

'Start talking.'

Dan's hand trembles as he clasps the wine bottle, tops up his glass. I think of that hand touching me. Has he touched Anna? I want to scream.

'It hasn't been easy for me, you know, the way you fell apart after Charlie.'

'*Poor* you.' My words drip with sarcasm.

'Grace, please listen. I had to be strong for you, but I found it difficult to cope when she died. I'd known her as long as you. Longer, even.'

'So it's my fault for grieving for my best friend, or her fault for dying?'

'Neither.' He sighs. 'Do you remember how it was just after she died?'

'Of course.'

'*Really* remember? Because you were so doped-up half the time I really don't think you can. You lay in bed for weeks. Shouted if I came near you, cried if I left you alone. I didn't know what to do for the best. You stopped cooking, cleaning, you couldn't even remember how to operate the washing machine.'

It sounds as though he's talking about someone else. Is that how it was? Medication and shock team together, making my memory so hazy it's like straining to make out a shape in the fog. You know something's there but you're not entirely sure what it is.

'I'm not blaming you, Grace. I'm not. But I missed Charlie; she was my friend too. I missed you and I didn't have anyone to talk to.'

'And then you met Anna?'

Dan nods. 'She started working behind the bar at the club. She was really friendly, really easy to talk to. I started staying behind after hours and she listened to me. Really listened.'

My teeth clench as I remember the nights I'd lain awake in bed waiting for Dan to come home.

'So you had an affair.' I shift in my seat, sit on hands that twitch with anger; my fingers want to claw his face.

'No. It wasn't like that.' Dan runs his hands through his hair. 'We were just friends, but then she started flirting. Making comments.'

'And you couldn't resist? You make me sick.'

'It wasn't like that. You remember when we won the match and I tried to get you to come to the club?'

'Yes.' It was the day I'd dug the memory box up – how could I forget?

'I was feeling sorry for myself. Chloe and all the other girl-friends were there. I must have drunk too much. I don't remember. I really don't. I can only remember odd fragments of the evening. I felt terrible when I realised what I'd done.'

'So terrible, you moved her into our home. Let me believe she was Charlie's fucking sister.' White shards of rage slice through me.

'I didn't want to. I fucking hate her. She blackmailed me. She said she needed somewhere to stay for a couple of nights until her new flat was ready to move into. A week at the most.'

'I don't believe you.'

'It's true. Remember I lost my phone that night? She took it. She filmed us having sex and threatened to send the clip to everyone in my contacts list. I couldn't risk you seeing that. My parents. Your grandparents. Your mum. My boss. How would we have survived that? I didn't want to risk losing you, Grace. Losing everything. I'd have had to leave the village. Find a new job.'

I lock my fingers together, place my palms over my stomach and lean forward. I feel as though he's punched me, hard and fast.

'But why… Charlie?'

'I knew you'd let her stay if you thought she had a connection to Charlie, and she does look a little like her. I didn't know how to explain her otherwise. I'm so ashamed, Grace. I thought she'd disappear after a few days and we'd write her off as a crackpot, resume the search for Charlie's real family. You weren't supposed to bond with her. I'd told her about your dad when I thought she was my friend. I never dreamed she'd make up a similar story to get you to like her.'

'I can't believe you've been so cruel. You've shared personal things with a complete stranger. And you knew how much it meant to me, finding Charlie's father.'

Dan looks pleading. 'I know. You still can. We still can.'

'There is no "we". Not any more.'

'Grace, please. I shouldn't have lied, but I panicked. I did it for you, for us.'

'And were you thinking of *us* when you fucked her?'

Dan's cheeks are wet. 'Please. It was a one-off.'

'And I'm supposed to believe that? You've probably been at it every time I've gone out. In our home. *IN OUR BED!*'

'No! I swear. It was just once. A stupid mistake. I don't even remember it. If she hadn't showed me the film, I'd never have believed it happened. We can work through it, can't we?'

'No.' My voice is controlled. 'Maybe we could have done if you'd told me the truth at the time, but you lied, cheated and manipulated me. I bet you both had a good laugh behind my back, didn't you?'

'No. I hated her being here. When I saw you were getting attached to her, I tried to make her leave but she wouldn't. It all got so out of control and I didn't know how to stop it.'

It's not only the fact that Anna slept with Dan, blackmailed him, that hurts so much. It's the lies she told. Letting me think I'd met someone who understood what it felt like to lose your parents at nine. The utter desolation and loss. The misplaced guilt and fear of abandonment. These were things I'd never shared with anyone else. Never thinking anyone else could understand, until I met Anna. We had so much in common, I thought – but it has all been a lie.

My head suddenly feels like a dead weight and I rest it in my hands.

'Why? Why did she want to stay here? She must have family? Friends?'

'She said not. Maybe she was jealous of how much I love you. I don't know. She's twisted. When I suspected she was doing things to hurt you…'

'What things?' But even as I ask, I count the ways my life has gone wrong since Anna moved in. Stealing my necklace, hacking my emails, the Twitter campaign. Could she have taken my keys and broken into the nursery? I dread to think.

'When she put nut syrup in your hot chocolate, I was really scared.'

'She could have killed me and yet you still let her stay. God, she probably poisoned my fucking soup, Dan. You're a coward.'

'I know. I didn't know how to get her out. I didn't know what she was capable of.'

'I do.'

Dan raises his head. His eyes – damp and red – meet mine for the first time.

'Look in the box, Dan.'

'What's in there?'

'Look.' My voice is steely.

He kneels before the coffee table, lifts the flaps on the box.

He gags. 'Grace…'

'Get out, Dan.'

'But we…'

'Get the fuck out!' I throw my wine glass as hard as I can at him. It misses his head by inches. Merlot runs like rivulets of blood down the buttermilk wall. Shards of glass embed in the carpet. I worry that Mittens will cut her paws, and then I remember that nothing will hurt her again.

'Get out!' I spray Dan with saliva and venom as I scream into his face.

Dan scoops up his keys, walks towards the door, head hung low. I stand at the window and watch his back as he leaves: I want to stab him in it.

Mittens has so many toys – mice, stuffed fish and tinkly balls – and I put them with her bowls inside the box. Then I gently cover the cat, who will never again feel the cold, with her fleecy paw-print blanket. As I carry the box outside, it feels as though I'm watching myself from high above. I struggle to make an impression in the soil with my fork. The earth is like stone, despite the rain. I thrust the prongs into the ground over and over, and shock waves travel up my arms, jolting my spine. It doesn't seem long ago that my hands blistered as I replanted the shrubs that I now know Anna deliberately uprooted, or that my shoulders ached as I dug up the memory box. Now I'm burying another box of memories. I blink away images of Mittens softly patting my cheek with her paw, purring as she rubs her face against mine.

I stab the spade into the earth over and over, wishing I were driving it into Anna. Causing her the same pain she's caused me. I wonder where she is, whether Dan will see her again, and I wonder why I care. They deserve each other. I drop to my knees and scrape earth away from the hole with both hands. It is deep enough now. I kiss the box and place it under the pear tree.

'Bye, Mittens.' I throw a handful of earth over the cardboard and mound soil back in the hole. Then I heave my ceramic pot, containing a budding miniature rose, over to the grave. It's heavier than it looks and the plant rocks back and forth as I inch it forwards. Leaves fall like teardrops onto the earth. Dizzy with exertion, I sit cross-legged on the damp ground. This time, I allow myself to cry.

And then I hear, from the front of the house, a sharp rap on the front door.

CHAPTER THIRTY-FOUR
Then

Siobhan was dead. She'd been found in the park, track marks in her arm. The police wanted to talk to me as I was the last person she'd called. Grandad drove me to the station and I texted Dan, Charlie, Esmée, with the words I was finding impossible to believe. Dan offered to come and meet me, but I told him I'd call him once I got home. Esmée was devastated and helpless – she was stuck in France. Charlie hadn't replied by the time we arrived at the station.

I left Grandad on the hard wooden bench in reception while I was led to an interview room. I had a horrible feeling I'd never see him again. It was hard to fight back tears as I sat in the windowless room, longing to turn back the clock. *Could I have saved her?* The thought that I might have been able to nestled inside me, as if it belonged there as much as my bones, my kidneys, my lungs. My skin would shed cells, my scalp lose hair, my liver repair itself. My body would refresh and renew in the years to come, but the guilt? I knew that would stay. Forever a part of me.

The police were kind. Water was fetched, tissues passed. The loss I felt was for the girl Siobhan once was, not the one she'd become. The girl who'd beaten me at hopscotch, who'd twirled the skipping rope with Esmée while I jumped in the middle with Charlie. But the tears I shed? They weren't for Siobhan alone. They were for all of us. For growing up. For growing apart. Our little foursome had splintered and shattered and it would never, could never, be the same again. The days of shaking hands with such force our shoulders hurt – 'Make friends, make friends, never ever break friends' – were over. Besides, now we were only three.

The police thought it was an accidental overdose. Jeremy and the rest of the Walking Dead had been brought in for questioning. Jeremy admitted to pressuring Siobhan into stealing the laptop so that he could sell it and buy drugs with the money. Siobhan hadn't wanted to try heroin, one of the gang said, but Jeremy told her if she didn't, she couldn't hang around with them any more. Some friends. Jeremy had wrapped his belt tightly around her arm until the vein protruded, but she'd got hysterical when he'd injected her and they'd all run off and left her. Went to a party, as though she didn't exist. And now she didn't.

I told the police it had been too noisy to hear my phone when Siobhan called and I'd had no idea she was in trouble. I thought I'd go to hell for lying. I probably deserved it.

It felt like days later that I was escorted back to reception. To Grandad. He held me against his chest; the buttons of his plaid shirt dug into my cheek as I sobbed. He stroked my hair, offering me comfort I didn't deserve. He'd rung Mum to tell her what was going on and she'd offered to come, but I shook my head. There was nothing she could do.

We drove home, trudged up the path and pushed open the front door. A white envelope lay on the brown hessian doormat. Please, not another one, not today. I picked it up, turned it over. It wasn't the same size envelope as before. It wasn't sent by the same person. My name was written on the front, this time in handwriting I did recognise. I pulled out the paper inside. Seven words were written in Charlie's looping script: *I'm so sorry, Grace. Please forgive me.*

Charlie's phone was switched off. I sprinted to my car, wrenched open the door. The engine coughed and spluttered before it juddered to life and I reversed out of the drive almost faster than I'd ever driven forwards. I sped through the village; the tyres squealed as they fought for traction. *I'm so sorry, Grace. Please forgive me.* Forgive her for what?

I racked my brains to think what Charlie might have done. I didn't believe anything had gone on with Dan. Neither of them would do that to me. She hadn't treated Siobhan any worse than any of the rest of us had. Charlie would be the first to say that what had happened was a horrible accident. What, then?

The temporary traffic lights at the crossroads were red and I banged my palms on the wheel. 'C'mon.' The roads were deserted; it seemed the whole village was at home nursing New Year's hangovers, and I slammed my foot down, squealed through the red light. My eyes flicked between the road and my phone and I jabbed the redial button, tossing my mobile on the passenger seat as the voicemail message kicked in.

I abandoned the car outside Lexie's house and skidded my way up the icy path, grinding to a halt as I tried to shoulder open the front door. It was locked.

I rapped my knuckles hard against the door, then furled and unfurled my fist to ease the pain.

'Charlie!' I slapped the door this time. 'Charlie!' I jigged up and down while I waited.

Lexie hardly ever went out. I peered through the letter box. I could see a light on in the kitchen.

'Lexie!' I thudded the wood with my fists. 'Open up.'

The light went out.

'Please. I know you're in there. I've seen you.'

Lexie shuffled, zombie-like, towards the door.

'Are you OK?' I asked, as the door opened.

Lexie had a glazed expression similar to those you saw on the news at the site of a natural disaster. Her face was bare and she looked younger somehow, without the slash of red that usually covered her lips.

'What do you care?' she mumbled; I had to lean forward to hear.

'Where's Charlie?'

'Gone.'

'Gone where? To mine?'

'Travelling.'

'What do you mean?' I snapped, frustrated with her monosyllabic answers.

Lexie lit a cigarette. 'Packed a rucksack and gone. Left.'

'She can't have left. Siobhan's dead.'

'So?'

'What do you mean, "so"? Does Charlie even know? I texted her but I've heard nothing back.'

'Does it matter?'

'Of course it matters. She wouldn't just leave. She's never mentioned going travelling.'

'You don't know everything.'

'I know she wouldn't leave without telling me…'

'Why? Because you're so bleedin' important? Sorry, I forgot the world revolves around you, Grace.'

The door swung towards me and I thrust my foot forward.

'She left me a note,' I said. 'It asked me to forgive her. Forgive her for what? I don't understand this. Tell me what's happening.'

'*She's* not the one who's done something wrong,' Lexie spat. 'Now piss off.' She opened the door wider and slammed it as hard as she could. I jerked my foot out of the way and sank down onto the step. Charlie had left me, just like my mum, just like my dad. Siobhan was gone. I sat motionless as snow fell from the gunmetal-grey sky, until I was as numb on the outside as I was on the inside.

'Please.' I rolled onto my knees and shouted through the letter box. 'Please, Lexie. I need to know the truth. What has Charlie done?'

CHAPTER THIRTY-FIVE
Now

Knock-knock-knock. *Get lost, Dan.* Fury boils and bubbles as I stamp down the hall, fling open the front door.

It's not him. A figure in a black coat is scurrying down the path towards the red Corsa parked in the lane.

'Wait!' Fuelled by the buckets of rage I can't direct towards Dan or Anna, I step out of the door. The figure hurries away. The dampness of the path seeps through my socks, and as the person who's been following me fumbles with the gate, it's the first time I've been thankful for the faulty catch. My hand snakes out and I grab their coat, twisting my fingers into their shoulder. There's a cry of pain and the hood falls back. A mass of blonde corkscrew curls falls free. I snatch my hand back as though I've touched something hot, and hold my wrist. It can't be.

She turns. It isn't Siobhan of course; how could it be? But the resemblance is so striking, it's as if I've been catapulted back in time. We glare at each other, Abby and I.

'You've been following me?' I don't need an answer.

'Yes.' She breaks eye contact and I remember the timid girl who used to creep past me in the school corridors, head down, rucksack slung over one shoulder. She'd never have said boo to a goose without her big sister at one time, but I suppose she had to learn to cope alone. She was three years below us at school, so she must be twenty-two now. What does she want? Revenge? Bring it on. I can't possibly feel any worse than I do already.

'You wanted to frighten me? Kill me? What?' I lean my face towards hers. 'Do your worst.'

She shrank back. 'I wanted to talk to you.'

'And you thought the best way to do that was to follow me? Watch me? Make me think I was going mad?' I'm screaming now, not caring if Mrs Jones hears, and I place my palms against Abby's chest and push her, hard. I've had enough of people's games to last me a lifetime. She falls backwards onto the gate. 'Piss off, Abby.'

'Grace!' Her voice is shrill. 'Please. Help me.' She steps forward as she utters the words her sister said seven years ago, and as much as I want to turn her away, I can't. We stand in the garden. The wind gusts against the gate, which finally springs free from the catch and slams into Abby's back, sending her tumbling to the ground. She looks up, rain streaking her face, hair plastered to her scalp.

'You'd better come in.' I turn towards the cottage.

Inside, Abby curls up in Dan's armchair – my armchair – and cries as though her heart is broken. I busy myself in the kitchen to give me time to think. I'm livid, but I'm not sure how much of my anger is due to Abby or because of Dan and Anna. It's a mixture of all of them, but Abby is the one crying in my lounge. She is the one who has lost a sister and it doesn't seem fair to direct all of my fury at her. I think the least I can do is hear her out. I boil the kettle, pulling cups from the cupboard, trying to drown out the sound of her anguish.

In the lounge, I place the tea tray on the table and clear my throat. Abby snuffles into the sleeve of her jumper.

'Sorry, Grace.' I don't know whether she means for scaring me half to death or for crying and so I don't reply. Instead, I pour tea that's not yet brewed, add a splash of milk and slide it towards her along with the sugar bowl and a spoon.

'What are you doing here?' I ask.

'We've moved back to the village. Grandad has Alzheimer's and Mum wanted to be closer to him.'

'I don't mean the village. I meant here.' I gesture around the room. 'What do you want with me?'

'Being back. There are so many memories. I wanted to talk about Siobhan.'

'Talk?'

'Yes.' She picks up her mug but her hand is shaking so much tea splashes over her lap. I thump a box of Kleenex onto the table before her.

'So why didn't you *talk* instead of behaving like a stalker.'

'I didn't know what to say. I was awful to you at school and I know you've had a rough time. I heard. About Charlie. I'm so sorry.'

I offer a curt nod.

'I practised my speech over and over in my head. Each time I rang and heard your voice I bottled out. Coming here. I thought it might be easier but it wasn't. I couldn't bring myself to knock on the door. Too scared you'd slam it in my face I suppose.'

'You almost ran me off the road, Abby. You could have *killed* me!'

'When I passed you and realised it was your car I was determined that I'd ask you. That I wouldn't chicken out again. I got myself really worked up. It was stupid and I'm so glad I didn't cause an accident. I never meant to hurt you, Grace.' Her face is blotchy and tear-stained and I sigh.

'Well here we are. What do you want to ask me?'

'Grace. Did Siobhan mention me when she called you that night?'

It's one of those times you have a split second to choose, and you know whichever path you take, there'll be no going back.

Abby's eyes are wide and hopeful. What can I say? That I refused to help? Hung up the phone? That I've regretted it ever since? Siobhan could be alive if I'd listened. I could tell Abby that, ultimately, I feel responsible for her sister's death. But what good would my admissions do? They can't bring Siobhan back.

I make my choice. 'Yes,' I say.

Is a lie still a lie if it brings comfort? I suppose it is, but I carry on nevertheless, not sure whether the story I'm fabricating is to console Abby or to appease my own guilt. 'I told her you were looking for her and you were sorry.'

Abby leans forward and twists the tissue she's holding in her hands. 'What did she say?'

'She said it didn't matter. She loved you anyway. She was going to come and find you.'

Lie upon lie. I could build a wall. Abby's body sags and I hold her as she cries. I fetch more tissues, more tea, and we swap stories of the big sister she once idolised. I never knew Siobhan used to have tap-dancing lessons when she was small. Abby didn't know Siobhan was the first person in our year to snog a boy. We all have different sides, I think. The things we share. The things we keep hidden. The good, the bad. The truth, the lies.

It's getting late and I'm exhausted. I offer Abby the spare bed but she wants to get back to her parents. They worry when she's out of sight too long and I can't say I blame them. It's a dangerous world out there, but at least I know there'll be no more shadowy figures outside my cottage, no more red Corsas parked down the lane. I hadn't imagined them. It's a huge relief to know that no matter what Google says about the side effects of my medication, I have a stronger grasp on reality than I'd thought.

'If you want to talk again, call me,' I say to Abby as she pulls her coat back on. 'And don't hang up next time!'

'I won't. Thanks, Grace. I can't tell you what a comfort it is to know Siobhan had forgiven me.'

I lean against the door frame until Abby's little red car disappears from view and I feel I might not have done such a bad thing after all. The truth hurts, doesn't it? And although I'm a long way from forgiving him, I can understand why Dan lied. I shudder when I think of Anna. I lock the front door and pull the chain across.

Hunger growls deep in my belly and I pick up the bag of Chinese food that is still sitting on the lounge table. *Waste not, want not*, Grandma would say. I scoop out some chow mein and put it in the microwave. As the plate spins and the food heats, I light some candles and put on a record. Nat King Cole rotates and crackles 'Maybe it's because I love you too much', and the lyrics slice me to the core. The pain of what Dan did, what Dan and Anna did, is still so raw.

The microwave beeps, my dinner steams. I fork noodles into my mouth but find I'm no longer hungry. I lift the needle from the record and flick the stereo off at the wall, blow out the candles and make a wish. The front and back doors are unyielding as I rattle the door handles, but I check they are locked again and again before I trudge up the stairs, sticking my head in Anna's room on the way, reassuring myself she is really gone. I'm fighting sleep, stifling yawns, but I strip our bed – my bed, now – not wanting to sleep with the smell of Dan. I tuck in hospital corners, ease the duvet into a fresh cover, before I slide between the cold cotton sheets. I curl into myself. My feet are freezing and, despite everything, I wish Dan were here to snuggle against.

CRASH.

My eyes spring open, dart from side to side, seeking out shapes in the blackness. The curtains aren't quite closed and shafts of moonlight slip into the room, casting shadows in every corner. I shudder as a shape looms out of the darkness, but it's only my dressing-table mirror. I've never lived alone before and my heart thump-thump-thumps against my ribs as I push back the covers and swing my legs out of bed. It's only a few short steps to the window but long enough for my mind to envisage a team of burglars forming a human chain, emptying the cottage of my belongings.

I peep out of the window. The lane is dark and quiet, my car the only vehicle I can see. A movement catches my eye and I jump as the wind swings the gate open, before slamming it shut. I berate myself for being so easily spooked and scuttle back to bed. My pulse is still racing; fear has driven drowsiness away and I click on my lamp, squinting in the mandarin glow. I open my book, promise myself no more than two chapters and locate my page, letting the words transport me to another time.

My heart has slowed and my eyelids are beginning to droop when there's a bang. Not the gate, but the front door. I freeze, gripping my book so tightly that the pages crumple. The lamp goes out and the room is plunged into darkness. I whimper and cover my mouth with both hands, trying to stuff the sound back inside. I screw up my face, listening for the telltale creak of the stairs, but the cottage is still. I'm rigid with fear as I sit upright in bed, not daring to move, not wanting the squeak of my mattress springs to give my presence away. My lower back spasms and I shift my weight slightly, wincing as the floorboards below the bed creak. I hold my breath, wondering who's here, whether they've heard me. There are no footsteps tiptoeing up the stairs; the only thing I can hear is the blood whooshing in my ears. I'm beginning to wonder whether I have imagined the whole thing when I begin to cough.

Smoke.

Time slows, logic deserts me and it seems I sit frozen for an interminable time before my hand darts out, scrambling around in the blackness for the phone I cannot locate. Cold water saturates my pyjama sleeve as I knock over my glass, and my feet sink into the sodden carpet as I leap out of bed and run towards the door. My toe stubs against the pine bedstead and I cry out in pain, tumbling forwards, landing heavily on my hands and knees. I stumble to my feet, flicking on the light switch, praying that my lamp has just blown a bulb – but the room remains pitch-black.

My heartbeat pounds in my ears and my palms are slick as I reach the door. I hesitate before I touch the metal handle, but it's cool. For a split second, I think everything's fine, but as I pull the door open, acrid smoke attacks my throat, my nose, my chest. My eyes sting and I slam the door shut, lean my back against it as though I can keep the fire out. My coughing is violent and painful and I'm doubled over, but I propel myself forward, drag the duvet from my bed, and drop to my knees to plug the gap at the bottom of the door. My pyjamas are drenched as sweat pours down my chest and back. The smoke seems thinner nearer the floor and I crawl on my belly over to the window, cling to the radiator and hoist myself to standing with thighs that feel like rubber. The sash window is stuck; it hasn't been open since the summer. I howl in frustration as I thrust upwards over and over until it gives. I lurch forward, and am left half-hanging out of the window, panting for air, like a dog in a hot summer car.

The lane is unlit and still. The solitude I usually love now seems menacing. I scream for Mrs Jones, knowing it's fruitless, that she will likely be asleep, will be unable to hear me over her TV if she isn't. *I'm going to die.* The bushes rustle and I think I see a figure creep from the shadows. I rub my smoke-sore eyes, but when I can focus again, the figure has gone. Every fibre of my being urges me to stay next to the window, to breathe in the air, but I need to find my phone. I crawl over to my bed, feeling around the damp carpet where I spilled the water, and I pray my phone is not wet, is still working. I fumble around; my throat is raw with coughing and just as it feels I can't possibly go on, my hand connects with something cold and hard: my mobile. My thumb presses a button, illuminating the screen and I almost cry with relief. I crawl back to the window – my movements are slower now – and force oxygen into lungs that burn with the effort of keeping me alive.

I punch out 999.

'Emergency, which service do you require?'

I open my mouth to speak, but the solace of hearing a human voice causes my words to clump together and I cannot spit them out.

'Which service do you require, please? Fire, police or ambulance?'

'Fire. Please. Quick,' I rasp.

I'm asked for my name and address. The operator sifts through my garbled sentences, confirms my details. She tells me her name is Mia, reassures me that help is on the way. I describe the layout of my house, let her know which room I'm in. Mia's voice is soft and soothing, her questions gentle, but I'm choking so much I cannot answer them all. I swing my right leg over the ledge, sitting as though I am riding a horse, staring into the blackness below. I tell Mia I'm going to jump. She assures me the engines are close, minutes away, but every cell in my body is fighting for survival. I tuck the phone between my ear and shoulder, grip the windowsill and try to hoist my left leg. My movements are slow, despite the screaming terror inside me. It feels as though I'm stuck in quicksand.

The sirens are faint at first. It's hard to hear over my ragged breath, but I see blue lights flashing down the lane and, as I shriek for help and raise my hands to wave, I feel myself slip and I scream as I fall into blackness.

CHAPTER THIRTY-SIX
Now

I'm hot, so hot. My skin is peeling, flesh melting, dripping from my bones. I open my mouth wide but something is stifling my screams and I'm choking, clawing at my neck, writhing from side to side, trying to release the pressure from my chest.

'Grace.' Warm hands grasp mine, squeezing gently. 'Grace, can you hear me?'

Grandma? It's an effort to open my eyes, they water and blink in the fluorescent strip lighting. Everything's stark and white. I'm tucked too tightly in a bed; the sheets are stiff and hard.

'There's been a fire; you're OK, but we thought…' Grandma's voice wavers. I try to pull my hands free, to sit, to pull out the tubes in my throat.

'Stay still, pet.' Grandad gently presses back on my shoulders. 'I'll fetch the doctor. Your mum's on her way.'

The doctor looks far too young to be qualified. A little boy in an oversized white coat and tortoiseshell round-rimmed glasses. He consults the clipboard at the end of my bed, clears his throat as though he is worried his voice may break mid-sentence. 'Grace, you're a lucky girl.'

I cannot answer, not sure I'd agree if I could.

'Don't be concerned about the tubes; your air tract is slightly swollen from the smoke inhalation and we just want to keep it open. There's no excess fluid on your lungs, no infection. You should be able to leave hospital in forty-eight hours.'

Grandma strokes my palm rhythmically with her thumb and I fight fruitlessly to stay awake.

I float in and out of fitful sleep, haunted by disturbed dreams of swirling flames and spiralling smoke. Grandma tucks a lavender bag under my pillow, but no matter how deeply I inhale, I can only smell soot. I'm never alone. There's an armchair next to my hospital bed and each time I wake, sweat-drenched and panicked, there's always someone with me: my grandparents, my mum, Lyn. I revisit the cottage again and again in my mind. I remember lighting the candles, but not blowing them out. My thoughts spin like a tornado trying to whisk me off to Kansas. I wish I could click my heels three times and go home. *Am I to blame? Am I always to blame?*

The tubes are removed and I vomit blood-streaked bile into a cardboard bowl. My stomach is tender inside and out. It's a relief to pull off the scratchy hospital gown and shower, standing on a tile floor that was once white, the grout now pigeon-grey. I tenderly touch the purple bruising on my abdomen and chest, and tears fall freely as I wonder what would have happened if the fire crew hadn't arrived when they did, if they hadn't carried me to safety when I fell unconscious onto the bedroom floor. I shake out a clean nightgown Grandma has brought in, and hold it to my nose, testing my sense of smell. I get a whiff of Comfort fabric softener. Grandma's smaller than me; the nightdress that is floor-length on her falls to just below my knees, presses against my ribs. I don't know whether all my things are burned and I'm too scared to ask.

Borrowed pink slippers slide from my feet as I shuffle back to the ward, feeling like I've run a marathon. I half expect someone to race up to me and wrap me in a tinfoil blanket. My lungs rattle, my breath rasps and pain darts through my chest.

Grandma folds the sheets back, plumps up my pillow and helps me back to bed. Mum tucks me in like she used to when I was small.

'I know you can't swallow properly yet, but you'll be as right as rain before you know it.' Grandma peels the lid from a Tupperware box, showing me thick slices of lemon drizzle cake.

The citrus smell makes me cough and Grandma dabs my eyes, handing me a Kleenex to blow my nose. The tissue turns black and I scrunch it into a ball. Aim it at my bedside table.

'Will you be OK on your own for a few hours? Denise is poorly and can't deliver the meals to the old folks. I've offered to help. Your mum is going to help me. Grandad's gone to get the car.'

Grandma may be seventy-two but she helps the 'old folk' whenever she can.

I nod.

'I can stay if you want me to?' Mum asks, but I shake my head. My throat hurts too much to talk. I watch them bustle down the ward and through the swinging doors before I curl onto my side, closing my eyes. My dreams are bright and vibrant. Impulse body spray tickles my nostrils and I dream that Charlie and I are running through the forest. Leaves rustle and branches bend to tell me their secrets. I strain to make out their hushed tones.

Saliva has deserted me and I prop myself up as I wake, reaching for my water jug. On my cabinet is a present, wrapped in shiny gold paper. My name is scrawled onto a label in writing I vaguely recognise but can't identify. The box rattles as I shake it. I glance around the ward to see if anyone is watching me before I ease the tape from one end and lift open the flap. I slide the present out.

I drop the box on my bed and recoil, as though it's a snake that might bite me. I press myself back hard against my pillow as I stare in horror at the box of chocolate brazil nuts. There's only one person who would have bought me nuts, who has bought me nuts before. *Anna.*

Grandma tucks the purple and pink crocheted blanket around my legs, despite the lounge being at least twenty-five degrees. This is the blanket that covered me when I had German measles and tonsillitis. I pull it up to my chin. The TV blares to life as I zap it on with the remote control. I search for the right button to turn the volume down: Grandad must have been the last person to watch it.

Grandma pulls out the smallest of the nest of mahogany tables and places it next to the sofa, then sets down a glass of Ribena and a plate of party rings. I feel about six but am grateful to be here, to have slept in my old bedroom last night, free from the clattering of trollies and the stage whispers of the nurses. Mum has gone back to Devon, reassured there's no lasting damage. Not physically, anyway.

I'm enthralled by *Jeremy Kyle*, equally horrified and fascinated by the drama as I suck on a biscuit, the sweet pink icing dissolving on my tongue. Grandma pretends she isn't watching, that she's just knitting, but every now and then the needles stop clicking and I hear her tut.

There's a rap at the door and Grandma heaves herself out of her chair. It seems she has aged in the past few days. She closes the lounge door behind her but I hear a male voice resonate down the hallway and I smooth my hair, brush crumbs from my nightgown, thinking it must be Dan. I breathe into my cupped hand, trying to remember if I've cleaned my teeth today, wishing I'd showered and dressed.

The door starts to open and I arrange myself on the sofa, feeling ridiculous that I still want Dan to find me attractive.

'Grace…' Grandma gestures to the men behind her. I don't recognise them. 'I'll get Grandad.'

'Grace, I'm DS Harry Mills and I'm in charge of the investigation into the origin and cause of the fire at Rose Cottage,' says the taller of the two men. 'My colleague is Fire Investigator Mick Walker from Oxfordshire Fire and Rescue Services, who also has some questions to ask.'

I squirm like a child before a headmaster and pull my blanket higher.

Grandad bustles into the room, drying his hands on his dark brown cords. 'Sit down, gentlemen, please.'

The men sit in armchairs but don't lean back. Their long legs stretch out in front of them and the room seems small and cramped.

There is the chinking of china and Grandma hands out cups and saucers, pours tea from the Royal Doulton teapot she saves for best. The party rings are whipped away, replaced with dark chocolate digestives that no one eats. I wait, twisting my fingers through the holes in the blanket, for the questions to start.

'What time did you go to bed on the night of the fire, Grace?'

I can't exactly remember and I feel heat rise to my face as though I have something to hide.

'About eleven, I think,' I croak and Grandad shifts up the settee towards me, passes me a glass of water.

'Was anyone else in the house with you?'

'No.'

'And when you left the lounge, everything was switched off? Appeared normal?'

'She's been brought up not to waste electric,' says Grandma.

I grip Grandad's hand. 'I thought I turned everything off, blew out the candles…' I study the carpet. Grandad squeezes my fingers.

'Where were the candles?'

'On the mantelpiece.'

'The origin of the fire was the wastepaper bin next to the table. Were there any candles or ignition sources nearby?'

'No.'

'There was a match in the bin – do you smoke, Grace?'

'No.' I shake my head, trying to dislodge my confusion. 'I don't keep matches in the house; I never use them.'

'Are you aware there was no battery in the smoke alarm in the hallway?'

'No…'

'There was,' Grandad interjects. 'I check it regularly, only replaced it a couple of weeks ago. Duracell, too. Worth the extra money for peace of mind.'

'Was the building secure when you went to bed?'

'Yes. I checked the doors several times.'

'The firefighters had to break in.'

'I don't understand?'

Mick takes off his silver-rimmed glasses. His eyes lock onto mine. 'We believe that the fire was started deliberately. The fact that the property was secure when you went to bed and was still secure when we arrived indicates that either someone who was already in the house, or another keyholder, set the fire. The chain was still across the front door, so entry wasn't gained that way. Who has keys to the back door, Grace?'

Icy tendrils kiss the back of my neck; the hairs on my arms stand to attention.

'Anna,' I whisper. 'Anna does.'

CHAPTER THIRTY-SEVEN
Now

Grandad whips his handkerchief from his pocket and dabs Grandma's eyes. She snatches it from him. 'I've already got enough wrinkles, thank you, without you pulling at my skin.' Grandad pulls a face behind her back. As much as it feels as though everything has changed, it's reassuring to believe, however naively, that some things never will.

An almost indecipherable voice announces that my train will be departing imminently. My case is small but heavy and I strain to pick it up. I pat my pocket, reassure myself my ticket is safe inside.

'You don't have to go,' says Grandma. 'That Anna doesn't scare me.'

'Well, she should.'

'You could stay,' Grandad says.

'It's better I don't. Not until the police catch her.' I offer one-armed hugs. 'I'll text you when I'm there.'

I heft my luggage aboard the train, swivelling my head around to make sure I'm not being followed, and stand in the carriage doorway, scanning the other passengers for a glimpse of shiny blonde hair. Satisfied that Anna isn't on board, I move a discarded newspaper from a seat peppered with cigarette burns – despite the 'no smoking' signs peeling from the windows – and sit. The floor is grey with dirt. I rest my handbag on my lap and place my case on the seat next to me. The doors slide shut, trapping in the stagnant air, awash with smoke, perfume and body odour. I peer out of the streaked window and wave my goodbyes.

The train rumbles as we begin to move, rattles as we pick up speed. I rest my head against the grimy glass and watch fields flash past. The book I brought for my journey remains unopened and I am lost in my own thoughts until we reach King's Cross. I stand and gather my belongings while the train is pulling in, clenching my buttocks to stabilise myself as I rock from side to side. I disembark and grip the handles of my bags tightly as shoulders jostle me; every inch of space seems to be accounted for. I jump with each nudge, terrified it's Anna. There is a hand on my shoulder. I swing around with a cry.

'It's me.' Esmée envelops me with her slight arms, squeezing me close. She's stronger than she looks. *Now we are only two.* I haven't seen her since Charlie's funeral, but I don't hug her back. Determined not to let my emotions out on a busy platform. Scared that if my sorrow is released, it may flood the tracks, engulfing everyone in its path, it feels so enormous.

'You're safe now,' she whispers into my hair, and I try to think of something happy to stop myself from crying.

'Let's get you home.' Esmée takes my case and I'm glad to have someone take charge. The journey has wiped me out. I don't think I've recovered properly from the fire yet.

Esmée navigates the Tube with a confidence belying the shy girl she once was. I slump, exhausted, in my seat, staring at the map on the wall. Red, blue, green strands of spaghetti twisting through the capital. Yet another thing I cannot make sense of; I could make a list. I close my eyes. The vibrations are soothing and I yawn.

'It's our stop next.' Esmée pats my knee.

I stand and lurch forward, grabbing Esmée's arm to right myself. I glance around but no one's looking at me, and I take comfort from my anonymity. We walk through littered streets. I press myself close to Esmée, flinching at the cacophony of honking horns. I breathe in the smell of exhaust fumes and fast food, and long for clean country air.

Esmée slows and stops in front of a row of shops.

'Home sweet home. Don't let the outside put you off.' To the left of a launderette is a canary yellow door, its flaking paint covered with graffiti. Esmée slides her key into the lock, twists, and kicks the bottom of the door. 'It always sticks.'

My case bumps off the walls as we ascend the narrow staircase, and it's so gloomy I strain to see where I am going, despite the naked bulb swinging from the ceiling. Esmée unlocks a solid grey door at the top and we're there.

The flat is matchbox-small, tastefully decorated in soft cream. Esmée has inherited the effortless stylishness of her Parisian mother. The lounge, diner and kitchen are tiny sections of the same room. Esmée crosses to the window in four steps, hefts the sash upwards. Warm air merges with warmer air.

'You're lucky you've come in spring. The heat from the dryers downstairs means it's always hot in here. Lovely in the winter, but quite unbearable in the summer. I'm not often here in the day, though. Have a nose around while I make a cuppa.' Esmée strides to the kitchen area. 'You can take the bedroom, hun; I'll use the sofa bed.' Esmée waves away my protests with one hand, pulls black glossy mugs from a cupboard with the other.

I open the first of two doors leading from the lounge. Every wall in the bathroom has been tiled white, the floor a chessboard. The door can only close once I've shuffled between the basin and toilet. I can almost reach out my arms and touch both sides of the room at once. The glass shower cubicle gleams. It is filled with Molton Brown products and I suddenly feel grubby from my journey. I move on.

The bedroom has eggshell walls, mirrored furniture and turquoise silk bedding. It will be my cocoon. I might emerge a butterfly.

'I'm lucky to have a separate bedroom. Many don't.'

I start as Esmée appears behind me. I take the mug she offers.

'Of course, I could get a three-bedroomed semi for the same price at home, but who wants to be stuck in a place that's too big to be a village, too small to be a town, where the most exciting thing to ever happen was when the pipes burst at school and we all got the week off?' She shrugs. 'This is London, baby. There are new faces every time I step out the door, and if I happen to sneeze, there aren't three people on my step within an hour, bearing casseroles and circulating rumours that I've caught the plague.'

'It's perfect, Esmée. I really appreciate it.' And I do. 'But don't you miss home at all?' I like knowing everyone nearby, I think. The gossip, the collective outrage when the post office cut their collections back to once a day. It was all anyone could talk about for weeks. Boring, some might say, but it felt safe to me. Well, it did. Before Anna.

'Sometimes, but I love living here. There's such a buzz. Always something going on. The village never felt the same without Siobhan. And now Charlie… I can't see me ever moving back properly. I feel I belong here.'

'I don't know where I belong any more.' I slurp tea, try to swallow the tremor in my voice. 'Can I take a shower?'

'You don't have to ask.'

The jet of water that falls from the showerhead is so powerful, I find myself gasping for breath as I rub water from my eyes, and twist the dial to turn the pressure down. Esmée's shampoo smells of ginger, but it doesn't matter how many times I lather my scalp, I still smell the faint tinge of smoke in my hair.

The towel is as fluffy as cotton wool and I rub myself dry in the bedroom, examine the contents of my case strewn over Esmée's bed. I contemplate getting dressed, but pull on pyjamas instead. The carpet is soft underfoot as I pad barefoot to the lounge.

Later, plates heaped with spinach lasagne balance on our knees and we chortle through a re-run of *Friends* while we eat, marvelling at how little Jennifer Aniston has aged. I'm grateful for the normality, the pretence that this could be a social visit. Despite Esmée's objections, I crowd beside her in the kitchen, drying the plates that she's washed squeaky clean, stacking them neatly on the narrow work surface.

'So how are you, really?' Esmée dries her hands, pours me a glass of Pinot, ushers me over to the sofa.

'I'm fine.'

Esmée raises an eyebrow.

'OK.' I sigh. 'I've been better. A few months ago I had a great job, a cat, a fabulous home, a boyfriend who I loved. I really did love him.'

Esmée squeezes my hand.

'He came to my grandparents' house to try to see me,' I say. 'Grandad had to stop Grandma clobbering him with her rolling pin.'

'He's a dickhead.'

'I know, but he was my dickhead. He keeps calling me.'

'To say what?'

'I don't pick up.'

'Good girl.'

'He texts, too. He wants to meet. To explain.'

Esmée raises her eyebrows. 'There's no explanation for what he's done. He's not the Dan I thought I knew.'

'Me neither.' I rest my head on Esmée's shoulder. 'I can't believe what he's done, and I don't understand why Anna hated me so much.' I glance around the room, as if she might spring out from behind the furniture.

'I don't know. Maybe she was jealous, hun. In love with Dan?'

'He's adamant it was a one-off; it didn't mean anything. But even if that is true, I guess she could have still developed feelings for him. '

'Perhaps she couldn't stand being rejected?'

'Maybe. I'm so glad I didn't introduce her to Lexie. Imagine what that would have done to her, thinking there was a piece of Charlie still living on, and then finding out it was all a lie?'

'Anna's insane. You don't have to worry about her any more.'

But we both know that's not true.

'She'll be locked up for a very long time, Grace, you'll see. You can't go around trying to murder people.'

I shiver. 'It was arson with intent to endanger life, apparently.'

'Same thing. Crazy bitch.'

'I just wish the police could find her.'

Esmée coaxes the last few drops of wine into my glass, then fetches another bottle from the kitchen, shakes Kettle Chips into a bowl.

'And the cottage? Have you lost everything?'

'No, thankfully. The fire was contained, the carpet is burned and some of the furniture scorched, but everything's mostly smoke-damaged. Grandma's washed the clothes in my wardrobe three times but…' My voice cracks. 'There was so much smoke.'

'You're very lucky.'

'So I've been told.'

'What happens now?'

'The cottage is sealed. All my valuables are in Grandad's garage. The police have all they need, so it's in the hands of the insurance company now. It'll be about a month before it's ready.'

'You're welcome to stay as long as you want.'

'I appreciate that. I didn't want to go to Mum's. Oliver's daughter practically lives there with her kids and there's barely enough room as it is. Once Anna's caught, I can go home, stay with my grandparents. The police said I'd get priority response if I called them again, but I just couldn't risk it. I don't want to endanger anyone.' I crunch a crisp; the salt and vinegar stings my sore throat. 'Anna won't look for me here.'

'Of course she won't,' Esmée says, and we fall into silence as we drink our wine. I try not to flinch as a car alarm sounds outside, reassuring myself that I'm safe, that Anna won't find me. But I can't help wondering where she is.

CHAPTER THIRTY-EIGHT
Now

The coffee pot steams and bubbles and I pour scalding liquid into Esmée's travel mug, hand her a banana. She unplugs her mobile from the wall, drops it into her cavernous bag.

'What are your plans today? It'll be really uncomfortable here. They've forecast a mini heatwave. Typical. It's boiling in April, and when I'm off in August it will most likely rain.'

'I might go out.' I lie. This is our daily script. I wait for the part when Esmée tells me to have a good day and I smile brightly and say I will, but instead she slaps a shopping list on the worktop.

'Can you pick up a few bits then, hun?'

'I'm not sure…'

'Grace, there are approximately ten million people living in London. Even if Anna knew you were here, which she doesn't…'

'You don't know that.'

'You've been here nearly a week. If she was going to find you, she'd have done it by now.'

'You don't know her.'

'Neither do you, not really. What are you going to do if they never catch her? Stay in forever?'

I chew my thumbnail. Esmée sighs, her hand spiders over the list and she scrunches it up.

'Sorry, Grace. I don't want to push you. I just hate seeing you like this.'

I cover her hand in mine. 'Leave the list. I'll try.'

'You don't have to…'

'I know. Now scoot or you'll miss your train.'

I bow my head, smoothing the crumpled paper as she gathers her keys, picks up her coffee.

'Have a good day, Grace. Feel free to rummage through my wardrobe for something summery.'

I blink away tears, smile brightly. 'I will.'

Esmée's heels click-clack down the wooden staircase and I shut the door to the flat, pull the chain across. Seeds scatter over the worktop as I drop granary bread into the toaster. I scoop them into my hand, drop them into the sink and I flick through Esmée's DVDs as I wait: *The Shining*, *Poltergeist*, *Halloween*. Movies I'd watch from behind a cushion at the best of times. The toast pops, making me jump. I tweezer it out with a thumb and finger, spread thick layers of butter and Marmite. I eat standing, palm scooped under my chin to catch the crumbs. The day stretches before me, long and lonely. I swallow the last of my breakfast, rinse my fingers. My phone vibrates, skittering across the counter. It's Dan. His calls have tapered off but he still rings at least three times a day. I don't answer, I never do. The phone stills, its battery almost drained even though I haven't used it once since I got here. I haven't got my charger and Esmée's is not compatible with mine.

The windows rattle in time to the drilling outside and I rub my temples, trying to ease away the headache that's snaking its way around my skull. I study the map Esmée has left me, trace the underground routes with my index finger. Work out which line I'd need if I were to venture out. *If.*

I curl on the sofa, punch numbers into Esmée's landline.

'Grace, how are you?'

'I'm OK. Any news?' Grandad's been calling the police daily.

'Not yet, but they'll catch her. Don't you worry.' He coughs and I hold the receiver away from my ear.

'Are you OK?'

'Fine. We both have a bit of a cold, but it's nothing. Grandma's out sorting donations at the charity shop. Mrs Jones has had a fall.'

'Oh, no. Is she OK?'

'Needs a new hip. Luckily the decorators heard her banging on the wall with her walking stick. She's in St. Anne's. Don't want to visit and take my germs in.'

'I'll go and see her when I come home. I might go out today.' I wait for the protests. For the 'it isn't safe's.

'Fresh air will do you good.' Grandad has never been to London.

'The air here…' But there is a buzzing against my ear and then nothing.

'Grandad?' I can't hear anything so I dial again, am met with silence.

I jolt as there is a thumping at the door downstairs. The phone thuds to the sofa and I drop to my knees. Cover my mouth with my hands. The banging comes louder this time and I crawl over to the window. Raise myself until I am peeping over the ledge. There is a figure below with a baseball cap on. I can see a glimpse of blonde hair sticking out from beneath the New York Yankees logo. Heat whooshes through my body. The thumping comes again and the figure steps back, looks up.

I dart down, but not quickly enough; they have seen me, I have seen them.

I clatter down the stairs, open the door a crack. Nod as the workman tells me he is replacing cables, that I may experience temporary problems with my phone line.

The door clicks behind me and, as I lock it, I wonder when I became so frightened. Whether it's purely because of Anna or if the fear runs deeper. I don't think I've felt properly safe since Dad died. I've always carried a sense of unease. I think of Grandma, carrying on regardless, despite Anna, despite feeling ill, and I want her to be as proud of me as I am of her. A quiet courage creeps over me. Maybe this new life I've been thrust into isn't what I'd have chosen, but maybe, just maybe, it'll be the right one for me.

Esmée has a flowing floral maxi dress that fits me and I slip her sandals onto my feet. I try to fold the map but it doesn't seem to fit together, so I concertina it as best I can and tuck it inside my messenger bag. I gather my keys and my courage and venture into London on my own for the very first time.

The brick wall presses hard against my spine as I flatten myself against it, fighting the urge to return home. I've never seen so many people jostling for space before. No one makes eye contact, everyone's in a rush and I'm not even in the centre yet. I inch my way to the Tube. My whispered apologies are unacknowledged and it takes an age to get to the station.

Two trains rumble past before I have the courage to hop on, darting out of the way of the door before it closes. I plant myself in the centre of the carriage, feet hip-width apart, and clutch the pole with both hands. I barely wobble as the train sets off and I chalk up my first victory of the day. *Baby steps, Grace.* A muffled voice announces we're at Charing Cross and I follow the crowd – sharp elbows and banging briefcases – to the ticket barrier, before I climb the steps to daylight. It's bright outside and I blink as I'm propelled forward, clutching my bag. *London is rife with pickpockets, Grace*, Grandma warned me.

My borrowed sandals slap against the pavement. I have nowhere to go, nothing to do. It's liberating and unsettling all at the same time. There's a mishmash of shops lining the streets. The smell of incense merges with the aroma of hamburgers and Lush soaps. I spot a phone shop on the opposite side of the road, jab the crossing button with my finger and wait for the green man.

'I'd like a new iPhone.'

'Certainly, madam; do you wish to keep your existing number?'

'Absolutely not.'

The sheer magnitude of the crowd is overwhelming and, as I wander around, I can't shake the sensation that I'm being followed. I think I see a figure in my peripheral vision. The hairs on the back of my neck prickle. I stop dead and spin around, but there's nothing but a sea of irritated faces swerving past me and I tell myself to stop being so paranoid.

The pigeons strut around my feet as I sit on the steps of Trafalgar Square. I fling them some chips. There's just enough battery left in my old phone to scroll through my contacts, transferring the numbers I want to keep. I'll send them a message so they have my new number. I feel a pang as I reach Dan's, but I remind myself why I'm getting a new phone and fight the urge to text him. A fresh start. The plastic casing of my old mobile snaps off easily. I remove the SIM, scrunch it inside my empty chip wrapper and toss it in the nearest bin. I can never remember numbers, and although it wouldn't be too hard to find out Dan's if I really wanted to, it feels like a step forward.

It's ridiculous to think it's only April. The heat is oppressive; it builds and builds. My feet swell and my sandals squeeze tight. I pass a man on the steps bundled with his belongings, a cap before him cradling coppers and a chewing-gum wrapper.

'Is this any good to you?' I hold out my old phone. 'It's Samsung's latest model. Can you pawn it? I don't have the charger, but…'

The man swipes the phone. Stuffs it in his rucksack.

There's a cafe in front of me, and I sit at a round table, shielded by a blue and white striped umbrella, and sip at a berry smoothie, playing with my new phone. It's over. Dan and Anna can't contact me, won't find me.

'Stifling, isn't it?' The waitress wipes her brow with her apron. 'Do you have everything you need?'

'Yes,' I say. 'I think I do.'

As much as I want to see Big Ben, the Tower of London, all the things I've read about, I'm exhausted – feet hot and swollen – and I still have to find the things on Esmée's shopping list. I trudge towards the Tube, and notice a neon pink tattoo sign flashing. I push open the door. It's time to spread my wings.

'Can you fit me in without an appointment?' I cross my fingers behind my back, even though I'm not quite sure what I want the answer to be.

'What do you want?'

'A small tattoo of a butterfly, here.' I point to the back of my shoulder.

'Yeah, no problem. Look through these design books, see if anything takes your fancy while I finish my coffee.'

'Thanks.' I thumb through pages of swirling designs, Celtic bands and intricate lettering, stopping when I see a tattoo similar to Charlie's. 'That's the one.' I tap the image with my finger.

'Nice and simple. My name's Rick. Follow me.'

The room is small and private and I slide Esmée's dress off my shoulder and lie on my front. A fan whirrs in the corner and every few seconds I'm hit by a blast of warm air.

'Ready?' Rick asks.

'Yes,' I say. I am.

The needle touches my skin and I tense. It hurts but it isn't unbearable. I unclench my hands, take deep breaths through my nose.

Look at me, Charlie. I'm flying.

*

My shoulder stings and I can't help but pat the dressing again, as if reassuring myself that I'm really that brave. When I lost my virginity, I thought everyone would know just by looking, that there was something different about me. That I'd changed. That's how I feel now as I stand on the platform, waiting for the Tube. Self-conscious but proud – it's an achievement of sorts. I glance around, almost expecting someone to question me, to ask about my dressing, but it's not like home – people don't just strike up conversations in the city. I half smile at a couple standing next to me. They both have tattoos. *Look,* I want to say. *I'm one of you.*

That's when I see her. Next to the archway. A flash of shiny blonde hair, a baby-pink leather jacket and then she's gone. *Anna.*

I crane my neck. Stand on tiptoes. But fear has made me dizzy and I stumble backwards. My fingers drum against my thigh – *think, Grace, think*. My head jerks from side to side, frantic eyes searching, as I breathe in to the count of five, exhale slowly. I tell myself that I shouldn't be scared, not here. I'm surrounded by people. Safety in numbers. It's when I am alone I should be frightened. When every shadow screams danger.

I can't see her. I scan the crowd, picking out blonde women. None of them wearing a pink jacket. None of them Anna. My heart begins to slow as I think I might have been mistaken. That it isn't her. Couldn't be her. But then I see it again. The swinging blonde hair. A glimpse of pink. A surge of anger floods my veins, drowning out my fear. She killed my cat. Destroyed my home. Ruined my relationship. What more does she want? I loop my bag across my body and shoulder through the passengers, ignoring the throbbing as my new tattoo is knocked. The hunted becomes the hunter.

My arms are stretched in front of me like an Egyptian mummy as I fight my way through the throng, thinking of what I might do when I catch her – but then I shake that thought away. I've lost sight of her. There are too many people, scowling and swearing as I push forward, and my adrenaline ebbs away. I stop, suddenly aware I've been muttering to myself. I must look crazy, and I wonder if I am. I think, I should go.

There is a juddering and a roaring. A sudden whoosh of air. I turn towards the Tube train thundering towards me. Step closer to the edge. I can't wait to get back to the flat. Train lights rocket from the blackness to my right. Hands slap against my shoulders, shoving me forwards. My body instinctively pushes back, trying to right itself, but it's too late. I'm thrust forward. My arms windmill as I fall. The tracks race up to meet me and I screw my eyes up tight.

CHAPTER THIRTY-NINE
Now

Esmée paces the carpet as I stretch on the sofa, cupping a mug of tea, trying to calm myself.

'You were deliberately pushed?'

'Yes.'

'It wasn't just someone knocking into you? I know how busy the platforms get.'

'I thought I saw…'

'Grace, I believe you think you saw her, but realistically, there are thousands of blonde women in London; millions, probably.' Esmée spins to face me. 'Are you sure?'

I close my eyes. See flashes of blonde. Pink leather. But no matter how hard I try, I can't see her face.

'I had a really strong feeling.'

'Grace.' Esmée crouches down to my level, the way I used to do at work with the small children. 'If you think it was her, we need to call the police.'

'And say what? I think someone tried to kill me but I didn't see them, there are no witnesses and I'm fine.'

'What about the lad that saved you?'

Who'd have thought that a pierced teenager, the sort I'd normally cross the road to avoid, would save my life? He'd grabbed my messenger bag, jerking me upright like a marionette. I can still feel the strap of my bag where it sliced into my skin as I was wrenched back to safety.

'He jumped on the train before I could thank him.'

'Let's call your grandad. See what he thinks.'

'No. He's not well; neither is Grandma. He'd only worry. They both would.'

Esmée presses the heels of her hands against her eyes. 'They'd want to know. What about your mum?'

'She's too busy with Oliver's family. Look, I'm fine. I probably just got knocked in the crowds like you said. I'm jumpy at the moment, anyway.' I put my mug down, the tea now cold and unappealing. Turn my mouth into a smile. 'It was an accident. Anna doesn't know I'm here, she can't.'

But as I plump up the cushion behind me and lean back, I can still feel the imprints of hands on my spine. The shove. The fall. The fear.

My tail bone rises and head lowers as I stretch my body into downward dog. It's been far too long since I've practised yoga. I'd forgotten how much I enjoy it. I exhale, transition into child's pose. Tension eases from my body and my breath is slow and even. Crashing waves sound from the iPod dock and a warm breeze flows through the open window. I inhale, prepare to move into cat pose.

There's a thudding on the outer door and irritation skitters through me. I focus on my breath again, try to reclaim my inner calm. Close my eyes. Listen to the waves. Whoever it is will go away. There's a few seconds of silence before the thudding begins again. I crawl over to the window on my knees, raise my arms to lower the sash. There's another knock. I glance down. Freeze, as I recognise the hand fisted towards the door. My arms are suspended in mid-air.

'Dan.' I blurt out his name before I can stop myself. He tilts his face up, pale and unshaven. 'How did you know I was here?'

'I rang Esmée.'

'She told you?'

'She said she hadn't seen you, but she was really abrupt with me. I didn't believe her.'

'What do you want?'

'Can I come in?'

'No. I've got nothing to say to you.'

'Then just listen, Please, Grace.'

'No.'

'I love you.'

I catch the words and screw them up, before throwing them back down at him in their new form. 'I hate you.'

'You don't, and I'm not moving until I've said what I came to say.'

'Suit yourself.' I try to slam the sash down but it sticks and I have to rock it left to right to inch it shut. I feel my face burn as Dan pleads on the street below. His voice grows fainter as the window closes and I swish the curtains together, sit cross-legged on the floor with my back against the radiator. Part of me wants to hear what he has to say, but I don't move to let him in.

The flat grows darker although it's only two o'clock, and a bolt of lightning illuminates the room, rumbling thunder hot on its tail. Rain lashes against the windows and I tug the curtains apart, peer out onto the gloomy street below. Dan is shifting his weight from foot to foot, hands thrust into pockets, hair plastered to his scalp. A white van zooms past and a sea of water covers him. He splutters, wipes his eyes.

'Please,' he mouths as he spots me at the window.

I hesitate, nod and pull on a hoodie, run a brush through my hair before I open the door.

*

Dan peels off his T-shirt and rubs a towel hard against his skin. I busy myself carrying the kettle over to the sink, even though I know it already contains enough water to make tea. I don't want to look at Dan's chest. See the freckles I've kissed. The shoulders I have cried against. I set mugs on the coffee table and perch at the opposite end of the sofa. The silence expands between us, filling the room, sucking out the air. I chew the inside of my cheek. I won't be the first to speak. I'll listen to what Dan has to say calmly and then I'll watch him leave as I stay here with my dignity.

Dan drains his tea. Leans back. He clasps his fingers together and rests them behind his head, elbows jutting out to the side. He may look relaxed but his right knee is jiggling up and down and I know that inside he is squirming. He clears his throat.

'My behaviour was inexcusable.'

'Which part? Letting me believe I'd found Charlie's sister or bringing your mistress into our home?'

'She was never my mistress, Grace. It was a one-off. A mistake.'

'A mistake that I've paid for. You killed my cat, destroyed our home. I nearly died. Is that what you wanted? To get rid of me?'

Dan looks stricken. 'No. I didn't. I want…'

'I don't care what you want.' I'm sick of his excuses.

'I don't blame you…'

'That's big of you.'

'Grace, please…'

'Please what? Please forgive me even though I'm a lying, cheating bastard? Why… Are… You… Here?' My pulse is rapid. I lean forward. 'What the fuck do you want?' Molten lava flows through my veins.

'To talk.' His voice is low and quiet.

'I don't want to listen!' I'm afraid of what he might say, but at the same time I'm desperate to hear. I don't know what to do.

'So why did you let me in? Look, I know that I've been—' his voice breaks. He inhales, begins again. 'I know that I've been a dick.'

I nod. That much, at least, is true.

'When Charlie died, you became so insular. So separate. I didn't know how to reach you.'

'I'm so sorry my best friend died, she…' Sarcasm drips from my voice.

'She wasn't just *your* friend though was she, Grace? But my feelings weren't important. It was all about you.'

I sit back, speechless.

'I'm not saying that's wrong. I know Charlie dying brought back memories of your dad. You had a lot to deal with, but so did I.'

I twist a tissue in my fingers.

'Remember, Grace. Remember how it was. You completely shut yourself off from everything. I was trying to support you emotionally, keep the house going, do the cooking – and you know how crap I am at that. I was scared to take time off because they were making redundancies. I wasn't sure if you'd ever go back to work and I was worried we'd only have my wage to rely on. I was so stressed.'

'You never said,' I mumble.

'You never asked how I was. Not once.'

I raise my head and his eyes, dark-ringed and bloodshot, lock onto mine. The same eyes that have watched me grow up, seen me grieve, drank in the sight of my naked body.

'I'm sorry,' I say and I am. 'But… Anna…'

'Anna meant nothing to me. She served pints and listened and it felt good to be listened to. To be able to talk about Charlie, and she seemed interested…'

'Interested in you.'

'It wasn't like that. I wish I hadn't…'

'Fucked her.'

'Yes.'

'Dan, why did Charlie leave so suddenly when we were eighteen? What did she mean by the note? What did she need to be forgiven for? I know I've asked you before, but if you're holding out on me, you have to tell me.'

Dan scrunches his face in confusion. 'I don't know. But…'

'Why did you move Anna into our home?' I fire questions at him, not giving him time to think. He normally clasps his hands together like he's praying whenever he lies, but his palms remain on his knees.

'I didn't want to. I was so scared she'd forward the film to everyone. You were doing so well: back at work, we were getting closer again. I didn't want to blow it.'

'She must have family, friends. Has she never heard of a hotel?'

'She said she had no one. I thought about paying for a B&B, but you'd have seen it on the credit card statements. I couldn't have explained it.'

'Pretending to be Charlie's sister, though? That was deliberate and cruel.'

'I panicked. She called the night we set up the blog and everything. I didn't know how I'd explain her any other way. I told her she could store her things and sleep in the spare room but not to get friendly with you.'

'Friendly? She almost killed me.'

'What she did was unforgivable, but…'

'What you both did was unforgivable.'

'I know. I never meant to hurt you. I thought she'd stay for a few days until she got herself sorted and then she'd go. You'd

never find out about us. I've come to say I'm sorry. I really am.'
Dan drops his face into his hands and I know he's crying, but I
can't comfort him, I just can't. I collect up the mugs. Flick on
the kettle.

When he is still and silent I pad over to the sofa.

'Dan, you have to go.'

'Come home with me.'

'I can't. It isn't safe. Not that it's safe here.'

'What do you mean?'

His forehead creases as I tell him what happened at the Tube
station.

'My God. Come back, Grace. Let me look after you. Please.'

He lifts a tendril of hair and tucks it behind my ear, trails the
tips of his fingers along my cheekbone.

'Dan…' I draw back, but he cups my face, rests his forehead
against mine, and I don't move, can't move. My breathing is
ragged; the rest of the room is sucked away until there is Dan,
only Dan, and our lips touch, feather-soft. He releases my face
but I don't move; I groan as he thumbs my nipples. My thighs are
wet and I squirm in my seat. Clothes are tugged, heaped on the
floor, and I straddle him, his hands clasping my waist. It is quick.
He grunts my name and pulls me close to him. Afterwards, I
can't believe what just happened. I scoop up my clothes, holding
them in front of me like a shield.

'I'd forgotten how beautiful you are,' says Dan. 'Don't get
dressed. Where's the bedroom? Let's lie down.'

The word 'lie' echoes around the room, bouncing off every
surface until it slaps me to my senses. No matter what happened,
or why, he deliberately tried to cover up what happened with
Anna and I can't forgive him for that.

'I can't do this.' I wriggle back into my knickers, clasp my bra.
'This was a mistake.'

'It didn't feel like a mistake. We're good together.'

'There has to be more than good sex…'

'Great sex…'

I zip up my hoodie. 'Things haven't been right between us for a long time, Dan. It's not just about Anna.'

'I know. There's Charlie…' Dan pulls his T-shirt on.

'It isn't about Charlie, either. We've grown apart. I like staying in; you love going out. I like things tidy; you think I have OCD. I've always been too clingy, terrified of being alone, scared of losing you the way I lost my dad.'

'You haven't lost me…'

'But I did, and you know what? The world didn't come to an end. I'm still here, and I think, that despite everything, I'm doing OK. I think I need this. To be on my own. Figure out what it is I really want. Be honest: were you happy, before this, before Charlie?'

The words spill from my tongue and come to rest in a giant question mark in front of Dan, demanding an answer.

Dan pauses for the longest time. 'No, I wasn't.'

There's nothing to be heard but the sound of our own breathing. Of hearts that used to beat together now marching to their own separate rhythm. Strangers become friends, become lovers, become everything – and then become nothing. A full circle.

'You should go.' I feel as though I could sleep for a week.

He stands. 'I am sorry, Grace. For everything.'

I nod. 'I know.'

'But you're wrong about one thing.'

'What?'

'You've gone through life thinking you needed me. That you couldn't cope if I were to leave you, like your dad did, like Charlie. But it doesn't matter how anxious you get or how afraid you feel, you keep going. You never give up. It wasn't you that needed me, Grace. It was me that needed you. You're the strong one. You can do anything. You've got to stop blaming yourself. None of it was your fault.'

His words slap me and I feel dizzy as he opens the arms I once never wanted to leave. I step into them and inhale his Dan-scent. It's over and we both know it. Memories of us will dwindle and fade until Dan becomes just a boy I once knew.

'Friends?' he whispers into my hair.

'Maybe.'

Tears blur my eyes as I watch Dan slouch down the street until he disappears from view. My mobile vibrates and I half hope it's him, asking if he can come back, until I remember that he doesn't know I have a new phone. It's a text from Lexie and I slide my thumb right to display it.

Urgent – I'm in hospital – can u come?

CHAPTER FORTY
Now

We could be anywhere as we rumble through the midnight-blue countryside. I peer out of the train window but all I can see is my pale, worried face reflected back at me. I lace my fingers together on my lap, try to relax.

Lexie was agitated when I called her, said she'd fallen down the stairs but was OK, just anxious to be discharged. Her neighbours heard her screaming – her lodger was away – and they called an ambulance. She said she's already fed up of the 'bleedin' nurses fussing round', and the 'bleedin' scratchy hospital gown', and having 'nothing to bleedin' do'. She said she has something important to tell me but is insistent that she talks to me face to face. It's about Charlie, she said. Visiting hours will be long over by the time I get back, but despite my wheedling, she wouldn't give anything away on the phone, said she'd see me tomorrow at ten o'clock.

I ring Grandad from the train to tell him I'm on my way home but he doesn't reply. Minutes later I get a text.

We can't talk, our voices have disappeared. We're tucked up in bed x

I reply: *Do you need anything? X*

No, having a hot toddy, we're going to go to sleep soon x

Night xx

I decide not to tell them I'm coming back. It doesn't matter how poorly she feels, Grandma would get up and change sheets, bake a cake most likely. I'll let them rest and call in to see them tomorrow. It'll be a nice surprise. The cottage sounds habitable, anyway. The downstairs is finished. Grandad's been overseeing the decorating, chivvying along the men as they clean and paint. Project manager, he calls himself. Grandma packs him off each morning with a Tupperware stuffed full of scones and flapjacks to placate the workmen.

I rest my head back, close my eyes, feel my body vibrating to the rhythm of the train. I can understand why children are lulled to sleep by moving vehicles. It only seems like seconds later that my head jerks upright as though I've received a small electric shock. The train is motionless. I wipe my mouth, hope I haven't been dribbling, stretch, and recognise the station sign outside the train window.

'Shit.' I grab my bag, stumble down the steps. Home. I zip my jacket up, huddle on a bench and call for a cab.

There's always noise at Esmée's flat: the whirring of the dryers below; traffic whizzing past the window – even in the dead of night there's the sound of sirens; lads on their way home, hollering at each other, dribbling empty cans down the road. The village, in contrast, is still and silent, as if a zombie apocalypse has taken place and all the residents have fled. Most of the houses are in darkness.

It's late but I'm not tired and I ask the cab driver to drop me at Lexie's. If the key's still hidden in the same place, I can pick up her nightgown and toiletries, some of the trashy magazines she pores over, take them with me when I visit. The torch on my phone illuminates Brian the gnome, dull and chipped, forever grimacing as he fishes. Weeds have grown around his base and I yank hard to dislodge him. The silver Yale key is still underneath and I turn the cold metal over in my hand before unlocking the door.

I flick the light switch – dust motes dance under the weak electric bulb – and trudge straight up the stairs. The door to Charlie's room is ajar and I resist the temptation to peek my head in, mindful that it's now someone else's space. Lexie's room has hardly changed: clothes are still strewn over every surface, much as they had been when we used to play dress-up in here. I remember Charlie wriggling into a Lycra mini skirt and bra top, stuffing the cups with toilet tissue. *Look at me, dah-ling, I'm fabulous.* I wait for the sting of tears, for the lump in my throat – but instead, find myself smiling at the memory.

A tiny black silk slip trimmed with lace is stuffed under Lexie's pillow, and I pull open drawers trying to find something more suitable for the hospital; something that will, at least, cover her bottom. The clothes in here are neatly folded, barely worn, and I find a large white T-shirt, 'RELAX' written across the front in bold black lettering. There's a hessian bag on the floor and I place the T-shirt inside, add clean underwear and toiletries, the latest copy of *Cosmo* and, because it's Lexie, a red lipstick and hairbrush. I'm just about to leave, am pulling the door behind me, when I think of slippers. There was nothing by Lexie's bed and I try to recall whether I've ever seen her wearing slippers. I don't think I have, but I remember Grandma buying her some moccasins one Christmas. I bet they've never been worn.

Back upstairs, I slide the doors to the wardrobe open and step back as clothes avalanche from the top shelf. I fold them, stack them neatly and then drop to my knees, looking for the shoebox with the slippers in. There are several boxes at the back and I ease them out, pop lids off. Some of the shoes look brand new: red shiny stripper heels, gold gladiator sandals. I lift the lid from the last box. Papers spring up and tumble to the ground. I bunch them together, putting them back, when I notice a birth certificate, and smooth it open. CHARLOTTE ELIZABETH FISHER,

BORN 1ST SEPTEMBER 1990. MOTHER – ALEXANDRA CLAIRE
FISHER. FATHER – PAUL MICHAEL LAWSON. I take care to stick
to the original creases as I fold it back up, but then I notice an
identical piece of cream paper. I think it must be Lexie's birth
certificate, but as I read the name, I can't quite believe what I'm
seeing.

ANNABELLE LAURA FISHER, BORN 1ST SEPTEMBER 1990.
MOTHER – ALEXANDRA CLAIRE FISHER. FATHER – PAUL MI-
CHAEL LAWSON.

The same birth date as Charlie. Annabelle. Belle. She's real.
Charlie's imaginary friend. Belle.

Annabelle. Belle. Charlie's sister.

Anna.

Letters scatter over the threadbare carpet as I upend the shoebox. I grab the one nearest to me, pull the paper from the envelope.

> *Mum,*
>
> *Why won't you answer my letters? What did I ever do
> wrong? Why didn't you keep me?*
>
> *Belle x*

I read another.

> *Dear Bitch,*
>
> *I know you were there when I came to see you – why didn't
> you answer the door? Have you any idea how much the
> train fare fucking cost?*
>
> *I hate you.*
>
> *Belle*

I feel as though I'm on a fairground ride. My head spins and I can't properly focus. I sink back onto my heels. Anna. Annabelle. Belle. I call Lexie's mobile. This can't wait until morning, but it goes straight to voicemail. I ring the hospital direct. Tell them it's an emergency, that I need to see Lexie, speak to her at the very least, but when they ask who I am, I stumble and stutter before I hang up the phone in frustration. I should have prepared a story. I never could lie. Not like Lexie. *Not like Anna.*

The kitchen smells of rotting food but I don't care. The table is littered and I sweep piles of unpaid bills, nail varnishes and empty cigarette packets to the floor. An ashtray shatters as it hits the floor; shards of glass scatter like confetti but I don't clear them up.

The fridge is empty but I find vodka in the freezer. I rinse out a glass, cough as the icy alcohol hits my chest. It's only when I am halfway down my second glass that I sit, study the postmarks on the envelopes and put the letters into date order. I read the earliest.

Dear Mum,

I hope you can read my writing – my hand's shaking with excitement!!!

At last I'm eighteen!!!! I'm sure you've been waiting for this day as much as me. I know you're not allowed to make first contact and I bet the time has passed so slowly for you. The adoption bastards wouldn't give me your details so I saved up all my babysitting money and used a private detective agency just like in a film! They found your address straight away. It cost a fortune, but it will be worth it when we're together, won't it?

I don't remember much about you but can recall sitting on your lap, your pink hair tickling my neck as you sang to me.

I don't know if my sister was adopted or just fostered like me, but perhaps the agency I used can find her too if you don't know where she is and we can all be together?

I can't wait for us all to be a family. It's all I've ever wanted. I've been dreaming of this FOREVER!!!!

Write back and let me know when I can come. I've already packed!!!

Lots of love,

Your daughter,

Belle xxxxxxxxxxx

The letters are all different. Some are loving, some are pleading, some are hateful. It's clear that Lexie never replied.

The last letter sends shivers down my spine.

You think you can ignore me? Think again.

CHAPTER FORTY-ONE
Then

I shuffled downstairs in my dressing gown, scooped up the post from the mat. There was a postcard of the Trevi Fountain. I flipped it over: *Back in Rome, can't keep still! Love you lots, Charlie xxx*

I'd hung a corkboard in the kitchen especially for the postcards that had arrived regularly over the six years since Charlie left. Each time one arrived, I felt a mixture of relief that she was still alive and fury that she never came back. The cards were piled on top of each other and the pins struggled to hold them in place. Often, I found them strewn all over the kitchen floor.

I hadn't seen her since we were eighteen. I'd never found out why she left, or what she had done that she wanted forgiveness for, but I followed her progress as she flitted from country to country, always going somewhere and not quite real to me any more. It was nice to be able to look forward to the post. The threatening letters had stopped once Charlie had left. I tried not to think about that too carefully. Tried not to jump to conclusions. *Look at the facts*, my old counsellor Paula would say. Siobhan's parents had moved away straight after her funeral. Took Abby somewhere remote. Somewhere they thought they could keep her safe. Was there such a place?

I sprinkled porridge oats into a pan, added milk. A proper breakfast to face the challenge today would bring. While it bubbled, I swished open the curtains in the lounge. Picked up Dan's empty Foster's cans and pizza box. The porridge steamed and I stirred in blueberries, poured orange juice and took my breakfast to the pergola outside. August had been dismal but September had brought an Indian summer. The sky was aquamarine blue and the clouds were white and fluffy. There was a slight breeze today; I'd be glad of that later.

'I'm off.'

Dan stuck his head outside the French doors.

'I didn't think you'd go today?'

'I always play on a Saturday.'

'I thought you'd come and support me.'

'I've sponsored you, haven't I? How often do you come to a match any more?'

'Maybe if I wasn't so busy cleaning up after you…'

'Don't start this again,' Dan sighed.

I clattered my spoon into my bowl and swept past him. 'See you later, then.'

He scuttled out the front door before my tears fell.

My legs felt leaden as I clumped up the stairs. This constant bickering Dan and I had fallen into was exhausting. Would it have been different if Charlie had stayed or would she had been driven away by our fighting? I supposed that even if she'd stayed it didn't mean she'd still be living with us. By now, she might have met someone and got married. It was hard to think of Charlie being married. Of being anything except the eighteen-year-old girl who loved to stand on the pub stool, waving a bottle of Bulmers cider around as she sang along to Madonna, Mike shouting at her to get her mucky feet off his upholstery. The pain was sharp when I thought Charlie had a whole life I'd never be a part of. A new best friend, most probably.

It took three attempts to hoist up the sash window in the bedroom. When I did, I stuck my head outside, letting the warm breeze ruffle my hair. It was the hottest September for years. I remembered the last one. We'd been due back at school but instead Charlie, Esmée, Siobhan and I had sat in the woods, dangling our feet in the stream, pooling our packed lunches. It had felt so daring to skip school, and even though Grandma had found out and grounded me for two weeks, I'd thought I could do anything with the support of the others.

Now, with Siobhan dead, Charlie god knows where, and Esmée living in London, there was only me, and I found I wasn't so brave after all. Often, I had thought I could pack a rucksack. Go to the places on the postcards Charlie sent. Try to find her. But I knew I wouldn't. Too scared I wouldn't find her. Too scared I would. Besides, there was Dan, and underneath the sniping about leaving the cap off the toothpaste, the grumbling that the toilet seat was left up again, I did love him and I hoped he felt the same.

The shower was cool, and afterwards, I lathered my summer-dry skin with lavender shower gel, shaved my legs. I didn't always bother shaving any more, but they'd be on display today. My T-shirt smelled of fabric softener as I pulled it over my damp hair. I looped a scrunchie around my wrist for later, and headed out towards the village green.

Grandma, Grandpa and Mum were already sat behind a rickety trestle table, handing numbers out to a queue of runners. I was pleased Mum had come. She was so happy with Oliver it seemed sometimes she'd forgotten Dad, but when I'd told her of my plan she'd been thrilled and said she wouldn't miss it for the world.

'Morning. It's a good turnout already.' I shaded my eyes as I scanned the green.

'Fifty registered so far. Who'd have thought the first village games would draw such a crowd? It was a fantastic idea, Grace.'

'Thanks. I think the beer tent might help. I'm glad Lexie's singing later.' Lexie's hostility had softened over the years and we were uneasy friends. I didn't want to lose anyone else.

'It'll be great. Where's Dan?'

'Football. He'll be here later.' I crossed my fingers behind my back.

The bark of the oak tree was coarse against my palms as I leaned forward, stretching out my hamstrings. A hand tapped my shoulder and I straightened up.

'Grace?' The voice was soft. I stared at the trunk as adrenaline raced around my body. *It can't be.* I didn't dare look.

'Grace?'

I slowly turned.

Charlie's mouth turned upwards but her eyes didn't light up, her skin didn't crinkle. Tiny shorts hung from her hips, and collarbones jutted out beneath her vest top.

A grubby pink rucksack thunked to the floor. 'Ta-da!' She fluttered jazz hands. Her smile slipped. 'Say something.'

I opened my mouth and closed it again.

'A hug, at least?' She stepped forward, opened her arms. I could feel her heart thudding, her ribs pressing against me. Her body juddered; the shoulder of my T-shirt was sodden. I pushed her away harder than I needed to.

'Why did you go?' I dug my nails into my palms. Tried to lower my voice. 'Not one bloody phone call…'

'It's complicated.'

'I'm listening.' I crossed my arms.

'I'll explain everything. I promise. I've missed you.'

'You disappeared without telling me. Ran off the minute Siobhan died.' My hands twitched and I wasn't sure whether I wanted to slap her or hug her.

'Didn't know what to say.'

'You couldn't think of anything in the last six years?'

'The longer I left it, the harder it got.'

'The first race, the 200 metres, will begin in five minutes.' Grandad sounded like a Dalek over the speaker system.

'I've got to go. Look,' I said, softening, 'will you stay and watch? We'll talk properly after. Your mum's singing later. Does she know…'

'No.' Charlie's face clouded. 'But look.' She gestured towards the crowd. 'It's a bit of an occasion, isn't it?'

'Grandma and I organised it. Didn't expect it to be quite so popular.'

'What's it in aid of?'

'It's for charity. For head injuries.'

'Your dad?'

I nodded. 'It's the fifteen-year anniversary soon. You know…'

'I'll run with you.'

'You sure? You look knackered.'

'I want to, unless you're scared of the competition?' Charlie grinned and I couldn't help grinning too. She was so unmistakably Charlie. Unmistakably back. We'd sort everything out later.

'Bring it on,' I said. 'I'll even sponsor you.'

At the start line, Charlie and I elbowed our way to the front. I knelt to tie my laces in a double knot. 'You should do the same,' I nodded towards her feet. She shook her head and jogged on the spot.

'Are you back for good?' I asked

'I hope so. I never wanted to leave but I felt I had to.' She bit her lip. 'I did something terrible, Grace. I hope you can forgive me.'

The starting pistol fired and I pumped my arms and legs as fast as I could, as if I were chasing her words. My ponytail swished against my neck. The sky was cloudless, the air muggy. I could hear the chant of the crowd. I didn't look. I couldn't take my eyes off Charlie, afraid she'd disappear before she had explained.

What had she done? She was ahead of me. Ignoring the stitch in my side, I urged myself forward.

'Come on, Grace!' Grandma's voice warbled my name, egging me on. The finishing line was ahead. With a final spurt, I lengthened my stride. I was practically level with Charlie now. Another push forward and I'd overtake her. We both reached out our arms. Out of the corner of my eye, I saw her fall. She should have tied her laces properly. My hand swatted the yellow ribbon. I crossed the line, and as I tried to look behind me, I sprawled to the ground. There was a searing pain in my left ankle. Grandad jogged towards me as I whimpered on the grass, my hands massaging my swollen skin, and then past me. I turned. Charlie was lying motionless.

'Call an ambulance!' someone screamed, as I stumbled to my feet and limped towards Charlie. It might have been me that screamed.

She was still.

Too still.

Lexie pushed past me. She knelt at her daughter's side. 'Charlie? What the fuck?'

Get up. Get up. Get up.

I felt an arm around my shoulder. Dan had come to watch after all. I shook him off, kneeling beside my best friend. The first-aid course the nursery had sent me on momentarily deserted me, but as I checked her pulse, everything came flooding back. I puffed air into her mouth and compressed her chest. *One, two, three, four, five.*

'The ambulance? Where's the fucking ambulance?' I could hear Lexie screaming, but still I counted as I breathed into Charlie's dry lips. *One, two, three, four, five.*

Charlie didn't respond. Her skin was waxy, and despite the heat of the sun she grew cooler. I counted as Lexie sobbed. I counted as Charlie didn't move. The paramedics came and took over from me and when they eventually stopped and shook their heads I was still counting.

CHAPTER FORTY-TWO
Now

It's two in the morning before I lock Lexie's front door and stuff the key under the gnome. I scurry through the village, whimpering as a cat darts out from between two parked cars. I see Anna everywhere: behind branches that sway and whisper in the wind; crouching in shadowy bushes; lurking in darkened doorways. I pass through the centre of the village, the street lights less frequent now, and as I reach the outskirts, they disappear completely. I pause at the top of my lane. It stretches out before me like a gaping black mouth. The sky is clouded and I can't see my cottage. My knees jerk as a bang shoots down the lane like a bullet. I'm about to run away when I hear it again, realise it's my gate. *Bloody Dan.* My fists furl and unfurl by my sides and I sprint, stumbling over potholes, the carrier bag full of letters bumping against my thighs. I hurl myself at my front door, jab the key towards the lock once, twice, three times – and then I'm in. I slam the door behind me. Lean my back against it as I wait for the burning in my chest to subside.

The fug of fresh paint catches in the back of my throat and I tramp upstairs, crack open the window in my bedroom; it doesn't smell like home. Grandma has taken down the curtains to clean. My Laura Ashley wallpaper is soot-stained and peeling – the lemon and cream flowers are hardly recognisable – but I barely notice my surroundings as I sit cross-legged on the bare mattress, the coverless duvet draped around my shoulders. I sift through the letters, trying to make sense of the timeline. Anna started writing to Lexie a few weeks after she had turned eighteen. From memory, I think that was around the time Lexie changed. Previously just a social drinker, she had become drunk all the time, snappy and tearful. This was also the time I started getting threatening letters. Were they from Anna?

Anna wrote to Lexie over a period of six months, tried to visit, but then the letters stopped. The letters to me stopped, too. Why? Had Anna met Lexie, met Charlie? Is that why Charlie disappeared? *I've done something terrible, Grace. Please forgive me.* The words swim together as I try to focus through puffy eyes. I stifle my second yawn in less than a minute, pull on pyjamas that smell of Grandma's washing powder, topple into bed and snap off the lamps.

When I was small and couldn't sleep, my dad would perch on the side of my narrow bed, his face glowing orange from my night light, and stroke my hair. 'Think of ten nice things that have happened today,' he'd say, and I'd list them one by one, never once letting on that the nicest thing of all was the sense that we were the only two awake in the world, safely cocooned in my sunflower-yellow bedroom.

I feel anything but safe tonight. Despite the exhaustion that has seeped into my bones and the amount of alcohol I have drunk, sleep evades me. I lean over the side of the bed and rummage around for my handbag, pull out my sleeping tablets and shake one out – then think about the day I've had and rattle out a second. I hesitate as I read the warning on the bottle, thinking about the amount of vodka I have drunk – more than I'd usually have – but then I toss the tablets onto the back of my tongue and wash them down with the warm dregs from a bottle of Evian I bought at the station. I snuggle down, pulling the quilt tightly around my shoulders, breathing slowly, until sleep claims me.

When Charlie and I were fourteen, my grandparents took us to the Isle of Wight. The wind bit my cheeks and blew my hair into my mouth as I swayed on the deck of the ferry, arms outstretched, licking droplets of salt water from my cherry chapsticked lips. I remember how disorientated I became: there was solidity beneath my feet and it seemed we were barely moving, but I was off balance. Saliva flooded my mouth and Charlie held my hair back as the contents of my stomach rocketed into the frothy slate sea.

For a moment, I think I'm back on that boat. I have the same sense of movement and stillness and I feel nauseous. Soft fingers stroke my hair and hot breath warms my ear. My nostrils inhale the scent of Impulse body spray.

'Grace,' soothes a voice. *Charlie?* I know I'm dreaming, and blackness swirls and spins and tugs me under once more.

Light slices through the windows and I massage my eyelids with my fingertips, trying to rub away the grogginess I feel. The smell of emulsion and gloss is suffocating; I can almost taste the paint. The back of my throat stings and my temples pulse with pain, but there's another smell wafting into the room and I tell myself I'm mistaken, inhale deeply – but there it is again. Bacon.

I jerk my head off the pillow, push myself to sitting, drawing my knees up to swing my legs out of bed. There is something cool and tight around my right ankle, slowing my movements. Throwing back the quilt, my mouth dries at the sight of an iron cuff, its chain trailing off the end of the bed. I think I must be sleeping still, and dig my nails into the soft flesh of my belly, but I don't wake up. I spring forward onto my knees and hoist the chain with both hands. It's heavier than it looks and it clanks as I tug it, but it doesn't move. It's hooked through the carvings at the base of my bed frame. There's a second chain, an identical empty cuff. For my left leg? What's going on? I reach for my phone but it's missing; so is my lamp. I lean over the bed and my head spins. My handbag has gone too.

Footsteps thud up the stairs and the bedroom door swings open.

'Morning, Grace.' Anna sashays into the room carrying a breakfast tray, except she doesn't quite look like Anna any more. Her hair is white-blonde, shorter, bobbed. She's wearing Charlie's orange tie-dye T-shirt and, despite the freezing temperatures, her tiny white denim shorts. She looks just like the Charlie in the photograph downstairs.

I scramble backwards, pressing my spine against the headboard.

'The orange juice is freshly squeezed, just the way you like it. There's brown sauce in the sandwich.'

Terror has lodged in my throat and I try to scream, but whimper instead like a tormented puppy.

'Are you OK? You had a late night. You really shouldn't take these.' She rattles my tablet pot. 'It's not a natural sleep.'

Anna sets the tray down on the floor and as she leans forward, I notice my missing chain with the two broken half-hearts swinging from her neck, glinting in the light.

'You fucking bitch.' Fury shoves fear aside and I lunge towards her, but my reactions are dulled, clumsy and I'm too slow. Anna sidesteps to the door. The chain rattles, tightens, and I howl as I fall to the floor next to my breakfast, the metal cuff biting into my skin, the carpet grazing my knees. The smell of bacon makes me gag and I vomit over the tray.

'That's fucking ungrateful,' Anna snaps and sweeps out of the room, leaves the door open as she clatters down the stairs.

I remain on my knees, resting forward on my elbows, until the room stops spinning and I sit back, wipe my mouth with my sleeve. I clasp the chain with both hands and yank as hard as I can until my shoulders burn in their sockets, but the solid pine bedstead my grandparents bought as our house-warming present doesn't move. Dan had wanted a faux-leather one where the TV rises up like flotsam at the touch of a button – he'd seen one on MTV's *Cribs* – but I'd thought it tacky, out of place in our cottage. Now I wish I'd listened to him. I wish he were here. I try the cuff instead, find the join and strain to prise it apart, wincing as I rip my nail to the quick.

Nausea rises again and I drop my head onto my knees. My breathing is too rapid, too shallow, as I wonder whether Anna will come back. I'm petrified she will. I'm petrified she won't. I force myself to calm down. Footsteps pound back up the stairs and the ball of dread inside me grows.

'Here.' Anna rolls a beige bucket towards me. Grains of sand spill out onto the carpet. Dan laughed at me for keeping a fire bucket outside the back door, but the plumes of smoke generated as he cremated hot dogs and burgers made me nervous.

'Don't say you haven't got a pot to piss in,' Anna cackles and the hairs on the back of my neck stand on end. 'You can clean up your mess, too.' A roll of black sacks begins to unravel as it flies through the air, landing with a thump next to the tray.

'Anna, this is crazy. Unlock me and then we can talk.' I keep my tone calm and measured, blink back tears and try to stretch my mouth into something resembling a smile.

'I'll be happy to.' Anna reaches into the pocket of her jeans, pulls out a silver key and dangles it in front of her. 'As soon as we've sorted things out. We've got off to a bad start but I want us to be friends, Grace. Sisters, even. Family's important, don't you think?'

'Yes.' In this moment I'd agree to anything. 'We can start again. Be friends. Just unlock me.'

'I can't yet.'

'You can. There's no harm done. I know it was a mistake about Mittens. It's fine, really…' The words stream from me. I can't stop babbling.

'It isn't just about Mittens though, is it, Grace? It's about you stealing my life.'

'I don't…'

'It should have been me growing up with Charlie, not you. *Me!*' She thumps her chest and I shrink back.

'I'm sorry.'

'You will be.'

'I'll scream if you don't let me go.'

'Go ahead.' Anna crosses her arms.

'Help! Help!'

I yell until my throat smarts and I'm drenched in sweat. My cries get weaker until they're replaced with the sound of rasping as I pant with exertion.

'Finished?' Anna's mouth twists into a smile. 'Who do you think's going to hear you? It's Saturday, there are no workmen coming. Mrs Jones is in hospital. No one ever just walks past here. I thought you wanted to be friends?'

'I do,' I whisper.

'If you want to be friends, you have to make amends.'

'How?'

'You'll see.' Anna spins on her heel and walks away.

'Anna,' I croak. 'Come back.' But I am alone.

CHAPTER FORTY-THREE
Now

I contemplate my options. The chain won't reach the window. I can scream all day, but Anna's right, no one will hear me. The lane doesn't lead anywhere. No one ever just passes by.

What am I going to do? I swallow hard; my mouth tastes sour. My hand is shaking as I pick up the orange juice, rotate my wrist in tiny circles and check the liquid for vomit as it sloshes around the cup. It seems to be OK and I take a sip, swoosh it around my mouth as though I have just cleaned my teeth, and spit it back out again. There's no way I'm actually drinking anything. It's probably full of ground nuts. My bladder is full already and I'm not pissing in a bucket.

I examine the cup: green and plastic, it's usually wedged at the back of the cupboard in case friends with young children visit. My sandwich is on one of the paper plates we keep stacked in the pantry for impromptu barbecues. Anna has used the flimsy plastic tray from the greenhouse – I usually stand seedlings on it – rather than risk the heavy silver-plated one that I dust off when we have visitors. There is nothing heavy or sharp. Nothing I can use as a weapon. Did Anna know I'd be home this weekend? She can't have, unless…

Unless Lexie's accident wasn't an accident.

How long will it be before anyone misses me? Before anyone finds me? The workmen will be here on Monday. I'm not exactly going to starve to death. What has Anna got planned?

I can't let myself imagine. *Deal with the facts in front of you, one at a time,* Paula, my old counsellor would say. And I try, but I feel like I'm on a waltzer at the fair, spinning round and round. I press my palms hard into my eye sockets. *Think, Grace.* I stand. Blood rushes to my head and I splay out my hands as I sway. I step forward with my left foot, drag my right, see how far I can go, wondering whether I can reach my drawers, find something to help me. The chain tightens, the cuff rubs against my bone, jerking me backwards. I try lying on my front, elbows digging into the carpet, and inch forward as far as I can. If I could just reach the bottom drawer. I stretch out my fingers, but I'm still nowhere near.

I crawl back onto the bed. I examine the cuff, point my toes and try to slide it from my ankle. I wonder where it has come from, remember that Anna has read *Fifty Shades of Grey*, and shudder. I thrust the cold metal towards my heel again and again until my skin is split and blood drips onto my mattress. There's no way it'll fit past my ankle bone. I shiver as I remember Charlie and me watching *Misery* on video after school one day. I'd hidden my face behind a cushion as Kathy Bates smashed a sledgehammer into James Caan's feet. 'You can hear the bones cracking,' Charlie had squealed.

My head drops onto my knees. I run my fingers through my hair, pull out the scrunchie I'd been too tired to remove last night. A hairgrip drops to the mattress and hope swells. I pounce on it, manipulate the metal until it's straight. I struggle to keep my hand still as I insert the grip into the lock of the cuff, slide it around. *C'mon.* I wipe the sweat from my forehead. Try again. I've seen this in the movies so many times. How hard can it be? My bicep burns with the effort of keeping my arm still, my hand steady, but there's no click. The cuff doesn't spring open.

I run my fingers down the chain until I reach the bedstead, trace the carvings with my fingers. I wobble the wood where the chain is looped through. It's not as solid as the legs; the carvings are the bed's weak point. I might be able to break the wood. I shuffle back up the bed. Lying on my back, arms by my sides, I pull up my knees and take a deep breath as though I'm preparing for a yoga move. I straighten my legs, smashing my feet into the wood, and I scream as pain radiates into my hip sockets.

I think I might be sick again. The wood hasn't cracked, isn't even splintered. I roll onto my side, wait for the nausea to pass; strain my ears, waiting for footsteps to bang up the stairs, but the cottage is silent. The only discernible sound is my heart hammering against my chest. I place both hands over it as if it is a frightened animal I can soothe. I draw my knees up, curling into a ball. I'm not sure whether it's stress or the after-effects of the alcohol and sleeping tablets, but my eyelids flutter and close and I fall into a restless sleep.

The electric light is dull through the smoke-stained shade but it still wakes me and I blink rapidly, curl up into a ball.

'I've made dinner.' Anna has placed the tray by the side of the bed and stepped back before I've even sat up.

'Anna,' I croak. It's painful to talk. My throat's raw from all the screaming. 'Please let me go.'

'It's pasta,' Anna says, as if I haven't even spoken.

'What do you want? How did you know I was here?'

'I was at Lexie's last night, sleeping in Charlie's room. I followed you back.'

'Lexie gave you a key to her house?'

'No. The neighbour let me in. I told her I was Lexie's niece. She said the family resemblance is striking.' Anna fluffs the bottom of her hair. 'What do you think? It seems short to me.'

'I think you're crazy. Let me go.' I tug weakly at the chain.

'Not yet.'

'Grandad's expecting me for dinner tonight,' I bluff. 'He'll know something's wrong if I don't turn up.'

'Really?'

I nod.

'Funny, that.' She pulls my mobile out of her pocket. 'As he's in bed ill, and he thinks you're still in London.'

'Esmée…'

'Thinks you're at your grandparents'.' Anna waves my mobile. 'Look, you even sent her a text to say you got there safely. Aren't you the considerate one? Now, eat your dinner before it gets cold. And clean your mess up. It stinks in here.'

'Anna. Anna. Please!'

'SHUT UP!' she roars, and slams the door behind her. I tremble as I listen as her footsteps fade away.

My bladder feels like the water balloons we used to throw at school: too full and ready to explode. I look at the bucket and begin to cry with frustration, but I don't have any choice. I step out of bed. I'm not sure whether it's exhaustion or fear making my legs shake, but I have to sit before I can wrench down my pyjama bottoms and squat over the bucket. Sweat pricks at my skin as I release a stream of urine into the plastic and I vow never to tell anybody about this – then wonder whether I'll ever see anyone again to tell. I jerk my pyjamas back up and lie back on the bed, sobbing into my pillow so Anna doesn't hear.

It's unfathomable that I slept again but I must have, because when I wake, the moon shimmers high in the sky. I'm glad I don't have curtains, because I can see the twinkling stars, notice how beautiful the world is. There's a growling in my stomach and I realise I haven't eaten in over twenty-four hours. I pick up the plastic bowl of pasta, and fork cold fusilli and congealed cheese into my dry mouth. The toilet flushes in the bathroom next door and my throat suddenly closes up. I drop the bowl onto the floor and huddle under my duvet as if a layer of cotton and feathers can protect me. It's awful not to feel safe in my own room and I wonder if I'll have to move after this. If there'll be an after this – and I shake the thought away. Urge myself to stay positive. Anna has to let me go, doesn't she?

CHAPTER FORTY-FOUR
Now

The stench in the room is acrid and sour: vomit mingled with urine. Stale sweat clings to my skin and pyjamas and I wish I could reach the window to gulp in fresh air. The rain drums against the panes and I'm desperate to be outside, to feel the drops splatter onto my upturned face, trickle down my neck. My grandparents will welcome the downpour. Grandma was worried the dry spell was lasting too long, and it's almost time for Grandad to plant the bulbs; the earth will be nice and soft if he's well enough to do it today. I wonder how they are, if I'll ever see them again. I feel light-headed and I clutch the duvet to quash the sensation that I'm floating away.

The bed in the spare room creaks. Anna's footsteps march across the landing and the bathroom door squeaks as she pushes it open. My heart rate doubles. I haven't cleared up the mess from last night yet and I daren't risk making her angrier. I quickly sit up, lowering my feet to the floor. My body aches like it did when I first started yoga, and my movements are jerky as I shuffle to the bucket. My quad muscles quake as I squat and wee. I push the bucket as far from the bed as I can reach, pick up the roll of black sacks and tear one off. I slide the tray into the sack and tie the neck. I consider tossing it across the room but tuck it under the bed instead. It's not heavy, but I may be able to hit Anna with it, surprise her somehow, and wrestle the key from her. I take this idea and bundle it with all the other straws I've clutched at.

My muscles tense as the door swings open.

'Morning.' Anna smiles. 'Sleep well?'

I bite back my sarcasm. 'I've been thinking. How about we go to Charlie's grave today? You and me. Or we can take Lexie, if you want to. It's unfair that…'

'That sounds great,' Anna beams.

'Really?'

'No,' she snaps.

I flop back onto my pillow. 'How about a cup of tea at least?' I could throw it in her face, I think.

Anna's eyes narrow. She picks up the bucket and leaves without a word; the toilet flushes and her footsteps thunder down the stairs. Much as I hate the bucket, I panic that she might not bring it back. I close my eyes and strain to hear what she's doing. Water gushes through the pipes as the kitchen taps are turned on. I feel like Spiderman with my heightened senses. Anna returns wearing my Cath Kidston apron, one hand clasped around a plastic cup, the other carrying the bucket. I pick at a piece of stray cotton trailing from the seam of the duvet and watch her out of the corner of my eye. How's she going to get the tea to me without a tray? She walks slowly towards the bed. Adrenaline courses through my body. I place my palms on the mattress and shift my weight slightly, angle my legs, getting ready to kick her as hard as I can. She stops. Puts down the bucket. Places a hand in the apron pocket and pulls out my paring knife. Its blade glints, and bile rises in my throat.

'Just in case you get any funny ideas.' She puts my tea on the bedside table and backs away, her eyes locked onto mine.

I break her gaze and pick up the cup, but I can't suppress the violent shaking of my hand and beige liquid slops onto my thigh.

'It's cold.' I sip the tea to double-check. It's a risk drinking anything she's given me, but I'm so thirsty now, I gulp it down.

'Of course. Do you think I'm stupid?'

'No. You're upset. Understandably so. Let me go, Anna. I won't tell anyone. The decorators will be here tomorrow, anyway.' I'm whining like one of the toddlers I look after at Little Acorns when they get over-tired, but I can't help it.

'Don't worry, Grace.' Anna runs a finger along the spine of the knife, taking a step towards me. 'It will be over very soon.'

The walls feel like they're closing in on me, the ceiling coming down. There's not enough air in the bedroom. When Charlie died, all I wanted was to be with her, but now I'm so scared I'm going to die, I realise how much I want to live.

And then the doorbell chimes.

Anna strides from the room, slamming the door behind her, and I kneel on my bed and scream and scream until I feel I'm about to faint. Two sets of footsteps thud up the stairs and I'm giddy with relief that I've been heard, that I'll be saved. I put my hands on my hips and lean forwards, panting as though I've run a marathon.

The door bursts open and Lexie is framed in the doorway, arm in a sling, cheek swollen and bruised. She looks small and frail. Thin bare legs poking out of a once-white hospital gown. Anna is shadowed behind her.

'Grace.' Lexie limps towards me. Freezes as she notices the chain running from my ankle to the bedstead. 'Belle, what the fuck are you doing? Let her go.'

'Not until we've talked. You owe me some answers, *Mum*.'

'We'll talk when you haven't got Grace chained up like a bleedin' animal.'

'Oh, poor Grace. Everyone just loves her don't they?'

'She's done nothing to you.'

'She wouldn't introduce me to you. You were supposed to get to know me through her, get to like me, and then I'd have told you who I really am. We'd have been a real family, but no. Grace wanted to keep you all to herself.'

'It wasn't like that…'

'Shut up.' Anna steps towards me. 'I wanted to like you, Grace. I really did. I tried to be nice, but you kept pissing me off. The more I listened to your stories about how much you loved Charlie, the more I hated you. Everyone loves Charlie. Everyone loves Grace. Who the fuck loves *me*? But' – her mouth twists into a smile – 'I'm prepared to give you a second chance. Charlie isn't here any more, but we can still be a family of three, can't we?'

'No.' Lexie's voice is cold and hard. 'Let her go or I'll call the police.'

'Go ahead. By the time you hobble to the nearest phone, I'll be long gone, and Grace?' She pulls my paring knife from the apron pocket, swishes its stainless steel blade through the air. 'Grace might still be here. Well, some of her might. Now get on the bed.' Anna thrusts the knife towards Lexie, as though prodding cattle. Lexie stands firm, but as the blade jabs into her shoulder, droplets of blood soak through her gown and she stumbles backwards.

'Anna, you're hurting her.' I try to reach Lexie but the chain is too short.

'I'm hurting her… That's rich.'

Lexie clambers on the bed next to me. Anna grasps her left leg, opens the other cuff and snaps it around Lexie's ankle.

'What do you want, Belle?'

'I want to spend some quality time with my mother. Is that too much to ask? I'm going to cook a nice meal, then we can all sit down and get to know each other properly.'

Anna slams the bedroom door on her way out.

'You're bleeding.' I reach out my hand but Lexie swats it away. 'I'm fine.'

The crimson stain spreads, and as I watch it, the contents of the room swirl and merge together until my peripheral vision disappears. There's a roaring in my ears as though I'm listening to waves in a shell.

'Breathe, Grace.' Lexie rubs my back in small circular movements. 'You're only breathing in. Breathe out.'

I huff out air, hiss it back in again. I can hear Lexie murmuring, feel the warmth of her hand on my spine, and gradually my body stops jerking. My sight is restored.

'OK?' Lexie squeezes me tightly with her arm.

'Yes.'

'Good.' She lets me go. 'No offence, but you stink.' She shuffles away.

I flop back onto my pillow and Lexie tugs at the chain, pushes against the bedstead with her one good arm.

'I've already tried that.'

Lexie sprawls on her back. Kicks off her shoes and places the soles of her feet against the carved wood. I shuffle down the bed, place my feet next to hers.

'Ready?' she asks.

'On three.'

We push and kick until my thighs ache too much to move, and scream until my ears ring. There isn't so much as a hairline crack in the wood.

'Fuck.' Lexie rubs her feet. 'How the hell do we get out of this?'

I look into her eyes and see my own fear reflected back at me.

'I don't know.'

CHAPTER FORTY-FIVE
Then

Six days after Charlie died, the morning sky was grey and black like an angry bruise. Mist shrouded the church spire that was usually visible from my window. Everything seemed muted somehow, dampened down. Even the birds were uncharacteristically quiet. Charlie had taken the sunshine with her. Dan brought me tea I couldn't taste and toast I couldn't swallow. I should have been dressing in party clothes – it was Charlie's twenty-fifth birthday – but instead, I wore black to attend her funeral. The shift dress I'd worn the Christmas before had been snug when I'd bought it, but now zipped up with ease; the material skimmed my body rather than clinging to it. I'd barely eaten a thing since Charlie died. Dan wore his interview suit and a borrowed black tie: a little boy dressed up.

A taxi took us to Charlie's house; we were both too shaky to drive. As there was no other family, it had been decided that we'd ride in the funeral car with Lexie. Mum and Oliver had driven down. They'd meet us at the crematorium with Grandma and Grandad. I pushed open the door to what had once been my second home and followed the clouds of cigarette smoke. Lexie sat at the kitchen table, one arm crossed in front of her, the other holding a cigarette, her eyes fixed on an overflowing ashtray. I touched her shoulder. She slapped my hand away. I glared at Dan. *Say something.*

'I'll make some tea,' he said.

While the kettle boiled, I ran hot water into the slimy washing-up bowl and began to scrub the dirty mugs and plates that covered every surface. I filled the silence with sloshing water and clinking china. Dan carried the milk over to me, holding it up so I could smell it. I sniffed and wrinkled my nose. He tipped it down the sink, congealing yellow lumps that I prodded down the plughole with a teaspoon. He made steaming cups of black tea that nobody drank. I dried up whilst Dan emptied the stinking bin and stacked the wine bottles and lager cans outside the back door for recycling.

There was nothing left to do but wait. The three of us sat around the kitchen table, silent and avoiding eye contact. It was a relief when there was a rap at the door. Dan jumped up to answer it and Lexie's eyes bore into mine. She was bristling. Her anger engulfed my sadness.

'I need some air,' I told her and joined Dan in the narrow hallway, clinging on to the back of his belt while he talked to the driver, so that I wouldn't float away in a bubble of grief.

The gleaming hearse contained the oak coffin and flowers: Charlie's name in white carnations. Grandad had helped organise things with Lexie. I suspected he'd contributed financially too; she'd never been good with money. Lexie got in the car first, then Dan, then me. I stared out of the window as we made our slow journey to say goodbye to someone who had been so full of life I still couldn't quite believe she was gone. I watched the people in the street talking, laughing. It seemed inexplicable that their lives remained unaffected. This was just another ordinary day for them. I envied them.

The sky was an iron-grey shroud of anger, full of weeping clouds. A large crowd, mainly dressed in black, waited outside the oak double doors of the chapel, dabbing eyes and blowing noses. Wreaths were studied and cards were read. Everyone looked as dazed as I felt.

We waited in the car until everyone had gone inside and then the funeral director came to escort us in. I hadn't cried by this stage. It all seemed so surreal. We made our sombre walk into the crematorium as Eva Cassidy promised blue skies. 'Somewhere Over The Rainbow' was Lexie's choice; Charlie would have made a face – 'What's wrong with a bit of Madonna?'

We sat on wooden benches designed to make bottoms as numb as hearts. At the front of the chapel, crimson velvet curtains trimmed with gold hung behind the plinth where Charlie's coffin sat. On top of the coffin was a silver-framed photo of a laughing Charlie on Cromer beach. I remembered Grandad taking it.

A middle-aged man who'd clearly never met Charlie led the service. Generic words such as 'warm', 'funny', and 'kind' were bandied around, and then it was my turn. My jelly legs somehow carried me to the lectern and I faced row after row of eyes bright with tears. I cleared my throat. 'Charlie was my best friend,' I began. I recounted the day we'd met; how she'd filled Dan's jam sandwiches with ketchup. There was tentative laughter at this point. I described how I knew from that moment that she'd be one of the most important people in my life.

'Why then?' Lexie's voice rasped through the crematorium, sounding as though she hadn't stopped chain-smoking since Charlie died.

My mouth hung open, my words ripped from me.

'Why?' Lexie stood now, her voice louder. Her face dark and twisted.

'Why?' I repeated. Not understanding what she was asking of me.

The congregation's gaze flicked between Lexie and me as though they were watching a macabre game of tennis.

'Why did you kill her?'

Lexie stared at me with such hatred that I stumbled backwards. Dan rushed to my side. I'd twisted the same ankle I'd hurt at the race, but it wasn't the pain that was making me cry.

'Lexie, it's understandable you're upset today.' Grandad stepped in, his voice even and calm.

'I'm upset every day because that fucking bitch killed my daughter. Killed Siobhan. It's her fault. Everything's her fault.'

'I didn't. I don't understand…' My eyes darted wildly around, searching for an answer.

'Siobhan's death was ruled an accidental overdose. Hardly Grace's fault.' Dan's hand felt scorching hot as he rested it against my spine. 'And I can't see how you can possibly blame Grace for Charlie.'

'If Charlie hadn't left…'

'Why did she leave, Lexie? She's your daughter – enlighten us.' Dan's voice got louder and Grandad placed a hand on his arm.

'It's not the time or the place, son. Lexie, do you want to come outside with me and get some air?'

'I don't want some fucking air; I want my fucking daughter back.' Lexie fell to her knees, keening.

The funeral director smiled at us, although his eyes were cold. 'I think you should go.'

People fidgeted in their seats, straining their necks for a better view.

I was shaking with shock. Dan supported me like I was ninety, one arm around my waist, the other gripping my elbow as I limped towards the door.

'I'll never forgive you, Grace,' Lexie screeched behind me.

Outside, I clung to Dan's arm.

'I'll fetch the car.' Grandad dashed over to the car park while Dan rubbed my back. Mum, Oliver and Grandma huddled together, too stunned to speak.

By the time we got home, I'd used up all the tissues in my bag. My throat was raw and my eyes felt gritty.

'What about the wake?'

'Do you want to go?' asked Grandad.

'No,' my voice was hoarse. 'But Charlie—'

'Charlie loved you. She'd understand.'

I climbed out of the car and stood on legs that didn't quite feel like mine.

'Are you coming in?' I asked.

'I think we should go to the pub and check on Lexie,' Grandad replied.

'Fuck Lexie.' Dan's voice was hard.

'She has no one else,' Grandad said. 'But we'll stay if you want us to?'

I shook my head. Grandad did a three-point turn. Oliver's car followed.

'We'll come back and see you before we head back to Devon,' Mum called out the window.

We stood in the hallway, not quite sure what to do.

'Tea?' Dan asked.

'Something stronger.' I wanted to drink myself numb. I unzipped my dress that smelled like the chapel and cloaked myself in a fleecy throw. Even though it was twenty degrees, I was chilled.

Dan handed me a vodka and Coke and we sat side by side on the sofa and toasted the girl who would now forever remain twenty-four.

CHAPTER FORTY-SIX
Now

'Don't suppose you've got a fag?' Lexie asks.

'No.'

'Thought not.' We lie in stunned silence. There's a wall of unanswered questions dividing us and I don't know where to begin knocking it down.

'I knew when you didn't turn up for visiting yesterday that something was wrong. When I got your text first thing—'

'Not my text.'

'From your number anyway, asking me to come here, I did a runner. Hitched a ride from a bakery van. You've met my Belle, then?'

'Anna.'

'Anna?'

'Dan…'

'Dan? You're not making any bleedin' sense, girl. Spit it out.'

'Dan has… He was unfaithful.' The knot of anxiety in my stomach twists tighter and tighter as words tumble out of me.

Lexie's eyes glisten as I go back to the beginning and tell her how much Charlie wanted to find her father. Her brow creases as I admit I stole the photo of Paul, tried to trace him through social media, but she sits silent and still. By the time I've told her how Anna got a job behind the bar she knew Dan drank in, how she seduced and blackmailed him, how she moved in and led me to believe she was Charlie's half-sister, Lexie's face is as white as the pillow she rests against.

'She deliberately targeted Dan?'

'Yes. She filmed them having sex. Dan says he can barely remember the night at all. I didn't believe him, but I do now. I think she's crazy enough to have spiked his drinks. She probably thought if she wrote to you, you'd ignore her… Again.'

Lexie flinches.

'I think you owe me an explanation, don't you? I take it from the birth certificates that Belle and Charlie were twins?'

'Yeah.'

'And Charlie never knew?'

'No.'

'Why?'

'It's complicated,' Lexie snaps. She picks at a stray thread on her bandage and pulls until it begins to fray.

'Complicated?' I explode. '*I'll* tell *you* what's complicated. *Your* daughter lost me my job, my relationship, killed my cat and then tried to burn my cottage down with me inside.'

'What? How did…'

I raise my hands as though her words will just bounce off them.

'You. Start. Talking.'

Lexie sighs so hard her body judders. 'I told you the truth, you know.' I have to lean forward to hear her hushed tone. 'About Paul being the dad. But he didn't know I was pregnant. He didn't leave because of that. He left because he thought his ex-girlfriend was pregnant and he wanted to go home to talk her into having an abortion.'

'Why?'

Lexie pauses for the longest time and I fight the compulsion to grab her shoulders and shake the words from her.

'Have you heard of Marfan's?'

'No.'

'It's a hereditary disease. Paul was a carrier. He didn't want a family of his own. Didn't want to risk passing it on. I didn't know too much about it, but he said it can cause sudden heart failure, especially during exertion.'

'Charlie. The race.' I cover my mouth with my hands.

'Yeah. That's why I blamed you. If she hadn't run, she probably wouldn't have died. Not then anyway.'

'But I didn't know…'

'I know. Neither did she. I wasn't being fair. It was easier to blame you than to look at my own failings. I didn't know she had it. There were symptoms to look out for. Being really tall…'

'She *was* really tall.'

'But not fucking giant-like, was she? She wasn't tired. Didn't get aches and pains. Stretch marks. She had none of the signs. None.'

'Isn't there screening? Couldn't she have been tested?'

'I didn't tell the doctors it was a possibility. I was young and shit-scared. Tried to pretend I wasn't pregnant, didn't go for any check-ups, but I was huge. Looked like I had a bleedin' watermelon stuffed up me jumper. Me parents slung me out, never spoke to me again and I slept on friends' sofas until I went into labour. The worst experience of me life. Then as soon as one came out, the pain started again and they said there was another on the way. Fucking twins! I was seventeen. Nowhere to live, no money, but I loved them as soon as I saw them.'

'So what happened?'

'I got a council house, benefits, some cash-in-hand cleaning. I was knackered all the time, but we got by. I was scared, though, always scared they'd be ill. I found it hard enough to cope with two healthy babies. Didn't know what I'd do if one of them was sick.'

'And was Belle? Sick?'

'She was different. I didn't know if it was the disease. Never happy. She cried all the time when she was a baby and as she got older she had massive tantrums.'

'That's normal.'

'She'd smash things up and lie to my face, deny it was her. I couldn't sleep, couldn't eat.'

'Did you see a doctor?'

'She said I was depressed. That Belle would grow out of it, but then Charlie started being naughty too. She never was before. Said Belle told her to do things. Whenever I told Belle off, she'd hurt Charlie: biting, punching. I caught her playing with me fags and matches one day. Gave her a slap round the legs. I was hanging out the washing later on when I smelled the smoke. Belle rushed outside. Charlie was up at the bedroom window. I thought I'd lost her.' Lexie's voice cracks and I almost feel sorry for her, but then I remember how outraged she had been when I asked her about the fire Charlie remembered. How she'd lied to my face. How she'd convinced Charlie that she had an overactive imagination, that all her memories were false.

'Social services got involved then. Placed Belle in temporary foster care to give me a break, but it was so much easier without her. Charlie was happier. I was happier. I refused to have her back. Tried to pretend she never existed. Every time Charlie mentioned her, I told her Belle was an imaginary friend: not real.'

'I can't believe she fell for that.'

'Can you remember being four?'

I think. 'No.'

'Children have short memories; believe what you want them to believe.'

'So when Anna got in touch…'

'It was such a bleedin' shock. I panicked. Didn't know what to do. How to tell Charlie I'd kept her sister hidden all these years. Tried to drink myself into oblivion.'

'I think that's when Anna involved me, when she didn't get a reaction from you. Remember those notes I got?'

There's silence. A sigh. 'They weren't from Belle.'

'Not Charlie?' Horror rises. *I've done something terrible.* How could she?

'No.' Lexie shakes her head. 'They were from me.'

'You?' I recoil as though she has physically struck me.

'I'm so sorry, Grace.'

'You? You sent me a box of dog shit? Why?' I'm shaking with rage and I sit on my hands to stop myself from grabbing her straggly hair and yanking it from her scalp.

'I was a bleedin' mess at that time. At your eighteenth party you came into my room when I was crashed out on the bed. I overheard you tell Charlie you'd help her find her dad, egging her on, and I panicked. That's the last thing I wanted. Thought if I distracted you, then you'd forget. But you didn't. All that Jeremy Kyle shit. The "a girl in our class found her dad" conversations. Did you think I was stupid? After the first letter, I couldn't stop. It all got out of hand. I didn't want Charlie to meet him. To find out she might have an illness that could kill her. To look into birth certificates and find out about Belle. I didn't want her to hate me. I loved her so much. But I drove her away.'

'Why did she go? *What did you do?*' I'm shouting now, but I don't care.

Lexie's face is bone-white, her cheeks hollow. There's a thin layer of sweat beading on her top lip. I'm glad she looks as bad as I feel.

'Charlie was putting my shoes back in my wardrobe after the New Year's party and she found a half-finished letter I was making to send you, the cut-up newspaper and glue. She was inconsolable. I promised I'd stop. Begged her not to tell anyone. She said she wouldn't betray me by telling you, and I thought it'd be OK, but then Siobhan had to go and die.'

'She didn't "go and die"; she OD'd because she was so lonely. We all blamed her for the letters. Nobody talked to her. Those junkies were her only friends.'

'Charlie said Siobhan would be alive if I hadn't sent the letters. She was furious. I was terrified what might happen if the police got involved and the truth came out. I begged Charlie to promise that she'd never tell anyone, especially you, Grace.'

'She hated liars. You turned her into one.'

'She didn't want to lie. She wanted to tell you the truth, but I said she had to choose. You or me. And she promised me she'd never tell but said she couldn't stay. Couldn't bear to look at me. Or face you.'

Please forgive me, Grace. I've done something terrible. The promise she'd made... The secret she'd kept. How could I ever have thought she had sent the letters?

'You're disgusting.'

'I know, Grace, but I...'

She reaches out her hand and I slap it away. 'Don't fucking touch me.'

'Fine.' We spend the next few moments lost in our thoughts.

'Let's just get out of here,' Lexie says.

'Oh, I hadn't thought of that. What would I do without you?'

'Drop the attitude, Grace. It doesn't suit you. We need to make a plan. Work together.'

The silence is thick, broken only by the clattering of Anna moving around the kitchen downstairs.

'What can we do?' I ask. 'We can't break the wood. There's no one to hear us scream. I couldn't pick the lock...'

'Pick the lock?'

'Look.' I pull the hairgrip from under my pillow.

Lexie snatches it.

'I've already tried.'

'There's an art. Dagenham Dave taught me.' The tip of Lexie's tongue pokes between her teeth as she eases the grip into the lock of her cuff, twists it around.

'Gotcha.' Lexie opens the cuff, frees her ankle. 'Even one-handed I've still got the knack.' She grins and, despite myself, I grin back.

'Do mine. Quickly.'

Lexie leans over, fumbles with the hairgrip. There's a click and I almost cry with relief as the pressure on my ankle eases.

'Let's go.'

But footsteps crash up the stairs and the bedroom door begins to swing open.

Lexie's feet are on the floor but I grab her arm and frown.

'The knife,' I hiss. 'We need to wait.' Lexie nods. She swings her legs back into bed and I drape the quilt over our feet, hoping that Anna doesn't check the cuffs and chains. My pulse gallops as Anna enters the room. I can feel the tension radiating from Lexie and I pray that she won't do anything rash. Anna clanks the tray down on the dressing table and picks up the knife with one hand, a bowl with the other.

'Pasta.' She hands the dish to Lexie, backs away, fetches a second for me.

My stomach lurches as Parmesan and garlic mingle in my nostrils. The mince is clumped together; grease pools on the surface.

Anna drags my dressing table stool over to the door and perches on the floral seat. I'd been delighted when I discovered that stool in the little second-hand shop on the high street. I'd spent ages rubbing down the legs and varnishing them, before choosing the fabric from John Lewis to upholster the seat. Now I want to burn it.

Anna picks up a third bowl and forks pasta into her mouth. 'Eat,' she mumbles.

I pick up the bowl. Swirl spaghetti strands around. Promise myself that if I ever get out of here, I'm never eating pasta again.

'I'm not fucking eating.' Lexie throws the bowl across the room. It falls before it reaches Anna. Tomato sauce soaks into the smoke-stained carpet.

'You. Just. Can't. Be. Nice. Can you?' Anna slams her food down. The dressing-table mirror vibrates. Sweat trickles between my breasts.

'Nice? You've chained me to a bed.'

'At least I didn't give you away.' Anna's hand spiders over the knife; her fingers curl around the black handle.

'At last, she gets to the fucking point,' Lexie says. 'What do you want? An apology? I'm sorry, all right?'

'I want…' Anna's breath judders. 'I wanted a meal with my mum. And now it's spoiled.' She raises the knife. I draw my knees up, ready to spring to Lexie's defence, but Anna drives the blade into her own thigh, slicing the skin open. Blood stains Charlie's white shorts crimson. I realise that the scars I'd seen on Anna's body at the spa must all have been self-inflicted.

'Belle!'

Anna lifts the knife. Thrusts it down, scraping it across her skin, drawing the perfect cross. Her face is as white as the shorts once were.

'Belle, don't. I am sorry.' Lexie's voice is pleading.

'Why didn't you love me?' Anna sounds desperate, and as much as I want to hate her, I can't help feeling sorry for her.

'I did love you. I do. I thought it was for the best.' Lexie's voice wobbles. 'I thought you'd have a better life.'

'Why give up me and not her? What did I do that was so terrible?'

Lexie reaches out and takes my hand. Her palm is clammy. 'I don't know. I'm sorry. I couldn't cope with both of you.'

'Nobody could cope with me.'

'Was it your foster parents who were killed?' I ask.

'Killed?'

'In the car, on the way to the seaside.'

'I made that up so you'd feel sorry for me. There were no foster parents. I was shoved from pillar to post. "Oh Belle's so disruptive." "Oh, Belle's a bad influence." When I got to twelve, no one wanted me; they wanted the cute ones. I lived in a care home. Oliver fucking Twist. Do you know how depressing those places are? The only thing I had was the photo you left. We looked so happy in it: you, me and Charlie. I slept with it under my pillow every night. I couldn't understand what had gone wrong.'

'Oh, Belle,' Lexie says. 'I've fucked up. I know. But this isn't the answer, keeping us here.'

'It was the only thing I could think of to make you listen. For years, the only thing that kept me going was the thought that when I turned eighteen I could find you, Mum. We could find Charlie together. But Charlie was with you all along. You kept her. Having a great time, while I…'

'I wasn't having a great time. I gave you up because I was depressed…'

'Were you still depressed eighteen years later? Why didn't you answer my letters?'

'It was a shock.'

'I hated you then, wanted to hurt you, make you suffer, make…'

'Why didn't you?' I interject. 'You broke contact for six years. Why?'

'Because I stopped needing her. I had a family of my own. People who loved me.'

'You have a family?'

'I married a boy from the home, Sam. We were so happy. We got a flat. Not a council one, either. Ground floor, with a garden. I made a little rockery, planted some herbs.' Anna stares into the distance as though she can see something we can't. 'Sam wanted a pond with some fish in, but I really wanted a kitten. He brought one home from work one day. He always let me have my own way. She was black with white feet. We called her Socks. He never did get a pond, was afraid she'd eat the fish.'

'Sam sounds nice.' I keep my tone soft.

'He was. We were saving up for our own house. The flat wasn't big enough, not with Lucas.' Anna closes her eyes.

'Lucas?' Lexie grips my fingers so tightly I'm afraid my bones might snap.

'We had so many baby toys. There was barely room to move. I couldn't stop buying him things. Sam told me off. We were supposed to be saving, but I loved Lucas so much. I wanted him to have all the things I'd never had.'

'What happened, Anna? Where's Lucas?' I am cold. I already know the answer. Lexie presses against me. I can feel her trembling.

'We'd been swimming.' Anna's voice is small and tight. 'He loved the water. I'd sit him in his orange duck ring and he'd kick his legs and giggle like mad. He fell asleep on the bus on the way home. I carried him up to bed. Switched the monitor on. I thought I shut his door. Went downstairs to do the ironing, but I was tired. I was always tired. I lay on the sofa and closed my eyes. Didn't wake up till Sam came home. I panicked when I saw how late it was. Lucas never napped for longer than an hour.' Anna pauses and I hold my breath. 'I ran to his room. He was so still. My beautiful boy. Socks was purring in the cot next to him. Sam was screaming that the cat shouldn't be in the nursery. He scooped Lucas from the cot – he was so floppy – and breathed into his mouth, but…' Anna is rigid. Panting. 'They took him away. I didn't want them to take him away.'

Lexie covers her mouth with her hands, but she can't contain her anguished cry.

'It was my fault. I should have been more careful. Sam left me.' Anna's body convulses as she wails. 'Everyone leaves me. I just wanted my mum. I just needed my mum.'

The knife drops onto the carpet as Anna covers her face with her palms. Rocks backwards and forwards, keening like an injured animal.

'Oh, my poor baby girl.' Lexie slips from the bed. Drops to her knees in front of Anna, wrenches off her sling and wraps Anna in her arms. 'I'm here, Belle, I'm here.'

'Mummy.'

'Shh. It wasn't your fault. It was probably genetic – there's a disease, a genetic disease. Charlie had it; you could have had it, passed it on. There's nothing you could have done.'

'Genetic? So it's your fault? *YOU KILLED MY BABY!*' Anna screams, pushes her weight forwards and Lexie topples backwards.

I feel suspended, like the marionette I used to own: strings tight, unable to move without direction. Lexie screams and I remember Dan's words. *You can do anything.* I throw back the covers, jump out of bed. I land awkwardly and pain rips through my left ankle – the one I twisted during the race against Charlie – and I'm splayed on the floor. My ankle burns and for a moment, I'm back in that day. Charlie on the ground. The fear. The panic.

And then I'm clutching the drawers, hoisting myself to my feet, lurching towards Anna. Her hand curves over the knife, her fingers clasp the handle, and I hurl myself forward, grab her wrist. The blade slashes my thigh and I feel the pressure but don't feel any pain, am surprised to see a crimson line stain my pale pink pyjama bottoms. I get hold of the knife handle over Anna's fingers and don't let go, but I step back as it swishes through the air again.

'It's OK, sweetie.' Lexie clings on to Anna like a baby monkey with its arms wrapped around its mother's neck. 'Mummy's here.'

'Mummy.' Anna's fingers slacken and sobs wrench through her body. I whisk the knife away. Stumble downstairs to find a phone.

EPILOGUE
Five months later

I close my eyes and let my fingers glide over the keys as I practise Beethoven's 'Moonlight Sonata'. It was one of Dad's favourites. The doorbell rings before I've quite reached the end and I close the lid of the piano, hauling myself to my feet.

'Morning. Want this straight in your car?' Lexie rattles the old crisp box she's holding.

'Please. Mine's already in there.' I point the remote at my new Honda, listening for the click as the boot opens.

My new neighbours are climbing in their car and I wave: she's a paramedic and he's a policeman. I find that reassuring, although I hope to never need them in a professional capacity. Mrs Jones lives with her daughter now, but I visit her often.

My bag's in the lounge, and as I pick it up, I stroke the black and white kitten curled on my warm piano stool.

'Bye, Moppet. I'll be back later. Be good.'

I sling my things on the passenger seat. Turn to face Lexie.

'You gonna be all right on your own?' she asks.

'Yes.'

'Belle asked after you yesterday.'

'How was she?'

Lexie visits the unit frequently, but I don't want to see her. Not yet. Maybe not ever.

I'm trying to forgive Lexie. She's having counselling, has stopped drinking, is trying to make amends for the past. To be a good mum. I try to push away the part of me that thinks how very differently things might have turned out if she hadn't sent those notes. If Charlie hadn't left. *You can't live in the past*, Grandma says, and I've realised that's where I've spent most of my time. Wishing things were different. Blaming myself. Thinking I might die jolted me into the present, and that's where I'm trying to stay. I have a lot to live for.

'She's groggy. She's on a new medication, but she spoke to the psychologist yesterday instead of ignoring her. It's a start.'

I want to reassure Lexie. To tell her that Belle will be fine, but the words stick in my throat. I know how grief can twist and change a person, leave invisible rocks of guilt to shoulder. I can't begin to imagine the horror of losing a child.

I place my hands over my stomach, inhale sharply.

'You OK?' Lexie asks.

'He's kicking.'

'He?'

'Yep. Had another scan yesterday. It's definitely a boy.'

'Bet Dan's pleased.'

I nod. I never thought I'd see Dan again after he came to Esmée's flat, but when the nausea that flooded my body didn't ease, the doctor thought it might be more than anxiety, and he was right. I shift my weight as an elbow or foot jabs me again. Dan was thrilled when I told him. He proposed at once, has proposed weekly ever since, but I'm content to be on my own for now. Living alone has bought a freedom, a peace, that I hadn't envisaged. I've shed the all-consuming feeling of loss that's cloaked me for over half my life and I'm happy. I'm not sure if Dan and I will ever be an 'us' again, if too much water has passed under the bridge – but we're friends, and committed to being the best parents we can be, and that's a start.

'We've picked a name.'

'Do tell.'

'Charlie.'

Lexie nods, blinks back tears. Squeezes my arm. 'Safe trip.'

I climb into my car. Stretch the seatbelt across my ever-growing bump.

The motorway is quiet and my satnav tells me I'll be there in another hour. I click on the radio. ELO's 'Mr. Blue Sky' rumbles out of the speakers and I smile as I think fondly of my dad and crank up the volume. I warble along. 'It's a beautiful new day, hey, hey.'

I think I'm here. I turn down a dirt track, bump the car towards a farmhouse, pull up behind a Volvo estate. A black and white dog sniffs my ankles, wags his tail. I pop open the boot.

'You must be Grace.' Familiar green eyes lock onto mine.

His hair is grey and he has a beard, but the resemblance to Charlie is startling.

'Paul Lawson.' I smile.

I'd kept up with the social media postings and just when I was beginning to give up hope of ever finding him, I had a reply. Lexie was livid at first, but finally conceded he had a right to know about his daughters and spent hours on the phone to him, trying to explain. He was furious, of course; devastated when he learned about Charlie, about Lucas. He's coming to meet Anna – Belle, I need to get used to calling her that – next week. But today, I'm here for Charlie.

Paul carries the boxes from the car, places them on a large farmhouse table. I pull off my jumper – the room is Aga-warm – and unpack piles of photos and videos, produce a Tupperware containing a cake.

'My grandma made it,' I explain. 'As it would be Charlie's twenty-sixth birthday today.'

I'd brought Grandad's old video recorder with me just in case Paul didn't have one, but there's one in the kitchen, a pile of *Monty Python* videos stacked next to it.

Paul slots in a tape. It whirrs and crackles and the screen goes snowy before an image appears, hazy at first but becoming clearer. It is of the school talent show. Charlie is on stage in a silver sparkly leotard, pink tights and purple leg warmers. She discos her way around the stage, high-kicking and shimmying her flat chest for all she's worth.

'She wasn't shy, then!'

'Not in the least. It was supposed to be a duo, but I was quaking behind the curtain. She won.'

The screen goes blue for a moment and then cuts to Charlie and me on the beach, building a giant speedboat out of sand.

'She always came on holiday with us,' I tell Paul. 'She was happy.'

We laugh and cry in equal measure through birthdays and Christmases, Easter egg hunts and picnics, and when there is nothing else to watch, I light the candles on the cake and we sing 'Happy Birthday' to the girl who wanted nothing more than her father at her side as she blew the candles out. As it is, he blows them out for her, his eyes glistening.

We found him, Charlie. We found him.

LETTER FROM LOUISE

Hello,

I can't thank you enough for reading *The Sister*, my debut novel. It's both exhilarating and terrifying to send my first book out into the world and I'm really grateful you chose to spend precious time with Grace and Charlie.

The Sister began life as part of a challenge at a writers' group, where I was given ten minutes and three words and the bare bones of Chapter One was born. Driving home, my mind was full of questions: What was Grace's secret? How did Charlie die? What was in the pink envelope?

That night, sleep wouldn't come as Grace stamped her feet and demanded her story be told, and the following day, stifling yawns, I tentatively put pen to paper, exploring the aftermath of Lexie's lie.

I'd love to hear your thoughts. Did you end up feeling sympathy for Anna? Compassion for Lexie? Should Grace give Dan a second chance?

I'm horribly embarrassed to mention reviews but they're so important, so if you've enjoyed *The Sister*, it really would mean the world to me if you could leave a review.

You can also connect with me via my blog where I regularly post flash fiction and insights into a writer's life.

Finally, I do so hope you join me for book two – there's a chapter of it at the end of this book if you want to dip in.

Love,

Louise xx

f fabricatingfiction

🐦 @Fab_fiction

www.louisejensen.co.uk

ACKNOWLEDGEMENTS

I've so many people to thank, it's difficult to know where to start. Firstly a massive, massive shout out to the whole Bookouture team, especially Lydia Vassar-Smith my editor, for believing in me enough to give me this chance, Natasha Hodgson, and the other Bookouture authors who are such a fabulous support network. Thanks, also, to Catherine Burke and the team at Sphere.

Louise Walters, my mentor via the fabulous WoMentoring Project, whose encouragement gave me the confidence to try and write a novel.

The Wordpress blogging community who have critiqued with kindness and allowed me to develop as a writer, in particular Lyn Churchyard (you know why!).

Mick Rodden from the Northants Fire Service for his valuable input into the fire and hospital scenes. Any mistakes are entirely my own.

Andrew Lockhart for his words of wisdom, Gary Tipping for keeping me calm at the last hurdle and Jane Isaac for always being on the end of the phone to answer my frantic questions.

Thanks to my early readers Leah Gee, Ceri Wickens, Michele Harris, and Karen Coles, and to Lee Harris for his proofreading skills. Thanks cuz!

Mick Wynn, with whom I bounced around many an idea. I actually think he ended up reading my manuscript far more times than me.

The beautiful Bekkii Bridges who helped me shape the end.

My lovely friend Natalie Brewin who was happy to read early versions and listened to me whinge like a child on more than one occasion.

My sister Karen Appleby for her (often brutal) opinion and my mum for producing us both!

Tim, possibly the most patient husband in the world who never complained when he had to do the school run or pull together a meal at short notice while I wrote 'just one more page.' Thanks for your unwavering belief that I could. I did!

My gorgeous boys Callum, Kai and Finley who are always the driving force behind everything I do. I love you and am so proud of you all.

And Ian Hawley who always encouraged me in everything I've ever wanted to do. You always told me I could write a book. I wish you were still here to read it.

Read on for the beginning of
The Gift, *Louise Jensen's next bestseller*

Run.

It's dark. So dark. Clouds scud across the charcoal sky, blanketing the moon and stars. Dampness fills my lungs and as I draw a sharp breath nausea crashes over me in sickening waves.

My energy is fading fast. My trainers slap against the concrete and I don't think I can hear footsteps behind me any more, but it's hard to tell over the howling wind.

I steal a glance over my shoulder but my feet stray onto soft earth and I lose my footing and stumble, splaying out my hands to break my fall. The side of my face hits something hard and solid that rips at my skin. My jaw snaps shut and my teeth slice into my tongue flooding my mouth with blood, and as I swallow it down, bile and fear rises in my throat.

Don't make a sound.

I'm scared. So scared.

I lie on my stomach. Still. Silent. Waiting. My palms are stinging. Cheek throbbing. Rotting leaves pervade my nostrils. My stomach roils as I slowly inch forward, digging my elbows into the wet soil for traction. Left. Right. Left. Right.

I'm in the undergrowth now. Thorns pierce my skin and catch on my clothes but I stay low, surrounded by trees, thinking I can't be seen, but the clouds part and in the moonlight I catch sight of the sleeve of my hoodie, which, unbelievably, is white, despite the mud splatters. I curse myself. Stupid. Stupid. Stupid. I yank it off and stuff it under a bush. My teeth clatter together with cold. With fear. To my left twigs snap underfoot and instinctively I push myself up and rock forward onto the balls of my feet like a runner about to sprint. Over my heartbeat pounding in my ears, I hear it.

A cough. Behind me now. Close. Too close.

Run.

I stumble forward. I can do this I tell myself, but it's a lie. I know I can't keep going for much longer.

The clouds roll across the sky again and the blackness is crushing. I momentarily slow, conscious I can't see where I'm putting my feet. The ground is full of potholes and I can't risk spraining my ankle, or worse. What would I do then? How could I get away? The wind gusts and the clouds are swept away and in my peripheral vision a shadow moves. I spin around and scream.

Run.

CHAPTER ONE
Now

Every Tuesday, between four and five, I tell lies.

Vanessa, my therapist, nudges tortoiseshell glasses up the bridge of her nose and slides a box of Kleenex towards me, as if today will be the day my guilt spews out, coming to rest, putrid and toxic, on the impossibly polished table between us.

'So, Jenna.' She shuffles through my file. 'It's approaching the six-month anniversary – how do you feel?'

I shrug and pick at a stray thread hanging from my sleeve. The scent from the lavender potpourri irks me, as does the excess of shiny-leaved plants in this carefully created space, but I swallow down my agitation as I shift on the too-soft sofa. I can't keep blaming my medication for my mood swings, can I?

'Fine,' I say, although that couldn't be further from the truth. I have so many emotions waiting to pour out of me, but whenever I'm here, words tie themselves into knots on my tongue, and however much I want to properly open up, I never really do.

'Have you been anywhere this week?'

'I went out with Mum, on Friday.' It's hardly news. I do it every week. Sometimes I can't understand why I see Vanessa at all. I've completed the set number of appointments I was supposed to, yet still I arrive on the dot each week. I guess it's because I don't get out much and I do like my routine, my little bit of normality.

'And socially?'

'No.' I can't remember the last time I had a night out. I'm only thirty but I feel double that, at least. I wasn't up to socialising for ages afterwards and now I prefer to be at home. Alone. Safe.

'Emotionally? Are things settling down?'

I break eye contact. She's referring to my paranoia, and I don't quite know what to say. At almost every hospital appointment the cocktail of drugs I am taking to stop my body rejecting my new heart is adjusted, but anxiety has wrapped itself around me like a second skin, and no matter how hard I try, I can't shake it off.

'The urge to…' she consults her notes, 'run away? Is that still with you?'

'Yes.' Adrenaline pricks my skin and the underarms of my T-shirt grow damp. The sense of danger that often washes over me is so overwhelming it sometimes feels like a premonition.

'It's not unusual to want to escape from your own life when something traumatic has happened that is difficult to process. We have to work together to break the cycle of obsessive thoughts.'

'I don't think it's as simple as that.' The fear is as real and solid as the amber paperweight that rests on Vanessa's desk. 'I've been having more…' I'm not sure I want to tell her but she's looking at me now in that way of hers, as if she can see right through me, '… episodes.'

'Are they the same as before? The overwhelming dizziness?' She lifts her chin slightly as she waits for my answer, and I wish I'd never mentioned it.

'Yes. I don't lose consciousness but my vision tunnels and everything sounds muffled. They're getting more frequent.'

'And how long are these episodes lasting?'

'It's hard to say. Seconds probably. But when it happens I feel so…' I look around the office as though the word I am looking for might be painted on the wall, '… frightened.'

'Feeling out of control is frightening, Jenna, and it's understandable given what you've been through. Have you mentioned these episodes to Dr Kapur?'

'Yes. He says panic attacks aren't unheard of on my medication but if all goes well at my six-month check he can reduce my tablets and that should help.'

'There you go then. And you're due back at work…' she glances at her papers, '… Monday?'

'Yes. Only part-time though. At first.' Linda and John, my bosses, have been more than generous with the time off they have given me. They're friends of Dad's and have known me most of my life, and although Linda said I shouldn't feel obliged to return I've missed my job. I can't imagine starting afresh somewhere new. Somewhere unfamiliar. I'm nervous though. I've been away so long. How will it feel? Being normal again. I'm jittery at the thought of mixing with people. I've got too used to my own company, being at home, filling my time. 'Pottering around,' Mum used to call it; 'hiding myself away,' she says now, but in my flat the jagged unease I carry with me isn't quite so sharp. But life goes on, doesn't it? And if I don't force myself to start living again now I'm afraid I never will.

'How do you feel about going back?'

My shoulders begin their automatic ascent towards my ears but I stop them. 'OK, I think. My parents aren't keen. They've been trying to talk me out of it. I can understand that they're worried it will be too much, but Linda has said I can take it slowly to start with. Leave early if I get too tired and go in late if I've had a bad night.' I've always had a good relationship with Linda, even if she hasn't visited me in the past few months. She doesn't know what to say, I suppose. No one does. The fact I nearly died makes people uncomfortable.

'And the donor's family? Are you still trying to contact them?'

I shift in my seat. Over the past few months I have poured my thanks into letter after letter that was rejected by my transplant co-ordinator. I'd inadvertently revealed too much. A clue about who I was, where I live. But without those details it all seemed so cold and anonymous. Eventually I paid a private investigator to find them and wrote to the family directly. It cost a small fortune just for their address but it was worth it to be able to express how grateful I am and how much their act means to my family, without filtering my words. I wasn't going to bother them again and never expected to hear back but they replied straight away, and seemed genuinely pleased to have heard from me. I know Vanessa won't like what's coming.

My mouth dries and I lean forward to pick up my glass. My hand trembles and ice cubes chink and water sloshes over the side and trickles onto my lap where it soaks into my jeans. I sip my drink, conscious of the tick-tick-tick of Vanessa's clock, discreetly positioned behind me. 'I'm meeting them on Saturday.'

'Oh, Jenna. That's completely unethical. How did you trace them? I'm going to have to report this, you know.'

My face flames as I study my shoes. 'I can't tell you. I'm sorry.'

'You know contact isn't encouraged.' Disapproval drips from every word. 'Especially this early on in the process. It can be incredibly distressing for everyone, and it could set you back several stages. A simple thank you letter would have sufficed but meeting – I just…'

'I know. They've been told exactly the same thing, but they want to meet me. They do. And I need to meet them. Just once. It feels as though someone else is inside of me, and I want to know who it is. I have to know.' My voice cracks.

'It's become almost an obsession and it's not healthy, Jenna. What good will it do you knowing whose heart you have?'

The colours in the painting behind her, something modern and chaotic, swirl together and the gnawing agitation inside me grows.

'It would help me to understand.'

'Understand what?' Vanessa leans towards me like a jockey on a horse, pushing forwards, sensing a breakthrough.

'Why I lived and they died.'

* * *

There's an indent in my chocolate leather couch marking the place I've spent too many hours. There might as well be a sign, GIRL WITH NO LIFE LIVES HERE. I light a berry-scented candle before flopping down in my usual spot. I always feel so drained when I've been to see Vanessa, and I'm never sure whether it's from the emotions that bubble to the surface when I sit in her immaculate office, or the effort of keeping them inside.

From the coffee table, I pick up my sketchbook. Drawing always relaxes me. I stream James Bay through my Bluetooth speaker and as he holds back the river I tap-tap-tap the pencil hard against my knee, staring at the bland walls as I wait for inspiration to hit. I've been meaning to decorate since Sam moved out nearly six months ago. Make the flat my own. Cover up the magnolia with sunshine yellow or rich red: bold colours that Sam hates. It's not like he's coming back although I know he'd like to. He never wanted us to split up but I couldn't stand the look of sympathy in his eyes whenever he looked at me after my surgery, the way he fussed around asking if I was all right every five minutes. I didn't want him to be stuck with someone like me, 'helping me through' as though we're old and there's nothing more to life. Cutting him free was the kindest thing I've ever done, even if my stomach still twists every time I think about him. We're trying to be friends. Texting. Facebooking. But it's not the same, is it? I add decorating to my mental list of things to do that I'll probably never get around to. The days when I had to take it easy have passed but I'm stuck in a rut I can't get out of and, truth be told, I'm scared. Despite the hours of physio and the mountain of leaflets I was sent home with, there's a hesitancy about my movements. An enforced slowness. My body is healing well, my doctor says, but my mind doesn't seem to believe it, and I'm terrified I will push myself too hard. That something will go wrong, and what would I do then? I picture myself lying on the floor. Unable to reach the phone. Unable to move. Who would know? I pretend to Mum I'm fine living alone. I pretend to everyone. Even myself.

What can I draw? I flick through the pages of my pad. Initially there is image after image of Sam, but lately my drawings have become darker. Menacing almost. Forests with twisted tree branches, eyes peering out of the gloom, an owl with beady eyes. I sigh. Perhaps Vanessa is right to be concerned about my mental health.

My mobile beeps. It's a text from Rachel, and I know without opening it she'll be asking what I'm doing later. I'll tell her I'm having a night in and to have a drink for me at the pub. It's our weekly routine, like Punch and Judy. The same every time even though sometimes you itch for a different ending. *I could go*, I think to myself but then I bat the thought away. It seems fruitless to try to fall back into the same habits. I'm not the person I was before, and besides, people treat me differently now, never quite meeting my gaze, not knowing what to say. I'll see Rachel at work on Monday.

Nearly six months ago, someone died so I can live. My world has become so small it sometimes feels as though I can't breathe. Who was it that died for me? I squeeze my eyes tightly closed but the thought still juggernauts towards me and I don't know how to make it stop. I shiver and cross to the window. The breeze blowing in is freezing but I am grateful for the fresh air. I have been home for weeks now but the heavy smell of hospital seems to have embedded itself into my lungs, and whatever the weather I always have the windows cracked open. I peer out of the slatted blinds into the dusk and a chill creeps up my spine. A shadow shifts in the doorway across the road, and the urge to run I told Vanessa about swamps me. My breath quickens but the street is still. Quiet. I slam the window and close the blinds and am cocooned by the dim light in my living room. My world is shrinking; my confidence too.

Back on the sofa, my hands are shaking too much to hold the pencil steady. *I'm safe*, I tell myself. So why don't I feel it?

CHAPTER TWO

Ten months ago, we'd both been ill. A virus had rocketed around Sam's office, and I'd come home from work one day to find him huddled on the sofa, duvet draped over him, a pile of scrunched-up tissues on the floor. Radiators belted out heat, and I'd thrown off my coat and jumper.

'I think I'm dying, Jenna,' Sam croaked, stretching his arm towards me, and I'd laughed but as I took his hand it was slick with sweat, and I pressed my palm to his forehead. Despite the fact his teeth were rattling together with cold, he was burning up.

'Man flu.' I'd grazed my lips against his hot cheek. 'Be back soon.'

I'd dashed out to the late-night chemist and stocked up on Lemsip and aspirin, and at home I warmed through chicken and sweetcorn soup. A couple of days later my throat stung, eyes streamed and I shivered so furiously I bit my tongue. We stayed in bed for days. The air grew thick and sour as we binge-watched box sets, volume blaring to drown out hacking coughs. We took it in turns to shuffle to the kitchen, slow and purposeful, like zombies, and fetched snacks we couldn't swallow, drinks we couldn't taste. It was such a relief to feel better. To hoist open the sash windows and let the cool breeze sweep away the stench of ill health. Under the shower, hot needles of water peppered my skin and I believed the worst was over.

Sam's strength returned day by day, but mine didn't and after about a week I felt so exhausted I was napping in the car during my lunch break, falling asleep on the couch as M&S ready meals blackened in the oven. At night, I'd wake gasping, trying to force oxygen into my lungs, and I'd stick my head out the window and gulp fresh air, wondering what was happening to me.

'I've booked you a doctor's appointment,' Sam said one day. 'Five o'clock. No arguing.'

I was too drained to protest. I sat in the GP's waiting room, the fug of illness stale and oppressive. The doctor barely listened to my symptoms before he scratched his salt-and-pepper beard and told me what I was experiencing was completely normal and I just needed to rest. He reassured me that my energy would return.

Three weeks later I barely had the strength to get out of bed. I hadn't been to work in over two weeks.

'This doesn't seem right to me,' Sam said as he stood over me, his face etched with worry. 'I've booked you an appointment to get a second opinion. I'll be back to pick you up at lunchtime.'

Later that morning I'd hefted myself out of bed and was shuffling to the bathroom when I stopped to scoop the post up from the doormat, and that was the last thing I remembered. Apparently, Sam found me on the hallway floor, lips drained of colour, and I was rushed into hospital, sirens blaring, blue lights flashing.

The next few months were a blur. On one level, I was aware of what was going on around me. I had viral myocarditis which had aggressively attacked my heart function; and a transplant was my only option. Sam was permanently curled up in a ball in the chair next to my bed. Mum plastered on her bright, happy smile and visited every day. Dad paced around the room, hands in pockets, head bowed. The beeping of the machines was the last thing I heard at night and the sound I woke up to in the morning, wondering where I was until I inhaled. There's nothing quite like the smell of hospitals, of disinfectant mixed with decay; hand gel mingled with hope. I was too weak to read, and I couldn't focus on the TV.

'Kardashians or soap stars?' Rachel would ask as she read aloud from the gossip magazines, but I'd drift in and out of sleep and never could quite keep up with who was divorcing who, or which actress was currently too fat. Too thin. It all seemed so trivial, the things we used to laugh about in the pub, but I was grateful for her company. None of my other friends came to see me.

Before indistinguishable meals arrived on rattling trolleys Mum would prop me up against pillows. I never equated the fact she could hoist me up in bed with the amount of weight I'd lost. She'd cut soft hospital food into small pieces and I'd swallow them whole, too exhausted to chew. What must have run through her mind? Memories of the chubby toddler I was, strapped into my white plastic highchair, mouth open wide like a baby sparrow. How did she cope? I never saw her cry, not once. What no one told me was the doctors thought it was highly unlikely a heart would be found in time. I was dying. The transplant lists were flooded, and although I wasn't well enough to go home, I wasn't a priority either. How do you prepare for the worst? I can't imagine. And I ache when I think of what they must have gone through: Mum, Rachel and Sam sitting around my bed, fingers laced together, as they prayed to a God they didn't believe in. Dad, helpless and frustrated, visited every day but never stayed for long, and when he spoke there was an edge to his voice as if he was permanently furious, and he probably was. You don't expect to watch your only child fade away in front of you, do you? Time was interminable: doctors consulted, nurses fussed and notes were made until, one day, a miracle happened.

'We've found a heart,' Dr Kapur announced.

The heart was a perfect match but there was no celebration as I was prepped for surgery; everyone painfully aware this gift of life only came to fruition through another family's grief.

The trolley wheels squeaked as I was rolled down the corridor, harsh overhead lights so white it was as if I could be sucked into their brightness and transported to an afterlife I desperately wanted to believe in.

I didn't think it was possible to feel any worse, but when I woke two days afterwards in intensive care, I felt so ill I almost wished I'd died. Fluids were fed through tubes in my arm, and my chest drain felt as heavy as lead.

One day, by the side of my bed, Sam dropped to one knee, and at first I'd thought it was through exhaustion. I'd reached for the buzzer to call for the nurse when I noticed the black velvet box resting on his palm. A ring – oval sapphire surrounded by sparkling diamonds – inside.

'This isn't the romantic setting I'd envisaged, but marry me? Please?' he'd asked.

'Sam?' I didn't know what to say.

He had lifted the ring from the box and held it towards me. I ran my finger over the stone which was as deep a blue as the ocean.

'It was Grandma's. She wanted me to start a new tradition. Passing it down along the family.'

I swallowed hard. My head battling my heart.

'I can buy another if you don't like it?'

Sam looked uncertain, younger than his thirty years, and it took every ounce of willpower not to cry. I curled my fingers to stop him sliding the ring on. I knew I'd never want to take it off.

'I can't marry you,' I whispered. 'I'm so sorry.'

'Why not? We've talked about it before.'

'Everything is different now. I'm different.'

'You're still you.' He stroked my cheek with such tenderness it was all I could do not to fall into his arms. Despite my unwashed hair, my stale breath, he gazed at me as if I was the most beautiful woman in the world. It tore me apart to look into his eyes and see worry reflected from the place lust once sat.

'I don't want to be with you any more, Sam.' I forced out the words that hurt more than the scalpel that had sliced through my skin.

'I don't believe you, Jenna.'

'It's true. I'd been having second thoughts about us before all this.'

'It's just because you're ill…'

'It's not. I've been having doubts for ages. I'm so sorry.'

'Since when? Everything was fine before?'

Before. Such an innocuous word but there would always be a divide. Before and after. A glass wall separating the things I could do then with the things I couldn't do any more.

'Jenna, be honest. Do you love me?'

I was at a crossroads. Truth or lies.

'I don't love you, Sam.' I chose lies. 'I'm so sorry.' It was the right thing to do. For him. Sam began to speak but I couldn't meet his eye. I twisted the starched corner of the bed sheet between my fingers and willed myself to stay strong. He would be better off without me.

He put the ring back in the box, and I jumped as he snapped it shut and crossed the room, his shoulders slumped. I longed to call him back and tell him, of course I loved him, but the words were shackled to my tongue. He hesitated in the doorway and I bit the inside of my cheek hard to stop myself crying his name, my mouth full of metallic blood and regret, and as he carried on walking my gifted heart and guilt pulsed away inside of me.

* * *

Four weeks after my transplant I was discharged from hospital. Mum picked me up.

'Where's Dad?'

She ignored the question. She had settled me into the back seat of a taxi showing as much care as the new fathers leaving the maternity wing, clutching car seats cradling newborn babies, and dreams of a perfect future. Mum clicked my seatbelt into its holder despite my protests that I could do it myself and shook out a cotton-wool-soft plaid picnic blanket, placing it over my knees.

'My daughter's had a heart transplant. Please drive slowly,' she said.

'Blimey.' The cabbie twisted the dial on his stereo and the music grew fainter. 'You're a bit young for that love, aren't you? Kids! Always a worry, aren't they? I've got three myself. Grand-kiddies too.'

The taxi rumbled forward, and the traffic light air freshener swung from the interior mirror, its smell sickly-sweet. We'd crawled along at a snail's pace – Mum not flinching at the cacophony of horns demanding we speed up – towards the three-bedroom bungalow I'd grown up in.

'Paint It Black' began to play: the Rolling Stones were one of Dad's favourites, and over the music Mum chatted to the driver about what a mild winter it was so far. I closed my eyes, resting my heavy head against the window, slipping off into sleep. The vibrations from the engine made my cheeks tingle.

The sound of shouting roused me. Hard, angry voices climbing in pitch. Dazed I started to push myself upright, forcing open my eyes when the car lurched forward, its wheels gathering speed, and I was thrown back in my seat. Dizzying blackness engulfed me as my head lolled and cracked against the window.

'*No. No. No!*' A woman's terrified screams rang in my ears and fear raced through my bloodstream.

The brakes screeched. Glass shattered and there was the feeling of flying, my skin burning, bleeding, as shards of glass sliced into my flesh.

My hands flew upwards to cover my face, and then came stillness. Silence. Music? I splayed my fingers and peered out. I was still strapped in my seat. The cabbie's head bobbed up and down along to 'Paint It Black'. Mum was telling him how a hard frost was predicted for the coming weekend.

I scrutinised my palms, turning my hands over. No blood. I'd been warned to expect a myriad of side effects with my medication, and as I tried to analyse what happened my head felt fuzzy and I wasn't sure if I'd imagined the whole thing. The lull of the engine teamed forces with the medication and I rested my head back once more and stared blankly out of the window for the rest of the journey. I must have been dreaming, mustn't I?